The Wind

It lifted Biddy's spirits to come down the slope towards the shrouded glen and glimpse smoke rising from the chimney of her sister's house, to see the neat hedges that Michael had planted, the wooden shed where the hens roosted and, straggling off on the seaward side, the peak stack and the drying-green with washing flapping like bunting on the sagging ropes. She could smell sheep and whiffs of peat smoke, and cooking. And she could hear, among the bleating from the pastures, the cries of her two little nieces, Rachel and Rebecca, as they played about the yard.

The little girls, aged four and six, called her Auntie Bridget. Innis, of course, still called her Biddy but to Michael and the boy she was always Mistress Baverstock or now and then, when something displeased them, they would address her, straightfaced and straight to her face as 'your ladyship', as if to exaggerate the distinctions that lay between them . . .

*Also by Jessica Stirling and
available in Coronet Paperbacks*

The Spoiled Earth
The Hiring Fair
The Dark Pasture
Treasures on Earth
Creature Comforts
Hearts of Gold
The Penny Wedding
The Marrying Kind
The Workhouse Girl

as Caroline Crosby
The Haldanes

About the author

Born in Glasgow, Jessica Stirling has enjoyed a highly
successful career as a writer. She now lives in the
Stirlingshire countryside.

The Wind From The Hills

Jessica Stirling

CORONET BOOKS
Hodder and Stoughton

Copyright © 1998 by Jessica Stirling

The right of Jessica Stirling to be identified as the
Author of the Work has been asserted in accordance with the
Copyright, Designs and Patents Act 1988.

First published in Great Britain in 1998 by Hodder and Stoughton
A division of Hodder Headline PLC
First published in paperback in 1998 by Hodder and Stoughton
A Coronet Paperback

10 9 8 7 6 5 4

All rights reserved. No part of this publication may be reproduced,
stored in a retrieval system, or transmitted, in any form or by any
means without the prior written permission of the publisher,
nor be otherwise circulated in any form of binding or cover
other than that in which it is published and without a similar
condition being imposed on the subsequent purchaser.

All characters in this publication are fictitious and any resemblance
to real persons, living or dead, is purely coincidental.

A CIP catalogue record for this title is available
from the British Library.

Printed and bound in Great Britain by
Mackays of Chatham plc, Chatham, Kent

Hodder and Stoughton
A division of Hodder Headline PLC
338 Euston Road
London NW1 3BH

CONTENTS

BOOK ONE
BIDDY

BOOK TWO
INNIS

BOOK ONE

BIDDY

ONE

The Barren Hind

I n the long summer of 1891 there was hardly a man came to Fetternish who did not have his way with Mrs Bridget Baverstock: that, at least, was how the stories went. But you know what stories and islanders are like, how if you put one with the other you can wind up with a fact that's as far from the truth as Land's End is from John o' Groat's.

Indeed, some imaginative scandalmongers even suggested that Willy Naismith was closer to his mistress than a house servant had any right to be; that the widow of Fetternish now and then borrowed him from his good wife not so much to share her bed as to fertilise it, not to scatter his seed, of which by then there was a great deal less than there used to be, but to put a kind of charm on the sheets so that the select band of suitors who *were* invited to warm the widow's four-poster might be endowed with uncommon potency and with a single cast of the rod, as it were, land Fetternish an heir.

It was all nonsense, of course, pure fancy, a skein of lies spun by folk who envied Biddy Baverstock her wealth and still resented the fact that a fisherman's daughter had inherited the estates of Fetternish without doing a stroke to deserve them; as if it were her fault that her poor, love-struck husband had dropped dead only six weeks after taking her to be his bride.

However you chose to interpret her behaviour you could not dispute that Biddy Baverstock was just the sort of woman whose dash and daring encouraged such scurrilous tales, a woman to whom men were drawn like moths to candle flame, not only for her beauty – sea-green eyes, auburn hair, a face and figure that would have tempted an anchorite – but also for her determination to prove herself as good, if not better, than any other landowner on Mull.

So far even the most spiteful gossips would have to admit that she had used her talents and advantages well. In the dozen years since her husband's death she had resisted several underhand attempts by her husband's family to wrest Fetternish back from her and had defied the temperamental climate and impoverished soil that had sent previous owners of Fetternish skulking back to the mainland vowing never to set foot on the island again.

Unlike them, of course, she thoroughly understood Mull's quirky character. She had been raised on the cattle croft of Pennypol, less than two miles from the great, handsome house on the cliff that, together with all its shaggy acres, she managed with the assurance of someone who had never been afraid to look a gift horse in the mouth, even to the extent of prising its jaws apart and totalling up its teeth. She had gradually cultivated and fructified most of the glens and headlands of the north quarter, had brought them under her sway and made them yield profit, just as she brought everything under her sway and made it yield profit.

Even Nature, it seemed, could not stand up to Biddy Baverstock; except that Nature, reluctant to be outfoxed, had pulled one grim little trick by way of revenge and had so far denied her that which she most wanted in life – a child of her own, an heir to Fetternish. By any reasonable standards Biddy was not old. But she lived in a community where women tended to marry early and expend what there was of their youth on bearing and rearing children, so that the schoolhouse in Dervaig was crammed to capacity and the fields about Crove contained almost as many toddlers as sheep. Or so it seemed to Biddy who, entering her thirty-third year, had abruptly woken up to the fact that she was half-way to being left on the shelf and that the best of her breeding years might already be behind her.

You would never have guessed to look at her that she was, or could possibly imagine herself to be, a dried-up old husk.

She was tall and broad-shouldered and if not wide at least not narrow at the hips. She glowed with robust good health. She was out and about in all weathers and had recently developed quite a passion for outdoor sports; so much so that even with the aid of the latest cold-creams and complexion lotions and dust-storms of French powder she could not disguise her naturally high colour or cool her propensity to perspire when taking any sort of exercise.

'Radiant,' the shooting gentlemen would declare, without a hint of criticism. 'By God, Bridget, you look positively radiant today.' By which, Biddy imagined, they were politely informing her that she looked no better than a boiled beetroot.

Although she was still arrogant she had shed much of her conceit. These days she did not have time to mope at her dressing-table and now and then would experience a wave of revulsion at the battery of jars and pots that she had accumulated and would instruct Margaret, who deputised as a lady's-maid when she wasn't too busy elsewhere, to sweep the lot out of sight so that the temptation to paint herself up like some haggard Edinburgh dowager would be temporarily removed. What she did not tell Margaret to do, though, was to wheel away the cheval-glass that stood in a corner of the dressing-room. In the slanted glass Biddy would examine herself whenever the mood stole over her and the faint wistful longings that had troubled her in the early years of her widowhood flared up into something very close to panic.

She did not strut before the glass, did not exhibit herself for her own pleasure or to rehearse the pleasure she might give to the favoured few who were admitted to her bedroom. In those private moments of contemplation she did not dwell on thoughts of marriage but, rather, on its consequence, on the eighth or ninth month of pregnancy when she would be lovely and swollen with a child of her own. Then, back arched, belly thrust out, she would realise just how false her posing was and what it signified and would pivot and pad away, cursing her foolishness and trying desperately to staunch the tears that trickled from the corners of her eyes.

So, while many women envied Mrs Baverstock there were

many women whom Mrs Baverstock envied, not for the simplicity of their lives, not for the tasks at which they toiled, of which she had done more than her fair share, not for the smoky cottages in which they dwelled nor the plain fare on their tables, but for their babies, their children, the girls and boys with which the island was seeded now that burnings and land evictions were things of the past and the economy more settled. It was, Biddy thought, Mull's growing season, a time of sprouting, when the next generation would take root in ground of good heart.

And there were children, children everywhere.

And not one of them hers.

Of the eight children to whom Biddy was related the ones that she loved and coveted most were the three that her sister Innis had borne to Michael Tarrant who, a long, long time ago, had been Biddy's first lover and who, if he had not been a Roman Catholic and she had not been so infected by her father's prejudices, she might have married in preference to Austin Baverstock.

The Tarrants seldom came to the big house and were never invited to any of the grand parties that marked the social season. Even so, Biddy visited them almost daily, walking the mile to Pennymain cottage over the narrow wooden bridge she'd had built across the glen at the rear of their holding, over the lush, watery ravine that was called in Gaelic *Na h-Vaignich* which, roughly translated, meant 'The Solitudes'. When Michael had first lived there alone, and Biddy had crept into his bed in dead of night, the name had seemed appropriate to the isolation of the place. Now it had changed, had become a hub of liveliness, with dogs, hens and children darting about, so that its only stillness, its only sullen centre was Michael himself, more dour and silent than he had ever been, as if marriage and fatherhood had not cured his loneliness but had in some way exacerbated it.

It lifted Biddy's spirits to come down the slope towards the shrouded glen and glimpse smoke rising from the chimney of her sister's house, to see the neat hedges that Michael had planted, the wooden shed where the hens roosted and, straggling off on the seaward side, the peat stack and the drying-green with washing flapping like bunting on the sagging ropes. She could smell sheep and whiffs of peat smoke, and cooking. And she could hear, among the bleating from the pastures, the cries of her two little nieces, Rachel and Rebecca, as they played about the yard. From her Tarrant nephew Gavin, though, she heard nothing, for even at the age of ten he was silent and guarded, like his father.

The little girls, aged four and six, called her Auntie Bridget. Innis, of course, still called her Biddy but to Michael and the boy she was always Mistress Baverstock or now and then, when something displeased them, they would address her, straight-faced and straight to her face, as 'your ladyship', as if to exaggerate the distinctions that lay between them.

Biddy's nieces and nephew were by no means the only youngsters to inhabit the quiet back roads of Fetternish. In fact the only dwelling on the estate, apart from Fetternish House itself, that did not contain new life lay beyond Pennymain in the crook of the arm of Pennypol bay, the broad, well-watered acres that had once belonged to Biddy's mother, where Vassie and Ronan Campbell still lived. There was no smoke, or precious little, hovering above the Campbells' turf-roofed cottage, no cats or hens skittering about in the shadow of the high drystone wall that Vassie had once built to keep the Baverstocks' sheep off her property. There were dogs, though, a pair of yellow-eyed, skulking mongrels that, when not work-ing the herd, were kept locked up in what had once been the byre; fierce cattle dogs that answered to no one except Vassie and would, at the first sniff of an intruder, snarl so savagely that not even brave, dour little Gavin dared come near them.

It wasn't the dogs or the big-horned cattle that roamed along the foreshore that made Pennypol seem inhospitable, however, so much as Vassie herself, Vassie and her drunken husband.

Even Biddy and Innis preferred not to pass too close to the house, for they were disgusted by the sight of their father sprawled on the doorstep, a whisky bottle hugged to his chest like a cherished child, motionless as granite or, rather, some soft and crumbling substance like lignite or grey lava. They of all people knew that it wasn't drink but brute pride that had torn him down, that had soured his marriage and turned family love to family loathing. And there were secrets too, dreadful, whispered secrets that Vassie still kept to herself while she patiently watched him shrivel and decay before her vengeful eyes.

On paper Vassie Campbell still owned Pennypol, including water rights and rights of access but many years ago she had leased it out to Fetternish, an arrangement that Biddy had augmented by taking the sheep off the low grazings and purchasing enough cattle to establish a small, high-quality herd over which her mother had sole charge. Now there were cows to be milked once again, calves in the calf park, bullocks braying along the foreshore and Vassie restored to her natural element. Except that her children were gone and would never return to live with her in Pennypol. And the moor had been closed off with stobs. And the dike at the top of the calf park had been rebuilt, the old jetty repaired and the fish-shed, Ronan's last sanctuary, had been torn down and replaced by a fine new slate-roofed byre. Improvements, expensive improvements that Biddy had commissioned and paid for and whose benefits Mam did not acknowledge, not even grudgingly, as if she somehow still blamed Biddy for all that had gone wrong, for all that had been irretrievably lost.

No one stepped uninvited on to Vassie's patch, not Biddy, not Innis, not Hector Thrale, the factor, not even amiable Willy Naismith who was friend to everyone on the estate. Nobody came closer than the end of the wall for if they did then the dogs would bark and Ronan would stir and roll his head and moan, uttering those unintelligible sounds that only Vassie seemed able to interpret. And she would come whisking out of the cottage or out of the byre waving a stick in her fist and would shout, 'Who is it? What do you want with us?' and all along the foreshore the cattle would lift their snouts and roar too as if she was not just their keeper but their leader, as dangerous and unpredictable as they were, only female.

'Mam, it is me. It is Innis.'

'I cannot see you.'

'I am here, by the new gate.'

'Who is it that you have with you?'

'I have brought Gavin to see you, and Rachel.'

The stick would be lowered but not discarded. Vassie would abandon the protection of the cottage and scuttle, crab-like, along the path by the wall. Her skin-and-bone build and leathery complexion made her appear ancient but her restless energy remained inexhaustible. She wore a greasy black cotton dress with a canvas apron tied around her waist and a ragged shawl knotted at her breast in traditional style. Now that her sons and daughters had gone she neglected herself and her home shamefully and the cottage had deteriorated into something not much better than a hovel. Only her fondness for the cattle, which she never neglected or ignored, seemed to be keeping her sane.

She peered at everyone with such suspicion that her brown eyes appeared to have receded into her head and left nothing but empty sockets under the fringe of hair that cut across her brow. There was nothing wrong with her eyesight – she could still spot an ailing calf at three hundred paces – but there were many things she chose not to see, visitors to Pennypol among them.

'Where is the little one? Where is Rebecca?'

'She is asleep at home.'

'Do you tell me that you have left her alone?'

'Biddy is with her and will stay until I return.'

'Why have you come here, bothering me? Have you no work of your own to be doing?' Vassie would say but not snappishly, not now that she had come close to her little girl grandchild and to the boy, the boy so solemn and watchful that she could not even begin to guess what he thought of her. 'And you, Gavin, is there no school for you to be going to today?'

She addressed him in Gaelic, knowing that he would only answer in English, for teaching in the day school in Dervaig was mostly done in the modern tongue. He could understand the old language of the islands well enough but he would not deign to have it on his lips. He was his father's son through and through, Vassie thought, more Lowlander than Highlander, with a sallow, clear-eyed handsomeness that would give him the air of a saint or a martyr once his growth had come upon him.

She longed to brush the curl of hair that licked his forehead but she had practised the role of hostile old wife for so long that even Gavin, brave as he was, would surely flinch if she stretched her hand towards him. He was polite though, well-mannered enough to answer, 'I have no school today because our master has had to go home to Oban where his father is unwell.'

Vassie leaned on the stick, claw-like hands folded on top, elbows cocked. 'Is there no other teacher to be giving you your lessons?'

'There is one lady but she is only there for the children.'

'I see, I see,' said Vassie. 'Do you mean for the babbies?'

'Aye,' her ten-year-old grandson answered. 'For the babbies.'

Rachel was quite unafraid of Vassie and, unlike her brother, did not appear to disapprove of the old woman. She was, however, bashful. She clung to her mother's skirts and peeked up at her grandmother in a way that reminded Vassie of her youngest, of Aileen, in the days before anyone had realised that she was fey. There was a sweetness in Rachel, a generosity that Vassie failed to recognise as a quality that she herself had once possessed, long, long ago now, before she had sacrificed *her* father's love for love of a worthless man.

Innis indicated the wicker basket at her feet. 'I have brought you some eggs and a jug of stock for broth and a loaf or two from yesterday's baking.'

Vassie grunted; the most Innis could expect by way of gratitude.

The Campbells were by no means poor. On the contrary: income from the hirings was more than enough to keep them on easy street. But there was no will now, no urge or purpose in Vassie, nothing she seemed to want. Ronan, of course, was too far gone to care about anything but whisky. In fact, it was considered a miracle that he was still alive at all.

'Bread, Gran,' Rachel said. 'Mammy bakit it.'

Innis was the good wife that she, Vassie, had once supposed herself to be. Only Innis was more loving, more expert and efficient; a better cook, a better baker, better with sewing-needles and knitting-pins, better too in her management of time. When Vassie contemplated her middle daughter she sometimes wondered how she could have produced such a paragon of virtue – or if it was Innis's conversion to Catholicism that had mysteriously endowed her with all these skills.

No matter how empty her heart, how steely her determination to keep her daughters at arm's length – for their benefit, not her own – Vassie could not help but soften to the girls and half-grown boy who, poor souls, had flowered from the fruit of her loins. She smiled at Rachel in spite of herself, let her face tighten, so that the mass of fine wrinkles that mapped her cheeks was smoothed away and she looked no longer fierce like an old witch woman but just enough like Mammy or Auntie Biddy to reassure her grandchildren that she would never do them harm. She said, 'And did you help your Mam with the baking, dearest?'

'I mixit the flour,' Rachel answered, her fist, like a cat's paw, kneading her mother's skirts, while her brother stared gravely down at her. 'I mixit the flour, Gran, and I ated the butter.'

'You should not be eating the butter,' Gavin said.

'In spite of the butter,' Innis said, 'she is a grand help to me in the kitchen. I can get through a baking in twice the time when I have Rachel's assistance.' She winked at Vassie who, though she well understood the joke, did not respond.

Gavin, though, uttered a tiny priggish sound, a *huh* of disapproval, and without warning separated himself from the group and walked away, hands behind his back, as if he was too sensible to associate with the silly females for one minute longer.

He moved towards the crest of the track where it spilled in streaks of sand and crushed shell towards the steepest corner of the calf park. His eyes, like his brain, were quick-focused.

He noticed rabbits nibbling in the shadow of the edge of the bracken, the dense almost impenetrable wave of fern that swarmed against the fence and broke against the escarpment of clean grey rock that marked the end of Olaf's Ridge. He was looking, at first, for his father. For he should have been with his father. Except that he had his duty to do, his manly duty to visit the ugly old woman of Pennypol, to be seen by her, admired by her, not for what he could do – snare rabbits, shoot pigeons, catch and pin down a struggling ewe – but only for how he looked; which sort of attention, being merely a boy, both flattered and embarrassed him.

In August sunlight Pennypol's pastures seemed so lush, so fertile that he could feel their weight within him, the colour of it all, the iridescent haze of insects, the fur-feel of the rabbits, the flat, spectacular expanse of the horizon that he, in an instant, blotted out. He had no liking for the sea, no curiosity about it. It just lay there doing nothing, or roared in at him, a nuisance, a waste, unconnected, Gavin felt, to ground that would feed sheep.

He frowned, creating a tiny blemish on his silky, implacable brow. He experienced a sting of anger at the sight of so many pestilential rabbits consuming good grazing grass on land that his father had informed him would one day belong to him – not rented, but owned – when the ugly old woman and the smelly bundle of rags that was his grandfather finally withered to dust and, like puffballs, were blown away by the wind.

He frowned at the rabbits, the nibbling rabbits, seeing nothing else now, all focused and concentrated, the voices of his mother and the ugly old woman, the stupid giggles that his sister emitted, fading off, fading out, until all he could hear was a clicking little pulse inside his head, like the *sneck* of rabbits' teeth; and he raised his arms and took aim with an imaginary rifle – like Mr McCallum's, big and heavy and satisfying – and fired, and whispered under his breath, '*Bam, bam, bam*. Die. Die. Die.'

Biddy recalled that one of the signs of Aileen's mental disorder had been an inclination to sleep more than was natural, to sidle away from field work and crumple up in the lee of a stook or on the bare, cattle-splattered track, to stick her thumb in her mouth and be unconscious within seconds. It worried Biddy that the deficiency that had affected Aileen's brain might have been handed down to the next generation and she was unduly concerned that her sister's youngest still seemed to require an afternoon nap.

When Biddy thought of herself as a romping child she thought of pace, of whirl, of action, of the need to throw herself about, to trail after Dada or Mam or their old dog Fingal, who been a pup in those days but had been dead now for eight or nine years, to run towards the vastness that was the shore or the greater, frightening vastness that was the sea. And how much she had hated it when her brother Neil had come along and then Innis who, Biddy had imagined in shrieking panic, was trying to eat Mam's udder.

Nevertheless, she was delighted to be left in charge of Rebecca for an hour or so. To sit in the doorway of Innis's cool, scrubbed, neat-as-ninepence kitchen with the little girl asleep beside her in the boxed cot that Michael had hammered together, Rebecca snoring softly under the cool net-lace coverlet in the shadow of the doorpost. She would peep frequently into the cot, see the rosy blush on the sleeping cheek that hinted that little Becky might be abashed by her innocent dreams or even by her own fairness. And she would rearrange the net-lace with the tip of her pinkie or gently dab perspiration from the child's upper lip and wish with a fierce, almost frightening longing that the little girl belonged to her.

Biddy sat on a three-legged nursing stool in the open doorway and looked out at the garden and the flank of Olaf's Hill and wished rather that she might be here in Innis's stead when Michael came home. He would not come home, though, if he even suspected that she might be there. Michael avoided her with an ingenuity that in another employee would have struck her as churlish.

She still wore her fancy hat – the cock's feather amused Becky and Rachel – and a short skirt and jacket and a silk blouse that maintained an air of authority without fuss. She preferred blouses and short skirts to the heavyweight evening gowns or frilly tea-dresses that her social position often required her to wear. Best of all she liked the sporting, figure-hugging light tweed coats, knickers and leggings that gave her a feeling of freedom without being too mannish.

In a month or so she would be free to wear what she liked, for she would no longer be plain Biddy, no longer Becky's aunt or Innis's sister; she would be Mistress Bridget Campbell Baverstock, guest of Lord Fennimore at Coilichan Lodge in the deep dark glen of the Tormont deer forest. She would consort on equal terms with other land-owning gentlemen and their ladies, fanatical shots who, at this very hour, were gathered on a Sutherland grouse moor banging away at the birds. She could have been with them; Iain Carbery had invited her by personal letter. She had refused though, not because she was coy but because she was still first and foremost a farmer and the early August month was busy with harvests and sales. She was also still a Campbell as much as a Baverstock and as happy to be here on the stoup of Pennymain cottage as anywhere.

Innis and Rachel appeared at the wicket gate by the side of the garden. There was a general springing about of cats and a clucking of hens and a yapping from the pet spaniel, Fruarch, who regarded himself as part of the family and probably not a dog at all. Fortunately Michael had taken the sheepdog, Roy, with him for Roy had no patience with the inquisitive, undisciplined little pup and would roll him over with his nose to teach the youngster who was boss. Roused by the hubbub Rebecca wakened with a little yawn and a stretch, then sat upright, shedding the net-lace coverlet like gossamer. Though she was no longer a baby Biddy picked her up and carried her out into the sunlight to greet the arrivals.

'I did not see you come over the Ridge,' Biddy said.

'We came along by the shore path,' Innis said.

She steered Rachel before her through the gate then released the little girl who, with the spaniel weaving and bounding playfully about her legs, went off into the leek beds with a handful of scallop shells to add to the decorative border.

'How is she?' Biddy said. 'Mother, I mean?'

'Much the same as always.'

Rebecca showed no signs of wishing to be put down. She had hooked a chubby leg around her aunt's waist and draped an arm around her shoulder and, with the cock's feather tickling her nose, peered down at her mother from lofty heights.

'Did you see Dada?' Biddy enquired.

'No.'

'He would be there all the same.'

'Oh, yes,' said Innis, shrugging. 'Where else would he be?'

Biddy put her niece down, watched the little girl trot forward and throw herself affectionately against Innis's skirts. Becky would surely grow up to be Innis's double. Already she had her mother's oval shape of face and straight, rather severe brows, together with an observant demeanour that suggested that she too might turn out to be a cottage scholar. Although Biddy loved the girls dearly there were times when she could not help but feel alienated from them. Raised in the Catholic faith they were already familiar with rituals that she had been taught to regard as idolatrous, rituals that seemed to have given Innis a dimension to which she, Biddy, for all her wealth, could never hope to aspire.

Touched by a guilt that was never far beneath the surface, Biddy said, 'You know that I would take Mam to live with me, if I could.'

'I know it,' Innis said.

'But not him, not after what he did to us.'

'I know it,' Innis said again. 'You must not be thinking, Biddy, that I blame you for what has happened.'

'Happened? What do you mean?'

'To Mam.'

'What of Michael; does he blame me?'

'Michael?' Innis said, surprised. 'I do not believe he even thinks of these things. He has never – never that I have heard – said a word against you.'

'Because I pay his wages and he knows better.'

'Biddy,' said Innis with the faint ring of chastisement that Biddy had always found patronising, 'what is wrong with you these days? You have not been at all yourself this past half year or so.'

'Nothing is wrong with me,' Biddy said. 'I am perfectly well.'

'Yes, may be, but you do not seem,' Innis paused, 'content.'

'I am as content as any farmer ever is,' Biddy said. 'I would be even more content if the market for beef was not so depressed and if the dealers in Oban did not have teeth like sharks.'

'I thought you were transporting mutton directly to Glasgow, now that the railway has been extended to Oban?'

Relieved that the conversation had veered away from her peculiar, and obviously noticeable, restlessness, Biddy said, 'Has Michael not told you what it costs to ship live meat by rail?'

'Michael seldom talks to me about his work.'

'Does he talk to you at all?'

'Biddy!' another soft, chiding exclamation.

Biddy said, 'If he does talk to you, you're fortunate. He throws hardly a word in my direction. He sends Barrett as his emissary instead.'

'Well . . .' Innis glanced towards the garden where Becky had joined forces with her sister and, hunkered on the dirt path, was planting the afternoon crop of scallop shells along the border of the rows.

'Well what, Innis?'

Innis shook her head. 'I promised I would not say anything to you.'

'About what? About me?'

'It is not you. It is . . .'

'For God's sake, out with it.'

'It is about the men who visit you.'

'Hoh!' said Biddy, pursing her lips. 'So that's it. I'm to be condemned just because I entertain gentlemen at my house. Is that what Michael has been telling you? Who does Michael think he is? My keeper? I do not have to answer to your husband – or to you, for that matter – for having guests at Fetternish.'

'It is not that, not that at all.'

'What is it then?'

'It is who they are.'

'Damn it, Innis, it's no business of yours who my friends are.'

'Michael is not the only one who is concerned.'

'Is he not? I suppose they are all burning with curiosity. Well, damn them! I do not have to explain myself to servants.'

'They are concerned in case you marry the wrong sort of man.'

'What?' Biddy shouted, loudly enough to startle her nieces. 'How *dare* they! How *dare* they tell me who and who not I can marry. I suppose they will be wanting me to ask *their* permission before I invite somebody to stay?'

'Biddy, the children . . .'

Biddy caught herself just in time. When she had been younger her temper had been her downfall, a furious red mist that had smothered her common sense and almost blotted out her reason. She had thought that she had outgrown tantrums now that she had matured or, at worst, had reduced them to a necessary firmness. It had been years – well, months – since she had yelled at any of the house staff, though just last week she had been forced to give Angus Bell a tongue-lashing for carelessly crippling one of the breeding ponies.

With Innis, though, it was different. Innis had seen her in fits often enough to know what to expect. Even so, she sucked in a deep breath, gained control of herself, and said, 'Do you suppose that if I were to marry – and nobody has asked me yet – that I would give up running Fetternish?'

'Give up the sheep, perhaps?' Innis suggested.

Biddy shook her head. 'If you mean would I be tempted to turn Fetternish into a shooting estate like Tormont – never.'

'Is that not what your Mr Carbery would like you to do?'

'He is *not* my Mr Carbery,' said Biddy, coldly. 'Even if he were, I would not be inclined to let a husband tell me how to manage my property. No, Innis, you can assure your husband that his job is safe, at least while I'm still breathing – which, God willing, will be for a long while yet.'

Innis said, 'I did not mean to offend you.'

'I am not offended,' Biddy lied. 'I understand Michael's anxiety. Do you remember how Mam used to fret every time

Fetternish changed hands? It is a natural thing in us to worry over every little shift in the wind.'

'But Mr Carbery . . .'

'Is a friend. I shoot with him, that's all.'

'And Captain Galbraith?'

'Same thing,' said Biddy. 'And Mr Parker. And Mr Poole.'

'You do seem to have an awful lot of gentlemen friends.'

'Would you rather I had no friends at all?' Biddy was fidgeting to be on her way. What had started out as a pleasant enough conversation had somehow deteriorated into an argument. 'I must go now. I have a very great deal to do.'

Knowing that she had upset her sister, Innis walked with her through the gate and out on to the sward behind the house that dipped into the gloomy gash of the glen. There appeared to be no breeze at all, yet the mass of shrubs that clung to the wall of the glen stirred as if they were being shaken not from above but from below. In the quiet of the afternoon the sisters could hear the snarking of rooks, the squeal of gulls, ewes baaing in the pastures, the beat of the sea like a distant pulse, and they paused, Innis's hand upon Biddy's sleeve, faces turned towards the glen which seemed to suck all other sounds down into it.

Innis said, softly, 'Is it true, Biddy?'

'Is what true?'

'That nobody has asked you to marry them?'

Biddy snorted. 'Nobody that I would have in a gift.'

'I'm – I am sorry.'

'For what? For me?' Biddy gave herself a shake, almost a shiver, and quickly withdrew her arm. 'I am not in need of your pity, Innis. There are more things to be doing with one's life than throwing it away on some man or other.'

'And children?'

'Children?'

'Are you not wanting children, Biddy, children of your own?'

'Whatever gave you that idea?'

'I have seen how much you love the girls. I just thought . . .'

It was all Biddy could do to contain herself, not to let Innis see how accurate the observation had been and how much it had hurt her. She could hear the rooks mocking from the trees in the glen and the spaniel pup yapping in the garden. She drew herself up again, took another deep, controlled breath and said, 'I would be obliged if you would keep your nose out of my affairs, Innis, you and your husband both. What I do and what I want are not matters that need concern you. If and when I do choose to marry it will not be to please my servants and employees – not even you.'

'I am sorry, Biddy,' said Innis again. 'I did not mean to offend you.'

'I am not offended,' Biddy said. 'I'm busy. Now – goodbye to you.'

'Goodbye, dear,' said Innis with that patronising air that sent Biddy off with anger in her heart, anger and frustration and, for some reason that she could not explain, remorse. 'Will we be seeing you tomorrow?'

'Hah!' Biddy exclaimed and, without turning, plunged down towards the narrow wooden bridge that hid itself among the trees.

As usual Willy was waiting for her. He seldom accompanied Biddy when she called upon her kinfolk. He was fond of Innis and the children and would meander down there on his own account, with hidden in his pocket a square of sugar tablet that Queenie the cook had made or an orange or banana that he had snaffled from the fruit bowl; something a wee bit out of the ordinary that would appeal to children so that Innis Tarrant's bairns, even po-faced Gavin, would look forward to his appearances and give him a welcome he did not otherwise deserve. When Biddy went walking in the south-west quarter, however, Willy stayed home, for visiting her relatives was something that his mistress preferred to do alone.

Besides, Michael Tarrant was a blasted pain in the neck and Willy couldn't stand to see how Biddy looked at the shepherd, not with love but with a cold kind of longing as if she both hated and desired him at one and the same time. Neither did he go with her on her rare visits to Pennypol, because the sight

19

of the ramshackle cottage and the whisky-sodden wreck that had once been Ronan Campbell – in whose downfall he, Willy, had played a small but significant part – made him feel guilty and disgruntled.

When Biddy returned from her filial visitations, however, Willy would always be waiting on the doorstep to greet her, waiting as attentively as he had ever done for Austin and Walter Baverstock. He treated Biddy exactly as he had treated his masters all those years ago. Met her on the front doorstep, took her hat and handed her a clean linen cloth with which to wipe the perspiration from her brow or, if the weather was unkind, the raindrops. Sat her down on the bench in the front porch and removed her boots, not stiff, clumsy riding-boots but light, laced things that fitted snugly about a lady's ankles. He would grasp Biddy's calf, plant the half-boot in his lap, unpick the lace and ease her foot out as gently as he might slide an oyster from its shell.

It was not the sort of attention that male servants usually accorded their mistresses and, indeed, there were precious few mistresses who would condone such familiarity; but the bond between Mrs Bridget Baverstock and Mr William Naismith was unusually close, for no one, not even her sister, understood Biddy quite as well as he did.

At sixty-one he was easily old enough to be her father. His trim beard and thick-curled hair were snow-white now but there was still a glimmer in his eye and, Biddy suspected, enough of a glow in the coals of the hearth to satisfy his second wife, Maggie, the household's third resident servant.

'Shy Margaret,' as she had once been known, was shy no more. Anyone who had shared Willy Naismith's bed for a dozen years couldn't possibly remain inhibited. It was not that Willy was coarse or rambunctious. Far from it. He was a model of courtesy and discretion, except when a certain tactful inform- ality was called for. Then he could still reveal a glimpse of the wild, romanticising rover that he had been in his younger days in Sangster when he'd slept with everyone and anyone, in- cluding Agnes Baverstock Paul, and had fathered umpteen bairns, in and out of wedlock, all of whom he had seen settled before he had left with his masters for Edinburgh and, later, for Mull.

No other man would have dared offer headstrong Biddy so much sound advice. He was her protector, her grand vizier, her champion. She trusted him not only to know his place but to know *her* place too and to keep her to it, to ensure that her impetuosity was held in check and that her temper did not land her in too much hot water. She was also well aware that Willy admired her as a woman but, unfortunately, age and a happy marriage had put him beyond her reach, just as her position as the female laird of Fetternish had put her beyond his.

Willy said, 'Was it your sister Innis you were visiting?'

'It was.'

'Is she well?'

'She is seldom anything else.'

'Aye, you're hardy examples of a hardy race, Mrs Baverstock.'

'Are you mocking me, William?'

'Certainly not,' Willy said. 'I just wish I had a pair of feet like yours.'

He sensed her dispiritedness. It was not unusual for her to return from Pennymain unsettled and 'down'. He clasped her heel with his left hand and stroked his right downward over her toes.

She gave a little groan as her tension eased, and said, not sharply, 'And what's wrong with my feet, pray?'

'Not a thing, Madam,' Willy answered, without looking up. 'Perfect, they are, even if they could do with a wash.'

She laughed. 'It's a warm day.'

'It is, indeed.'

'Have Maggie draw me a bath.'

'Already being done.'

'I will be changing for dinner, of course. Has Maggie . . .'

'The light grey silk, I think.'

'Good.'

He eased on her kid-skin slippers and, though she was young and flexible, offered her his arm. She took it because it was her

21

due, hoisted herself upright and wafted through the open door of the hall.

Willy followed on behind.

The hall was cool, the coolest place in the house, with the exception of the larders, on stuffy summer afternoons and in winter, the warmest. No large windows, only two small square 'spy-holes' flanked the main door. From the gravel drive outside the ground-floor aspect of Fetternish House was less imposing than stolid, as if it had been fortified not against marauding Vikings but against hordes of discontented tenants trooping up from Crove. Nobody could quite decide which was the front of the house and which the rear. All the elegant and magnificent architecture was concentrated on the seaward aspect where the huge windows of drawing and dining-rooms gazed over tiered grass terraces to the distant isles and peninsulas and the eternally changing sea. Willy, a self-taught scholar, thought of the views as Homeric but even he had to admit that during equinoctial gales, when the house shook and trembled, the only places to be were plastered against the stove in the kitchen or here in the great hall which was as snug as snug could be.

There was no more than a wisp of smoke in the massive fireplace this afternoon, though, and the doors to drawing and dining-rooms had been left open and the tops of the windows lowered so that the lazy breeze that came up from the sea could find its way into and through the big house and take away its stuffiness. Water was running in the bathroom upstairs, a pleasant trickling sound accompanied by knocking in the copper pipes, for pressure was not all it should be and there were no plumbers on Mull who could fix such advanced examples of indoor sanitation.

Biddy slipped out of her jacket and passed it to Willy who folded it carefully across his arm before he stepped to the oak table and poured a glass of gin and water from the jug there. He freshened it with lemon juice, a sprig of mint and a handful of the crushed ice that had been coaxed from the infernal machine in the cellar, and gave her the glass.

Biddy drank thirstily while she sorted through the letters and packets that Willy had spread out upon the oblong table.

'When did the post arrive?' Biddy asked.

'About half an hour ago. Barrett brought it up from the village.'

Bills from seed merchants, catalogues from sellers of horse rakes and prize cultivators, a day-old edition of the *Scotsman*, a copy of a garish sporting magazine to which Biddy subscribed. Letters: one from her brother Neil in Glasgow, another from Captain Galbraith, a young military gentleman who thought that he might be in love with her, and the last from Iain Carbery, bearing, ominously, an Oban postal mark.

Biddy pressed the rim of the glass against her under lip and nibbled on a sprig of mint, moving it from side to side with her strong white teeth.

Willy watched his mistress carefully from the corner of his eye.

Iain Carbery was much given to ostentation and despatched his correspondence in huge tusk-coloured envelopes almost as thick as cardboard. Embossed insignia decorated both front and back and the address was scripted in black Indian ink in deep, slashing strokes, as if the writer had used a sabre in preference to a pen.

'Ah!' Biddy said.

'Hmmm?' Willy said.

'I do believe Mr Carbery has found time to write to me.'

She put down the glass, lifted the tusk-coloured envelope and tapped it thoughtfully against her lips. It smelled not of violets or lavender but, albeit faintly, of black powder, as if Iain had written it in the butts, which, knowing Carbery, was not beyond the bounds of possibility.

'Are you not going to open it?' Willy asked.

'I will read it later, at leisure.'

Willy hesitated. 'Perhaps Madam should open it now.'

'Why?'

'In case madam has failed to notice,' Willy said, 'I do believe it's stamped with an Oban postal mark.'

'Is it?' Biddy studied the envelope. 'So it is.'

'I was under the impression that Mr Carbery was in Sutherland?'

'He was,' Biddy said, frowning. 'At least I thought he was.'

Willy removed a brass letter-opener from a hanging drawer and slid it along the woodwork. Biddy fielded the dagger, slit open the envelope, unfolded the letter and scanned it hastily.

'He is coming here,' Biddy said.

'I thought that might be the case,' Willy said. 'When's he due?'

'Tonight.'

'Tonight?'

'On the evening boat. Will we pick him up at Tobermory?'

'I'll send Angus down with the dogcart – or would you rather I went personally?'

'No, Angus will do it. Meanwhile, will you . . .'

'Make ready the guest room?'

'Yes – and do we have beef, good beef in the larder?'

Biddy was flushed but not flustered.

There was no apparent reason for Iain Carbery to visit Fetternish at the start of the grouse-shooting season. He was an apparently well-to-do sportsman whose itinerary was governed by whatever there was to shoot at. Between times he would indulge in a spot of salmon fishing or ride with one of the Border packs. Biddy had not expected to see him before the beginning of September.

'Aye, we have a whole side of beef in the larder,' Willy answered.

'He'll be here by six. I must hurry.'

'If I might enquire, Madam,' Willy said, in the dry voice he used when pretending to be a proper butler, or when something got under his skin, 'why is Mr Carbery visitin' us on short notice?'

'I have no notion, William,' Biddy lied.

'Is there nothing in the letter to indicate his purpose?'

'Nothing.'

'He's after something, if you ask me.'

'After something? After what?'

Willy opened his mouth to blurt out '*You*' – then thought better of it.

Soberly, he said, 'Dinner at eight then, Mrs Baverstock?'

'Yes, William, dinner at eight,' Biddy answered and, wheeling, headed for the main staircase at something approaching a gallop.

The water in the big box-sided bath was peaty brown. Some visitors regarded it as dirty, especially after heavy rain turned it the colour of beef broth, and insisted on it being 'purified' with handfuls of soda crystals but there were no such indulgences for Biddy and, fortunately, none for Mr Carbery.

In fact, Iain Carbery was not much given to horizontal bathing. He preferred to lope down to the sea in his maroon-and-black striped bathing costume and plunge straight into the briny. If the sea wasn't available in the vicinity of his temporary accommodation then he would cheerfully wade into a loch or river or, failing that, stand out on somebody's lawn clad in nothing but a towel while ghillies and servants, working a chain, flung buckets of cold water upon him as if he was in imminent danger of bursting into flames like an old hayrick.

When Biddy thought of Iain Carbery – which she did quite often – it was that image of him that she held in mind. Hardly a locket portrait. Certainly not one Iain would have chosen for himself for there was something comical about his great shivering shouts of enjoyment, his hearty towelling-downs, the liquorice-striped woollen costume clinging to his not inconsiderable parts like a clootie dumpling drawn dripping from the pot.

There was also a kind of mortification in Carbery's demonstrations, as if he was whipping his body in punishment for unspecified sins. Bathing outdoors in all weathers was also part of a more general assertiveness, however, for Iain always had to be last out of the saddle, last in from the river, last down off the hill. And if any man dared challenge his right to be so then, by God, he would outlast them too, come hell or high water. What Iain was intent on proving, of course, was an ability to outlast all other males *anywhere* and illustrate to any woman who agreed to mate with him that she would become the receptacle not only of prolonged pleasure but of a substance so strong and powerful that her babies would come whirring from the womb like driven grouse or leaping out like fresh-run salmon.

Biddy had to admit that she found this aspect of Iain Carbery attractive; together with his size. He was almost as tall and broad-shouldered as her grandfather, Evander McIver, and he undoubtedly emanated potency; a river, a veritable flood of vitality that might cause the dainty ladies of Edinburgh to tremble and even swoon but that gained him nothing but admiration from the hard-drinking, hard-riding men and women with whom he usually associated. As to the view that he cherished of her, it was probably not of Biddy Baverstock sprawled on a tartan plaid in the heather above the Coilichan or even as she was now, bobbing, sleek as a seal, in the peaty waters of her bath – yes, he had been here and seen that too – but groaning in child-bed, for, Biddy suspected, Iain Carbery regarded her not as one of his conquests but as one of his failures.

Seven times they had joined in illicit union. Seven times Iain Carbery had given of his best. Seven times the widow of Fetternish had responded as only a woman of her passionate nature could, with, in fact, an enthusiasm that had left Mr Carbery gasping and exhausted. And *still* there was nothing to show for it, not a hint or sign that a single armour-plated Carbery tadpole had found its way upstream to surprise the slumbering ovum that nestled in Biddy's insides.

As she lay in the bath and studied her limbs through the pale brown water Biddy had no doubt as to why Mr Carbery had abandoned the grouse moors of Sutherland and hastened south and west to Oban and hence, by one of MacBrayne's steamers, across the Firth of Lorne. It was too early in the season for deer stalking. The attraction, therefore, must be game of another sort. Namely, and unashamedly, herself. Obviously she presented a more rewarding challenge to Iain's sporting instincts than any of the creatures of moor and mountain. Obviously he had been unable to resist the prospect that, with August waning, she might come late into season and be there for the taking.

Certainly she was there for the taking. These days she was always there for the taking. In that assessment at least the gossips were accurate. Iain Carbery was not her first or only lover. She'd had several transient affairs in the past half dozen years, liaisons that had given her pleasure but that had not, alas, led to courtship and marriage, even although the gentlemen had all been eligible bachelors and had declared themselves madly in love with her and ready to throw up everything to help her manage Fetternish. She did not require an estate manager, however – Hector Thrale still performed that function very well – but only someone to father her child and who, when that momentous event was confirmed, would whisk her to the altar double quick to provide the child, her child, with a name.

In exchange for the service, for, you might say, being willing to put the cart before the horse, the fortunate fellow would receive a fair share of all that Fetternish had to offer; a table to put his feet under, a pillow upon which to rest his head, a bed to lie down on and a handsome wife to keep him warm on cold winter nights.

Bearing this in mind Biddy was careful only to entertain men who were free to marry and with whom she felt she could cobble up some sort of friendly relationship. But as the summer of her thirtieth year wore on and *nothing happened*, not even with virile Mr Carbery, her desperation increased to the point where she began to feel that her inability to conceive might be some sort of divine punishment, that she might after all be compelled to take on a husband and trust to God, fate, luck or whatever factor controlled such things to ensure that she would do within wedlock that which she could not do out of it, namely, conceive and carry a child.

She soaped her breasts, trickled warm water on to her belly, lifted one long, smooth, muscular leg and studied it. She waggled her toes. Every visible part of her seemed to be in perfect working order, ready for the fray, ready and eager to be fructified.

She sighed and leaned back, resting her hair on a damp towel, and thought of Iain Carbery poised on the deck of the *Dalriada*, ploughing up past Duart Point and Fishnish Bay, past Salen and round Calve Island, his bushy hair fluttering in the salt sea breeze, his great, bushy, buffalo-horn moustaches twitching as he sniffed the wind, scenting her, perhaps, across all the miles of moor and shore, scenting her eagerness, her readiness, thinking, as she was, *Now is the time. Tonight, tonight. Now is the time, tonight.*

Biddy rose abruptly from the peat-brown water.

'Maggie,' she called. 'I'm coming out.'

TWO

A Family Man

It seemed to Innis that Michael was just the same as he had always been, that he had not changed one iota since that afternoon thirteen years ago when he had come straggling down the moor track behind Pennypol in the wake of the Baverstocks' first flock, those big, soft-looking Cheviots that nobody had thought would survive the intemperate climate but that had thrived and multiplied under the care that Michael had lavished upon them in return for his wage and allowances.

Mrs Baverstock was a generous employer, not just to her kinfolk but to all her tenants and servants; a fact of which Michael was well aware.

No matter how intimate Biddy and he had been in the past, though, he would not permit her to favour him over his fellow workers when it came to cash. He was not so proud and stubborn, however, that he refused the little extras that Biddy put in his or, rather, in Innis's, way; an extensive garden, a potato patch, repairs to the cottage roof, additional outbuildings, a substantial allowance of peat and coal and other small benefits, like the free use of a dogcart or trap to take the family to chapel in Glenarray one Sunday in the month.

Thrifty and industrious, God-fearing, abstemious, skilled in sheep-rearing, Michael Tarrant was a man much respected but not much liked, for he kept himself to himself both on the estate and off it and had no truck with the villagers at all. He had, after all, a wife and children to provide him with company and whatever else you might say about him you could not deny that he was first and foremost a family man.

That August afternoon he arrived home late, so late that the first hint of gloaming had gathered in the glens and, out to sea, the sun floated in strands of velvet cloud like a blow-fish, so lazy-looking that it seemed that it might slip no further and might elect not to set at all.

In spite of what Innis thought, Michael Tarrant *had* changed. He was still neat and well-scrubbed but so spare now that he appeared almost emaciated, as if he was being eaten away by a wasting disease, which, of course, he was not. Still, there was nothing of him, no pick of flesh on ribs or belly, only sinew and bone and flat muscle. His hands and arms, face and neck and the hairless vee of his chest were stained brown by wind and weather but the rest of him was so pale that when he stripped to wash he seemed almost skewbald, like some strange half-camouflaged animal. Gavin was rounder and smoother in limbs and belly, his complexion pink where his father's was brown. Otherwise he was a fair copy of Michael, except that his black hair had no little flecks of silver above the ears.

Father and son arrived together. They were always together, communicating, for the most part, not by word or gesture but by an invisible link, like the submarine cables that carried the telegraph, so that each seemed to know just what the other was thinking without a sound being uttered.

Haddock pie in the oven, a soup pot bubbling on the iron stove, an enormous kettle of warm water steaming on its hook over the fire in the brick-lined hearth; the kitchen was stifling, Innis and the girls red-faced.

Innis pulled a tin bath from the corner and propped it on trestles by the open door. She hoisted the kettle, disengaged it from its hook, carried it to the bath and emptied out its contents. She placed a bar of soap and two towels on the end of the trestle then went out into the open yard at the rear of the cottage to refill the kettle from the pump that brought water up from the glen.

By the time she returned to the kitchen Michael and Gavin were towelling themselves dry and the girls, Becky and Rachel, had taken up their customary positions, crouched on the stone-flagged floor. They looked up at the menfolk with awe, not expectation, for they knew that they would not be given sweetmeats or a coloured pebble or something, anything, that Daddy had found for them that afternoon. They waited only for a word of recognition, a sign that Daddy had noticed them at all.

Michael put on the clean flannel shirt that Innis had laid out and turning his back on the girls tucked the tail into his breeks, cinched the narrow leather belt about his waist and jerked it tight.

Then he said, 'Gavin tells me your sister was here this afternoon?'

The girls were still, very still, crouched on their heels, Rachel's arm draped over Rebecca's shoulder. Grunting, Innis took all the weight of the kettle on one arm, swung the blackened hook through the blackened handle and released the vessel over the peat fire. A small pot of tea water was already boiling on the top of the iron stove. Innis wiped her hands on her apron, stepped from hearth to stove and carefully scalded the earthenware teapot. She was not put out by Michael's undemonstrative tone, the Lowland accent that made questions and answers and statements all sound exactly the same. Her only concession to years of taciturnity was not to answer at once, for she knew that few of his utterances were ever expanded into full conversation.

'Yes, she was,' Innis said, at length.

'Gavin tells me you went to Pennypol?'

'I took over some baking.'

'I ated the butter, Daddy,' Rachel whispered, rocking on her bare heels. 'I told Gran I ated the . . .'

'Gavin says you left Becky with her,' Michael went on.

'She was asleep. Becky, I mean.'

He nodded. 'I thought I told you I didn't approve of your sister being left alone with the children.'

'Aye,' Innis said, 'but you have never told me why.'

Michael drew out a chair and seated himself at the table. Gavin followed his father's lead, then the girls scrambled from the floor and climbed on to their stools while Innis ladled soup from the pot, placed a bowl before each of them and, standing motionless by the table, bowed her head. Michael muttered Grace. They all, even Becky, added 'Amen'. Innis seated herself and lifted her spoon.

She said, 'You have never told me why, Michael.'

'I do not have to give you a reason.'

'Do you think that she will steal them?'

He paused, said, 'She's not a good influence.'

'Oh, is that it?' Innis said. 'When did this become apparent to you?'

He paused again. 'She has another one – no: the same one – staying with her tonight.'

'She said nothing to me about visitors,' Innis said.

'She is too ashamed to talk of it, no doubt.'

'Which one is it?'

'Carbery.'

'Is he not residing at Coilichan Lodge?'

'I tell you, he's staying at Fetternish.'

'Is this the only reason why you do not want Biddy to . . .' Innis glanced at her daughters and bit her lip. 'That is no reason at all, Michael.'

'He is not her husband.'

'Not yet at any rate,' Innis agreed. 'But he is her friend and there is no reason why he should not be lodging at Fetternish. It is what people like Biddy do – they share hospitality with others of their kind.'

'Aye, and what else do they share, I wonder?'

Even when they were alone, without Gavin's censorious eye upon them, Michael seldom strung so many words together. She knew what was troubling him, of course. It was not the everyday fact of Highland hospitality that irritated him. Biddy might have any man she chose to stay at Fetternish, a whole battalion of them. Provided they were not eligible bachelors. Innis well understood the anxiety of the Fetternish workers, their concern that they might soon have a master as well as a mistress and that the new master might sweep all before him, including Biddy, and that they would find themselves unemployed because of it. If there was more to Michael's irritation than that, something darker and less petty, then Innis ignored it and adopted an innocence to which she was not strictly entitled, a mildness at odds with her intelligence.

She said, 'I still do not understand what it has to do with our children.'

Michael pushed away the empty soup bowl. 'Biddy is morally tainted.'

Taken aback by the ridiculous statement, Innis said, 'In the eyes of God are we not all morally tainted?'

'I'm not starting to argue with you about religion,' Michael said. 'Is there no more for my supper than soup?'

'There is fish pie,' Innis told him. 'Are you ready for it now?'

'Yes.'

Her mother would have flayed Michael for his peevishness, delivered sarcasm so caustic and obvious that even Michael would be forced to take notice. But Innis lacked her mother's bitterness, the resentment that found its release in scathing irony. Even in his cups, her father would quail before Vassie's scolding and, pushed far enough, would discard all self-control and lash out, not with his tongue but his fists. At least Michael had never struck her which, Innis believed, meant that he still cared for her.

Quickly she dished out the pie, scraping the ashet on to her husband's plate. She put a bowl of boiled potatoes on the table and told Gavin to serve his sisters which, precisely as instructed, he did.

Seated once more, Innis said, 'How is it that you know that Mr Carbery is staying at Fetternish?'

'Angus Bell has gone with the trap to meet him at Tobermory pier.'

'Do you think,' Innis said, teasing a little, 'that Mr Carbery may have arrived without warning because he intends to ask for Biddy's hand in marriage and he is hoping to be catching her off guard?'

Michael uttered a muffled *huh*. 'He is after Fetternish, that's all.'

'How is it that you can be so sure?'

Staring straight ahead of him, Michael ate in sullen silence.

33

'Perhaps he might be in love with her,' Innis suggested.

'He has no money.'

'Who told you that?'

Again no answer.

Innis longed to lead him back to the subject of morality, to invite him to define precisely what he meant by 'tainted' and to explain why her sister's courtships – for that is how Innis chose to see them – should be regarded as different from the wooings that went on in the back rooms of cottages, behind byres or out among the heather. Courtship was the way of the world, not of itself a wickedness. And if Michael still felt guilty over what he had done with Biddy all those years ago then surely he had amply compensated for it by becoming a loyal and loving family man.

'Michael, who told you?'

'Thrale.'

'Perhaps it is not money that Biddy is looking for.'

'I'm sure it's not.'

'Why are you so set against her all of a sudden? Are you fretting in case she takes a husband who will change the way the estate is run?'

Michael turned his head and stared at Innis as if he was seeing her for the first time that evening. He said, 'If she has a child . . .' That was all. The sentence trailed away and yet somehow it sounded complete, as if all his apprehension and disapproval were contained in those five simple words.

He put down his fork and knife and got to his feet.

'I have work to do,' he said. 'In the hut.'

'What about your tea?'

'I will get it later.'

When his father moved towards the door, Gavin spooned the last of the pie into his mouth and leapt to his feet. Cheeks bulging he looked, for once, not just boyish but childish.

'Daddy,' the little girl murmured, 'I bakit the bread we took to Gran.'

'Yes, Rachel,' Michael said. 'Gavin told me,' then, with his son dogging his heels, he threw open the cottage door and vanished into the dusk.

The fears that Biddy's servants harboured in respect of Iain Carbery's motives were by no means groundless. He *was* after money, a soft billet, and Fetternish, he'd decided, would provide him with one.

Fetternish was not a sporting estate, however, and never would be. Its lochans teamed with small brown trout and the sea-fishing from the rocks of its sundry headlands provided mild entertainment. But it had no mighty salmon rivers running through it and its moorland ridges had long ago been cleared of primitive red deer and given over first to cattle and then to sheep so that game of any size, any challenge, was scarce compared to what could be found in the mountainous country around Ben More and in the black gash of the Horsa.

The house and its occupant more than compensated for the lack of game and Iain had to admit that more profit could be made from cattle, sheep and pony breeding than from hiring out shootings that were hardly worth hiring out at all. Even so, he had persuaded Biddy to employ a gamekeeper, Mr McCallum, who had done a good job of ridding the estate of its vermin and had begun to rear pheasants and attend the welfare of the grouse that fed on the heather where the moor rolled away towards the Dervaig road.

Iain had all this in mind, and a lot more besides, when he bade farewell to Lord Fennimore and abandoned Sutherland for Mull. There was a drawing power to Mull, to Fetternish, that Iain found hard to resist. He wondered sometimes if Bridget's ill-famed sister Aileen, whom had never met, had conjured up a love spell specifically to lure him back to the Hebrides. He travelled, as always, without a servant and arrived at Fetternish bearing no more than he could carry on his broad shoulders: one Anson shotgun, one greenheart fishing rod, a bulging oilskin dunnage bag, a brace of pheasants and two bottles of Ferntosh whisky to present to Bridget Baverstock, the light of his life and his hope for the future.

'*Bridget!*'

'*Iain!*'

They embraced on the gravel drive like long-lost lovers.

Angus Bell witnessed it. Angus Bell was shocked.

'Terrible, it was, terrible,' he would tell his father, a man so narrow in his views that Calvin seemed libertine by comparison. 'Never have I been seeing such a display of bridleless passion. It is painful for me to be telling you, Da.'

'No, son, it is better if you are rid of it so that it will not curdle in your memory and drive you to the taking of the drink.'

'Drink? Why the drink?'

'Never you be troubling yourself about why the drink, just go on and tell me what it was that she did to him.'

'She kissed him.'

'On the mouth!'

'Right on the mouth, Da.'

'And did she open her lips?'

'I will swear that she did.'

'Did he put his hands . . .'

'Aye, around her back.'

'Low on her back?'

'Very low, Da, very, very low.'

'There will be a judgement on that shameless woman one of these days, mark you. I do not know how our Maggie can be putting up with it and her so pure and modest in her ways. What would they be doing to each other next?'

'He gave her a nice brace of pheasants. She put her arm about his waist and they sauntered into the house by the front door.'

'Willy, where was Willy all this while?'

'At the door, waiting to attend to the luggage.'

'What did Willy make of it, do you think?'

'I canna say, Da, but he was smiling.'

Indeed, Willy had been smiling.

Willy did not entirely disapprove of Iain Carbery. Of all the suitors who braved the ocean to bend the knee before his mistress, Carbery was probably the least objectionable. He was, of course, an obvious scoundrel and far too callow to be devious. Willy, in fact, had Carbery pegged as a man who would take what he wanted not by strategy and scheming but by sheer persistence. But at least, Willy thought, you knew where you stood with a fellow like Carbery or, in Biddy's case, where you lay.

They met. They kissed. They sauntered into the great hall arm-in-arm and, before Willy and Angus could even fetch the luggage in from the trap, they had gone upstairs, probably to put in a wee bit of practice before dinner.

It had not occurred to Biddy just how much she had missed love-making, divorced from any happy consequence that might result, until Iain had her on the bed with his trousers about his ankles and her skirts thrown up.

There was nothing romantic about it, nothing romantic at all, yet his haste expressed a strange kind of poetry; the poetry of greed, of uncultivated longing, coupled with a complete lack of pretence. It was as if he had travelled half-way across Scotland driven by sheer need of her. And Biddy, dispensing with all the falderals, all the hop-skip, fan-fluttering nonsense of genteel and hypocritical courtship, was just as eager as Iain was to get on with it. It was, after all, her house and her body. She was at liberty to do as she wished with them, while the servants – not even tutting – kept an inquisitive world at bay.

'*Biddy, Bridget, Biddy, Bridget . . . ah-hah, ah!*'

She wrapped her arms and knees about him and locked him fast.

He was not large in that part but he was strong. If she had been a less liberated sort of woman or lacking experience of the male then his ardour might have seemed frightening, even cruel. Recalling Austin, though, and, more recently, dainty Captain Galbraith, she revelled in and responded to Iain's onslaughts without fear that he would be offended because she was enjoying herself too. When it was over and she lay back, panting, she experienced no revulsion or regret, only gratitude and an almost majestic rapport with the brute who lay upon her, still snorting like a grampus.

'God,' Iain said, hoarsely. 'God, but that was . . .'

'Good?'

37

'Excellent,' Iain Carbery said. 'I mean – *most* excellent.'

He rolled on to his elbow and looked down at her. He still wore his lined tweed waistcoat and flannel shirt, the collar jutting out behind his ear. His face was sleek with perspiration and he smelled, Biddy thought, faintly fishy as if he had been too close to the *Dalriada*'s kipper boxes. She did not mind, not at all, for under the fishy smell, she thought, lay the powerful odour of black powder and that other indefinable fragrance which had to do with maleness, with endowment.

She sat up and smoothed down her skirts. Her stockings were wrinkled about her knees but she would attend to them shortly. She would not bathe before dinner, however, for later that night Iain would take her again and, like Eve and Adam, she would be naked and he would be naked and neither of them would give a fig how they smelled while their essences mixed and mingled.

Iain drew in a deep breath and, tilting his hips, eased his parts back behind the lug of his lambswool combinations.

He settled his hand on Bridget's waist and asked, seriously, 'What d'you think, sweetheart?'

'I think we must wait and see.'

'And try again?'

'Of course,' Biddy said, without blushing. 'And try again.'

Commercial intercourse between Scottish Border towns and the markets of America had been hard hit by the imposition of stiff trading tariffs and the profits of the tweed-manufacturing firm of Baverstock, Baverstock & Paul had slipped considerably in recent years. With the French also threatening to erect protective barriers Willy Naismith feared that his old masters, the Baverstocks, and his present mistress, Biddy, might soon find themselves in queer street.

Willy was privy to all Biddy's financial secrets. He had even taught her how to read a balance sheet and how to interpret the ebb and flow of international trade from share prices published in *The Times*. Fortunately Willy had been raised with the Baverstocks and knew a thing or two about investment. During his years of service in Edinburgh he had even been incorporated into a caucus of highly-placed house servants who exchanged confidential information on money and markets and some of them – not Willy, alas – had built up healthy portfolios of their own.

For some time now Willy had suspected that the source of the capital that Biddy used to improve her island kingdom was in danger of drying up. He had written on the q.t. to his eldest daughter in Sangster to learn just what, if anything, Walter Baverstock and Agnes Paul planned to do about the slump in trade, for if the foreign markets went west then demand for sheared wool would also fall and the golden years, such as they were, would be over.

To an outsider, though, everything on Fetternish seemed tickety-boo. Willy doubted if Mr Carbery had a clue as to what he might be letting himself in for by pursuing the widow of Fetternish and just what might be required of him, apart from fathering sons, if and when he managed to drag Biddy to the altar. It was not dislike of Carbery, then, or even serious doubts about his intentions that brought Willy out at the ungodly hour of half-past six o'clock on a misty August morning, with the hounds, Odin and Thor, snuffling down the path before him, the sea calm as a pond and not a sound to be heard except the odd gull cry and Carbery's muffled yodelling as he vigorously towelled himself down after an early-morning plunge.

For once Carbery had elected not to trot back to the house in a wet bathing costume and Willy, quite unintentionally, came upon him as he was peeling himself out of the clinging woollen garment.

'Ah, Naismith! Thought I heard the dogs.' Iain massaged his hair with a sodden towel. 'Is this your usual?'

'Usual?' said Willy.

'Beat – for a constitutional, I mean.'

'Yes,' said Willy, to avoid explanations. 'How was the water, sir? Cold?'

'Not in the slightest. Very pleasant, very refreshing. You don't . . .'

'No. I don't,' said Willy, whose antipathy to salt water was legendary.

He watched the gentleman unconsciously display himself, turning this way and that as he wriggled the towel between his legs and down over his calves. Willy found not the slightest appeal in the sight of a nude male body but he was nonetheless gratified to note that the outlandishly well-muscled curves of Carbery's buttocks were not matched by anything out of the ordinary on the port side. Odin, the bolder of the two ageing hounds, came sniffing about the stranger and Carbery, still naked, crouched and clasped the animal by the ears and hugged and petted him for a moment while Odin yawned and yielded without so much as a growl of protest.

After a minute or so of play Carbery got to his feet, plucked up his shirt and pulled it over his head. 'I take it that Mrs Baverstock is still asleep?'

'She is,' said Willy. 'At least, she hasn't put in an appearance. It's a wee bit on the early side for the mistress.' He paused. 'May I enquire, Mr Carbery, how long you'll be stayin' with us this time?'

'That depends.'

'On anything in particular, sir?'

'Does it matter to you, William, how long I stay?'

'Not in the least, sir.'

'Are you expecting – I mean, is Mrs Baverstock expecting other guests?'

'None that I know of,' Willy said.

He had had no face-to-face confrontations with Iain Carbery before now. Although he knew that he had the measure of Carbery he was not at all sure that Carbery had bothered to take *his* measure yet. It was to rectify this omission that Willy had sought the man out.

'In that case,' Iain Carbery said, buttoning his trousers, 'I will be here as long as Mrs Baverstock cares to put up with me.'

Odin had joined Thor and the pair were intent on exploring the roots of a gorse bush. Those rabbits that McCallum had not yet shot or trapped would be well away, leaving nothing to intrigue the hounds but lingering scents and occasional droppings. Willy glanced towards the haze from which the skerries were beginning to emerge like clumps of horsehair. As casually as possible, he said, 'I take it, Mr Carbery, you're aware what Mrs Baverstock requires of any man who may have ambitions to become her husband?'

'I don't see what business . . .'

Willy interrupted. 'The truth is, I'm what Mrs Baverstock has instead of a guardian.'

'Are you threatening me, by any chance?'

'It's not my place to threaten the mistress's guests.'

'What then? A warning?'

'Advice, Mr Carbery, that's what I was hoping to offer you.'

'I do not require advice from a – a steward.'

'In that case,' Willy said, 'I'll apologise for having interrupted your ablution and will be on my way.'

'Wait.' Iain Carbery draped the towel around his neck and spread his bare feet like a pugilist. 'Tell me, Naismith, did Mrs Baverstock send you out here to find me? Is there something she wishes you to tell me that she's too modest to say to my face?'

The notion of his mistress as modest brought a smile to Willy's lips. He was tempted to say, No, Mr Carbery, I'm no white-haired Cupid. Instead he hid his amusement by stroking his beard and said, 'Mrs Baverstock does not know I'm here, nor did she send me. However, you have my assurance that she wouldn't be unduly disturbed to learn that we'd had a conversation of sorts.'

Carbery performed a little shuffle and waggled his bottom impatiently.

'Come to the point, Naismith, if you please.'

'The point, Mr Carbery, is that Fetternish is not a gold mine.'

Iain Carbery's brows shot up and the buffalo-horn moustaches, glossy with salt water, twitched. 'Ah! Ah–hah!'

'The wool market . . .'

'Do not talk to me about the state of the market,' Iain Carbery blurted out. 'I've suffered more than anyone from the ups-and-downs of trade, particularly trade with the damned Americans with their mania for *ad valorem* duty. Protectionism? A plague on poxy Yankee protectionism, if you ask me.'

Willy hesitated, then said, 'Am I to take it, Mr Carbery, that you're an investor in woollen goods?'

' 'Course I am.'

'May I ask, sir, in which particular commodities?'

'Wherever there is money to be made or, should I say, *was* money to be made. Ladies' dress goods, for instance, had a twenty-thousand turnover last year. This year, two thousand so far. Oh, high-class American tailors will still pay the price for a fetching novelty but no one can survive on that.'

'Does Mrs Baverstock know what you do?'

'Come now, Naismith, a gentleman doesn't discuss his business with a beautiful woman, or with any sort of woman, come to think of it.'

Somehow Willy had assumed that Carbery was a dunderhead whose conversation was limited to occasional cries of 'Shoot, boy, shoot!' He had also assumed that Carbery had some sort of private income but had imagined that it would take the form of a parental remittance. Mention of wool caused Willy's ears to prick up, for while he might not know the first thing about shearing a sheep, he knew a great deal about how to fleece a wool-grower.

He looked out to sea again and selected one single question from the host that clamoured in his mind.

'Ever been to Sangster, Mr Carbery?' he asked.

'Sangster?' said Carbery, quickly. 'Where's that?'

'In the Border country,' Willy said.

'Ah, yes, I believe I have heard of it,' Iain Carbery said. 'Never set foot in the place, though. Sorry.' And Willy thought, You damned liar!, and wondered why the Baverstocks, Walter and Agnes, had picked such a transparent idiot to do their dirty work.

Innis had raised her son and daughters with a healthy respect for the faith that had claimed her. She had taught them that they were different, not necessarily better, than other little boys and girls for Innis did not doubt that her children would soon encounter prejudice. There was too much evidence of it, in small ways if not large, to sustain a belief that Mull folk were tolerant in matters of creed. The handful of Catholics on the island were scattered far and wide and hardly ever came together. Even the most holy days were celebrated in sparse huddles with Father Gunnion trotting from one mass to another before collapsing into bed in the back room of the Inglis sisters' run-down boarding-house in the lane behind the Mishnish Hotel in Tobermory.

Innis chose to make the cross-country haul to Glenarray to attend mass in the isolated community hall in which she had first received instruction and within whose walls she had married Michael. On one Sunday in the month she would settle her children in the cart that Biddy loaned them and would drive through the hills, sometimes with, but more often without, Michael at her side.

Innis had a warm affection for Father Gunnion and in turn Father Gunnion had a special affection for Innis Tarrant and her children. She was his only island convert and in his opinion – which he kept to himself, of course – the better half of the marriage, for she had fulfilled all the vows that the ordinances had required of her and grown more loving in the Lord as the years went by. Of Innis's husband the priest was less sure. Tarrant was a dour soul, aloof and sullen, who made his rare appearances at mass as if he was conferring a favour on the Church.

Pennymain cottage contained only a few indications of the household's religious persuasion. A small, rather plain crucifix rested on the shelf by Innis's bed, an ebony-framed depiction of the Blessed Mother on a shelf above the children's cots. And that was all. Now and then, when she had the cottage to herself, Innis would light a candle before the Blessed Mother's picture and would offer up special prayers for those she loved and she never failed to commemorate that winter's day when, a dozen years ago, her brother Donald had drowned in Arkle bay.

She made no issue of prayer and seldom prayed for herself. Careful reading had informed her that she was no sinner and that what she discovered in Catholicism was, rather, a source of grace. She worshipped not out of fear but in gratitude for all the gifts that had been showered upon her. She would have liked to believe that Michael had brought about these changes, that he was the source of her contentment but she knew that this was not so and she would not lie to herself, not even a little.

So she carried her sense of well-being like the rosary curled in her pocket, and no longer expected anything of Michael that he was unable to give. She no longer expected him to love her as yieldingly as she loved him for she knew now that he was bound to her by a sense of responsibility. She respected him for that at least, and ungrudgingly maintained her side of the marriage bargain.

Until, that is, a certain Sunday in August in the year of '91.

It would have taken a bold man indeed to tell the Reverend Thomas Ewing that he was beginning to look like what he was – a typical minister of the Church of Scotland.

First he would have bridled at the suggestion that his appearance had become a matter of comment and secondly, having an enquiring mind and an analytical disposition, he would have demanded a precise definition of the word 'typical' since in his experience of the world there was no such thing as a typical anything. He would probably have gone on to expound on the folly of sticking labels on folk just because of what they were or what they did and he might even have worked himself up into a full-blown harangue against pseudo-scientific systems of categorisation and the perils of applying such risky principles to any individual organism, be it fish, fowl or clergyman. By which time the unfortunate ignoramus who had passed the remark in the first place would be hot-footing it away down Main Street or doing his best to slither over the wall into the kirkyard, blushing like a tomato.

However sad, the fact remained that Reverend Tom Ewing *did* look like everyone's idea of a Church of Scotland minister now that he was approaching fifty – assuming, that is, that everyone's idea of a Church of Scotland minister had been shaped by a half-remembered glimpse of a plate or engraving of John Knox, the sixteenth-century divine, who had railed against the Tudors and the monstrous rule of women and had interrogated poor, sweet, tragic Mary Stuart half to death, all in the name of Reformation. Tom, though, would have been quick to point out that Knox had also penned an excellent treatise on Predestination as well as the famous *First Book of Discipline* which had influenced the whole thrust of Scottish educational theory ever since and still presented an ideal worth striving for.

When it came to appearance, though, Tom didn't have a leg to stand on. Middle age had rendered him scrawny and rather shabby and, when robed, slightly fanatical, as if all the milk of human kindness that had once flowed in his veins had been curdled by disappointments too numerous to mention. He did not walk now; he stalked. He did not preach; he ranted. He seemed, in fact, to have become the epitome of every melancholy bachelor who had ever occupied a rural manse or ruled with rod of iron an unrepentant Highland parish.

The truth was that Tom's shabbiness was less a sign of self-neglect than the run-down-ness that manifests itself in falling hair, flaking skin, chipped teeth and eyes ruined by too much reading; in other words, of growing old. His critics also tended to forget that the stipend of the parish of Crove amounted to hardly much more than the poverty grant and most of the items in the minister's wardrobe, like the poor chap himself, were hovering on the verge of being irreparable. And as if all that suffering, all that hardship was not enough to heap on one man in his lifetime, Tom Ewing had been unlucky in love, not once but twice. He had loved both Campbell girls in turn, though his yearning for Biddy had been triggered less by the heart than by another part of his anatomy and he had known from the first that he had no chance of snaring the widow of Fetternish; but that hadn't stopped him dreaming.

Before he became infatuated with Biddy he had been in love with Innis. But that was love of a different order entirely, something tender, cautious and sincere. He had failed to press his suit with her only because she was so much younger than he was that he felt she could not be expected to regard him as anything other than a friend. So he had lost Innis to a dour incomer. And also to Roman Catholicism, a conversion that put her beyond his reach forever. He still saw Innis from time to time, but not often. He had no reason to visit Pennymain now and trips to Fetternish were usually made at Biddy's behest for they were both still pillars of the community and obliged to work in harmony in spite of the fact that, eight years ago, he had made a complete ass of himself by asking her to marry him.

She had been playing the piano by candlelight on a dreary November evening; a little lullaby by Brahms, sheet music pinned to the scroll and firelight flickering in the big, warm drawing-room. He had been at her shoulder, turning the pages, his usual hurricane of longing reduced to a pure aesthetic appreciation of her beauty, so calm, so fitting, so proper that he had suddenly heard himself say, 'Bridget, will you marry me?'

For a moment or two she had continued to play, then with a rather violent little *plink* she'd stabbed an elbow down upon the keyboard and brought about a deathly hush. 'What did you say?'

He had been so shocked by his unpremeditated proposal that he had been unable to open his mouth, let alone repeat the question.

'Say it again, Thomas?'

'I – I'd rather not.'

'*Say it again.*'

'It was a mistake, an ill-considered . . .'

'Do you wish to kiss me?'

'No.'

'Do you wish to take me to bed?'

'No, I . . .'

'Do you wish to give up your pulpit and spend your days helping me to run Fetternish?'

'Bridget – Biddy, I'm sorry. I don't know what came over me.'

'Did you not mean it?'

'I suppose – well, yes, I suppose I did. But not – not seriously.'

'Good,' Biddy had said. 'Because if you *had* meant it seriously then I would have felt obliged to give your proposal serious consideration.'

'Really?'

'Of course.' She had positioned her fingers on the keyboard, had found her place in the music and had softly played a few bars of melody. 'I have always had the greatest respect for you, Thomas. And it is no secret that I am not averse to the idea of remarriage – to the right man.'

'But I am not the right man?'

'Perhaps it is more a case of me not being the right woman.' She had stopped playing again and had turned and offered him her hand. He had taken it and held it. 'I am no more cut out to be a minister's wife than you are cut out to trail about the sheep pastures on my coat-tails.'

'I suppose that's true.'

'In addition to which,' Biddy had gone on, 'you were always much more attracted to my sister than you were to me.' She had squeezed his hand. 'Now, do not deny it, Tom. It was obvious that you were in love with Innis and would have done anything for her. Even,' another squeeze, 'to the extent of letting her run off and marry a Papist without lifting a finger to prevent it.'

'I doubt if I could have prevented it.'

'Why did you not try?'

'She was too young, Biddy.'

'Nonsense! Innis is only a year or two younger than I am. Be that as it may, even if you were not in love with Innis, I could not marry you, Tom, for the simple reason that we are not compatible. No: that's not what I mean. I mean that you know too much about me.'

'Oh, I hardly know you at all.'

'Would you not like to share my bed then?'

From somewhere, Lord knows where, Tom had suddenly found the wit to extricate himself from the ridiculous situation in which he had placed himself. 'Certainly, I would like to share your bed. What man would not?'

'You see?' She had sighed. 'That's the burden I have to bear, to be desired without being loved.'

The undercurrent of longing and the appreciation of her beauty were still present in him but the rancour had gone. He had seated himself on the piano bench and had taken both her hands in his.

'Are you saying, Biddy, that you no longer trust anyone?'

'That is precisely what I am saying.'

'Because Austin died in your arms? Because you think he let you down?'

'No, no, no. Because I have too much money.'

Tom could well understand her confusion, how her worth as a woman had been reduced by the ownership of land. Through no fault or wish of her own she had become powerful – and isolated. Even he had been unable to separate what he wanted from her from what she might need from him.

'Well,' he'd said, 'you can trust me.'

'Can I?'

'Always.'

'And the question you asked me?'

'Is tactfully withdrawn.'

He had never asked that question of Biddy Baverstock again. But when rumours of her promiscuity began to circulate he was quick to defend her and to protect an ideal of womanhood that was no ideal at all. He asked nothing in return except her friendship and whatever she chose to give, through him, to the church and the community. He remained lightly in love with Biddy as he remained lightly in love with Innis and had never met another woman who could compare with Vassie Campbell's daughters. So he grew older, alone in the manse at the bottom end of Main Street with only Mrs McCorkindale to come in each day to see to his needs and not much to look forward to except the day when some ignoramus would come up to him in the street and tell him that he was beginning to *look* like a typical minister and thus at a stroke transform mere eccentricity into cantankerousness.

Then on a Sabbath afternoon in mid August in the year of 1891, between the close of Sunday School and preparation for evening service, Tom glanced up from the book he was reading on a bench in the manse garden and saw Innis Tarrant at the gate and piled up behind her on the Fetternish dogcart, like a little troupe of monkeys, five or six children and, in their midst, the stranger whose arrival would change all of their lives forever.

If Michael had been with her it would never have happened. He would have guessed at once what was on her mind. He would have reached across and grabbed the reins and urged the horse – a strong animal, one of Biddy's best – past the ragamuffins who were strung along the side of the track.

'Too many,' Michael would have said. 'Too many for Biddy's horse to pull,' and would have left the little tribe to trudge on through the sultry heat without so much as a wave or a nod by way of greeting.

They were strangers, of course, very obviously strangers, and Michael would have no truck with strangers. But Michael was not with her, and the girls, if not Gavin, seemed to understand her need to be charitable.

'Look, Mammy, look.'

The Glenarry track was white with dust. It scribbled like spilled milk up through heather hag and bracken past the great, grey shapes of glacial boulders to the frieze of pines that stood out against a sky the colour of raw cotton. The air throbbed with the hum of insects. The black cattle and Blackface sheep that picked across the open slopes seemed flattened by the sullen heat and nothing seemed to be moving except the three or four buzzards that circled lazily high above the saddle of the pass.

'Who are they, Mammy?' Rachel asked.

The girls were standing on the board by Innis's side, braced against the iron handrail. Gavin was behind them, standing too, his hands out to steady himself as the cart rocked on the rough surface.

'Tinkers,' Gavin said. 'Just tinkers. Pay them no heed.'

But Innis was already reining the horse, reducing its pace

from that of a jog to a walk, to less than a walk.

One by one the tinkers stepped back into the ditch or on to the hummock that backed the ditch, and warily watched the cart approach.

Five of them; three children, a young woman and a man. They each had a sausage-shaped bundle roped to their backs, even the littlest, who could not have been much older than Rachel. She was a small, round-faced creature almost hidden by a man's hat, a floppy, wide-brimmed felt, torn and holed, that was tied beneath her chin with twine. She had charge of a pup on a string, a short-legged, chubby mongrel that whined at the cart's approach and, still too young or too weary to be nimble, rolled and flopped to find protection behind the skirts of the little girl's coat.

The boy next; seven or eight years old, dressed only in a vest and tweed breeches that had been cut off at the knees, a slight, pale-skinned boy who reminded Innis of her cousin Quig, except that this child was skinny and his eyes and his smile were feverish and eager. Then a girl, ten or thereabouts, in a faded cotton frock, her crushed straw bonnet prettily decorated with wild flowers and her long fair hair spilling over her narrow shoulders like a cascade of sand. Then the young woman, older than the others but not by much, rake-thin, bare-headed and bare-legged, one shoulder awkwardly hunched to balance the weight of her bundle. And then the man.

He wore a rusty black suit with the jacket slung over one shoulder. His collarless shirt was sweat-plastered against his ribs. He was barefoot like the rest of them. Little cuticle-shaped spectacles clung precariously to his nose and he dabbed at them from time to time to prevent them slipping, dabbed with his forearm not his finger, for he carried two bundles, not on his back like a packman but one in each hand like a washer-wife. Like the boy, he smiled at Innis as the cart came abreast but his smile was not feverish, not eager-to-please, just candid and friendly, asking for nothing.

Innis drew tight on the rein and halted.

'Mother!' Gavin hissed in her ear.

Innis ignored him. Rachel and Rebecca crowded against her,

staring with unabashed interest at the strangers.

'Good day to you, ma'am,' the man said. 'It's a hot one, is it not?'

'It is all that,' Innis said. 'Are you going far, you and your family?'

She addressed him in English for she assumed that the stranger would not be familiar with Gaelic. She did not climb down off the board, though. She had heard tales of marauding gangs and of violence done to travellers. Then she thought, On Mull? One grown man and four children? And, because her fears were so patently daft, she smiled.

'Aye, a far piece yet I'm thinking,' the man answered. 'But we have food enough and the weather seems set for another day or two so it will be no hardship for us to spend the night camped out of doors.'

They had not banded together around the man, Innis noticed, but remained strung out along the trackside like a little battalion of militia not quite licked into proper shape yet but ready to march on at a moment's notice. Even the spongy-legged pup seemed primed to make another mile or two before dusk and stood upright by the little girl's legs, leaning into her, not whining now but growling softly in his throat.

'We are going towards Dervaig, if that is in your direction?' Innis said.

Gavin pressed himself against his mother's shoulders, squeezing his face between his sister's heads, and whispered, 'No.'

'It is, it is,' the man said.

'I cannot take everyone on board the cart,' Innis said, 'for the horse will not be able to make the long pull up to the pass. But I can take the baggage, if it is not too weighty, and all the youngsters. My son . . .'

'*No!*' Gavin hissed.

'. . . my son, Gavin, will be walking with you.'

'How far is it to Dervaig?'

'Six miles or thereabouts.'

'I have no wish to impose but – well, it *would* be a great help to us if you're willing to take the luggage and the youngest bairns. The boy,' he indicated with his head, 'is not so sure at walking as the rest of us and, as you can see, my wee girl – Evie – does not have very sturdy legs.'

'And you, are you not weary?'

'Not I. Free of the luggage I'm good for the rest of the day.'

'Mother,' Gavin said again, flat-voiced, 'what are you doing?'

'A kindness,' Rachel told him. 'Is that not right, Mammy?'

'That's right, dear,' Innis said; then, to the tinker, 'Load on the luggage and as many bodies as you can, and we will be on our way. Gavin.'

'*Yes*.' Realising that argument was futile, Gavin hopped over the passenger rail and strutted off along the track, sulking, while the tinker's children clambered eagerly on board the Fetternish cart.

THREE

The Empty Road

Innis could not explain why it gave her pleasure to have a cart full of children behind her, all tucked down safe and secure amid the luggage.

She could hear Rachel and Becky chattering away, exchanging inconsequential information with the strangers as they petted the puppy. It occurred to her that the raggedy band were not tinkers after all, at least not tinkers of the usual sort. There was none of the truculence or obsequiousness that she associated with the travelling kind. She had nothing against tinkers, of course, but they rarely came to the north part of the island where there were few crops to harvest. The stranger's children had broad accents, though not as guttural as some she'd heard, and she guessed that they were not from a farming community but were city dwellers. The conversation between Rachel and the boy soon confirmed her initial impression.

'What's 'at?' the boy asked.

'That is a stirk,' Rachel answered.

'A cow?'

'No, it is a bullock.'

'What's a bullock?'

'A stirk, a stirk. My Gran has a lot of stirks.'

'We ca' them cows where we come from.'

'Where do you come from?'

'The Greenfield.'

'Where's that?'

'Over – over yonder. Behind yon hill, I think.'

'The mainland?'

'Aye, where we got on the boat.'

'Well, here we are calling them stirks.'

'Is that the same as men cows?'

'Men cows?' Rachel considered. 'Yes, I think it might be, since they are not able to be giving the milk and do not drop calves.'

'You speak funny.'

'So do you.'

The elder of the girls on board laughed suddenly, then for no reason that Innis, a mere adult, could fathom, a gale of laughter and giggling blew up behind her. She glanced round and saw that Evie was holding up the pup between two hands while the little animal made water, the tiny unformed curlicue between its hind legs twitching as it dribbled.

'Ach, Pepper, have ye no manners at all?' said the elder girl. 'Peeing in somebody's else's cartie. You'll get flung overboard, so ye will.'

'Nah,' Evie cried in alarm, swinging the pup away. 'Nah, nah.'

'I didna mean it, Evie. Honest!'

'We have a dog too,' said Rachel, diplomatically. 'His name is Fruarch.'

'What sort o' a name's that for a dog?' said the boy.

'It's a good name.'

'Is it a big dog?'

'Bigger than him. But not very much.'

'Can we see your dog?'

'Yes, if you are coming to our house.'

'Can we go tae her house, Tricia, can we?'

Tricia did not answer for, Innis thought, she does not know where she is or where her father is leading them or perhaps why. Innis glanced down at the man who walked by the side of the cart. He kept up with the pace of the horse almost, it seemed, without effort. Far ahead, dwarfed by the shoulder of the hill, Gavin strode on alone. She had had no concern for her son. He had been a determined walker almost since he was out of napkins and could keep up with and even outstrip his father on occasions. She would have been prouder of him, though, if he had not been so proud of himself. She felt aggrieved that he had not been more polite.

The children were giggling again. The man glanced up at Innis, winked and gave a little waggling wave of his hand. He had removed his hat and carried it by his side, wafting it across his face from time to time to fend off the black flies. He was taller than she had first thought, all legs, but not angular or awkward. He had begun to lose his hair, though. The sweat-shiny dome above his brows, coupled with the eyeglasses, gave him a scholarly air that jolly winks and waves could not quite disguise. The young woman walked twenty or thirty paces to the rear, watching the back of the cart in case any baggage or children might inadvertently tumble out and need to be retrieved.

Innis said, 'I do not think that you have told me your name, sir.'

'My name is Gillies Brown.'

'Are they all your children, Mr Brown?'

'Indeed they are.'

'I am called Innis Tarrant. The two girls and the sulky boy are mine.'

'I am very pleased to meet you, Mrs Tarrant, and not just because you have been kind enough to offer us a ride.'

'Have you been to Dervaig before?'

'No, never.'

'There is not much there for a man seeking work.'

'Dervaig is not our final destination,' Gillies Brown said. 'We are aiming for the village of Crove which, according to my map, is some two or three miles further along the road to the north-west.'

'Crove?' said Innis. 'It is not far from Crove that I live.'

'Then,' said Gillies Brown, 'I take it you're acquainted with Mr Ewing, the parish minister?'

'I know Mr Ewing very well,' said Innis. 'I have known him since I was a child. Are you a friend of Reverend Ewing's?'

'Hardly. In fact, we have never met.'

'I see,' said Innis, though, of course, she saw nothing of the sort and her bewilderment and curiosity were only increased

55

by his answer. She suspected that Mr Brown might even be teasing her a little. She let the cart roll on slowly for the horse was labouring a bit now that the track had steepened. She said, 'I am wondering what Mr Ewing could be wanting with tink . . .' She stopped herself just in time. 'I mean, with a labouring family – if that is what you are, Mr Brown?'

'Oh, aye, Mrs Tarrant, that's just what we are – a labouring family.'

He glanced round again at his eldest and gave her a reassuring wave. She was stooped too, thrusting into the hill, her sharp, intelligent face intent with effort. Fortunately it was no great distance to the summit. Gavin had already vanished down the other side and would probably be haring down the long hill, past Corm's farm and the steading at Ardinish, eager to get home to report to his father that there were tinkers in the neighbourhood.

Innis said, 'What is it that you labour at, sir?'

'Education,' said Gillies Brown, casually.

'Education?'

'The instruction of the young.'

'I am aware of what education is, Mr Brown. It is just that I cannot see what employment an educator might hope to find in our village? Are you sure you are not the replacement teacher for Mr Creggan, who has gone to Oban to look after his father?'

'No,' said Mr Brown. 'I am not the replacement teacher for Mr Creggan who has gone to Oban to look after his father.'

Innis waited, lips tight to her teeth. She had never thought of herself as a gossip before, driven by a desire to pry into other people's business, but she was consumed with curiosity nonetheless and just a bit annoyed at Mr Brown for his apparent reluctance to tell her what she wanted to know.

He smiled to himself and flapped his hat at the flies.

Innis resisted for the best part of a minute, then blurted out, 'What *are* you doing here, Mr Brown? There is no church school in Crove. In fact, there has been no school at all for the past eight years, not since Mr Leggat retired and no replacement could be found for him, at least none that would satisfy both the parents and the School Board.'

'Well, a teacher has been found at last,' Gillies Brown said. 'Apparently the Argyllshire Education Board have decided that the school at Dervaig is overcrowded and they are going to reopen the schoolhouse in Crove. Mr Ewing, I gather, will be the man responsible for confirming the post.'

'It is the first I have been hearing of it.'

'It seems there are enough children in your parish now to justify spending some money.' He laughed. 'Whisky money, Mrs Tarrant, that's what will reopen your school for you.'

'Whisky money?' said Innis in astonishment. 'What's that?'

She leaned towards him, supported on one hand, the other just barely gripping the reins. He was adjacent to the forewheel, face upturned towards her, his expression no longer mischievous but perfectly serious.

'It's a Residue Grant that some councils have earmarked to provide free elementary education.'

'What does whisky have to do with it?'

'Because it originally derived from money raised to pay publicans' compensation; huge sums gathered by Customs and Excise from local taxes intended to pay publicans for loss of their licences and the closing of public-houses. But the Westminster Parliament didn't see fit to approve the Act and the money was subsequently distributed among local authorities to be used for the furtherance of education, particularly in rural areas.'

He did not lecture her with the granite gravity that had been the hallmark of her dominie, Mr Leggat, in the handful of years that she had spent at elementary school. Nonetheless, Gillies Brown explained things clearly and firmly and Innis did not doubt that what he said was fact. She was amazed, though, that she had heard no whisper of Reverend Ewing's plan to persuade the powers that be to reopen the day school in Crove.

Shoving herself round on the board, she surveyed the cartload of chattering children behind her. Five there to begin with, plus Gavin. Seven growing up in Barrett's family, three in Mr McCallum's, several sundry Bells at the stables. Two with the new tenants at Coyle. She could tally up twenty without having to rack her brains or stray far off Fetternish. For the past eight years the children had trekked into Dervaig each day. In winter, however, or in stormy weather many a day was lost and at the time of the harvests many lads who should have been occupying a school bench were working the fields instead.

Listening to Mr Brown, Innis felt sure that he would do well by the young folk who fell under his charge and that her old friend, her lost friend, Tom Ewing had pulled a rabbit out of the hat this time.

'I will drop you off at the manse, if that is where you are to go?'

'Is it not out of your way, Mrs Tarrant?'

'Not so far as all that,' Innis said. 'It is the least I can be doing for the new teacher.' She hesitated. 'Will Mrs Brown be following on once you are all settled?'

He shrugged, not casually. 'My wife died in the spring of the year.'

'Oh, I am sorry to hear it.'

'In Glasgow.' He looked up at Innis again, candid in his sorrow. 'Which is the sole reason that we are tramping through this glen today.'

'To get away from Glasgow?'

'Aye, Mrs Tarrant, as far from Glasgow as possible.'

'In that case, Mr Brown,' Innis told him, as the cart crested the rise, 'you have come to just the right place.'

The Tarrants sat down late to their evening meal. Slices of cold roast lamb, green salad and boiled potatoes. Bread too, a jar of blackberry jelly and, because it was Sunday, a big dish of junket flavoured with vanilla to slip down sweetly afterwards. It was stuffy in the kitchen. The evening, like so many on Mull, had become still and airless and the sea itself seemed to lie exhausted against the shore. Though it was several hours until sunset, dusk had already begun to sift down over the hills. It was half dark inside the cottage but, out of habit and for the sake of economy, Innis would not light the oil lamp until supper was over.

Gavin had returned to Pennymain two hours before his mother and sisters. He had come via the headlands, short-cutting along the edge of the bog and past the long rakes of peat that, in a week or so, would be carted off to the stacks. He had scrambled down to the shore and snaked past his grandmother's house and up over the nose of Olaf's Ridge, anxious to track down his father, eager to bring his father news of his mother's misdemeanour. He sat at the table now, hard-eyed and sullen, filled with pique that his tell-tale account had been not only inaccurate but incomplete.

Michael said, 'So they are not tinkers after all?'

Innis said, 'He is a teacher and his daughter – the eldest – is his assistant.'

'And was it Ewing who sent for them?'

'No, he was appointed by the School Board. Tom Ewing is, however, responsible for seeing him settled into the parish.'

'Did you speak to him, to Ewing?'

'Only a word or two. He did not expect Mr Brown until next week and he had a good deal to do to make them comfortable before he went off to conduct the evening service.'

Michael said, 'If Brown is a teacher, as he claims, why were they walking along that empty road?'

Innis said, 'I do not know.'

'Perhaps they do not have any money,' Rachel said. Still too young to be adept with a knife, she ate with spoon and fork.

'How do you know?' Gavin said.

'He told me. Bobby told me.'

'Are they so ignorant,' Gavin said, 'that they do not know that a steamer calls at Tobermory?'

Innis said, 'I think it may be that what Rachel says is true, Gavin, that Mr Brown *is* short of money. If he paid for steamer tickets only to Craignure or took the small boat to Duart then it would be a considerable saving on fares.'

'Teachers are not short of money,' Gavin said.

'Mr Brown has got whisky money,' Rachel said.

'What?' said Michael. 'Is this man a drinker then, like your father?'

Innis was still upset with her son for running off and for

carrying tales to his father. She sighed. 'No, it seems that the money comes from a publicans' fund that the parliament in Westminster did not need to use, after all.'

'Publicans an' sinners,' Rachel declared, nodding primly to her sister as if the biblical phrase explained everything. Intent on her food, Becky hummed her agreement.

Changing tack, Michael said, 'Where's his wife? Is she not with him?'

'She passed away earlier this year.'

'Is that what he told you?'

'What reason would he have to lie about such a thing?'

'It seems this schoolmaster could tell you anything and you would swallow it without salt,' Michael said. 'How do you know that he has not abandoned his wife and come to Mull to escape from her?'

'And brought his children with him?' Innis said.

She was tired. The stimulation of meeting new and interesting people had been smothered by Michael's antagonism. She had anticipated it, of course, but not to this degree. She had learned how to deal with him, though, by trimming her arguments to fit his mood.

'Publicans an' sinners an' Far-sees,' Rachel remarked to no one in particular. 'They've got a pet dog, like us.'

Becky said, 'Pepper is Evie's doggie. I like Pepper.'

'Girls, just eat your supper,' Innis said.

'So this "whisky money" has been used to hire a teacher and to reopen the old school building, has it?' Michael said. 'I suppose you'll be wanting to send the girls there, sooner instead of later?'

'It would certainly be more convenient.'

'To be taught by an incomer.'

'Are you not an incomer?'

'Aye, but the sheep do not know that.'

'We will have to be seeing what happens,' Innis said. 'I am surprised that Mr Ewing has said not a word to anyone about his scheme.'

'He wouldn't be consulting with you,' Michael said, 'since you have become a heathen.'

'Mammy, can I go to the school for to see Pepper?' Becky piped up.

'Perhaps,' said Innis, 'when you are old enough.'

'New Year?'

'Yes, after the New Year,' said Innis, just for the sake of peace.

Peace, Tom Ewing decided, was something that he would have to learn to do without, at least until he found some place for the Browns to stay.

There were billets in the loft of the McKinnon Arms but to the best of his knowledge nobody had lodged there in years and the drovers who came to the district would not even drink at the bar let alone doss there. He might have put the Browns into the Wingard Hall but he was wary of taking advantage of his civic position, particularly under the circumstances.

Late on a Sunday afternoon, therefore, Tom Ewing had no option but to invite Mr Gillies Brown and his children to put up at the manse and, distracted by thoughts of young Browns roaming loose about his domicile, he was consequently even more 'ranty' than usual that evening. He had obviously developed a bachelor's natural apprehension not just of the havoc that children could wreak but of the prying habits of women – well, girls – when set down in a new place and, despising himself for his caution, he had locked up not only the sherry and whisky decanters but had even put away his tobacco jar and pipes, as if he suspected that Mr Brown's daughters, being Glaswegians, might already be addicted to the smoking habit.

He would have preferred it if Mr Gillies Brown had not insisted upon attending the kirk to hear him preach. But, being a minister, he was obligated to encourage Christian duty. Besides, Mr Brown was a jovial soul, only too grateful for the offer of shelter and relieved to see his children safe and settled, albeit temporarily. Even so, Tom Ewing could not concentrate on his sermon and substituted loudness for exposition.

Frankly, he was already beginning to wish that he had never become involved in the council's plan to reopen the school,

61

although the number of children in the parish now amply justified it. However, last May the Provost of Tobermory and the Chairman of the School Board had covertly enlisted his assistance. They had, it seemed, already hired not just a teacher with a certificate but a teacher with a pupil-assistant daughter who would work in tandem for the niggardly sum of sixty pounds per annum.

The old school building had been all but abandoned and was currently being used as a corn store by Mr Sloan the local miller, who paid a nominal sum in rent for the privilege. The dominie's house, where Mr Leggat had once stayed, had been sold off by the council five years ago and there was little hope of repossessing it without a legal battle. Tom's brief, therefore, was to provide lodging for the teacher and his family until such time as permanent accommodation could be found in the proximity of the village; no easy task, since every croft and cottage was presently occupied.

Mr Brown was waiting for him at the gate of the church. It was no distance to the manse but the schoolmaster did not wish to be impolite by treating the minister's house as his own.

'A fine sermon, Mr Ewing. You were certainly in good voice tonight,' he said. 'It seems a pity that there were not more present to hear you.'

'It is not the best season for church attendance,' Tom Ewing said. 'As you will no doubt be finding out, folk have too much to do at the back end of the summer to give much time either to God or to learning.'

'I hope that I'll be able to change that,' said Mr Brown.

'How?' Tom said. 'By beating them into school with your strap?'

'Hardly, hardly,' said Gillies Brown, with a laugh. 'It's all a matter of instilling the right kind of discipline.'

'Oh, so you are a teacher of the old school, are you?'

'Mental discipline, is what I mean.' Gillies Brown remained where he was by the wall at the gate. 'I'm not a hard taskmaster, not a bully, but one sort of learning tends to lead to another.' He seemed in no hurry to return to the manse. He pointed. 'I take it that's the village?'

'We prefer to think of it as a small town.'

'Well, it's not quite a metropolis,' Gillies Brown said, ruefully, 'but it is a pretty sort of place to be on a warm summer night. Where's the school?'

'Do you see the lighted building on the right at the head of the street?'

'I do.'

'Well, that is the McKinnon Arms. The school building lies down a lane just opposite to it. It is more or less just another cottage, though a long one. As I recall it is partitioned into two rooms, each with a stove.'

'I will have a look at it tomorrow.'

'No, I fear you may have to wait a day or two, Mr Brown. The building is currently under lease to Mr Sloan, our miller, whose entitlement to use the place as a corn store does not expire until next Monday.'

'A corn store?'

'Oh, the corn sacks will all be removed, I assure you, and the building will be swept and whitewashed and put right for you. Benches and desks are on order from the carpenters in Tobermory and, I think, blackboards and slates too. In two to three weeks you will be able to assemble your first classes.'

'I will just have to be patient, I see,' Gillies Brown said. He pointed once more. 'Crove seems to be that sort of place – patient, I mean.'

Tom's nervousness eased a little. He followed the line of the stranger's finger and, for a moment or two, tried to see Crove through the stranger's eyes. An August moon outlined the rows of whitewashed cottages that led from Tom's church uphill to the 'other church', the United Free. Oil lamps glowed in the windows and, though it was not yet mid-evening, there was a feeling of night now, of rest beneath the tranquil slates. Peat smoke wreathed the air and away to the west, over the invisible sea, a band of clear blue light suggested that Hebridean tales of a blessed land across the waters might after all be true.

'It is not so peaceful as it seems,' Tom said. 'We have our conflicts here just as you do in Glasgow.' He hesitated. 'Is it to put the past behind you, Mr Brown, that you have brought your children to Mull?'

'I take it you've heard that I lost my wife last spring?'

'Yes.'

'Clara was eight months a-dying, sick all through the autumn and winter. When spring came, however, we began to think that she was on the mend. She seemed to be almost her old self again then, in a matter of a week, the illness returned . . . and she was gone.' He gave a little shrug. 'I don't blame Glasgow for what happened. My parents are from Coll originally but I was raised in the city. I don't think Glasgow is a wicked place. No, the wickedness was in me.'

'What do you mean by that, Mr Brown?'

'After Clara died I found I could no longer teach properly. When I looked at all those young faces in front of my desk I no longer saw eagerness and hope and optimism. I saw only the suffering and loss that lay ahead of them.'

'Surely you were grieving?'

'Of course I was grieving, but I could not shake it off. And I didn't want to contaminate small, impressionable children with my disillusionment.'

'Did the school board sack you?'

'I resigned.'

'And Mull, the post here?'

'My mother read the council's advertisement in the *Oban Times* and suggested it would be better for all of us if I made a clean break with Glasgow.'

'What did your children think of that idea?'

Again the shrug: 'You know what bairns are like, Mr Ewing. To them it was an adventure. Even Janetta, my fifteen-year-old, thought it would improve our lot. So here we are, and feeling better for it already.'

'You have been very frank,' Tom said. 'I admit that I had wondered why a teacher with your qualifications would apply for a post in a village school. Now, I will be equally frank with you. There is no dwelling-house attached to the school and, to my shame, I haven't yet found anywhere for you to stay.'

'Mrs Tarrant, it seems, did not even know the school was to be reopened. Why has there been secrecy?' Gillies Brown asked.

'Because the good folk of my parish will probably resist it.'

'Why? Is the school at Dervaig so highly thought of?'

'It is a fine school, certainly, but it's miles from Crove, far too far away for young children to walk there, especially in bad weather. To be honest, Mr Brown, in spite of the diligence of school board inspectors education has had a weak grip on our parish ever since Mr Leggat left.'

'I see,' said Gillies Brown. 'It would seem, Mr Ewing, that I have arrived just in time.'

'In time for what?'

'To save your parish from foundering in ignorance.'

Tom nodded. He had looked up Crove's main street so often that he had ceased to see the village for what it was; a haven, yes, but also a backwater, half asleep and dreaming of a time that would never come again. The erosions of an industrial century had finally reached the heart of Mull and the islanders would be unable to resist progress for very much longer. In Tom's book, progress meant education, whether his parishioners liked it or not.

'I hope you can, Mr Brown.'

'Oh, I can, Mr Ewing. I know I can.'

'Failure, I take it,' Tom said, 'is not a word in your vocabulary?'

'No, but supper is,' said Gillies Brown. 'Shall we go in now?'

'Yes,' Tom said. 'I think perhaps we should.'

Although some doubt remained as to his lineage, Robert Quigley – Quig – was, in fact, no blood relative to either the Campbells or McIver. He had not been bred out of the old man's loins in one of the reprehensible matings for which the old man had been famous in his youth. For all that, Quig was closer to the old man than any of his so-called cousins, male or female, for the heyday of the feudal island community was over and Evander McIver but a phantom now, a spectre of his former self. In this past year even his wits had begun to wander and

Quig, patient and indomitable Quig, had everything his own way at last.

He no longer had to consult the old man about which bulls to sell or which members of the mongrel clan should be told to leave Foss for employment on the mainland. The island, and all that stood upon it, were effectively his, even the two-storey, wooden-walled house with its stone chimney and the verandah that had begun to crumble in the big winds that roared in from the Atlantic. The snug parlour where McIver had taken his ease smelled damp now and the books that lined its walls were prickled with mould. Evander McIver was incapable of protest. Even before he had lost his wits he seemed to have accepted that when he finally faded into oblivion the old, individualistic way of life that he had created would fade into oblivion too.

Quig was twenty-six years old that summer. He was as slim and nimble as ever yet his calm, all-absorbing manner was too mature for someone who had seldom left the confines of the tiny green isle; a spot of land so small and far away that it seemed to be no more than the shadow of a cloud on the surface of the sea. He cared for the old man and he cared for the cattle and was father to Donald, Aileen Campbell's boy, though he had never bedded her and, of course, never would. He was also the intermediary between Foss and Mull. He saw to it that Vassie had hire of the best bull for six weeks every autumn and that Innis was informed of every downturn in her grandfather's condition, for Quig knew that Innis and he were alike in that respect and would never neglect their obligations.

On Monday, last day of the month, Innis sailed from Pennypol in the tiny black-hulled steam vessel *Gannet*, that carried mail and supplies to Foss. She would be ferried ashore on the sloping beach at the front of the bungalow and would stay for no more than the hour, then the *Gannet* would return her to Ulva ferry where Willy Naismith or Angus Bell would pick her up in the gig and drive her back to Pennymain.

Quig looked forward to his 'cousin's' monthly visits and would prepare for them thoroughly. Shortly before eleven he would trundle Evander's chair, tilted on its round wooden castors, across the floor of the sitting-room and into the bedroom. There he would pad the chair with blankets and the strips of bleached canvas that were needed to keep the old man upright, and would lift the old man carefully out of bed. The smell of decay and the reptilian touch of dry skin rubbing over fragile bones did not offend Quig in the slightest. He would dress his guardian patiently, place him in the chair and bind him tightly with the canvas straps. A shawl would be wrapped about his shoulders and a knitted cap pulled down over his hairless skull and Quig would wheel him out of the house on to the verandah where Aileen and Donnie waited.

The old man would not recognise them, would address them as if they were folk who had been young when he was young. 'My sweetheart,' he would say in Gaelic, stroking Aileen's hair, 'my sweetheart, how pretty you are today, Ishbel, how the sun sparkles in your eyes. Will you not be kissing me again, Ishbel, my dearest?' And, at Quig's urging, Aileen would force herself to kiss her grandfather's withered cheek and would not flinch when he looked at her, sly and half blind, and struggled to draw her down on to his lap, muttering words that even Quig did not understand so old and worn were they. Then Donnie would hold a glass of watered whisky to Evander's mouth and he would stretch his neck like a hen's and sup so greedily that the liquid would trickle through his beard and wet the shawl that cowled his shoulders. And he would say, 'Aye, Hamish, you are a brave, good man,' or 'Douglas, how can I thank you?' And Donnie would press the glass gently against the old man's lips so that taste and smell at least might comfort him. And when Innis saw her grandfather in this state she would weep into Quig's shoulder and say that it would be better if he were to let go his hold on a life that was a life no more. And Quig, wise Quig, would agree.

She was brought off the *Gannet* in the little boat that Donnie was old enough to handle by himself now. She carried with her soft fruit, fresh vegetables and cheeses in two baskets, one from Biddy, one from herself. She carried mail too, a bundle of correspondence that Quig would attend to later. She looked, Quig thought, prettier than ever, with her sallow, sun-dusted complexion, straight brows and clear, intelligent eyes. He had never been able to see the least trace of likeness to Innis in her sister Aileen whose innocence was a sign of emptiness and whose child-like prettiness was spoiled by petulance and bad humour. He no longer thought of Aileen as Donnie's mother for she had played no part in raising the boy and he, Donnie, was as smart as she was wanting.

Aileen sat by her grandfather's feet, cross-legged on the veranda, pouting and pretending to be shy, pretending that she did not recognise Innis. In the doorway, Mairi, Quig's mother, waited, arms folded under her bosom, her gypsy-dark hair hanging in thick tangles about her shoulders, while Donnie drew up the little boat and helped his aunt clamber over the bow on to the sand. He took the baskets and the mail and followed her up the beach and across the crackling tide-line to the house.

The old man was motionless, forearms hanging on the canvas straps. He peered at the girl who had once been his favourite as she climbed the steps and, who, after taking off her bonnet, stooped and kissed him on the brow.

'How are you today, Grandfather?' she asked.

'He is just as you see him, Innis,' Mairi said. 'You cannot be expecting him to change now.'

'Grandfather? Grandfather?'

'He cannot be hearing you.' Quig stood close so that when emotion overcame her he would be there to comfort her. 'He is neither worse nor better.'

'Are the nights still bad?'

'Yes, they are bad,' Quig said. 'He is still troubled by dreams.'

'I wonder what he dreams of?' Innis said. 'I wonder what it is that troubles him so much? Grandfather, do you not know who I am?'

'Vassie?' he said, frowning.

'He is still thinking that you are your mother,' Mairi said.

'Perhaps that is who he dreams about,' said Quig. Innis had no trace of tears in her eyes today. Quig experienced a certain disappointment that he would not get to feel her body against his. He did not love her with a grown man's passion, yet he regretted that she had married a cold fish like Michael Tarrant and not the minister of Crove who, so rumour had it, had been fairly and squarely in love with her at one time. He put his hand on her shoulder. 'He is seeing nothing real now, not even you, Innis. It is all inside his head now, in a place where none of us can reach.'

'Me,' said Aileen, without warning. 'I reach.'

She scrambled to her feet and lunged forward so that her face was no more than an inch from her grandfather's, the movement so sudden that he blinked and instinctively raised a hand as if to protect himself.

'I know, do I not, Grandad? I know. I know,' Aileen chanted, thrusting her face into his until Quig caught her by the elbows and pulled her back. 'I know what it is he is dreaming about. I can see. I can see.'

'Aileen,' Quig said. 'Behave yourself.'

He restrained her with an arm about her waist until she became calm and, giggling, nuzzled and gored him affectionately; while Donnie, who had seen too much over the years to be embarrassed by his mother's behaviour, carried Innis's baskets indoors.

It gave Willy quite a turn to find the minister on the doorstep. For an instant he was possessed by the idiotic notion that Iain Carbery had finally persuaded Biddy to become his wife and had sent post haste for Reverend Ewing to perform the wedding ceremony.

Out on the gravel, though, was the minister's gig and the stuffy little piebald pony that Biddy had gifted him four years ago, but seated in the gig was a total stranger who, even as Willy spotted him, lifted his hat from his head and waved it, as if arriving at Fetternish House was some sort of minor triumph.

Willy tossed the floral garland that he had been wearing on to the porch bench, wiped his hands on his apron and, still conscious of the stranger, gave the minister an awkward bow instead of the customary handshake.

'Well, Reverend Ewing, this is an unexpected pleasure.'

'Is Mrs Baverstock at home?'

'No, I believe she's out on to the moor with,' a delicate hesitation, 'with Mr Carbery.'

'Oh, he's still here, is he?'

'Yes, Mr Ewing, I'm afraid he is.'

'I suppose they've gone shooting?'

'What else would they be doing?' Willy said. 'Would you care to step inside and partake of a cup of tea – you and your companion?'

Tom glanced behind him as if he had entirely forgotten that he had a passenger on board. The stranger, still grinning, waved his hat once more.

Willy raised an enquiring eyebrow.

'My friend is not quite so daft as he looks, Willy,' the minister said. 'He is, in fact, our new schoolmaster.'

'Is he, indeed?' Willy said. 'He's a long way from Dervaig.'

'A new schoolmaster, for Crove. The schoolhouse is being reopened.'

'Ah!' said Willy. 'Not before time, Mr Ewing, not before time.'

'I wonder if Mrs Baverstock will also feel that way?'

'You can but ask her,' Willy said. 'What is it you're after, Minister?'

'After?'

'Something tells me this is not a social call.'

Tom shook his head. 'There is no putting anything past you, Willy Naismith, is there? Yes, I am eager to enlist your mistress's aid. The teacher, and his family, will be requiring a place to stay and there is nothing at all to be had in the village just at present.'

'I see,' said Willy. 'Have you spoken to Mr Thrale about vacancies?'

'I thought I would consult Mrs Baverstock first.'

'Aye, the horse's mouth,' said Willy. 'Well, Mr Ewing, unless your schoolmaster intends to sit out there all morning scaring the birds with that hat of his, I suggest that the pair of you come inside.'

'To wait for Biddy?' Tom said.

'No, to talk to me,' said Willy.

'Aileen is no better, I see?' Innis said.

'She will never be any better,' Quig said. 'She is quiet and biddable for the most part but she is scant of wits and there will be no curing that.'

Innis said, 'What will become of her after . . .'

'After Evander dies?' Quig said.

'It cannot be long now.'

'No, even he cannot survive another winter.'

'It would be a mercy if he were taken soon.'

'I agree,' Quig said.

'But what will happen then?'

'To Aileen?'

'To you, to all of you?'

'I do not know,' Quig said.

They were seated on the steps of the verandah with their backs to Evander and Aileen who squatted like a little jester beside the old man's chair. Nothing occupied her hands, no string of shells, no tatting needles, nothing. She stared vacantly over the shallow bay and hummed one of the tuneless old songs that Vassie had crooned to them when they were children, as if that might soothe the dying old man, as a lullaby does a baby.

Donnie had transferred the last of the supplies from the *Gannet* and had taken the boxes indoors. The rowing boat was pulled up on the sand ready to ferry Innis out to the steam vessel as soon as she received a signal from Skipper Morrison that the tide had turned. Perched on the flat roof of the *Gannet*'s tiny wheelhouse the skipper and his crew were eating their dinners from tin plates while all the gulls in Christendom circled above them, screaming for titbits.

'I think you do know, Quig,' Innis said. 'I think that you have already decided just what you will do when the time comes.'

'Will your friend Mr Ewing give him a Christian burial?'

'Yes, Tom made Grandfather a promise and I'm sure he will keep it.'

'Then I will see to it that Evander is buried here, where he belongs.'

'I mean,' said Innis, 'after that.'

'After that,' Quig said, 'after that . . .' He shrugged.

'Will you be staying on Foss, or will you leave too?'

'Where would I go?' Quig said.

'To the mainland.'

'If I do go to the mainland,' Quig said, 'have no fear that I will leave Aileen behind. I will take her with me, her and my mother and the boy. I will always look after them wherever I wind up.'

'You are under no obligation to take care of Aileen.'

'Aye, but I am,' said Quig.

They were silent, saying nothing. They were like sister and brother in that respect, each sensing the other's doubts. Together, knees and shoulders touching, they listened to the desperate screams of the gulls piercing the warm August noon.

Innis said, 'There is a teacher come to Crove. His name is Brown.'

'A teacher in Crove?' Quig said. 'Do not tell me that at long last they are opening up the schoolhouse again, or do they expect him to be setting up his class in the cow pasture?'

'No, the schoolhouse will be reopened and refurbished.'

'Well, well, well,' Quig said. 'A school in your parish, do you say? Will it be only for infants, or can anyone attend?'

'No, it is for junior and senior pupils too.'

Quig could not hide his interest. He leaned against her. He did not drink spirits or smoke tobacco and she could smell the inimitable Foss smell from him, clean as sea air. He said, 'Have you already met this schoolmaster then?'

'I have,' said Innis. 'He is . . .'

'What?' said Quig, giving her a little dig with his elbow. 'What? Handsome, is that what it is you are trying to say?'

'No, I cannot say that he is handsome.'

'What then? Come along, Innis, out with it.'

'Personable.'

'Personable! Pah! What sort of a feeble word is that to describe a man who makes your cheeks turn pink?'

'My cheeks are not pink.'

'If that is not a blush,' said Quig, 'then what is it?'

'I have barely met the man.' Innis paused. 'Besides, he has four children. He is staying with Mr Ewing at the manse until a proper house can be found for him. He has a daughter who will teach the younger ones.'

'And his wife, will she teach too?'

Innis laughed in spite of herself. She did not know why imparting this rare piece of local news to her cousin should give her pleasure. She might instead have chosen to tell Biddy of her encounter with the stranger but she was wary of Biddy, not of her elder sister's sensitivity but of her scorn. She had been holding the news to herself all morning long, though why the arrival of Mr Gillies Brown and his family should raise her spirits was a total mystery.

Quig said, 'By God, Innis, are you telling me there is *no* wife?'

'I am telling you just that.'

'What age is this chap?'

'Oh, I would think he will be thirty-seven or thirty-eight years old.'

'Perfect!' Quig gave her another dig in the ribs. 'Just perfect!'

'But I am a married . . .'

'No, not for you, Innis – for Biddy,' Quig said. 'An educated man with four children and no wife would surely be a perfect match for your sister.'

'Do you know,' said Innis, frowning, 'somehow I never thought of that.'

Biddy was not surprised that Willy was not at the door to greet her. Her nieces were being 'looked after' on Fetternish while Innis visited Grandfather McIver on Foss and Willy could not resist romping on the lawn with the two little girls, playing bat and ball or, more often, acting the part of a totem pole around which Becky and Rachel draped daisy chains and coronets of wild flowers. Margaret, Willy's wife, would be on hand to provide slices of buttered bread when hunger overcame the youngsters or, if an unfortunate tumble grazed a knee or an elbow, to offer the sort of matronly comfort that Willy, for all his enthusiasm, could not possibly match. No William then, but out on the gravel was the minister's gig with the piebald pony uncoupled and left to graze on the crescent of grass that fronted the house.

'Visitors?' Iain Carbery muttered. 'Who on earth can be calling on you at this hour on a Monday forenoon? Has your sister come back early?'

'I think it's Tom Ewing,' Biddy answered.

'Were you expecting him?'

'No.'

Iain made a tiny *tsking* sound, as if he was sucking a corner of his moustache. 'Will he stay for lunch?'

'Possibly.'

'I wonder what he wants this time?'

'He doesn't *always* want something, you know,' Biddy said. 'Perhaps he has just dropped by to see how we are faring.'

'Perhaps,' Iain conceded with as much tact as he could muster.

He had hoped for more rough shooting after lunch, for the morning had yielded nothing but a single mangy rabbit that Odin had flushed out of the brambles more by luck than intention. Not the sniff of a grouse or partridge, not even a pigeon or two, though the corn crop in the south quarter was heavy. All rather a waste of effort, in fact. Iain wished he had contented himself by covering Biddy out there among the heather. He had never been one to mix one sport with another, however, and had even made it clear to his friend Walter Baverstock that he would devote only so much time to wooing the widow of Fetternish, that if nothing cropped up in the breeding stakes before the start of the wild-fowl season on the Solway then Biddy, and the Sangster Baverstocks, would just have to twiddle their thumbs for another six months or so.

He loved Biddy Baverstock after a fashion but, he assured himself, he loved his Anson 12-gauge even more. Until, that is, he entered the drawing-room and saw Ewing, Naismith and the other fellow, saw Biddy laughing, her jacket flung open, hat in hand, her auburn hair floating like a halo in the sunlight.

Then he felt a sordid little pang of jealousy, quite unbecoming for a man of his sanguine temperament. He had put the guns away in the rack in the office but still wore his boots and tweeds, his pockets bulging with No. 6 shot as if he was nothing more than a lackey like, say, McCallum. By the time he reached the drawing-room the conversation had sparked Biddy into good humour and someone or something had already made her laugh.

'Ah, Iain,' she said. 'I believe you know Reverend Ewing.'

'Yes. Yes, of course.'

'And this is Mr Gillies Brown.'

'Ghillie?' said Iain, hopefully.

'No,' the man told him. 'Gillies.'

The men were standing now that Biddy had joined them but there were tea-cups and oatcakes on a side table and, in Iain's opinion, a sort of tap-room atmosphere as if the men had been interrupted in the middle of an entertaining, perhaps even risqué discussion. He strode forward, grasped Brown's hand, and resisted the temptation to wrench him on to his tiptoes. 'How d'you do?'

'How are you, sir? Good bag?'

'Huhmmmph!' Iain muttered. 'Not here to shoot, are you?'

Iain had divined immediately that whatever lesser claim to distinction Brown might have he was certainly no sportsman. He did not have that look about him, the keen eye, the alertness that marked the brotherhood of rod and gun.

'No, Mr Carbery, I'm here to work.'

'What? On Fetternish?'

'In Crove.'

Biddy laughed once more, as if Brown's simple statement had been a masterpiece of wit. For a dreadful moment Iain wondered if he was being made fun of. He ground his back teeth in a chewing motion and glanced from Brown to Ewing, Ewing to Biddy.

'Mr Brown is a teacher,' Biddy explained, 'who has been employed to reopen the school in Crove.'

'But,' Iain said, 'you have no children.'

'No,' said Biddy, dryly. 'I have no children. That, however, does not prevent me taking an interest in education. Talking of children, where are my nieces?'

'In the kitchen, Ma'am,' Willy Naismith informed her, 'helping Queenie make a batch of pancakes, I believe. Quite safe.'

'There you are, Gillies,' Tom Ewing said. 'Already you have two pupils for your infant class right on your doorstep.'

'Doorstep?' said Iain.

'Mr Brown is, I believe, lookin' for a place to stay,' Willy put in.

'Is he, indeed?' said Biddy.

'I thought you might have a croft or cottage lying empty,' Tom said.

'No,' said Biddy, not sharply. 'Nothing that I can . . .'

'There's the farm, Mrs Baverstock,' Willy put in.

'Farm? What farm?'

'An Fhearann Cáirdeil,' Willy said, using the Gaelic. 'It's not much more than a ruin.'

'Surely it wouldn't cost much to make one of the old cottages habitable,' said Willy. 'Bit of work on the roof, some mortar on the walls and it might be just the ticket for a man with a family.'

'Oh!' Biddy said. 'So you have a family, Mr Brown?'

'Mr Brown is a widower,' Tom Ewing said. 'With children.'

'How many children?' said Biddy.

'Four,' Gillies Brown replied.

'Four, do you tell me?' Biddy said and gave Iain Carbery such a look, as if it was his fault that he could not match the teacher in fecundity. 'Where are they now? In Glasgow?'

'At the manse,' Tom Ewing answered.

'Well, Tom, I see why you are so anxious to find accommodation for Mr Brown and his four children,' Biddy said. 'You will not be having much peace to meditate on your sermons with such a houseful.'

'There *is* the farm, Mrs Baverstock,' Willy reminded her.

'Yes, there is the farm,' said Biddy. 'My husband's favourite spot. He loved it there. I could never understand why.' She gave a little twirl, not gay, not effervescent, as if to shake off a memory that had alighted upon her like a cold hand. 'I presume, Tom, that you are looking for a contribution to

76

the community good, something for nothing?'

'Well, not quite nothing,' Tom Ewing said. 'Next to nothing, though.'

'I told you so,' Iain Carbery murmured.

Biddy ignored him.

She was uncommonly still and looked at none of the gentlemen who surrounded her. For a moment or two she stared out of the big window at the sea, as if she could already detect the changes that lay just beyond the line of the horizon. There was no sound in the drawing-room save the creak of a chair as Iain Carbery, impatient with this petty business, seated himself and stooped to unlace his boots.

'An Fhearann Cáirdeil,' Biddy said, half to herself. She turned. 'Do you know what it means, Mr Brown?'

'The steading where friendship is to be found,' Gillies Brown said. 'Or, more simply, Friendship Farm.'

'I see you have the Gaelic, then,' said Biddy.

'Learned at my mother's knee,' the schoolmaster answered.

She held the incomer with her gaze. At that instant Iain Carbery felt a chill of apprehension seep into his loins; a challenge, not from the tall, balding teacher but from Biddy, as if she had at last found someone against whom she could pit herself. Obviously fantasy, Iain thought, a fear unworthy of a gentleman of his prowess. But that was the trouble with Fetternish, with Mull, with this whole self-absorbed community; everything seemed so much larger and so much more significant than it did on the mainland. Already he resented Brown's intrusion and the attention that Biddy was giving him, more attention than the gangly weed deserved.

'Lunch,' Biddy stated. 'First we will have lunch then we will all be going out to Friendship Farm to see what there is to see.'

'If it's suitable for habitation, do you mean?' said Willy.

'Yes,' said Biddy, nodding. 'And just what it will cost to repair.'

And Iain Carbery, stooped over his bootlaces, groaned.

FOUR

Tupping Time

The test of love, as far as Michael Tarrant was concerned, was obedience. He did not have to coax obedience from his wife, who so far did everything that a man could expect of a woman. Cooked for him, cleaned his house, washed his clothes, raised his children and, in the spring season, doctored the weak lambs and sickly ewes that he brought in from the pasture. She also fed the hens and gathered eggs, weeded the vegetable plots, howked potatoes, pumped water, chopped kindling, lugged peats, read to the children and, in her leisure moments, said her prayers to the Holy Angel that watched over her.

No, he had no complaints about Innis. She was a model wife. If he had been a man of a different stamp, untrammelled by ambition and desire, then he would have been content with her. But he knew that she did not love him as Gavin did. His son obeyed him without question, blindly and devotedly, as if they were one flesh not just in the chant of the church but uniquely, inseparably joined in wish and will so that all he, Michael, had to do was state what he wanted and Gavin would see that it was done. He did not have that sort of obedience from his daughters. Did not have it from Innis who, however loyal and dutiful, was still a woman, still, in essence, fashioned in ways that he could not understand, still lacking one crucial quality – total selflessness.

It did not occur to Michael that the things that came between Innis and he were the very things that he had wished upon her – children, the house, her religious obligations, things that he might have shared with her if sharing had been in his nature. But sharing was not in his nature and, as the years rolled on, he came to believe that no one loved him, no one except his son.

Michael would say, 'I want you to go up to the big house and tell me who is there and what is going on.'

Gavin would not ask for a reason. He would be off at once, hurrying across the bridge and up through the birch trees and the pines, through the bracken, then down on to his belly, crawling through the grasses until he could see the gravel drive and crescent lawn; or if he lay below the house, the figures in the dining- or drawing-room windows, or the cook or Mr Naismith or Mr Naismith's wife, or even his aunt, Mrs Baverstock herself, pottering about in the walled garden. He would skirt the house in a wide arc, slithering through the grasses, and observe it from another angle, or would go down into the gully north-west of the house then up again on to the unreclaimed stretch of moorland where Mr McCallum might be setting traps for vermin or hanging the corpse of a crow or a buzzard on the gibbet at the end of a fence.

'Hey, laddie, and what are you doing with yourself today?'

'I am doing nothing in particular, Mr McCallum.'

'Have you been to the house?'

'No.'

'Aye, that's as well for there are some rum folk stayin' there just now.'

'Are there, Mr McCallum?'

'Aye, gey rum folk, I tell you.'

'Is he there, him with the Anson?'

'Mr Carbery. Aye, he is still there. The minister called again this morning, too, and there have been other people from Tobermory in and out.'

'What sort of people, Mr McCallum?'

'Council officers, I think, though I don't know them myself.'

Gavin would linger long enough to admire Mr McCallum's 12-bore and, if the gamekeeper was in the mood, would be allowed to heft it and take aim with it as if it were a rifle. He coveted the gun more than he coveted anything.

Then the Browns came to Fetternish.

They lived in a canvas tent out on the headland to the north of the house, in the ruins that his mother called An Fhearann Cáirdeil. Since school had not started he was despatched there by his father almost every day and would steal through the alder brake and undergrowth to observe what the Browns were up to and who might be with them. He would watch them cook and wash, watch them have a laugh with the workers that Mrs Baverstock had sent out to restore the best of the ruined cottages.

'How many were there today, Gavin?' his father would ask.

'Four of them. Mr Bell was among them.'

'Old Mr Bell, or Angus?'

'Angus. He was joking with them too.'

'What were they joking about this time?'

'I do not know.'

'What were they doing – the men, I mean?'

'Putting up posts for the roof.'

'It's it to be slate or turf?'

'Turf, I think. They are cutting out the turf from the back of the wood at Sorn.'

'Is Brown cutting turf too?'

'No, they are all still pulling stones from the ruins and putting them in piles where Mr Lawrence tells them to. Mr Lawrence has the mortar trowel out and a bucket of mix and he is plastering the wall.'

'Was Bid . . . was Mrs Baverstock there?'

'She came later.'

'With Naismith?'

'By herself. She brought them drink. Beer, I think.'

'Was the man Carbery not with her, son?'

'No. She came by herself and she left by herself.'

'I see.'

In spite of his arrogance, Gavin was not yet old enough to comprehend the meaning of what he saw. He did not even have the sense to consider why his father despatched him there at all.

To Gavin spying was still a game, though he too felt vaguely threatened by the presence of the Browns, felt as if he was helping to protect Pennymain from incomers who had already obtained a hold on Fetternish and might soon spill over the hill and claim more of the estate. What they – a teacher and his children – might want with grazing land or what they would do with it once they'd got it were not questions that Gavin paused to consider.

The school board had already announced that classes at Dervaig were to be split. In future, children from the parish of Crove would be taught in their own schoolhouse. Miss Anderson, an assistant at Dervaig, sang Mr Brown's praises and assured everyone that he had a fine 'parchment' even if his pronunciation of Gaelic was not as polished as a purist might wish. Gavin did not know what a 'parchment' was and cared nothing about Gaelic.

Gavin was not the only one to be disturbed by the Browns' arrival. Hector Thrale, the Fetternish factor, was furious because he had not been consulted. He informed Michael that he would not lift a finger to help the Glasgow tykes, as he called them, except in so far as his job demanded it.

Thrale was angry because Mrs Baverstock had taken labourers from field work just to provide a stranger with a sound cottage at a nominal rental of six pounds a year, with nothing expected of him except to keep Crove's girls and boys in order five and one-half days in the week. Aye, and cereal harvest and potato picking coming round too, to say nothing of the fishing. Every hand, however small, was needed to help out, as it had been in his, Thrale's, day and his father's day as far back as he could remember. He told Michael that he could not understand why the council and the school board had decided to squander money on such a pointless project and blamed Thomas Ewing for exerting undue influence.

All of this information Michael absorbed and stored away. He did not gossip, did not speculate. He spoke of it to no one, not even to Barrett. Certainly not to Innis. When Innis raised the subject of the Browns, Michael retreated into a silence that seemed to indicate disinterest. He did not even exchange a glance with Gavin, or the boy with him, so that Innis had no inkling that her husband had any special knowledge of the teacher, or that he, Michael, was keeping a close eye on what was going on at the big house and how it might affect Biddy.

When Gavin returned late one Saturday afternoon and told his father that he had seen Mammy out at An Fhearann Cáirdeil talking to Mr Brown, Michael said nothing and instructed his son to say nothing. He waited until supper was over and the girls were in bed, until he was sure that Innis was not going to volunteer to tell him where she had been that afternoon and then asked, 'Where were you today?'

After a split second's hesitation, Innis said, 'In Crove.'

She was lighting the paraffin lamp, the taper held in her left hand, the flame from the wick and the first curl of brown smoke outlining her profile in the gloom of the kitchen. She had put up her hair, Michael noticed, and wore the peacock-blue dress that she usually kept by for Sundays.

She did not look at him or at Gavin, though they were both watching her. She leaned towards the lamp and blew, blew gently on the wick, her gaze focused on the flame, her eyes clear and innocent.

Michael said, 'Who did you meet in town?'

'No one of consequence.'

'Did you not meet Tom Ewing?'

'No.'

'Or – what is his name – Brown?'

'No.'

'And where did you go afterwards?'

'I came straight home.' Innis settled the glass over the wick and with a soft motion of the wrist extinguished the taper. 'Why is it that you ask, dear?' But Michael, startled by the fact that his wife had lied to him, could do no more than shake his head.

And Gavin, of course, said nothing.

Iain Carbery had been to bathe in the sea twice that Saturday, once for his customary morning ablution and the second time to cool off after Biddy had abandoned him – no other word for it – in favour of the weedy schoolmaster.

For a woman of her stature in island society, Biddy Baverstock could be incredibly crass at times. Although he admired her self-sufficiency and individuality Iain had so far failed to discover the line that separated the lady from the fisherman's brat and, being but a half-baked gentleman, blamed *her* for *his* failure to come to terms with her manner of doing things. He could not, for instance, fathom why Biddy suddenly seemed to find a schoolmaster's company preferable to his own. He did not like being ignored in favour of some cashiered teacher who had probably never fired a gun in his life.

He wished now that he had not let his heart rule his head and that he had paid no heed to the blandishments of Walter Baverstock and Agnes Paul who were anxious – nay, desperate – to have him marry the widow of Fetternish and regain at least partial control over an estate that they still regarded, morally if not legally, as theirs.

Iain had known Walter since his bachelor days in Edinburgh when, together with Austin, they had been fellow members of the New Athenian Club. He had been present in the club on that auspicious afternoon when Fetternish had been put up for auction and had watched in awe as Walter and Austin had succumbed to impulse and had bid for the Mull estate, sight unseen. But he had never let on to Bridget that he had been acquainted with her late husband and that he still remained in occasional touch with Walter and Agnes.

His income derived from a small parcel of shares that Carbery senior had put together and divided equally among his children before he left to start life afresh in Chicago, along with his second wife. Unfortunately Iain had never acquired the knack of speculation that had raised his older brothers to positions of power on the London stock exchange, and he had struggled for years now to make ends meet. His domicile was a shabby, two-roomed apartment in a tenement in Edinburgh's Leith Walk, which was the reason he spent the best part of the year as an itinerant house guest, trading on his sporting talents and his charm.

Age, though, was beginning to catch up with him. His shares

had not been productive of late and he had grown weary of living out of trunks and being perpetually affable to every nit-witted nob who offered him bed and board. Biddy, of course, did not fall into that category. He had first encountered her at Coilichan Lodge a couple of years back and had been attracted to her from the outset. In fact, if he had been less addicted to the roving life at that stage he might even have invited her to marry him there and then; unaware, of course, that Biddy had already begun the bizarre process of 'testing' potential husbands and that he would just have to wait his turn.

Things had gone on from there, not so much casually as erratically, with Walter and Agnes Paul pushing from behind and Biddy leading him on by the nose like a prize bull.

Small wonder that Iain was confused.

When he returned like a merman from the sea late that afternoon he paused to listen at the door of Biddy's room, scowling at the notion that the fisherman's brat might already be putting the weedy Glaswegian teacher to the test and that he would hear noises of copulatory joy from within. Madness, of course: not even Bridget Baverstock was quite so indiscreet as all that. Even so, he paused; he listened; he heaved a sigh of relief and moved on, shivering a little, to dress for dinner.

When he came downstairs again a half-hour later he found Naismith hanging about in the great hall, pretending to put logs on the fire.

It was September and, though the weather had not deteriorated yet, there was an autumnal nip in the air. Soon, Iain thought, the stags would be roaring in the high hills, the hounds streaming out over farmland stubble, the geese beating down from the north. The best time of the year for a sportsman; those crisp, cold mornings and misty-damp afternoons, with hunt balls and shooting parties and the pot, socially speaking, being stirred in all the big houses across Scotland. And here he was, stuck on Mull, agitatedly trying to pluck up enough courage to persuade a fisherman's daughter to become his wife.

Naismith handed him a whisky and soda water.

'Where is Mrs Baverstock?' Iain asked.

'Gone into the village, I believe.'

'With the schoolmaster, I suppose?'

'I can't say about that,' Naismith told him.

The steward was hovering again, hanging about in that unobtrusive way he had, as if he suspected that he, Iain Carbery, might try to steal the silver. Iain seated himself in one of the Georgian chairs and tried to appear at ease.

'Did she take the dogcart?'

'She did, Mr Carbery.'

'Then she will have gone with the schoolmaster.'

'If I may say so, sir, you seem to be uncommonly concerned about Mr Gillies Brown,' Naismith remarked. 'It wouldn't be because Mrs Baverstock is spendin' so much time with him, would it?'

'Certainly not.'

'Because, Mr Carbery, that is her business,' Naismith said. 'I mean, to concern herself with the welfare of her tenants. Mr Brown and the new school will be assets to our community and it is to our community that Mrs Baverstock is responsible. That's the way it is on Mull.'

'I don't have to be lectured on a landowner's responsibilities,' Iain said, trying not to sound frazzled. 'I'm well aware that a gentleman, or a lady for that matter, has a duty to the parish.'

'Will I refresh your glass, Mr Carbery?'

'What? Yes.'

Warily, he watched the steward decant whisky into the crystal. He had never much cared for the elderly servant who appeared to have more of a grip on Fetternish affairs than seemed quite wholesome. Iain knew, of course, what Naismith had meant to the Baverstock brothers back in the old days. Walter still seemed to have a soft spot for 'the old rogue' but Agnes Paul hated him. Naismith's sons and daughters were still employed by the Baverstock Pauls but only in the woollen mill and the manufactory, no longer in the house. Agnes had seen to that.

'I know what you're thinkin', Mr Carbery.'

'Do you?' said Iain, guiltily.

'Aye, you're thinkin' that there are maybe more fish in the sea than you calculated, sir, and that the mistress will one day make one cast too many. Time's not on your side, Mr Carbery.'

'What the devil are you talking about?'

'Oh, I think you know what I'm talkin' about, sir.' Naismith leaned closer, as if the great, somnolent house was filled with ghostly eavesdroppers. 'Can you not do it, Mr Carbery? Can you not give her what she wants? She needs more than a man, Mr Carbery. She needs a husband. We all need a man here to run Fetternish. It is not a proper house without a man at the head,' Willy Naismith paused, 'and children, heirs for the future.'

'This is nonsense!' Iain got to his feet. He waved the whisky glass angrily. 'By God, Agnes Paul was right about . . .'

'Agnes Paul?' Willy interrupted. 'I was not aware that you knew Mrs Paul, sir. Well, well, is that not a strange coincidence?'

Iain opened his mouth, but as he had already put his foot in it, closed it again promptly.

Willy said, 'It must have been Edinburgh.'

'Edinburgh?'

'Where you had your conversation with Mrs Paul.'

'What? Yes, yes – Edinburgh.'

'I mean,' said Willy, 'it couldn't have been in Sangster, since you told me you'd never been there.'

Iain hesitated then deliberately buried himself in the Georgian wing-chair once more. 'Yes, in Edinburgh, at a friend's house, I seem to recall. *Not* that it is any business of yours.'

'I expect you know Mr Walter too?'

'No,' quickly; a pause, then, 'No, I don't believe we've ever met.'

'Mr Walter, my former employer, is not easily forgotten,' Willy said. 'Tell me, though, what did Mrs Paul have to say about me?'

'Naismith, I have more important things to think about than . . .'

'Whoa,' said Willy. 'Whoa there.'

'Whoa?'

'If you heard my name mentioned at all then it must have been in – what's the word? – in the context of mutual acquaintances. That suggests to me, sir, that you've been aware for some time that Bridget Baverstock and Agnes Paul are sisters-in-law – yet you've never mentioned this remarkable coincidence to my mistress. May I ask, why not?'

'It didn't seem . . .'

'Prudent?' Willy suggested.

'Yes, prudent.'

'Because Mrs Bridget Baverstock of Fetternish might assume that you were a friend, even an ally of the Baverstocks of Sangster?'

'Look, Naismith, I don't need to justify my actions to you.'

'That's true, Mr Carbery.' The steward smiled. 'After all, it's not likely that Mr Walter and his sister will be guests at your wedding – if there is a wedding. By which I mean, you're not liable to do anythin' that would cause my mistress embarrassment.'

Iain realised that he was being threatened but he could not for the life of him decide what he was being threatened with. He stared up at the elderly servant who, decanter in one hand and soda siphon in the other, stood between him and the fireplace.

'Will you tell her?' Iain said.

'Hmmm?'

'Tell your mistress that I am acquainted with her in-laws?'

'I'm only a steward, Mr Carbery, it would not be my place to carry tales about house guests to Mrs Baverstock.'

'Do you mean I should tell her myself?'

'Tell her what? That you once had a casual conversation with Agnes Paul? I mean, it's not as if you were a close friend of the Sangster Baverstocks, is it? No, Mr Carbery, if I were you I would keep quiet about it.'

'And you? Will you keep quiet about it?'

'That depends,' Willy Naismith said.

'On what?'

'On whether or not you decide to marry the lady,' Willy said, 'or, to put it another way, whether or not the lady decides to marry you.'

Iain closed one eye, squinting it shut as if he had just bitten into something sour. He said, 'And if she does?'

'Your secret will be safe enough,' Willy Naismith said, 'as long as I remain steward of Fetternish.'

'And if she does not?'

Willy Naismith grinned, the big, grey, hairy face seeming not so much foxy as vulpine. 'Then,' he said, 'I'd feel compelled to inform Mrs Baverstock that she had had a very lucky escape.'

A half-hour ago he had been worrying about the schoolmaster when all along he should have been worrying about the steward. As it was he did not know whether he was dealing with greed or devotion, could not fathom just what Naismith wanted or, indeed, just how much he knew.

'You don't like me, Naismith, do you?' he said.

'No, sir, I like you well enough,' Willy answered. 'It's just that I don't trust you – but then I trust no one very much. It's a quirk in my character that comes from having been brought up with the Sangster Baverstocks.'

'So,' said Iain, cautiously, 'it's a case of marry or be damned, is it?'

'Something like that, sir, aye.'

'And in the meanwhile?'

'My lips are sealed.'

Love did not burst upon Innis like a glorious red-and-gold Mull sunset after a day of torrential rain. There were no Aeolian harps, organ voluntaries or angelic sopranos warbling overhead every time she and Gillies Brown met. In fact, the process was so subtle that Innis was unaware that it was happening at all.

Prior to Gillies Brown's arrival she had not been discontented, or, rather, had not realised that an important element was lacking from her life. She had her home and her children to keep her occupied and the shifting seasons and the calendar of Catholic worship to add substance and structure to her days. The only disappointment, with which she had come to terms long ago, was that she could not rescue her mother from her embittered isolation. And she still clung tenaciously to the belief that in taking her away from Pennypol Michael had brought blessing into her life. She refused to recognise that much of what passed for happiness derived from her own equable temperament and that her contribution to the stability of the marriage far outweighed his.

When she first met Gillies Brown, therefore, she was neither miserable nor restless. She was simply – without knowing it – unfulfilled.

In the first weeks after his arrival Gillies was exceedingly busy putting together all that he would need to teach the children of Crove, to ensure that the demands of the school board would be satisfied and the commissioners' 'whisky money' well spent. He was also concerned with keeping his family comfortable while the cottage at Friendship Farm was made fit for habitation.

He was pleasantly surprised at the alacrity with which the work was carried out. He confessed to Innis that he had expected a certain slowness in the habits of the islanders, that all the stories that he, a townie, had heard about the Hebrides had led him believe that the Spanish principle of *mañana*, or its Gaelic equivalent, applied the moment you stepped off the mainland. He was also surprised by the friendliness of the folk, for he had also heard that the natives of Mull were subject to unpredictable mood swings that left an incomer not knowing quite where he stood. So far, though, he had met with nothing but kindness.

'You must not be thinking, Mr Brown,' Innis told him, 'that those of us who live upon Fetternish and serve my sister Bridget are typical of all the islanders. You must be prepared for a bit of trouble when the school opens.'

'Truancy, do you mean?'

'Oh, there will be that, and you must learn to live with it,' Innis said. 'Most of the families in this part of the world have great respect for education but there are a stubborn few who were glad to see the back of Mr Leggat.'

'Why?'

'Some of them still think that education will be putting the wrong ideas into their children's heads.'

'You mean that they consider knowledge itself as dangerous?'

'Yes, some folk would prefer to have everything cut and dried for their children just as it was for them, even if that means condemning their children to drudgery. They will always be looking backwards to find some excuse for not having to think at all. My mother is like that. She would have you believe that the ruin that has been brought upon the Highlands came only through the greed of the landlords and not through the laziness of the people.'

'But you don't agree with her?'

'Not entirely,' Innis said.

'What about the burnings and the land clearances?'

'Economically necessary, some of them,' Innis said. 'It was not the reason but the manner of execution that was unforgivable.'

'So I had better be careful how I teach history, is that what you're telling me?' Gillies Brown said.

'If, like Mr Leggat, you assure the children that they are victims of the English and that all the woe that they believe has come upon Scotland is not their fault then they will cheer you to the echo. They will fasten upon your praise of flawed heroes, upon the Wallace and the Bruce and Charlie, their Bonnie Prince, as if they were redeemers who might return at any time. But if those dead heroes *did* return they would be finding in the Scots just what they found all those centuries ago, suspicion and dissension, an idleness of thought that would doom any cause to failure before it could begin.'

'I gather that you will not be the one to raise Freedom's banner on Caliach Point, Mrs Tarrant?' Gillies Brown said.

'Freedom from what, Mr Brown?'

'Aye, that's a question that is difficult to answer.'

'Without education,' Innis said, 'without knowledge of what is going on in the world there are no answers.'

'If I may be so bold as to enquire,' Gillies Brown said, 'where did *you* receive your education?'

'I was four years attending the school here, before it closed. From the time I was strong enough to walk to Crove with my sister and brothers to the time my mother needed me to help with the cattle.'

'And your brothers?'

'They went to the boat with my father.'

'I find it hard to believe that you acquired all this wisdom in the local schoolhouse.'

'It is hardly wisdom, Mr Brown. Just common sense.'

'Aye, but common sense is also a scarce commodity,' Gillies Brown said. 'I think, Mrs Tarrant, that you are one of those odd creatures – an educated woman.'

'I am fond of reading, Mr Brown, if that is what you are meaning.'

'Where do your reading books come from?'

'From my grandfather. He used to send them to me.'

'Is he the cattle breeder who lives on Foss?'

'Yes, but he is old now and his mind has gone. He is dying, in fact.'

'I'm sorry to hear it. It seems to me, though, that's he's leaving a fair legacy behind him.'

'Foss, do you mean?'

'No, Mrs Tarrant, I mean you.'

'Me?'

'Aye, a woman who has been taught to think for herself and who will no doubt pass that gift on to her children. The gift of independence, I mean.'

'I am not independent of anyone or anything,' Innis said, not knowing whether to be insulted or flattered. 'I am just a shepherd's wife.'

'Then the shepherd – Mr Tarrant – is very fortunate.'

'It is kind of you to say so, Mr Brown, but I doubt if Michael would agree with you.'

They were standing together by the mouth of the track that led to An Fhearann Càirdeil. She had left Becky and Rachel with Willy for a half-hour or so while, drawn by curiosity, she had walked the quarter-mile to the headland to see what was being done to the old crofting community.

It had been more than a decade since she had been to the north quarter; one evening, one beautiful evening, Michael and she had walked there for no reason other than to admire the views across the Sound to Ardnamurchan. It had been the last time they had walked out together just for the sake of it for she had been pregnant with Gavin and after her son was born there had been no more evening strolls.

Friendship Farm had never been a proper farm, only a cluster of four crouching, turf-roofed black houses that hugged the edge of the scrub forest on the height of the headland. The cliffs were not sheer but fell steeply in a tumble of grass ledges and grey boulders down to an inaccessible shingle beach and lent An Fhearann Cáirdeil an impression of both protection and airiness. Thirty or forty paces in one direction brought you to the tuck of the woods; thirty or forty in the other carried you out to the point where ravens and seabirds twisted so lightly in the air currents that you thought that you too might be able to plunge outward into the teeth of the wind and, like the birds, take wing.

It had been a half-century since the crofters had abandoned Friendship Farm. They had left not under duress but by choice when Sir Ord Gunnarsby, who had owned most of the land at that time, had offered to pay passage to Canada for any tenant who cared to accept. According to Vassie, the three families of An Fhearann Cáirdeil had eagerly seized the opportunity to leave their desolate Scottish headland for the new Dominion and had gone before the troubles started.

Where were they now, Innis wondered, those exiles and their children and their children's children? Were they settled on the cattle plains in the icy shadows of the Rocky Mountains with never the cry of a seabird or the pounding of Atlantic waves to remind them of home, or were they labouring in the great wheatfields that spread across Canada from coast to coast? There was nothing of them left here but ruins, not even strange stone grave markers to make you think that the past was never quite past and that some twist or knot in the structure of time itself might one day bring them back.

She had never left Mull to visit the mainland. She probably never would. She had not been to Edinburgh, like Biddy, or to Glasgow to visit her brother Neil, so that when the strangers came – the Browns – they brought with them not echoes of an old life but something entirely original and exciting.

She watched Mr Brown's children play along the edge of the

wood, chasing the fat little pup, stooping to peer into the bracken as if the fern held secrets that town dwellers should know about, delighted at the adventure that Dad had brought them on. When Gillies Brown laughed too Innis had realised that they were sharing the moment and that he, a stranger, seemed to know exactly what was on her mind. And when she had looked up at him, he had winked and spread his hands apologetically as if to excuse his intrusion.

It was the effect of that gesture that Innis could not bring herself to explain and, lacking the words to do the job, had lied instead.

'I came straight home,' she said.

Barrett's name was George but nobody ever called him that. Like his father and grandfather he was known simply by his surname now that he had grown too old to be called 'the boy.' Not only had he grown too old, he had also proved himself more manly than either of his forebears for, by the age of just twenty-seven, he had already fathered six healthy children.

His wife, Muriel, was three years his senior. At one time she had been betrothed to Innis's brother, Donnie, who had drowned. She came originally from Leathan, near the head of Loch Mingary where Mishnish, Quinish and Fetternish touched. The Barretts' cottage was down that way too, a stout little stone house on a quiet shingle shore behind which the Fetternish rams were pastured; those big, docile, dreamy-eyed beasts that were pampered and spoiled from one year's end to the next for the sole purpose of providing Biddy Baverstock – via Michael Tarrant – with a lamb crop second to none.

Michael had learned his trade on the rolling hills of the Ettrick Pen in the Border country. Barrett, on the other hand, had been reared with Mull sheep, for his grandfather had switched from cattle-keeping to sheep-tending when the first of the big flocks was brought on to the island, and his father, still hale and hearty, presently had charge of Mr Clark's Blackfaces.

Michael and the moon-faced young man were not akin in

temperament but shared experiences and instincts had created an amicable bond between them. In fact, those times in the year when they laboured together at the dipping trough or in the clipping shed were happy ones for both of them. No less happy, though somewhat less strenuous, were the six weeks from September when the rams were painted between the forelegs with a mixture of linseed oil and red paste and driven gently from the sheltered lochside pasture to do their work in the tupping fields.

Michael and his assistant had few disagreements about the simple rules of husbandry. Old ewes with young rams, maiden ewes with experienced rams was a principle that they both agreed upon, though Michael set more stock in the quality of the ram than Barrett for he firmly believed that the commercial value of a flock lay in strong, milky ewes. They would argue about it in friendly fashion, exchanging little jibes, while parcels of ewes, sixty at a time, were gathered round the rams. The argument was without point for come February there would be few barren ewes and the lamb-crop, whatever the weather, would always be a good one.

That autumn, however, Michael took less pleasure in the tupping season than usual. In fact, he seemed to take no pleasure at all. He was disinclined to talk and even Barrett, an amiable fellow, found himself shut out not just for a morning or afternoon but throughout the whole of the month.

He complained to his wife about Michael's surliness but Muriel had never been enchanted by Mr Tarrant, whom she thought a sullen devil at the best of times, and he, Barrett, received no consolation or advice from that quarter. It did not occur to him until late in the month that the senior shepherd was nursing grievances connected with Crove's new schoolmaster.

'Are you sending your children to the school yet, Barrett?'

'I am, the three who are old enough. I see that Gavin and Rachel are there too, though they are not together in the classroom.'

'How would you be knowing that?'

'I have been there to see it for myself.'

'Have you now?' Michael said.

'If you go down with them, he will make you welcome.'

'Who will?'

'The schoolmaster, Mr Brown, or his daughter.'

'I have more to do with my time than tramp over to Crove just to look at a schoolroom.'

'It is a very nice schoolroom,' Barrett said, ingenuously. 'And I have heard that Brown is a very good teacher.'

'Who told you that?'

'Muriel. Have you not spoken to Mrs Tarrant about it?'

'No, I have not.'

'She has been there too. She has been to inspect the classroom.'

'Has she now?'

'Aye, more than once.'

'Has she also been out at the Farm?'

Surprised, Barrett said, 'Why would she be out at the Farm?'

But whether Michael meant Muriel – which was daft – or his own wife, Innis, Barrett never did discover, for Michael just shook his head and with no more expression on his face than a plank of wood, went stalking off with the dog at his heels towards the tupping field, his shoulders hunched against the insidious drizzle that had temporarily replaced the usual autumn storms.

They had experienced rain before, of course – Mull was seldom free from some form of precipitation for more than a few days at a time – but the late-summer rains that came whisking in as suddenly as April showers had been just as much a novelty to the younger Browns as everything else on the island.

They would whoop and shout warnings to each other and Bobby would grab Evie by the hand and Evie would cry out to Pepper, and Tricia would emerge from the tent or Dad from the door of the cottage, and Janetta, cross-legged on the grass, sewing or darning, would leap up and beckon and they would all of them run for shelter as if the sky was throwing down fire instead of water. They would dive shrieking into the tent or, after it had it become habitable, into the cottage that smelled darkly of peat smoke and paint, of earth and paraffin, and would stand with their faces raised towards the roof, listening to the thud of the big raindrops on the turf as if they were moles, not people at all. But after the transfer from tent to cottage, and after the school was officially opened and their days regulated by the long walk to and from Crove the weather soon lost its charm and they all, all except Evie, became aware that this was no holiday, no adventure and that as soon as winter broke – winter without towering brown tenements and closes and shop doorways to shelter in – their endurance would be sorely tested, and that Dad had not led them to the Promised Land after all.

The schoolhouse, however, was a haven rather than a prison for the Brown family. The younger ones were unaware of the dissension that Dad's arrival had caused within the narrow community, of mutterings from the taproom of the McKinnon Arms or Miss Fergusson's shop. Tricia, Bobby and Evie had no notion that Mr Ewing had been criticised for his part in restoring the schoolhouse, and if they had, they would not have understood why. Even Mr Ewing himself was unable to pin down the reasons for Crove's resistance to the school's reopening. There was, of course, no general reason. Perhaps a niggling fear that by educating the children, the children would become superior to their parents and would see the community for what it was, would pack their bags and leave for the mainland, and that the village would dwindle and die because its youth had been lost.

Mothers were less susceptible than fathers to the unspoken anxiety that education would bring disillusionment in its wake for, being merely women, they were unselfishly ambitious for their offspring and not inclined to pessimism about the future. They made Mr Brown and his daughter Janetta welcome and, along with some far-sighted fathers, took the opportunity to call in at the schoolhouse to greet the master and his assistant and peep into the classroom just to ensure that it was up to the standard that Mr Leggat had demanded in their day. Surly reactionaries – few of whom could read, or write more than their names – were soon in retreat and, within a week or two of its doors being opened, Crove Parish School was an accepted fact of village life again.

Out of the houses, out of the hills, trailing across the bridges and along wooded tracks the children would arrive, older ones in charge of younger ones, skipping and scuffling, sprinting and dawdling in a manner that seemed by turns purposeful and purposeless, schoolbooks wrapped in oilskins bouncing on their backs, dinners stuffed into their pockets or – for some dainty little Riding Hoods – packed into wicker carrying baskets. Forty-three of them all told, aged five to fourteen, most of them glad to be relieved of the long, long trek along the Dervaig road and many of them, the very youngest, just glad to be at any sort of school at all.

It was not just the children of the Parish of Crove who benefited from the arrival of Mr Gillies Brown and his daughter Janetta. The master and his youthful assistant received equal bounty from the island children, for this was not teaching as it was in Glasgow, with each class progressing by simple stages. This was 'mixed' teaching and demanded a great deal of concentration and attention in the preparation of lessons. Gruff, fluffy-chinned lads, who had put in four or five years at Dervaig, rubbed elbows with over-protected ten-year-old girls whose instruction had been at best spotty and at worse non-existent. And to cope with such an infinite variety of young minds Mr Brown had to put his gloom and depression behind him. There was simply no room for it in his head during those first weeks of autumn.

So, while Gillies and Janetta Brown worked hard to find their feet with the pupils, the pupils worked hard to adjust to the alien accents of the Lowlanders and to test out the limits of the teachers' patience – and, very swiftly, realised that discipline, decisiveness and direction were not only to be found along the road in Dervaig but had arrived in Crove too, and that neither Mr 'Glaswegian' Brown nor his tall, eagle-eyed daughter were going to stand any nonsense from a mere fisherman's son or a crofter's daughter.

The schoolhouse, then, was the hub of the Browns' existence, a warm place, lively and interesting if not always, in the beginning, entirely friendly. And the turf-roofed cottage on the headland at An Fhearann Cáirdeil was their refuge when the late-summer rains swept in and dusk came down early and they could snuggle altogether and wish now and then – though only now and then – that Mam had never been called away into Heaven and they were all back in Glasgow where they probably belonged.

It was only to amuse Iain that Biddy gave a dinner party for Mr Clark and his wife and their daughter Penelope who, accompanied by her two small sons, was on one of her frequent visits to The Ards.

Penelope was a charming young lady who, Biddy thought, might be capable of delivering the sort of society gossip that passed for entertaining conversation with gentlemen like Mr Carbery. She was also, of course, emphatically married and emphatically in love with her husband, a distinguished professor of mechanical engineering at the Glasgow Industrial Institute. She, Penelope, chattered on at some length about her husband's reputation and intellectual prowess while Iain, who had been quite prepared to flirt with her just for the exercise, grew more and more depressed by his inability to brag about his last bag of pheasants or his friendship with Lord Fennimore who, he gathered, Penelope Clark Crawford regarded as something of a joke.

The dinner party had not been a success. In fact, as far as Iain was concerned, it was a dismal failure and only served to highlight the failure of his entire – what? – mission to Mull, particularly when Penny Clark Crawford confessed that not only was she happily married but that she was also happily pregnant again.

'You did that deliberately, didn't you, Bridget?'
'Did what deliberately, Iain?'
'Brought that girl here to flaunt before me.'
'Girl? Oh, you mean Penny. Come now, she is hardly a girl.'
'What age is she?'

'My age, or a year or two younger.'

'Well, damn it, she *looks* like a girl.'

'That may,' Biddy said, 'have more to do with your age than hers.'

'Are you suggesting that I'm past it?'

'I am suggesting nothing of the sort,' Biddy told him, but without emphasis. She was seated at her dressing-table, clad in a night-gown, brushing her hair. She turned. 'Do not tell me that you feel "past it"?'

He had consumed more than his fair share of the table wines and had been tippling brandy all evening. He sat on the side of the four-poster looking, Biddy thought, like something from a Hogarth engraving, shirt flopping from his trousers, galluses dangling, a glass still cupped in both hands. His posture was not that of a drunkard, however, but one of dejection. Even his moustache had lost its vigour and drooped like that of an ailing walrus.

'You're one to talk, Biddy,' he mumbled.

'Am I? About what?' Biddy said, with a warning shrillness.

'About being . . .'

'Go on, Iain, say it.'

He heaved a sigh and drank, glanced up, prudently shaking his head.

Biddy put down the silver-backed comb, Her hair was not long, did not hang in tresses down her back but, kinked and curled in fashionable style, formed a dense, almost leonine mane about her head and shoulders. She got to her feet and approached the bed.

Lamplight silhouetted her figure through frills and ruffles and soft, pink, clinging silk. If the sporting gentlemen could have seen her at that moment they would have swallowed hard and growled, 'By God, but you're in prime condition, Biddy. Must say – prime condition,' and, even allowing for the equine phraseology, she would have accepted the compliment graciously. One sporting gentleman, however, appeared to be steadfastly unimpressed.

Iain did not so much as glance up as she padded across the Turkish rug and, stooping, plucked the brandy glass from his fingers and placed it on the bedside table.

He sank his elbows on to his knees and leaned into them. He was aware of the ripe curve of her stomach only inches from his brow and the underside of her breasts brushing his hair, but he remained indifferent. It was not pretence, not churlishness or sulk or even coyness that stayed him. And it certainly wasn't drink for alcohol only fuelled his ardour and did not smother it. He hung his head and let her rub herself against him like a gigantic tabby but he made no move to pull her down or to fondle the soft, strong parts of her that rounded out the silk.

'Are you bored with Mull, Iain, is that it?'

'Well, the weather – this constant drizzle . . .'

'Are you bored with me?'

Taking his earlobes lightly between her fingers and thumbs, she tilted his head back so that he was compelled to look up at her. He blinked and tried to smile but no amount of effort seemed able to lift the corners of his mouth and what emerged was a weak sort of rictus.

'Are you?' Biddy persisted.

'Of course I'm not.'

'Do you think I'm too old to bear children?'

A little more urgently, less jadedly: 'I didn't say that.'

'Did Penny Crawford not set you to thinking?'

'I hardly noticed her. She is not my sort, Biddy. Too – too . . .'

'Too much in love with her husband?'

'The professor – hah!' Iain said. 'Did you know that she was expecting?'

'Yes.'

'Are you jealous of her?'

'Yes.'

'I see,' Iain said. 'And consequently you are disappointed in me?'

'No more, I suspect, than you are in me.'

He sighed and tried to reach past her to the brandy glass but Biddy nudged his arm away with her hip and seated herself beside him on the bed. She put an arm, not seductively, around his shoulder.

'Take me to bed,' Biddy said.

'Are you – are you ready?'

'Yes.'

'You always say that.'

His voice was muffled, almost furry. She could feel his lips stir against the material of the night-gown as he blew a frill of lace away from his nose. Then he pulled away and, twisting on the bed, faced her squarely. 'Bridget, why will you not marry me? Is it because I cannot give you a child? God knows, I've tried.'

'You must not be blaming yourself,' Biddy said.

'Easy for you to say,' Iain told her, 'but if I do not blame myself, who am I to blame? No, Bridget, this entire situation has become unsatisfactory. Evidence suggests that you care for me enough to accept me as a husband – a husband in all but name. So let me ask you again – why will you not marry me?'

'I do not think I love you enough.'

'Think? Think?' Iain cried. 'Damn it, don't you know?'

Biddy, however, would not be drawn into giving a straight answer. She had acquired enough sense over the years not to confuse what she felt for Iain Carbery with love. In recent weeks, in fact, she had begun to realise that, for all his vigour, perhaps she did not much like the shooting gentleman. True, she had encouraged him and had certainly enjoyed his company, though more in bed than out of it. Perhaps she was just disgruntled because Iain had not swiftly delivered that which he seemed to promise.

Now, however, there were alternatives, for she had looked upon Mr Gillies Brown if not with lust or even longing then at least with speculation. He was a quick, intelligent and decisive man with a ready-made role in the community and, of course, had already spawned four children.

Biddy swung her legs up and, tugging back the covers, wriggled into bed. She thumped bolster and pillow, propped them against the bed-head and leaned back, arms folded. 'Are you coming into bed, Iain?'

Now he *was* sulking. 'Not until you give me a straight answer.'

'To which particular question?'

'Will you marry me?'

Though not noted for her quickness of wit, even Biddy saw the irony of their present situation. She gave a little, damning laugh, and shook her mane.

'I'm serious,' Iain said, petulantly.

'I know that you are.'

'Well?'

'Do you not see how silly all this is?' Biddy asked. 'Here you are in my bedroom, on my bed, telling me that you will not be sleeping with me unless I agree to marry you.'

'I don't find a proposal of marriage in the least humorous,' Iain said. 'If you must know, Biddy, I'm tired of being – being toyed with. I do have some sense of honour, you know, although it may not seem so to you.'

'It's not honour, Iain,' Biddy said. 'It's pride.'

'Whatever it is, damn it, I've had enough of your . . . *Will* you marry me?'

'If I say that I will not, what then?'

'I'll take my leave immediately.'

'There is no boat until the morning,' Biddy said. 'Will you be walking to Tobermory and spending the night on the pier?'

He got to his feet, rising to his full height beside the bed. Emotion had revivified his moustache. It stood erect. His colour was high. His eyeballs bulged slightly, not apoplectically but with something approaching dismay. He filled his lungs as if to bellow but when he spoke his voice was muted and gravelly.

'I'm tired of this nonsense, Biddy, although I am not tired of you. Indeed, I'm willing to give my life to you by making you my wife. Anything less will not be satisfactory to either of us. I can say no fairer than that.'

'Iain . . .'

'Wait,' he said. 'I haven't finished. I'm willing to give my life to you, Bridget, but I'm not willing to be laughed at or to have to submit to any more of this unseemly testing.'

'Iain, come . . .'

'No, I'll not impose upon you, Bridget, not tonight.' Despite the floppy shirt and dangling galluses he appeared almost

103

dignified. 'I don't like being measured against professors of engineering or – or schoolteachers, or anyone else for that matter. I am my own person and you know all there is to know about me. If you do not care for me as I am then I would be obliged if you would say so. I feel I'm due that much respect.'

'Iain, I'm sorry if . . .'

'I'm leaving tomorrow. And, no, I will not be sleeping on the pier.'

'Yes, that was . . .'

'I've business in Edinburgh, as it happens, and would have left at the week's end in any case. However,' he paused, 'I feel that we've reached a crossroads in our relationship and you must make a choice. My offer of marriage remains on the table. I'll allow you time to consider it carefully.'

Drawing up her legs beneath the covers, Biddy clasped them in the manner of a child, though she did not, not for a moment, seem childlike in any other respect. 'In the meantime,' she said, 'will you not be coming to bed?'

He hesitated; at least, Biddy thought, he hesitated.

Another lungful of air before he answered: 'I would prefer not to, Bridget. Under the circumstances I do not think it would be – correct.'

'I see,' Biddy said. 'Yes, I understand.' She cocked her head. 'How long will you be allowing me before you must have an answer?'

'I will be at Coilichan on the twentieth. I will expect an answer then.' He pursed his lips, closed his eyes then let them flutter open. In spite of his dogmatic stance he seemed nervous, almost despairing. He said, 'Unless – unless you have already made up your mind?'

Biddy rested her cheek against her wrists and peeped out of the arch that the drapery made, peeped at the window from which, in daylight, she could watch the weather skimming in from the west. She seemed, Iain imagined, to be contemplating a rejection here and now.

Aghast now at his bravura, he waited to be told that it was over, that he had lost not only his lover but his soft billet and his one chance of making good his debt to the Sangster

Baverstocks. He was tempted to recant, to throw it all overboard, to strip back the bedclothing and throw himself upon her, to show her that he was still man enough to take the initiative. But he *had* taken the initiative, had he not? Had forced a choice upon her. He could not go back on it now without seeming even weaker than he really was.

'Bridget,' he said, at length. 'I'm waiting.'

'The twentieth,' she said, 'will be time enough.'

'Do you mean . . .'

She turned her head swiftly. He glimpsed the baleful fire in her eyes, not so much anger, perhaps, as annoyance that he had clumsily forced an issue that she had been reluctant to confront.

'Yes,' Biddy said. 'I will be at Coilichan in September.'

'Will you tell me then what you've decided?'

'One way or the other,' Biddy said, 'I will be giving you my answer then.'

Early the following morning in the great hall Iain Carbery kissed Biddy on the cheek. He thanked her politely for her hospitality, reminded her of her promise, and with rod, shotgun and dunnage bag stowed safely behind him in the dogcart, rode out of Fetternish with an inexplicable sense of relief.

The nights were the worst. He would waken screaming in the wee small hours, his horror so great that even Vassie would be afraid and, no matter how often it happened, would leap out of bed in the alcove and sway, dizzy and disoriented, while his shrieks rang through the cottage, unmuffled, it seemed, by roof and walls, but ringing, ringing with a hard, marbly, terrified edge that cut through her hatred and into her heart.

She could not ignore him. In the night hours when the demons occupied his brain – or what was left of it – and delirium caused him to cower, quivering, in the corner under the loft ladder or to throw himself blindly upon the door, scratching and scraping until his fingers bled or, worst of all, forced him down on to all fours by the hearth to beat his brow upon the stones until the unhealed wounds of the previous week, or the previous night, reopened and blood flew everywhere – then she could not ignore him and abandon him to his punishment. Then, with the dogs barking a furious accompaniment from the shed, she would shake her head to dispel her dizziness and would run out through the canvas curtain, reaching for the rope as she went.

At first, four or five years ago, he had fought her off with demented fury. Once he had felled her with a blow from his forearm, not coldly and deliberately as he had done in the days before drink dragged him down, but randomly. He had struck her more than once in this manner, breaking bones in her wrist on one occasion and on another cutting open her head; not now, though, not these past months for although he still possessed a lunatic energy when the fits took him, his muscles were as wasted and weak as old straw.

Ronan's hallucinations should have represented the pinnacle of Vassie's revenge but there was so much of it, the territory so unknown, that her satisfaction was spoiled by pity and the need to prevent him doing himself harm.

So she would grab the rope of plaited straw from the hook by the dresser, would jink and jook about him in the half-dark until she could loop the rope about his chest and yank it up tight under his armpits. Still raving, he would strain away from her like a horse against the hames until she threw all her weight backward and pulled him sprawling on to the floor. If he was already crouched on the floor, though, she would drag him full length until she could stretch the rope to the post that supported the roofbeam and, like a bargee, would haul it round and make it fast. Then she would jink away again while Ronan pawed and screamed at whatever ugly devils flew before his eyes.

She would pull out a stool and sit on it, breathless and pained. She would watch him struggle against the binding and hear him shriek out the names of the fallen angels who tormented him, and only a dose of Vassie's black jallop or two or three big swallows from a fresh bottle of Old Caledonia would send them scuttling back to the shadows.

Nobody knew of the nocturnal trials that Vassie endured, not even Innis.

There were times when Vassie thought that he must surely fall against the plaited rope, shaking the roofbeam with his weight; that his brain would be extinguished like a candle, his heart stop, his engorged liver and shrivelled kidneys and the rotted bag of his stomach given rest at last. Ronan, however, did not die, did not slump against the rope, and would go on shrieking until the visions flickered out of their own accord, as if the demons had become bored with tormenting him and had decided to leave him hanging for another night.

Then Vassie would rise from the stool and mix a draught of the heavy opiate that Dr Kirkhope had prescribed, would pour it into a bowl, pull his head back by the hair and pour it into his mouth, holding his nose so that enough of the medicine would go down his throat and not be coughed up. Then she would pour out a half-cup of whisky and give it to him, and he would grasp it in both trembling hands and conduct it to his mouth and swallow it without spilling a drop. Then, and only then, would she slacken the rope and let him slither down on to the floor and sleep as Fingal had once slept, twitching and growling, in the circle of warmth by the hearth.

She had no notion what tormented him. Even in rare moments of lucidity he would not talk of it. She thought sometimes, in a vague mystical way, that he must be dreaming of Donnie, Donnie bloated, white and rotted as he, Ronan, had seen him before he was laid in his coffin; or of Aileen, his trusting girl-child daughter whom he had raped up there on the high, heathery moor; or of Biddy and Innis and how he had beaten them black and blue just for the pleasure of it; or of Neil, simple and trusting, who had been driven away by his father's wickedness and had never, not once, returned.

Did *they* come back to torment him, the living who were as good as dead or the dead who were living still?

She did not dare ask.

She did not dare pick up the pieces, to recompose the pattern that she had once thought of as her family. They were not hers now, not hers to call her own. She could not be possessed by them as Ronan was possessed by them for *she* knew where they were and how they were, all except Donnie, who had never gone away at all and who, for her, would always be the fair and handsome boy that he had been when he, and she, were young.

She was hoeing the potato patch when he came to her. She did not notice him swinging down the sheep track from The Ards, but if she had, her heart would have leapt into her throat and she would have turned dizzy with the spell that had been woven around her, the cruel, bright deception that the light played on her keen, old eyes, tricking her into hope and into happiness. He leaned on the rusted harrow that plugged a gap at the end of the long drystone wall and quietly watched her.

She felt rather than saw his scrutiny and, propped on the shaft of the hoe, swung round slowly, as if she too was moving in a dream, a daylight dream. She did not cry out in temper, did not shout at him. For a moment there was no sharpness in her, and no fear of anything.

She said, 'Who are you? What is it you are doing here?'

'I am Donnie, Grandmother. Do you not recognise me?

'Donnie?' she said. 'My Donnie?'

And it *was* her Donnie, her handsome boy come back to her, just as he had been before he first went out to work on the boat, small but strong-shouldered, with that straightness in his bearing and the steady, steady gaze that said that he was afraid of nothing. That faint air of cockiness too, as if he already knew that in a year or two all the girls would be mad for him and he would have to do nothing but be himself to win them over.

He did not know how to answer her, though, so he smiled instead.

She could not move, could not stir herself. She clung to the hoe, leaning into it, and felt a pleasant weakness ooze through her, a warmth, a softness that only the sight of Innis's girls gave her, and Gavin too. But not like this, not sweet and sudden like this.

He said, 'Can I be coming over?'

'Aye,' Vassie said. 'Aye, come, come along, son.'

She knew who he really was, of course, though she had not seen him for the better part of two years. He had not come over with Quig to deliver or collect the bull last time or the time before that. He was no longer a child but a boy, a boy who would very soon be a man. He had filled out, grown broader and his likeness to her son, to her Donnie, was uncanny.

She watched him unsaddle the pack from his back, throw it over the harrow and clamber after it, not quick and agile but with the same sort of caution as her Donnie would have demonstrated. He picked up the pack by one strap and rested it against his hip and came on down to the fence of the potato patch and climbed over it too. And it was all Vassie could do not to rush forward and embrace him, in spite of who his father was.

He smiled at her again and when she leaned towards him he kissed her cheek without hesitation and then, to Vassie's amusement, formally introduced himself: 'I am Donnie, Grandmother. I am your daughter Aileen's son. Do you not remember me from coming over with Quig and the bulls?'

'Sure it is that I remember you. It is just that you have grown since I saw you last and you – you look . . .'

'Like my uncle? Aye, Quig tells me that I am well named for I am my uncle's double, except that I am darker in the colour of my hair.'

'What does your mother say about it?'

He gave a little sigh, made with the lips, but he was not in the least embarrassed by the question. 'I do not know if my mother can be remembering her brother. You know how it is with my mother, Gran. None of us, not even Quig, can ever be sure what it is that she does and does not remember.'

'Does she not talk of him?'

'No, never.'

'Or of me or – or her father?'

'No, Gran, never.'

'What is it that she talks about these days?'

'She is not much of a one for talking at all,' Donnie said.

He spoke of Aileen as if she was simply something that was there on Foss, something curious and natural but not useful, something that had to be cherished and preserved but not necessarily loved.

It had been many years since Vassie had last visited the little green island that her father owned, many years since she had seen her youngest daughter. She had convinced herself that she was not welcome on Foss but the truth was that she could not bear to witness her father's inevitable decay, the withering that would ruin him before it took him to his rest. It was not a withering like Ronan's, though she had heard from Innis that Evander's mind played cruel tricks on him too and that he had also become helpless.

The main reason that she had avoided much contact with Foss, however, was that thirteen years ago she had told Tom Ewing that her Donnie had fathered the child on Aileen, for her son had drowned by that time and could not deny it. She had lied to protect Ronan from the penalty of the law and to protect herself from the terrible slanders that would accrue if ever the truth came out, but there was never a day went by when she did not feel shame at what she had done, at the lie she had told the minister.

Now with young Donnie standing before her she felt the first spontaneous wave of affection dribble away, leaving her shrewd and sharp – and melancholy – once more.

She said, 'Where is Quig? Is he not with you?'

'He is busy with the cattle and with looking after my great-grandfather. He sent me over on the ferryboat to Croig and I walked from there by myself.'

'For what reason are you here, Donald?'

'To go to school.'

'What is it you say?'

'I am to go to school, for two years.'

'Who is it put this idea into your head?'

'Dada – Quig, I mean.'

'Why is it that he has waited so long? Why did he not send you to the school at Dervaig before now?'

'He did not want Mam to be without me until I was old enough to go away on my own. And now I am.'

'Hah!' said Vassie. 'Have you no education then?'

'Aye, Gran, I can read and I can write and I have been instructed in the history and in the geography of the world, and in several forms of counting.'

'Who instructed you?'

'Great-grandfather, until he – well, until he could not do it any more. After that Quig read me my lessons and corrected my copybooks.'

'If you are so well instructed,' Vassie said, 'why is it that Quig feels that you are in need of more education?'

'He thinks I will be needing it.'

'Needing what?' said Vassie.

'The Certificate of Merit.'

'What good will that be doing you?'

'It will be getting me work if I ever need it,' Donnie told her, not, she noticed, by rote and rehearsal but as if he understood the value of formal, state-sanctioned education and approved of it.

'Do you not have work on Foss?'

'Quig says that there may not always be work on Foss and that we must all be prepared to do better for ourselves if we have to be moving to the mainland. Many of us have gone away already to work elsewhere.'

'Are you not a cattleman then?'

'Aye, Gran, I know something about the handling of the beasts and I can row a boat and set long lines and do a lot of other things. But I do not have any knowledge of the world and I am in need of education.'

'Quig told you that?'

'He did.'

'And has he sent you here, to Crove, to get some – some of this knowledge of the world? Is that it?'

'I am having to begin somewhere, Gran,' Donnie told her.

He smiled again, not smugly or patronisingly, not in the least insolent, unlike like Ronan or Gavin, unlike the smirk that the shepherd gave her if they ever happened to meet. It was, Vassie thought, like the smile her eldest used to have before Ronan wiped it away.

'I have letters,' Donnie went on.

'Letters from Quig?'

'Aye, to explain . . .'

'Does Quig not know that I cannot be reading letters?' Vassie said.

'There is not one for you, Gran. There is one each for Aunt Innis and Aunt Bridget and another one for Mr Brown, who is the new schoolteacher,' Donnie said. 'Quig said that you would point me to my Aunt Innis's house for I have never been there and do not know the way.'

'Is that where you will be put to lodge, with Innis?'

'No,' Donnie said. 'I believe it is Quig's intention to ask Aunt Innis to ask Aunt Bridget if I might be staying at the big house for a time.'

'Am I to be nothing in all of this but a signpost?' Vassie said.

'Oh, no,' said Donnie, disarmingly. 'You are my grandmother and that is why Quig told me to come here first of all so that I could tell you what Quig's plans for me are, to make sure you approve of them.'

'Quig's plans, aye,' Vassie said. 'Your Dada's plans.'

'Quig is not my father,' Donnie said. 'My father was a drover who took my mother against her will, as you of all people must remember, Gran.'

'I remember,' Vassie said. 'Sure and how would I be forgetting that?'

'Will you point me the way to Aunt Innis's house?'

'I will be doing better than that, Donald. I will come part of the way with you to make sure that you do not get lost.'

'I never get lost.'

'You are not on Foss now,' Vassie said, putting down the hoe and wiping her muddy hands on her canvas apron. 'You are on Mull, one step nearer to the mainland.'

'Aye, and the big wide world.'

She laughed, the sound grating and rusty as if her voice, like the old harrow, had been unused for far too long.

'Come,' she offered him her hand, 'I will be taking you the first part of the way myself.'

He took her hand and held it not as a child might but rather as if she, like his mother, was more in need of assurance than he was. So Vassie led him out of the potato patch and wide around the back of the cottage, just on the off chance that Ronan might be conscious enough to recognise who had come to stay or, more precisely, who had come at last to stake a claim on Fetternish.

For that, Vassie had little doubt, was part of Quig's plan too.

FIVE

Every Good Omen

The girls were very impressed with their cousin. They stood, quiet as mice, staring up at him while he spoke with their mother in the garden in front of their house. They did nothing to gain his attention, created no fuss, simply planted themselves – Rebecca with her thumb in her mouth – six inches in front of him and moved when he moved so that Donnie was soon engaged in a solemn little dance, less waltz than pavane, that only became untenable when Fruarch joined in too. He was no taller than Gavin, but even Becky sensed that the stranger was older than her brother even if he was not quite, or not entirely, grown-up.

Mammy had been surprised to see him but had given him a kiss on the cheek. She had even opened the gate for him and had taken away his pack and put it inside the kitchen door where Fruarch could not widdle against it. Then she had come out into the garden again and the stranger had given her a letter that he took from inside his shirt. Mammy had opened the letter and read it. And it was while she was reading it, while Fruarch was sniffing about the young man's legs, that the young man looked down at them and did what few other young men ever did – he spoke to them, not from up high but from down low.

He came down to them, bending his knees and sitting back on his heels so that he was right before them. Becky, still sucking her thumb, drew back a little bit, and then he smiled. 'Are you not sure who I am?' he said.

Rachel shook her head.

'I am your cousin, Donald. I come from an island called Foss. Perhaps you have been hearing about it from your Mam?'

Rachel nodded.

'What do they call you?' he asked.

'Rachel.'

'That is a very pretty name,' he said, and then reached out and took Becky's wet fist and very gently detached her thumb from her mouth. 'And you, what is it they call you?'

'B . . . Becky.'

He extracted a clean, red-spotted cotton handkerchief from the pocket of his shirt and, still talking, wiped saliva from Rebecca's cheeks and dried the little fist, one finger at a time. 'Do you go to the school, Becky?'

'N . . . New Year.'

'I go to the school,' Rachel put in.

'Is that the school in Crove?'

'Aye.'

'Well, I am here to go to the school too,' said Donnie.

'You are too big.'

'No, I am not. I am here to learn my spelling and my counting tables just the same as you.'

'I can spell big words,' said Rachel.

'Can you spell – dog?' he asked.

'Aye.'

'Spell it then,' he said.

'Dee – Aw – Gee.'

'Very good. Now, tell me, what is *this* doggie's name?' Donnie asked as Fruarch, pipped at being ignored, straddled his shoulder and licked his ear. 'Is it "Nuisance", by any chance?'

Rachel was quite old enough to understand the joke. She laughed while her sister, though not so sure, giggled, and the young man, with some difficulty, separated himself from the spaniel and got to his feet again.

Innis said, 'I think you have made two friends already.'

'I am hoping it will be no less easy when I get to Crove.'

Innis gave the letter a little shake. 'Do you know what it is that Quig is asking me to do?'

'Yes.'

'Why has he suddenly decided to send you to school?'

'He says it is necessary if I am ever to find work.'

'Is there not enough work for you with the cattle?'

'If Evander dies there will not be enough work for any of us, perhaps.'

'What reason does Quig have for thinking that?'

'I do not know, Aunt Innis. He did not tell me.'

'Is Grandfather worse?'

'He is much the same,' said Donnie.

Innis did not know why she was disturbed by Quig's letter. There would be no difficulty in finding lodging for such a polite and personable young man. Except that he was no ordinary young man. His precise relationship to the Campbells could not be properly explained and even she could not be sure – or did not wish to decide – whether he was her half-brother or her nephew, or both. She did not blame Donald for her confusion, of course, and held nothing against Quig who had done more for the Campbells than anyone by taking care of Aileen for so many years. Even so, she was concerned at Donnie's sudden appearance in their midst and just a little dismayed that Quig had not thought to warn her in advance what was on his mind in respect of the boy's future.

She said, 'Are you hungry?'

'Well, yes, Aunt Innis, I am.'

'Come in then,' Innis said. 'I will be giving you some supper and then when my husband comes in from the field I will be taking you up to Fetternish House. We will discuss the matter with Biddy – your Aunt Bridget – who I think Quig hopes will take you in.'

'If it is not convenient for me to stay at the big house,' Donnie said, 'perhaps I can sleep in your house for one night.'

'I have no bed for you, Donnie.'

'I will not be needing a bed. I can sleep anywhere, in the shed even.'

Innis shook her head and gave a little laugh. 'No, no, no,' she said, taking her nephew's arm, 'it is not the way it was in Quig's young days. We will not be having you sleep rough. You are a scholar now, Donnie, and scholars deserve the best of hospitality. Besides, you are also my nephew and Bridget's nephew and we can hardly be putting you out with the dogs, can we?'

'I also have a letter to give to Aunt Bridget,' Donnie said.

'Yes, I thought that might be the case,' Innis said, and shepherded her father's son indoors without more ado while Rachel and little Becky, still giggling, followed happily on behind.

Guiding his steps with a storm lantern, Innis conducted her nephew to the front door of Fetternish House. Dusk held no terrors for Donnie but he was struck dumb with awe when Willy Naismith opened the big oak door and admitted them into the great hall. It was all Donnie could do to remember his manners and hand over Quig's sealed letter to his Aunt Bridget while the hounds circled him, sniffing and snuffling curiously.

Biddy had taken supper at a little table in the hall. The night was not cold but had a moist, shivery feel to it that heralded a further shift from summer into autumn. She had had Willy build the fire so high that flames licked the breast of the huge stone fireplace, and hall, staircase and gallery danced with gigantic shadows. She was dressed in a loose garment of red wool. With Carbery gone and no one to criticise her for being unladylike, she had even kicked off her shoes. Thor and Odin had grown not fat but heavy in maturity so that they appeared ideally suited to the scale of Fetternish which, on that September night, seemed to Innis more like a medieval castle than a Victorian country house, and her sister, rich and red and beautiful, like a character from a poem by Tennyson or Scott.

Standing before the hearth, Biddy read the letter then, holding it down by her flank, said, 'Have you eaten, young man?'

'I gave him supper,' Innis said.

'William, take my nephew down to the kitchen and provide him with tea and, if he wishes it, some of the apple flan.'

'Aye, ma'am.'

'This gentleman is William Naismith. He is my steward. He

will see to your needs, Donald, while I discuss certain matters with your Aunt Innis.'

'Yes, Mrs Baverstock.'

'Do not call me "Mrs Baverstock". I think that addressing me as Aunt Bridget will be more appropriate.'

'Yes – Aunt Bridget.'

'Go now.'

'My pack?' Donnie said in a quiet, tremulous voice.

'Take it with you meanwhile – until we decide just what we are going to do with you.'

Donnie nodded and Willy led him away down the corridor towards the kitchen stairs. Biddy waited until she heard the door close before she turned to face her sister. 'Did you have anything to do with this?' Biddy said. 'Have you been plotting with Quigley behind my back?'

'I knew no more about Quig's plan than you did until this afternoon.'

Sweeping her skirt about her, Biddy seated herself on the end of the sofa, knees spread and the letter in her lap.

'I wonder what he is after? Quigley, I mean?'

'I would have thought that was obvious,' Innis said.

'It is not obvious to me.'

'He is just calling in his debt.'

'Debt? What debt?'

'The debt that he feels he is owed for taking care of Aileen.'

'Well, I certainly did not ask him to . . .' Biddy stared into the flames and sighed. 'Yes, I see what it is that you mean, Innis. If Aileen and her child had not been put away out of sight on Foss then you would have had to take care of her.'

'Or you,' Innis said. 'Because she could not have stayed with Mam and him at Pennypol.'

'And if Michael – or Austin for that matter – had known what was happening and what lay behind it . . .'

'That is all water beneath the bridge, though,' Innis interrupted. She came around the end of the sofa and seated herself beside her sister. 'It did not happen because Quig took her in.'

'No. Grandfather did.'

'Grandfather – Quig: what is the difference now?'

Biddy said, 'Is it to be the boy first, do you think, then Aileen, then, one by one, the rest of the Foss clan?'

'There is no Foss clan left, Biddy. Quig has sent most of them away.'

'Why has he done that?'

'Because he is aware that when Grandfather McIver dies there will be no living for them on the little isle.'

'The herd will still be there, will it not, the famous Foss bulls?'

'No, Quig knows that it was the famous Evander McIver that made Foss thrive, not the quality of the stud. When Grandfather goes it will all go with him, perhaps not at once but swiftly, very swiftly.'

Biddy hesitated. 'I have never asked you this question, Innis, because it is not a subject I find palatable but – Quig, does he sleep with her?'

'No, I am sure he does not. No decent man would take advantage of Aileen's condition and Quig is nothing if not decent.'

'Has she not changed then?'

'Only for the worse.'

Biddy drew her knees together and plucked her long skirt into alignment with her thighs. She smoothed the material down with the flat of her hand.

'This debt you talk of, Innis, is it money Quigley is after?'

'No, he is after making sure that Donald is part of the family.'

'By sending him to school?'

'By sending him here.'

'Does Quig expect me to look after him?'

'Where else would Quig send him? To Pennypol?' Innis said. 'If you do not want him, I will take him in.'

'I do not say that I do not want him,' Biddy said, hastily. 'I just cannot understand why Quig would send him here now. Why now?'

'Because Quig is now certain that he is all right in the head.'

'Unlike his mother, do you mean, unlike Aileen?'

'Yes,' Innis answered.

Biddy frowned. 'Still, I do not feel comfortable with him.

120

Oh, he is a handsome lad, no doubt, but . . .'

'Does he not remind you of our Donnie?'

'Too much, perhaps,' Biddy said. 'But what *is* he, Innis? How do I think of him? I mean, is he our brother or . . .'

'Think of him as your nephew,' Innis answered. 'Or, better yet, as himself.' She rose from the sofa and, without heat, said, 'I see that you do not want him here, Biddy. I will be taking him back to Pennymain with me. He can stay with us until he is finished with his schooling.'

'What will Michael have to say to that?'

'Michael will understand that I have responsibilities too.'

'I will take him,' Biddy said, abruptly. 'You have no room at Pennymain. I have plenty of empty beds. One half-grown boy will not take up much space. He can sleep downstairs. Willy will find him odd jobs . . .'

'He is not an unpaid servant, Biddy.'

'I'll wage him then, if that is what you want.'

'He is Aileen's son. We must look after him properly or not at all. I do not say that he will not put his hand to work – I expect he will – but he is a cattleman, remember, not a kitchen drudge. If you require someone to pay for his keep . . .'

'Do not be ridiculous. You are right, as usual, Innis,' Biddy said. 'We *are* responsible. We *do* have a debt to repay.'

'For Aileen's sake,' Innis reminded her.

'Yes,' Biddy said. 'For poor Aileen too.'

Gillies Brown had been prepared to adjust to a curriculum that was both rootless and roofless and had arrived from Glasgow armed not only with a selection of tried and true textbooks but also with a batch of test papers which he had filched from a cupboard in Greenfield School. Product of the best brains in the National Inspectorate, the test papers reflected the latest in educational theory. The questions were designed not just to separate genius from dunderhead but also to winkle out the so-called 'sluggish learners' and place a finger irrefutably upon those poor wights who had absolutely no intelligence at all.

Gillies Brown was sceptical. He was not convinced that such

rigid demarcations meant anything or that the presence of 'sluggish learners' in a classroom did not merely indicate a degree of sluggishness in the system itself. Nonetheless, during those early weeks in Crove he needed guidelines or, to stretch the metaphor, guy-ropes to keep his confidence from floating away over the sea never to be seen again. In fact, at times he was so bewildered that he even began to wonder if he had reached that perilous age when the brain cannot cope with novelty but demands only familiar and unvarying routine.

Janetta encountered no such problems in her teaching methods. She laughed at her father's confusion, told him that he was just being a silly old man and that the children of this rural community were better at testing him than he was at testing them and that, if he did not tighten his grasp, they would soon be having him on toast for breakfast, like a kipper or a fried egg.

It was not that the children of Crove were rowdy, at least not within the classrooms. At morning play and noon dinner-break, however, they struck out into the fields behind the schoolhouse yelling like Turks or Zulus and, until Gillies strap-ped the ringleaders, lit fires along the dikes and dug tunnels in the sand cliffs of the riverbank. The boys had five times more energy and ingenuity than their counterparts in Glasgow and a grisly aptitude for trapping rabbits and spearing crows, while the girls engaged in games that seemed, at least to Gillies, not just repetitive but positively ritualistic.

'They're only children, Dad, country born and bred,' Janetta assured him. 'They're not savages.'

'Oh, I know they're not savages,' Gillies told his daughter. 'Contrary to how it might appear, I don't really mind them firing the bracken or pursuing the odd bunny-rabbit with a sharpened stick, provided they don't do themselves any harm in the process.'

'What is it then?'

'It's the silence,' Gillies admitted. 'It's the silence, and the looking. You can't convince me that's a natural way for children to behave.'

'They're just listening.'

'Hoh-hoh-hoh!'

'They are. They're fascinated by what you're telling them, that's all.'

'They're sizing me up.'

'Of course they are.'

'I feel I'm being weighed up against the teachers from Dervaig.'

'You're just not used to such a mixture of infant, primary and elementary. I'm beginning to think you were spoiled in Glasgow.'

'Well, I'm not spoiled now,' Gillies Brown would say. 'I'm in the thick of it and I just wish they wouldn't be so damned – pardon – so blessed quiet all the time, just – just staring at me, saying nary a word.'

'Tell them that if they don't start larkin' about in class you'll belt the lot of them,' Janetta suggested. 'That should do the trick.'

'A reign of terror?'

'The rod of iron, Dad, that's it.'

He glanced at his daughter speculatively and it was not until she laughed again that he was entirely sure that she was making fun of him. She was a bright, fair-haired girl, not unlike her mother in appearance. When he looked at Janetta, when he listened to her speak, he was taken back to his early days as an untrained and unqualified teacher, before legislative provisions had allowed him an opportunity to improve himself and earn a living wage; and he recalled all the encouragement that Clara had given him to push ahead in his profession even when everything had seemed dead set against him.

'You're right, dear, of course,' he said. 'Pick me three or four of the very smallest and I'll do as you suggest.'

'Ooooh, but you're cruel.'

'Not as cruel as children can be, sometimes.'

'That's true,' Janetta agreed, as if her six months of teaching as a pupil-assistant carried as much weight of experience as his twenty-one years.

Gillies Brown was no Wackford Squeers. He had no prejudice against corporal punishment in principle but he was less than liberal in his use of the 'tawse', the stiff black leather strap the very sight of which, coiled like a snake on a teacher's desk, could hold a class in thrall. He applied the strap only to boys and only when social order was threatened or his own personal authority was severely challenged. Fires in the bracken along the borders of the schoolyard fell into the first category but, so far, he had not had to resort to strapping as a means of saving face.

Infants, five to seven, were under Janetta's charge. Some had already attended a term or two at Dervaig, but most were quite new to school and found that sitting still for the best part of a day was a difficult discipline to master. One or two had a habit of dropping off to sleep as soon as the classroom warmed up and would slumber away for ten or fifteen minutes at a stretch while Janetta pretended not to notice them.

In Gillies's classroom, however, nobody fell asleep. They were all far too busy staring at him, the round, nut-brown faces of primary pupils on the front benches uptilted, those of the older pupils slanted downward as if they had something to hide; collective guilt, perhaps, or just plain scorn for the incomer. The presence of the schoolmaster's children did not help, and Tricia, Bobby and Evie, though not bullied, were not made welcome at first. But it was not until the young man from Foss arrived in the Fetternish dogcart that Gillies Brown's troubles took definite shape and the began to comprehend the nature of the silent souls he had been employed to teach and to perceive that, even in the young, still waters could run very deep indeed.

The Browns, all five, had been in the schoolhouse for a good half-hour before Janetta took the handbell out to the doorstep to summon pupils from field and gate and spur those laggards who were still mooching up the main street into a final, breathless sprint. With Miss Brown still tolling away on the bell, Crove's hopes for the future swarmed into the unpaved yard in front of the little whitewashed building and formed into three units; infants in column of route at one end, junior girls at the other and, behind them, in line abreast, a raggle-taggle assortment of surly, sprouting males.

Just as the bell stopped and its echoes died away, the Fetternish dogcart appeared in the lane that led from the village street and Mrs Baverstock stepped out of it. She was swathed in a pleated tweed cape and had a fur-trimmed hat on her head. Everyone, even the youngest, knew how important Mrs Baverstock was, and everyone knew Mr Naismith, her servant and steward. But nobody recognised the young man who accompanied them through the gate and straight into the schoolhouse; nobody, that is, except Gavin Tarrant who had already been warned that his Foss cousin might turn up that morning.

Mr Brown did not have a desk in the headmaster's cubby. He had a table, though, and two wooden chairs that Mr Ewing had 'discovered' in the manse and had brought over to give the place a certain official clutter. There were also two narrow cupboards and an awkward sort of tallboy which left very little room for the widow of Fetternish, her servant and the new arrival who, Mr Brown was quickly informed, was Mrs Baverstock's nephew. Mrs Baverstock was not disposed to be friendly. She wore a haughty, almost supercilious air, as if she suspected that Mr Brown might turn her young relative away.

'What is your name, young man?' Mr Brown asked.

'I am called Donald.'

'Surname, please?'

'His surname is Quigley. His mother is my sister,' Biddy said.

'Are you from this parish, Donald?' Gillies Brown asked.

'I am from . . .'

'He is from the Isle of Foss,' Biddy put in, 'which falls within the jurisdiction of this parish.'

'Are you lodging in Crove?'

'He is staying with me at Fetternish,' Biddy said.

'Mrs Baverstock, if you please,' Gillies Brown said. 'I would prefer Donald to speak for himself.'

'I am staying with my aunt, meanwhile, sir,' Donald said, promptly.

'Have you had schooling before?'

'No, sir.'

'That does not mean he is ignorant,' Biddy put in.

'I am lettered, sir,' Donald said. 'My grandfather taught me from books.'

'Your grandfather?'

'Evander McIver.'

'Ah, yes!' Gillies Brown exclaimed. 'Now that he is – not himself, he has decided to send you to school, is that it?'

Biddy would have interrupted once more but Willy laid a hand on her arm and drew her back slightly.

'Aye, sir, that is how it is,' Donald said.

'Very well,' Gillies said. 'I will give you some tests to do to ascertain just how well you have been taught and what you do and do not know. And then . . .'

'You are not going to turn him away?' Biddy said.

'Of course I'm not going to turn him away. He belongs to the parish, even if he does live umpteen miles away across the Atlantic. And even if he did not, Mrs Baverstock, I would still take him in if his parents asked it of me.'

'Why are you testing him then?'

'To find out what he knows and what he should be taught.'

'Oh!' said Biddy.

'Now, ma'am, if you don't object I'll take Donald into class and find him a desk suitable to his size, and we will get on with the business of the morning.'

It was the first time that he had seen Bridget Baverstock play the part of laird – or was it lady? She did not relax her haughty manner, however, even after it became clear that her wishes were not being opposed. Behind her back, though, Willy Naismith pulled a face, lips pursed and eyes wide, and it was all that Gillies Brown could do not to laugh.

He cleared his throat.

'Did you bring your dinner with you, Donald?'

'Oh, God!' said Biddy, her hand to her throat. 'I forgot all about dinner.'

'No matter,' Gillies said. 'We will gather loaves and fishes and make sure that Donald doesn't go hungry.'

'Pardon?'

'He can share with my family,' Gillies explained.

He was puzzled by the woman's nervousness for that, he realised, was what lay behind her mood. She was not being autocratic just for the sake of it but, rather, to cover up an insecurity of feeling in respect of the boy. He waited for her to fuss, to tidy her nephew's hair, pick an invisible thread from his jacket, give him a motherly lick and spit to make him respectable. But Willy prevented her from embarrassing her nephew by drawing her back into the passageway that separated the classrooms.

From one room – Janetta's – came the murmur of a morning prayer. From the other – Gillies's – the usual abnormal silence.

'I must get in, Mrs Baverstock,' Gillies said.

'Yes,' Biddy said. 'I understand. When will I collect him?'

'Collect him?' said Gillies Brown.

'To drive him home. I mean, bring him back to Fetternish House.'

Willy made a face again and, wrinkling one eye, shook his head slightly.

'He can walk the road home with us, Mrs Baverstock,' Gillies said.

'What if it turns wet this afternoon?'

'Oh, I don't think he'll melt in the rain. Will you, Donald?'

'No, sir,' said Donald, patiently. 'I do not think I will.'

'You *will* see him safe home?' said Biddy, anxiously.

'Yes, Mrs Baverstock. I'll see him safe home,' Gillies Brown promised and, aided by Willy Naismith, ushered the doting auntie out into the yard.

He had seen his cousin before, of course. Had seen him briefly at Pennymain only the previous night before his, Gavin's, mother had served up supper and, carrying the storm lantern, had left to guide Donald to Fetternish house. If he had thought more of his mother he might have cried for them to wait for him. Might have accompanied them across the bridge up to his aunt's house and escorted his mother safe back home. But there was supper to be eaten and his sisters to look out for, though they had been put early into bed. He had done nothing, had said nothing. Not to his mother and not to the cousin from Foss.

In the classroom that morning his cousin had been kept apart. Lessons had gone on around him while Donald had sat at Mr Brown's desk which had been dragged over into the corner away from the door and the blackboard. Donald had perched up there on the high stool like a prince. Had received from Mr Brown three separate test papers and a dozen long sheets of lined foolscap and, with a new pen-nib in a new holder and a new piece of mauve blotting paper, had kept his head down and had written steadily, almost without pause, dipping the nib into the ink-well, while the rest of the class, Primaries and Elementaries alike, had peeped at him, amazed at the ease with which he wrote and the speed with which he calculated, this half-grown boy off the islet of Foss, where none of them had ever been.

The big girls murmured, the wee girls whispered. Gavin guessed they were already talking about Donald Quigley and thinking him a hero and that unless he was writing rubbish he would be put above them all in the top seat at the top of the class and the girls would all suck up to him. He was not even the son of a head shepherd either, just the son of some cattle-man who tended a herd of big-horned steers on the backside of the Treshnish Isles.

Gavin watched while he did his reading. Watched while he filled his copybook with the words that Mr Brown read out for the Elementaries to define. Watched while he drew a map of the two rivers – the Clyde and the Forth – that flowed across the central plain of Scotland. Apart from the spelling it was all quiet work that Mr Brown had them do that morning so Donald would not be disturbed. Gavin sat still and silent, watching, a small cold clod of anger thick in his chest at the recollection that his cousin had ridden in the Fetternish dogcart along with Mrs Baverstock and the realisation that that was something he had never done, not once.

At the dinner-break Donald was gathered up and swept away by the Browns. They kept themselves to themselves the Browns did, young ones and older ones, even the pretty one with long, straight hair called Tricia who sat next to Gavin in the back row. They had nothing much to do with anyone, except his sister Rachel who claimed she was their friend. Miss Janetta Brown came through from the Infants' classroom with Evie and the stupid slavering pampered pup that was kept out in the gardener's hut during classes. Miss Brown spoke to Donald and brought him two scones and a ripe, red apple and a beaker of hot tea and stood by the small desks talking to him for a long time.

At half-past three o'clock, when classes ended, Gavin hid in the maltman's close at the end of the lane.

He was waiting for the dogcart from Fetternish to come and pick up his cousin and to see if Donald Quigley would ride off and leave the others behind. But the cart did not come, and Gavin did not show himself though it was his job to find Rachel and take her home to Pennymain with him. The Browns would bring her. She would walk with them as far as the crossroads at Coyle. He would wait for her there, down the track apiece, because Mammy did not think it right that Rachel should come over the bridge on her own and Dad did not want to be indebted to the Browns for seeing her safe all the way to the cottage.

Gavin watched from the maltman's close as the Browns came out, all except Mr Brown, who often stayed behind. When Janetta Brown came out Donald and Rachel and the pup were with her. The pup was put down on the end of a rope leash and, laughing, the six of them started up the main street towards the head of the Fetternish road without even looking round for him.

He waited until they were out of sight, and then he ran.

He ran down the lane and across the common grazing and through the reeds at the edge of the wetland at the bend of the river. He ran fast, elbows pumping, the fisherman's bag thumping against his flank. He ran doggedly, grunting, round the back of the ragged wood and out on to the track well ahead of them so that when they arrived at the crossroads, he was already there, standing off apiece. Waiting, while they chattered and laughed and said goodbye to Rachel. Waiting, implacable and unyielding, with the small hard lump of hatred still throbbing thickly in his chest.

Now that the Browns had settled in at An Fhearann Cáirdeil Biddy did not see quite so much of them. She felt it would be unfair to intrude upon their privacy and did not walk out to the lonely headland or prowl the edges of the woodland with her gun as often as she had done in the past. Besides, she had Donnie to look after and that was much more of a responsibility than she had anticipated. Though the young man was polite and undemanding, his presence in the house had brought about changes in routine. When it came to caring for her nephew's welfare Biddy left nothing to chance and very little to Willy Naismith, and it was Donnie's timetable that now controlled the pattern of her days.

She did not object to Donnie spending time with the servants, did not dissuade him from walking over to the Browns on Saturday afternoons or dropping in on his Aunt Innis and his cousins at Pennymain. Nevertheless, she was just a wee bit jealous of the free time that Donald spent away from her and she would find herself peering out of a first-floor window or hanging about on the drive whenever he was due to return. She realised that she was being needlessly protective of a boy who had been raised to take care of himself but she could not help her feelings or disguise them.

In the evenings after school, as soon as he had consumed the hot chocolate and buttered toast that Queenie made for him, Biddy would make sure that he changed out of his damp clothes – even if they weren't damp – and that the dogs were shut away while Donald did his homework at the table by the fire in the drawing-room. At seven o'clock dinner was served in the dining-room, complete with damask tablecloth, candelabra and the second-best silverware; after which Biddy would escort Donald into the drawing-room again to hear his reading or grammatical interpretation or quiz him from the questions that were printed in the back of his history book. Now and then, she would treat him to a rendering of some jolly shanty or cotter's song at the piano before, reluctantly, she sent him upstairs to bed. In the morning she was first up and would waken Donnie with a knock on the guest-room door and a cheerful – too damned cheerful in Willy's opinion – cry of 'Come along, Donald, rouse and shine,' or 'Up and at 'em,' or some other daft phrase that Biddy misinterpreted as the best means of communicating with the next generation.

She was in fact in awe of her nephew, as once she had been in awe of Innis. Mr Brown had told her of his testing and marking and of the interpretation that he, an experienced teacher, put upon the results.

'Your nephew is a remarkably well-informed young man,' Gillies had said. 'His parents should be very proud of him, I mean, given that he has not had the benefit of any formal schooling whatsoever. His knowledge is considerable and, to be honest, his powers of ratiocination much higher than I would have expected under the circumstances.'

'His ratty what?' Biddy had said.

'His ability to deduce by reason.'

'Oh.'

'I'll be surprised if he isn't ready to sit for his Merit Certificate by the end of the summer term. After that I would suggest that he goes on to continue his education at a college on the mainland.'

'College? What sort of college?'

'Whatever sort of college he fancies.'

'He is not fifteen until the middle of next year.'

'Age is no barrier, or not much of a one,' Gillies had assured her. 'It'll mean leaving Mull, of course. Donald may not wish to do that.'

'Oh, he will, he will, he will,' Biddy had said. 'If it means going to college, he will. I cannot be thinking of any member of our family who had the brains to go to college on the mainland before.'

'Perhaps it wasn't brains but opportunity that your family lacked,' Gillies Brown had reminded her. 'In any case, Mrs Baverstock, I've promoted your nephew to head of the Elementary class and put him at the top desk.'

'This isn't – well, favouritism, is it?'

'Favouritism?' Mr Brown had said, as if he had never heard the word before. 'Favouritism? Why would I be inclined to favour Donald?'

'Well . . .' Biddy had been embarrassed by her obvious *faux pas*.

'Because he's your nephew, do you mean?'

'Well . . .'

'I assure you Mrs Baverstock I favour no one child over another. What would be the benefit in it; the benefit for the child, I mean? When Donald, or any of my pupils, leave school they'll have to deal with the world on the world's terms, not mine. Any knowledge that I've managed to impart will be theirs to use or to neglect, as circumstances and character dictate.'

'Yes, I – I apologise.'

'No apology required, Mrs Baverstock,' Gillies had said. 'Just look after that young man, will you? If he's given the right sort of encouragement in the next half-year or so he can go far in life.'

'And you will be giving him that encouragement?'

'Of course I will. Will you?'

'With all my heart,' Biddy had answered.

Naturally she had told Willy first of all. Then she had gone down into the kitchen and told Maggie and Mrs McQueen. Cook had said that she wasn't a bit surprised since she had known a few clever boys in her days in Edinburgh and Donnie was just like them. Next Biddy thought it necessary to inform Innis but now there was a proud, bragging note in Biddy's voice as if *she* had been responsible for Donnie's sound upbringing. Innis did not have the temerity to point out this fact, although she was well aware that her sister's pride in and affection for their nephew was excessive. Finally, on a cool, grey October day that smelled of ripe dung and winnowed straw, Biddy had girded her loins and had tramped down to the wall at Pennypol.

Sweetening the visit with a basket of bottled fruit, a bag of cane sugar and a box of tea, she had reported to her mother exactly what the schoolmaster said about Donnie and what a glorious prediction had been made for his future.

'Surely you cannot expect me to be surprised,' Vassie said at the end of her daughter's enthusiastic account. 'Donald will not be the first in the family to be having more than his share of brains. He is part of him a McIver, and the McIvers have always been renowned for their common sense.'

Biddy sighed and, somewhat deflated, glanced along the line of the drystone wall to the black house with its thin reek of peat smoke hovering at the chimney-hole and the bundle that was her father lying against an upturned barrow near the doorway.

'What about the Campbells then, Mam?' she heard herself say. 'What is it that they are renowned for? How many of them have ever been given the high seat in a school classroom or have been told that they are fit to being going on to study at a college?'

Vassie evaded the question with one of her own. 'What will Donald be studying in this fine college of his?'

'I do not know,' Biddy said. 'Agriculture, perhaps.'

'Agriculture, pah! Is there not enough of the agriculture around here for him to be studying without going off to fancy places on the mainland? Where is this college?'

'Mr Brown tells me there are three of them to choose from. Glasgow, Edinburgh or Aberdeen.'

'Aberdeen! It is all fish in Aberdeen.'

'If he went to Glasgow,' Biddy said. 'He could lodge with Neil.'

'Neil has enough trouble of his own without taking in more.'

'Donnie would be no trouble, I am sure.'

Vassie, who had been preparing the layers to store her potato crop, wiped her earthy hands on the bib of her apron, adding a smear of dirt to the sheen of grease. She looked ragged this morning, ill-kempt and unslept. There were great dark circles of fatigue under her eyes and her weather tan had an unhealthy greyish tint to it.

'Boys are always trouble,' Vassie said, grimly. 'Besides, has it not been occurring to you, Biddy, that it is not for you to dispose of his future and to be saying what is right for him? He is Aileen's son, remember.'

'Aileen? Oh, Mam, Aileen will not know what we are talking about when we suggest sending Donald to college. I doubt if she even knows where he is at present, only that he is not on Foss with her.'

'She is his mother,' Vassie said. 'But if she does not know what to be doing with Donnie, then Quig will. You must not be putting Quig to one side. He may have other things in mind for Donnie to do.'

Biddy shook her head. 'If you are meaning that Quig will want him to go back to Foss with his Merit Certificate then I think that you are wrong. Quig would not have sent him to school just to go back to being a cattleman. He has more in store for Donnie than that. He is ambitious, is Quig.'

'Has he been talking to you then?'

'No. I have not seen him for weeks.'

Along the line of the wall Biddy saw her father suddenly struggle to rise from his sprawled position against the wheel-barrow. She was shocked by his helplessness but even more shocked when he finally staggered to his feet and, supported by the cottage wall, jerked himself round to face her as if he had recognised her voice. Even though he was the best part of three hundred yards off, when he waved in her direction she took an involuntary step backward.

Vassie did not even glance round.

'Hoh!' Ronan yelled, hoarsely. 'Hoh, lassie! Are ye lookin' for a man then? I have a bottle here to suit both of us, if you will come over for a kiss.'

'He is still a fool, that man,' Vassie said.

'Does he not know me?'

'No, he cannot be seeing past his nose,' Vassie said. 'He will come no closer than the gable. He cannot stand upright for long since his legs are full of whisky and his head is full of water.'

'Can nothing be done for him?'

'Aye, we could be sending him to the college like Donnie, I suppose, to learn all about agriculture.' Vassie laughed without a trace of mirth. 'There is a brain for you, Biddy, a fine big brain, all swollen up with its own conceits.'

'If it was not for him I would take you to live in the house.'

'Is that what you would be doing?' Vassie said. 'Well, I would not be going to stay in your grand house if it was the last dwelling in the whole of Mull, not even if I was alone and did not have him to look after. Aye, Biddy, you might be the laird of Fetternish, or its lady, but that does not give you the right to go telling everybody what they must be doing with their lives. I can fend for myself. I am not needing your interference.'

'Mam!'

Her father leaned on the house wall now, very casual, very normal. His arms were folded and he had no bottle visible in his hand. Even at a distance, he seemed to be smiling at her in the old, easy, charming way that he had had when Biddy had been young, before she and the others learned what a blackness lay within him and how his charm would suck them in and deceive them as it had sucked in and deceived others, even strangers. With a shudder of revulsion, she remembered the feel of his tongue in her mouth, his hands toying with her breast. Remembered too whose son Donnie really was and, for a moment, felt her revulsion spread out like a great misty wave to engulf the boy too.

Vassie snapped a hand to the sleeve of Biddy's coat.

Gripping tight as a vice, she said, 'You must not be thinking it.'

'Thinking what?' Biddy said.

'That he is tainted, or that he is to blame for himself.'

'Who? Dada, do you mean?'

'I mean Donald.'

'I – I do not think anything of the kind.'

'Aye, but you do. It would not be natural if you did not. Bear this in mind, though, that he is *our* boy, *your* boy only for a short while and then he will be gone into the world and it will be of his own making.'

'I thought you said he was Quig's responsibility?'

'Aye, so he is. But he is a good omen for us, Biddy. Whoever his father is and however far from reason his mother may be, Donald is a good omen and we must seize on every good omen while we can. Just remember . . .'

'Yes, yes, that he is not my son,' said Biddy impatiently, while out there ahead of her her father lolled and beckoned, beseeching her to come to him again.

The library of the New Athenian club in Edinburgh's George Street was still its pride and joy. It lay on the upper floor of a handsome granite-pillared building at the top of a marble staircase broad enough to accommodate six Trojan horses, or six stalwart Clydesdales, for that matter, in line abreast. How this calculation had been arrived at was not one of the questions that New Athenian members tended to ponder, though after an afternoon of steady tippling or a night's carousal in the library bar some august gentlemen had been known to see a pink elephant or two descending the marble in front of them.

No pink elephants or Trojan horses for Walter Baverstock, however. Biddy's brother-in-law had always been a model of rectitude and temperance whose reward had been to grow more and more ascetic-looking as the years rolled past. Indeed, in certain lights he had even begun to resemble the blank-eyed busts of the ancient Greeks that guarded the alcoves and, with his beard gone plaster-white, might have been taken for a relative of Diogenes rather than the son of a Border town manufacturer. His companion that early autumn afternoon was infinitely more sanguine. With a fair quantity of second-rate claret poured down his neck Iain Carbery had more of the stamp of a Vandal or a Hun than a noble Greek philosopher.

The pair were not alone in the library.

Several elders drowsed in pitted leather armchairs in the proximity of the fireplace and several others were engaged in sombre discussion of the latest slump in share prices and the effect on world trade of the Franco-Russian *entente*. Baverstock and Carbery had gravitated to the niche at the end of the long room, however, and claimed sole occupation of the famous 'Wallace Settle', the legs of which were alleged to have been carved from the very gibbet on which Sir William had been hanged. History, legend and literature held no interest for the couple. Their conversation, which had begun over luncheon in the dining-room below, concerned Fetternish and had become as close to acrimonious as Walter would allow.

'Keep your voice down, Carbery, if you please.'

'Are you implying that I'm shouting?'

'No, no, of course not, but you know how sound travels in this place.'

'Let it,' Iain said. 'I have nothing to hide.'

This, in fact, was a palpable lie.

Iain had been nursing not merely a dreadful migraine for several days but also severe twinges of guilt, a condition less common than gout in men of his calibre. Even he had not had the gall to take himself back to Sutherland for the fag-end of the grouse-shooting season or the heart to impose himself just yet on any of his other sporting friends. The truth was that he had begun to miss Biddy almost before the boat had sailed out of Tobermory. He had pined his way down the Sound of Mull and sulked his way down the new railway line that linked Oban to Edinburgh via Callander and Stirling and, on returning home to his cramped, damp and lonely apartment had flung himself on to the bed and wept like a love-sick loon.

Shame enough in that unmanly incident, God knows, but more shame still at having hauled himself down to the Leith docks just to seek out company, something that he had not done in several years: company, specifically female company. A girl, specifically a thin-lipped, narrow-hipped girl with frizzy red hair: a girl no more like Biddy than a crow is to a swallow but active enough, and actress enough, to take his mind off Mull and relieve him, albeit briefly, of his sorrow and self-pity. He had sought her out again – she wasn't hard to find – and had conducted her back to his apartment and persuaded her to spend the night and had taken her roughly, almost frantically, two or three times and had paid her a lot more than she was worth to him, or to anyone.

'No,' Iain said, loudly. 'Nothing to hide and nothing to be ashamed of.'

'What on earth are you blathering about?'

'What do you think I'm blathering about?' Iain said. 'I'm

blathering about your dear sister-in-law which, as I seem to recall, is what we've been blathering about for the past hour and a half.'

'And who seems, for some reason, to have become a touchy subject.'

'Of course she's a touchy subject,' Iain shouted. 'If you had bothered to inform me just what she's like . . .'

'I haven't seen her in years,' said Walter, making a little gesture with the flat of his hand to soothe the irate sportsman. 'I cannot imagine that she has changed as much as all that. She was always rather grasping.'

'Grasping?' Iain threw all his weight backward, making the historic woodwork creak. 'Oh, no! Biddy's not grasping. Bit demanding, I'll concede, but not greedy, not in the sense you mean.'

'And still attractive to look at, I suppose?'

'Absolutely.'

'If you are so all-fired keen on her, Iain, why not pop the question?'

'I have popped the question.'

'Did she turn you down?'

'No, as I've explained before, she wants to be sure of children.'

'I'm afraid this "modern" approach to marriage is all rather beyond me,' Walter said. 'On the other hand, Bridget Campbell was never a girl to be bound by convention. That was how she managed to snare my late brother.'

'As you've told me a thousand times,' said Iain. 'What I want to know is how you and your sister hope to profit from my marriage to Bridget?'

'She stole Fetternish from us.' Walter gave a lift of the shoulders as if he had received a tap on the back of his neck. 'Ill luck for all of us that Austin died when he did. That, I admit, was not the Campbell girl's fault. But she was most unco-operative, most uncompromising thereafter. Looking out for herself, with no regard at all for her obligations to our family.'

'I thought your sister Agnes opposed the marriage?'

'She did at first, but then she relented.'

'That's not what I heard,' Iain said. 'Biddy has a different tale to tell. However, that does not answer my question: How will my marriage to Bridget restore control of Fetternish to the Baverstocks?'

'It won't, of course,' Walter said. 'Oh, my sister Agnes still cherishes the fond notion that one day the estate will return to our possession and that her sons will inherit it, but . . .'

'But you do not?'

'I'm perfectly prepared the let the blasted place go. Good riddance to it. I was never comfortable there and have no desire to set foot on Fetternish ever again.' Walter paused. 'I'm more concerned with the twelve percentage holding that Biddy Campbell has in our Sangster manufactory.'

'Biddy won't sell out to you, you know. She'll never relinquish her stock. She's a shrewd woman, Baverstock, damned shrewd. And she has Naismith to advise her if she feels the need of advice. In fact, the truth is that she would be better off without a husband at all.'

'If it weren't for children.'

Iain shifted uncomfortably upon the settle. The effects of the lunch-time claret were beginning to wear off and even talking about Fetternish and Biddy had become almost painful. The library's tall windows were streaked with sunshine but the cries of the street traders that gathered on the corners of St Andrew's Square had somehow become muffled and forlorn. A day for the hill, Iain thought, and yearned not for geese on the Solway or fox-hounds pouring over the stubble around Selkirk but for Mull, for Fetternish.

'If it weren't for her desire for children,' Iain agreed.

'Can you not – I mean, is it not possible to . . .'

'Oh, come now, Baverstock, you don't have to be so damned delicate. You mean, why have I not proved my worth in that department? Well, I've tried, God knows, but it seems that we are not suited, not – not medically, at least.'

'Medically?'

'Physiologically.'

'You mean, you can't?'

Iain glanced up the length of the room to the sleepers by the fire. He envied them their ease, their freedom from obligation. He almost wished that he had never met Biddy Baverstock or – no – that he had never undertaken to become Walter's spy in a house so filled with love. He scratched his hairy ear with his forefinger. Love? *Was* it love? *Was* he really in love with Biddy Baverstock? Good God! What an appalling thought!

Iain said, 'She's not going to yield up her holding in your factory, Walter, whether she marries me or whether she does not. In any case, I thought you needed the wool crop that Fetternish is contracted to supply?'

'We do – at the moment.'

'Trade's bad?'

'Dreadful.'

'I see,' Iain said. 'Do you resent the fact that Biddy is protected by sale of the wool crop at a fixed price? Would you prefer to see Fetternish turned over to cattle or deer? Or the planting of forests? Oh, no, surely not timber?'

'A husband, a strong, resolute husband who was also the father of her children could insist upon changes, could he not?'

'I doubt it.'

'I must say, Carbery, you've changed your tune.'

'Whether I have or whether I haven't is immaterial. Biddy won't marry me, and that's an end of it. I've wasted enough time courting, all to no purpose. I'm sorry, Baverstock, but there you are.'

'I'm disappointed in you, Iain. I thought you had more stuff, more determination than that.'

'Well, I haven't.'

'Are you not stalking this month?'

'Possibly.'

'Hasn't Fennimore invited you to Coilichan?'

'Sort of.'

'And Bridget Campbell? Will she not be there?'

'It's all so – so petty, Walter, this second-hand wooing.'

'It appeases Agnes,' Walter said. 'She hasn't mellowed with the years. She blames the Campbell girl for Austin's untimely death and will do anything, however petty, to make her life uncomfortable. She's still very bitter.'

'Is that it? Is that all?' Iain said. 'Spite? Female malice? Good God, Baverstock, how did I get mixed up in this silly game? I thought there was more behind it, some scheme or plan, some sort of deviousness. Now you tell me that it's all just a peevish ploy to appease your sister's sense of injustice. Do you imagine that marrying me would be a punishment on poor Biddy?'

'*Poor* Biddy? Why do you say *poor* Biddy?'

'Because she desperately wants a child and can't have one.'

'Can't have one? Are you sure?'

'Practically certain.'

'Hmmm!'

'Didn't you know?'

'No, I can't say that I did.'

'Well, it's a fact. No child, no marriage.'

'Or,' Walter said, 'no marriage, no child.'

'What?'

A pause, then Walter enquired, 'Will the shooting not be good on Coilichan this year?'

'How do I know?'

'Come now, Iain, you always know these things.'

'Yes,' Iain confessed. 'From all that I've heard, the stags are in prime condition.'

'You will go, will you not?'

'I doubt it.'

'Iain?'

He looked from the windows at the sunshine which had already turned back into rain. It was that time of year, of course, when even the weather was uncertain. He said, 'Well – perhaps. Probably.'

Walter's smile was deliberately restrained, hidden by his wispy plaster-white beard.

'You just can't resist her, Carbery, can you?' he asked.

And Iain, honest to a fault, answered, 'No.'

It was fast approaching bedtime and Becky was already nodding off over the supper dishes. In most other island households the younger children ate separately and it was one sign of growing up when you were invited to share the table with Daddy. This was certainly the habit in Barrett's cottage, a fact of which Michael would now and again remind Innis. But, as Innis would remind Michael, the Barretts had a brood of six scuttling about their feet and it was only thanks to Muriel's domestic ingenuity that any of them managed to get fed at all. No, Innis insisted, the Tarrant family must try to break bread together once each day, particularly in the four winter months when Michael and Gavin were in from the fields by half-past five o'clock: yet sometimes she would be late home from buying stores in Crove or just a little tardy in returning from a visit to Pennypol or Fetternish or even, now and then, from An Fhearann Cáirdeil, and the evening meal would not be served until six or six-thirty by which time, as now, Michael would have a face like phiz and Becky would be nodding off over her soup bowl.

There was never much conversation, never much exchange of information about the events of the day. Michael would be silent, sometimes grumpy, and Gavin, as always, would adapt effortlessly to his father's mood.

Only Rachel, bubbling like a little pot, would chatter away about all the things that had interested and amused her, until her father would tell her 'That's enough,' or Innis, sensing trouble, would quietly suggest that she eat her supper and not talk so much.

'Donnie gave me a treacle candy today.'

'Where did he get a treacle candy?' Gavin asked.

'Queenie made it for him. He brought me a piece to school. It was wrappit up in white paper. I ate it at the dinner time. See,' she fished in her pinafore pocket, 'I keppit the white paper.' She spread a torn square of Fetternish stationery on the table beside her and smoothed it out with her small fist. 'Is it not nice paper? It is Auntie Bridget's paper. She gave it to Donnie to wrap all the candy in. We all had bits, big bits, and we ate them at the dinner time. Were you not for getting a bit too, Gavin?'

'Rachel, please eat your supper,' Innis murmured.

'Gavin? Were you not for getting a bit of Donnie's candy?'

Gavin did not deign to reply. His shoulders were straight and his head bent. He had the habit, like his father, of sitting too close to the table, upright and tight-elbowed. He snipped with the edge of his fork at the slice of hot mutton that lay on his plate, lifted a fragment to his mouth and snapped it off the tines.

'Donnie has got the top desk now,' Rachel said. 'I have seen him at the top desk. He sits next to Tricia.'

School had changed Rachel; Innis was aware of it, even if Michael was not. What had until recently been ingenuousness in Rachel was now something else, not quite calculated and certainly not malicious, but with a teasing quality that someone less dour than her brother would surely have taken in good part; a verbal form of rough-and-tumble that Rachel had learned by imitating the Browns, who were forever ribbing each other and trading insults that affection rendered harmless.

'Donnie is the cleverest. There is Donnie and then there is Tricia and then there is Kitty. And then there is John Mackenzie and then there is Peter McLean and then there is Alice Williams and then . . .' She drew in a full breath. 'And then there is you, Gavin.'

'Rachel, that's enough,' Michael said.

'It is true, Daddy. Gavin is not on the top row now. Donnie says I will be in the top row when I am old enough. Donnie says . . .'

He swung his arm and with the knuckles of the hand that held the fork struck his sister a glancing blow on the side of the head. Her hair flew out in a billow and her thin neck curved backward, but before Rachel even knew what had caused the pain, and before Innis could catch the flying hand, Gavin was eating again, snipping and picking again, as if that sudden, swift snap of the hand had not been planned or even willed but had happened of its own accord.

Shock silenced Rachel at first. She angled her head towards her brother who continued to eat as if nothing at all had happened. She looked stunned and bewildered and two or three seconds passed before tears welled into her eyes, then she let out a low moan and, sliding from her chair, flung herself into her mother's arms. It was Becky who wailed. Roused by the sound of the slap, Becky screamed loudly while Rachel, sobbing, pressed her face into Innis's breast.

'*Gavin, don't you ever, ever do that again,*' Innis hissed furiously.

'Do what?' Gavin said, knifing at the mutton.

'*How dare you hit your sister, a wee girl like that. How dare you!*' Innis cried. She shifted Rachel just enough to accommodate Becky who, still howling, had flung herself against her mother too. 'If you ever . . . Michael, will you take him outside. It is a whipping he needs and you should be doing it.'

'Send them to bed.' Michael said.

'Did you not see what Gavin just did?'

'She deserved it,' Michael said. 'I'll not be whipping the boy for nothing at all.' He put down his fork, craned across the breadth of the table, pulled Rachel away from Innis's protection and, in a flat, dead voice, said, 'Get to bed, lady, or I'll be whipping you.'

'*Michael!*' Innis exclaimed in horror.

Then she noticed the glance that exchanged between father and son and in the tilt of the eyes and faint complacent smile realised that it might not be Aileen's boy who bore the Campbell taint but Gavin.

With a little gasp of disbelief, she thrust herself back from the table and, lifting both her daughters into her arms, carried them swiftly away.

Fetternish House was at peace with itself. Only the solemn ticking of the grandfather clock in the alcove below the stairs, a fall of ash in the fireplace and the soft-footed prowling of the south-west wind in the gallery disturbed the silence. Oil lamp in hand, Biddy lingered in the corridor outside her nephew's bedroom. She could see the strip of light beneath the door and knew that he was not yet asleep. She knocked tentatively and heard him call out, not in alarm, she thought, but sleepily. She turned the brass handle and went in.

It was the largest of the four guest rooms that occupied the first floor of the house and it had a fine view to the south and a tall iron fireplace and a chimney that did not smoke. She had furnished it with bits and pieces and the very best of the beds from the other rooms and had even purchased new blankets, great soft fluffy things from Jenner's catalogue and a brightly coloured quilt and coverlet that she thought a boy – a young man – might appreciate. Donnie was tidy in his habits and as self-sufficient as Biddy would allow him to be and he had settled quickly into his new life in the big house and gave no trouble at all. The only thing about him that Biddy found disconcerting was his resemblance to her dear brother for he had not been so much older than Aileen's son when he had drowned.

The little pot of tea – he was very partial to tea – and jug, cup and saucer were still on the round tray which he had put to one side of the bed. His clothing for the morning was laid out on a chair and he had even been sensible enough to smoor down the coal fire in the iron grate and attach the snark-guard to its hooks. The lamp, an Orly, burned on the bedside table and by its light Donnie was reading a tall tome bound in half leather that he had probably borrowed from the bookcase in the office downstairs. Propped up against the bolsters, his nightshirt tied over his chest and a cotton scarf wound about his neck to protect him from stray draughts, he looked both studious and virtuous.

He did not shift away or start when Biddy entered. He placed a taper of paper in the book and closed it, looked towards his aunt and smiled.

'Is it not time you were asleep?' Biddy said.

'It is, Aunt Biddy. It is,' he agreed. 'I got caught up in my reading or I would have had the lamp out a half hour ago.'

'What is it that you are reading?'

'It is a book on veterinary medicine. Aunt Innis lent it to me. Apparently it was given to her by Grandfather some years since.'

He looked at the volume as if he was half inclined to open it again. Instead he leaned out of bed and placed it carefully upon the rug beside the tea-tray.

Biddy noticed how strong he was, back muscles already filled out and tight under the flannel nightshirt. His forearms too were muscular and had a dusting of dark down upon them. He looked older than he did in his school-going clothes, neat and compact and not clumsy, as young men so often were. She felt suddenly self-conscious and awkward, unprotected by her matronly affection. She pulled her robe about her throat and set her lamp down by the door, went to him and seated herself on the side of the bed.

What was it her mother had said? You must seize on every good omen. Donnie was, without doubt, a good omen, and his coming to Fetternish had been the best thing that had happened in years. He was not surly, not tense in her presence, and seemed used to a woman's gentle attentions. Biddy wondered if Quig's mother, Mairi, had been mother to Donnie too, if she had come at night to kiss him and tuck him in.

Biddy said, 'Mr Brown tells me that you are clever enough, perhaps, to be going on to college at the end of the summer. Is that what you would like to do?'

'It is,' Donnie answered, 'if it can be managed.'

'What subject would you be inclined to undertake?'

'Husbandry,' he said, without a blush.

'Agriculture?'

'Yes, especially in its animal aspects.'

'What do you mean – if it can be managed?'

'Quig says that he will make provision for it, if I prove myself able.'

'Money, do you mean?'

'Aye, that is what Quig means.'

'Oh, if it is only a question of money . . .'

He touched her arm. He was obviously not as conscious of her as she had become of him. He touched her with a sudden, quick little gesture, a tap of the fingertips only, and at the same time shook his head.

'It was not for that purpose that Quig sent me here,' he said. 'I mean, not for money, not for the patronage.'

It was a queer word for a young man to be using, Biddy thought. But then she had had very little to do with her grandfather's ménage on the Isle of Foss, had no knowledge of how Quig thought or what subjects he and the others had discussed over the fire during the long, bleak winter nights. Perhaps they were grateful for their good fortune, fully aware that they had been favoured by Grandfather McIver's generosity, by his – yes – 'patronage'.

'We are not asking for charity, Aunt Biddy. Quig would not like you to be thinking that,' Donnie went on.

'No matter what Quig thinks,' Biddy said. 'I am your mother's elder sister and, fortunately, it would be no hardship for me to meet your college fees. It is something I would like to do.'

He shook his head again. 'Quig would not stand for it.'

'Well,' Biddy said, 'we will just have to wait and see.'

'Aye,' Donnie said and, to her astonishment, raised himself up from the pillow and kissed her on the cheek. 'You have been very kind to me already, Aunt Biddy, and I love you for it.'

'Nonsense,' Biddy said, blushing like a beetroot. She rose hastily from the side of the bed. 'Nonsense, stuff and nonsense.'

'Goodnight, Aunt Biddy.'

'Goodnight, Donnie,' Biddy said and, turning out his lamp, hurried out into the corridor before he noticed her scarlet cheeks and sentimental tears.

'It isn't right, you know,' Willy said.

'What is not right, dear?' said Margaret.

'The fuss she makes of that young lad.'

'He is her nephew after all.'

'Aye, but she spoils him.'

'If he was your boy, Willy, would you not be spoiling him?'

'I never spoiled any of mine when I had them. Not like that.'

'Perhaps it is because you never had the opportunity.'

'Maybe, maybe,' said Willy, with a sigh. He lay on his back in the bedroom in the little parlour apartment that Maggie and he shared in the servants' basement and stared up into the darkness. 'He's a personable young chap, I'll admit, but if you ask me she is becoming just too fond of him.'

'He is fond of her too, is he not?' said Maggie.

'Would you not be fond of someone who was fussing over you all the time?' said Willy. 'No, there is something – something not right about it.'

He felt his wife's round knees dig into his hip. 'Could it be that you are jealous of him, old man?'

'Aye, well, I am jealous of his youth.' Willy turned on to his side and put his arm about Maggie's middle. She was as warm as toast. He could feel the rise and fall of her stomach under the night-gown, soft and vibrant like a cat's purr. 'I'll wager you would like me to be his age again.'

'No, I would not,' said Maggie, stoutly. 'What would I be doing with a boy when I have a man beside me?'

'The same as you do with a man, only oftener,' said Willy.

He expected to feel a tremble of amusement in her muscles, her breath against his ear. Instead she edged away, just an inch or so, to be sure, but in the darkness and intimacy of the bed it seemed like a parting. She propped herself on an elbow and admitted a draught of chill air into the sheets.

'It is not too late to be changing your mind, Willy.'

'What do you mean?'

'I am not too old.'

He hesitated, then said, 'No, Margaret, but I am.'

'My father's uncle fathered a son at the age of seventy-one and he, by all accounts, was less than half the man you are.'

'Aye, but he was a Bell and the Bells are . . .'

'What? What are we?'

Willy fiddled with the sheets and blankets, closing off the gap that let in the cold air. It was not the first time that Margaret and he had had this sort of conversation and perhaps it would not be the last, though with every passing year the possibility of Maggie bearing healthy children became just a shade more remote. She would be forty soon – and that would be far too late in life to be safe. He could not bring himself to divulge the real reasons why he was so careful when they made love together. For instance, how could he explain that it would break his heart to have to leave a sturdy son or a pretty little daughter behind when he died. Maggie would probably say that he might

148

well live to be eighty or eighty-five and counting on her fingers would point out that their son or daughter would be independent by then.

Aye, Willy thought, but at seventy-five or eighty I will not be independent: I will be like a child myself, frail and cantankerous, a girning, burdensome old devil. Who would wish that on a son or a daughter?

There was more to it than callous selfishness. He was so terrified of losing Maggie that he would not risk making her pregnant, no matter how broody she became from time to time. He had already fathered his share of children. He had done as well as he could for them under the circumstances of his employment; yet he had not loved them or their mothers the way he loved Margaret Bell. He had never made any bones about not wanting children from the marriage. There had been no deception, no false promises on his part. He needed her all for himself and would not, not at his age, risk sharing her.

'What?' Maggie nudged him once. 'What is wrong with my family?'

'There's not a thing wrong with your family.'

'They are wondering why I have not borne children.'

'They are not,' said Willy, sighing again. 'Your brother is half-way to presenting them with a whole new generation so they aren't in the least concerned about you – about us.'

'I suppose you are right,' Maggie conceded. 'It is just seeing her with him, seeing how much he has changed her.'

'He will not be with us for long,' Willy said. 'He will soon be going away to the mainland to study, if what I hear is correct.'

'She will be breaking her heart when that happens.'

'I know,' Willy said, relieved that the conversation had swung back to Biddy Baverstock and her nephew. 'It is then that she will become desperate.'

'Desperate, dear?'

'Aye, for a husband.'

'I thought you said . . .'

'I know what I said, Margaret, but I know our mistress only too well. I'm sure that when Donald goes away she will be desperate enough to marry anyone who happens to come along.'

'Just for the sake of having a child of her own?'

'If she can have children at all.'

'What if she cannot?'

'Then she will be stuck with him, won't she?'

'Is it Mr Carbery we are talking about?'

'It is,' said Willy, 'but I wish it wasn't.'

'She could do worse,' said Maggie. 'Much worse.'

'True,' said Willy. 'But she could also do better, much better.'

'Who, for instance?' Maggie said.

But Willy would not answer his wife's question, for if he'd done so she would surely only have laughed.

SIX

The Highland Game

Edgar, Lord Fennimore had inherited thousands of acres of prime grazing in Scotland and Ireland, more land, it was said, than you could tour in a month. His estates were famous for their profitability. The ground value of 9,300 acres in Aberdeenshire, for instance, was worth more than ten thousand pounds a year and even his most modest holding, in County Tyrone, brought in the best part of a thousand. Now and then he contemplated clearing sheep and cattle from one of his wilder properties, turning off the tenants, and transforming it into a deer forest, but his mother, bless her heart, always talked him out of it.

She was of the old school. She believed that deer were best kept in parks and not on ground that God had given you to raise sheep and cattle, pigs, ponies and potatoes. For, she would say threateningly, if ever the Famine returned or Home Rule came about then it would be hereditary peers who would be the first to be lined up and shot and if you had a hall full of mounted heads and horns then it would surely be yours that would be joining them and you would not be tasting half so good as a haunch of venison, now would you?

Bowing to maternal Irish logic, Edgar, Lord Fennimore did not, therefore, shoot over his own ground but elected instead to lease one of the many sporting estates in which Scotland abounded.

Tormont on the Isle of Mull was owned by Mr William Poole whose occasional habit of winging a ghillie or scoring a pony-man with a stray bullet had earned him the nickname 'Blind

Billy', a sobriquet of which he seemed inordinately proud. Billy Poole might have been no great shakes with a rifle but, by gum, he had the magical touch when it came to minting profits from the shaggy expanse of hillside and misty mountain-top that had been his portion of the family inheritance.

It was not pretty country. Loch and river were dark and the confluence of mountains that divided the glen of the Horsa kept sunlight from the lower slopes for the best part of the day. Landowners and farmers among Billy's visitors were forever castigating him for not draining the wet mosses and scouring out the low heathers. But Billy knew better. Billy knew deer. He knew that mixed ground, rank heather, patchy woodland, stony corries and huge boulders suited deer perfectly and that cotton grass and moss kept the herds fed in the hungry weeks of early spring. When it came to the management of red deer, in fact, no man on Mull was wiser than Billy Poole and his judicious policies had improved the stock enormously, which is why experienced guns like Lord Fennimore were willing to pay forty pounds a day at the height of the season.

Billy also ran a famously good house. The isolated, twenty-roomed lodge at Coilichan was comfortable and the food, his Lordship declared, was better than you would find in most London clubs. Housekeepers, cooks and parlour-maids, as well as hill and river ghillies, stalkers, dog-handlers and ponymen were all permanently employed, though the lodge itself was closed from the First of November until Easter, its overstuffed furniture cloaked in dustsheets, its cisterns drained and its fireplaces empty.

For several years now Lord Fennimore had rented all six of Tormont's beats for the final fortnight of the stalking season. August, he felt, was too early for stags; besides which in that month he led a party on to the Kilnaury grouse moor in Sutherland and did not care to confuse one pleasure with another. Maud, his lady wife, was a keen shot when it came to the birds but disliked the egregious slaughter involved in taking down deer. She was also aware that Edgar needed to let off steam from time to time and that some willing wife or handsome widow would probably be included on the Coilichan guest list and that her own presence there would only cramp her husband's style.

It was Clarence Parker who had first introduced Bridget Baverstock into his Lordship's circle. At the time Fennimore had been entangled with rapacious Louisa Carnforth, wife of Sears Carnforth, the publishing magnate, and had watched with envy as the young, red-haired widow from 'down the road' had been wheedled away from Parker by bluff Iain Carbery. Now, however, with Louisa lugged off to America by an irate husband, he was free to take up other options which, of course, included the charming young widow of Fetternish.

Biddy was unaware that she had become the focus of Fennimore's amorous intentions. She thought of herself as only a fringe guest, fortunate to be included in such august company. She was flattered to be drawn into aristocratic society but was not foolish or vain enough to imagine that she would ever make a splash in the capital. She was, she realised, just part of the holiday scene, quaintly Scottish, like the ghillies and stalkers and commoners with whom his Lordship liked to surround himself during his Highland vacations.

She arrived at Coilichan in mid-afternoon, accompanied not by trusty Willy Naismith but only by her gamekeeper, McCallum. She had quarrelled with Willy, who had been opposed to the idea of her meeting Carbery again and resented being left behind to dance attendance on young Donald who, Willy complained, only had to be fed regularly, not wet-nursed. Biddy's feelings of anxiety were not entirely due to concern for her nephew's welfare, however. By showing up at Coilichan she had committed herself to giving Iain Carbery a straight answer to his proposition of marriage and she still had not quite decided what that straight answer would be.

She was tense as the Fetternish gig rolled into the yard behind the lodge and she found no friendly faces there among the guddle of dogs and stalkers and ghillies; no Mr Parker, no Captain Galbraith, no sign of Iain Carbery. She was not much comforted when Edgar, Lord Fennimore pranced out of the crowd and extended his long arms to her as if he expected her to jump straight into them.

'Why, Mrs Baverstock, what a pleasure to see you once more. I am delighted, delighted that you could join us again this year.'

'Thank you, your Lordship. I am grateful for the invitation.'

McCallum held the pony steady while the peer reached up and helped Biddy to the ground. He was a tall, willowy man, deeply tanned. He stood close to her, peering into her face, into her eyes, practising his fatal magnetism. He had always been quite friendly, of course. In disposition he was not unlike Iain, only more polished. Biddy had observed him in moods of vulgar good humour, roaring with laughter, singing with the ghillies' chorus and dancing wild reels in the hall with Mrs Carnforth as his partner. There was something different in his manner today, however, something Biddy could not quite put her finger upon but that she found faintly disconcerting and unpleasant.

It suddenly occurred to her that Iain had jumped the gun and had announced their engagement and that Lord Fennimore was about to congratulate her.

Fighting panic, she stammered, 'Has Iain – has Mr C-Carbery arrived?'

'Yes, this morning sometime.' Fennimore did not take his eyes from her. 'Come, let me show you to your room. No maid, I see. No matter. I'm sure we can find one for you. Come.'

He twined a long arm about her. He smelled differently from Iain. In spite of his fondness for dogs and guns and the outdoor life in general, his Lordship carried an aura that was very clean and piercing, like cologne. He had reached that age, fifty, when men of breeding are at their most assured and, in spite of her apprehensions, Biddy did not resist when he guided her towards the doorway at the side of the house.

'Where is Iain?' she heard herself enquire.

'Gone to bathe, I do believe.'

'In the river?'

'In the loch,' his Lordship said and, with an arm about her, led her past the ghillies, stalkers and dogs and into the stuffy lodge.

*   *   *

154

Now that the nights were drawing in Innis found it more difficult to justify her afternoon strolls to the crossroads where 'by chance' she would meet with Gillies Brown and indulge in five or ten minutes of casual conversation. In three or four weeks the dusk would come in early from the sea and Michael would expect his supper at five instead of six and there would be far fewer opportunities to steal away from Pennymain to meet the teacher.

It was still September, though, and on that quiet, cloudy afternoon the couple encountered each other as usual and, with the children milling ahead of them, lingered at the crossroads to talk.

'I take it you've heard that your nephew has been promoted to the top desk?' Gillies Brown said.

'Of course I have heard,' said Innis, smiling. 'Biddy has been telling everyone for miles around, as if it was her doing that he is so bright.'

'He is a very responsive student,' Gillies said. 'Someone has made sure that he has applied himself to his books.'

'That would be my grandfather, I expect – or Quig.'

Gillies poked at his spectacles with his forefinger. 'Tell me, Innis, where does Quigley stand in relation to the boy?'

'He has no proper standing at all, I suppose.'

'Is he not responsible for him?'

Innis hesitated. 'I know what it is that you are asking me,' she said. 'Donald is my sister's son but my sister is not possessed of all her mental faculties. If it will be saving embarrassment I will tell you that Quig is not her husband, nor the father of her son. We do not know who Donald's father is, for Aileen was – I do not know how to put it.'

'Taken advantage of?' Gillies suggested.

'Aye, that will do – taken advantage of when she was young. It was probably a drover at one of the fairs, some pig who never dared show his face on Mull again. I doubt if we will ever find out the truth of it.'

'Does Donald know this?'

'I am sure Quig will have told him by now.'

'Given the circumstances, he is a remarkably well-balanced young chap.'

'Quig has to be thanked for that, I've no doubt,' Innis said.

'I would like to meet Robert Quigley. Can it be arranged, do you think?'

'He will be delivering the Foss bull to my mother in the next day or two,' Innis said, 'and I will see to it that he receives your message. If it concerns Donnie's future Quig will be just as anxious to talk to you as you are to him.'

'Will you have no say in the matter?'

'None,' Innis answered

'What about Mrs Baverstock?'

'She is certainly very attached to Donnie.'

'That much is obvious,' Gillies said. 'I have seldom seen a woman fuss as much as she does over her . . .'

'Ah, but he is not her son,' said Innis. 'Perhaps that is why she fusses.'

'Has she never been tempted to marry again? Bear children of her own?'

Innis lifted her chin and glanced cautiously at the schoolmaster. Thirty or forty yards away the Browns, Innis's daughters and Donald had gathered in an elbow of the road, chatting too; a curious little circle with the dog, Pepper, squatting in the centre as if he too were taking part. Innis experienced a tiny pang of regret that Gavin was not among them. He, as always, had vanished as soon as school was over and sought no other company than that of his father or, now and again, Mr McCallum.

'I'm sorry,' Gillies said. 'I didn't mean to pry.'

'We do not discuss things, Biddy and I,' Innis said. 'However, since you have raised the subject I will ask the same question of you.'

'Hm?'

'Are you not inclined to marry again?'

'No, it is far too soon even to think of it. Besides, what sort of woman would take me on with four children tugging at my coat-tails?'

'A woman who liked children, I suppose,' Innis said.

A burst of laughter floated from the gathering down the road. Even Janetta, who was normally rather solemn, joined in.

'I wonder what the joke is?' Innis said.

'They're probably talking about us,' Gillies said.

'Oh!' said Innis. 'I am surprised they find us so funny.'

'Schoolmasters are perennially entertaining to young folk, especially if the schoolmaster also happens to be their father,' Gillies explained. 'I had better get them home before they become too obstreperous.' He hoisted the bag which contained his books and documents on to his shoulder, then asked, 'How long will Biddy be gone, all told?'

'Eight or nine days.'

Innis was tempted to add, *Will you miss her, Mr Brown?* But she had no justification for supposing that Gillies was romantically inclined towards anyone, let alone Biddy. Surely, Innis thought, he is far too sensible to fall for my sister's all-too-obvious charms and too decent a man to begin calculating her net worth. If she, Innis Tarrant, had been free, however, she would have taken on Mr Gillies Brown *and* his children without a second thought.

'It won't be the same here without her,' Gillies said.

Innis was astonished by the admission. 'Beg pardon?'

'Like Windsor without the Queen,' said Gillies with a teasing twinkle in his eye. 'Will you tell Robert Quigley I'd like to talk to him?'

'I will.'

He gave a wave of farewell, nothing too demonstrative.

'See you tomorrow, Mrs Tarrant?'

'If you are in luck,' Innis said, then, signalling to her daughters to join her, set off along the track to Pennymain feeling just a little let down.

Iain cried, 'What in God's name are you doing here, Biddy?'

'I came at your invitation, as I recall.'

'I don't mean here at Coilichan; I mean here on the second floor.'

'I was shown to this room,' said Biddy.

'By whom?'

'Lord Fennimore.'

'Good God! Doesn't the old buzzard know I'm billeted in the wing?'

'Wing?' said Biddy. 'What wing?'

'Where we usually are. Out of harm's way.'

'Harm's way? What on earth are you babbling about?'

'Fennimore must know that you are with me. Did you not remind him that you are my guest, my companion?'

'I may be your guest, in a manner of speaking,' Biddy said, stiffly, 'but I am not your companion.'

The non-appearance of a lady's-maid to help her unpack had not fazed Biddy one bit. She had hoisted her trunk on to the bed and had just begun to unfold gowns, skirts and blouses and hang them neatly in the mahogany wardrobe when Iain had burst in upon her. His hair was damp, he had a towel slung over one shoulder and was somewhat out of breath, as if he had taken the stairs two at a time. In fact Biddy had had warning of his arrival for, in spite of its stuffing and padding, the house echoed like a great hollow gourd.

Iain rubbed his moustache with his thumb and performed a little dance of agitation around the bed. 'You really should *not* be on this floor, you know.'

'Why ever not?'

'Because – because it's . . .'

The bedroom, like most rooms in the lodge, was not spacious. It had a low ceiling and a small bay window that looked out upon the Tormont saddle and the massive shoulder of Ben More. The light was fading, the room almost dark, the air itself almost as heavy as the mahogany furnishings. Iain stepped over a footstool, two travelling cases, a hatbox, squeezed himself past the dressing-table, knocking over a candlestick in the process, and reached out to sweep Biddy into his arms without so much as a by-your-leave.

'Stop it, Iain,' Biddy barked. 'What has come over you? Stop it, I say.'

He wore an unbuttoned waistcoat, tweed breeches and a linen shirt without a collar. He seemed massive in the cramped room and smelled cold and clammy, like a water-horse or kelpie.

So far he had addressed her only in a shrill, shouting tone but when he caught her by the shoulders and drew her close his voice dropped an octave.

'Biddy, Biddy! Don't you know that this room is part of Fennimore's suite? His dressing-room is next door and his bedroom just down the hall. You would be safer downstairs with me.'

'This is where I was put,' said Biddy; 'this where I will stay, thank you.'

She was not entirely unmoved by Iain's concern. She had been rather alarmed to be ushered into the main part of the lodge for she knew only too well that the second floor was occupied by Lord Fennimore, his staff and a few carefully selected guests – like Mrs Carnforth. She had made no protest, however, for she did not wish to seem unsophisticated or ungrateful.

Iain continued to hold her by the shoulders. She wondered what she would do if he tried to force himself upon her there and then. Meekly submit, she supposed. She had no passion in her, though, not a spark, only a flux of apprehension and uncertainty and a strong desire to be home again, safe home with Willy and Margaret, and Donald.

'Did you not tell Fennimore that we're engaged to be married?'

'But we're not,' said Biddy.

'Are we not?'

'No.'

'Is that by way of being an answer?'

She circled his wrists with her fists and broke free of his grasp. 'Iain, this is neither the time nor the place to discuss such a matter.'

'Fennimore is after you.'

'Please keep your voice down.'

'For two pins I would take you away from here right now.'

'Would you? Supposing I do not wish to go?'

'I see, I see. You intend to try him next, do you? Well, you won't break his heart the way you have broken mine.'

'Iain!'

'He wants nothing from you except the pleasure you can give him.'

She feigned horror. '*Iain!*'

He still smelled clammy, although there was a dew of perspiration on his brow as he reached for her once more. 'I'm in love with you, damn it.'

She took a pace backward. She would have retreated further but she was trapped in a corner formed by the bed and the wardrobe. She watched him lift his fists, thump them against his temples as if to knock some sense into his head. She was more distressed than alarmed now. It had not occurred to her that Iain Carbery had feelings, at least not the sort of feelings that a woman might recognise, let alone share. His sensitivity was not feminine, however. It seemed to her more manly than all his strutting and chest-beating had ever been.

She felt suddenly, horribly responsible for his anguish.

She just prayed that he would not weep.

She touched him lightly, rested her fingers against his cheek, which was not cold but hot, almost feverishly so. 'Iain. Oh, Iain, I'm sorry.'

He rejected her sympathy. Perhaps he thought that it was insincere. He dumped himself on the side of the bed, hands dangling between his knees, head bowed. Biddy touched his cheek again, then the side of his neck. She heard his breathing ease, flattened out into a chesty sigh.

He said, 'I don't know what came over me. I've no right to tell you how to behave. My only excuse is that I haven't been myself of late. Out of sorts. Under the weather, rather.'

She was sorry for him and also afraid of him. He had surrendered too much of himself to be dismissed as a fool. He had revealed how much hold she had over him, a power not calculable in pounds and pence, not defined by a shapely figure, auburn hair and eyes the colour of the sea.

Iain Carbery was *in love* with her and, having so willingly put the cart before the horse, she did not know how to compensate him for his devotion or, in all conscience, how to appease him.

Except by becoming his wife.

She was not ready for that act of commitment; not yet, not with Iain Carbery.

'I'll ask Lord Fennimore to allocate me another room,' she said.

Iain glanced up and said, sharply, 'No, you will not.'

'But I thought . . .'

'You will be more comfortable here than in the wing behind the kennels.' He tried, without success, to sound cheerful. 'Much as I love dogs, Biddy, I do not like sleeping next to them.'

'I will come to your room.'

'Then Fennimore will know that we're lovers.'

'I think he knows that already,' Biddy said.

'Does he know that I love you?'

'I doubt it.'

'Does he know that we are to be married?'

She placed a knee on the bed and put an arm about his shoulders, touched her cheek to his. He had not shaved that forenoon and his skin felt rough, as if the wild setting had already begun to affect him. She was only too aware what he wanted her to say now but she could not bring herself to say it, to console him with a lie about love.

'You are quite feverish. I hope you have not caught a chill with all that bathing in the loch,' she said. 'Why do you not go to your room and lie down for a little while before dinner?'

'I'm fine, Bridget. Really, I am.' He pushed himself to his feet and eased his way to the door. 'However, perhaps I should take a snooze. I'm not used to feeling out of sorts.'

'I hope you are fit by tomorrow.'

'Tomorrow?'

'For a full day on the hill,' Biddy said.

'Yes.' Iain sighed. 'Stalking *is* what we're here for, I suppose.'

'Among other things,' said Biddy.

The bull was a massive, docile beast with hair the colour of burned cork and the best pair of horns in the stud book. If he had been scaled he would have weighed in not far short of twenty hundredweight but Lear, as he was called, had never been exhibited in the show ring and only a handful of folk were aware that he had sired the best of the Pennypol crossbreeds.

He may have been all that a bull was supposed to be but he was emphatically no sailor. No matter how smooth the waters between Foss and Mull, Lear would arrive at the quay below Vassie's cottage snorting with indignation and rattling the chains that bound him to the puffer's deck. His broad-spanned horns were ornaments no more; Lear well understood what fine weapons were attached to his skull and how to use them. What he did not understand were gangplanks and the motion of tides. Many a rap on the forelegs and many a whack on the rump were required to bring him square to the posts before the chain was slipped from his nose-ring and he was free to slash and stab at the woodwork until another more interesting sight caught his attention.

Head lowered, he would finally stamp up the gangplank and kick and prance on the quay, distracted by shouting and barking and the white flash of the linen tablecloth that Vassie waved in his face.

Then he would lumber into a gallop, stiff and spraddle-legged but gathering speed by the yard, until finally he would thunder off the end of the quay, while Skipper Morrison and his crew crouched on top of the puffer's wheelhouse, peeked through their fingers, muttering, 'Jesus! Jesus!' and Vassie, trailing the tablecloth, raced like a hare for the gate.

Quig had never been able to dissuade the old woman from undertaking this dangerous manoeuvre. Even direct orders from Biddy were ignored. In Vassie's book the safest way of getting a bad-tempered bull off a short pier without damaging him was to use the tablecloth lure and, she said, she would not be denied the thrill since it was the most fun she had from one year's end to the next. There was no arguing that the method worked. Within a half-hour of storming into the pasture reserved for him, Lear would be calmly munching on the heap of oats and cotton cake that Vassie had strewn to welcome him and, an hour after that, would be loudly serenading the cows in the meadow by the shore like some great bovine troubadour.

That autumn's delivery would have been no different from

any other, no more or less risky, if Ronan Campbell had remained asleep.

It was all Ronan's fault. For months – years – he had lolled in the cottage doorway or sprawled by the big wall and only when nature drove him to it would he stagger out to the dry-earth closet to do his business. The upright, coffin-shaped shed, reeking of lime, was Vassie's one concession to sanitation, if, that is, you did not count the chamber-pots beneath the bed. She would bully Ronan out of the house and across to the shed whenever he showed the slightest sign of need. He went reluctantly, whisky bottle in one hand, pages torn from the *Oban Times* stuffed into his braces and he often fell asleep while seated on the planking, head resting on the wall, trousers looped about his ankles.

Perhaps he was asleep when the puffer arrived. Perhaps he was even dreaming when a bellow from Lear or Vassie's cries of '*Hoh. Hah. Here, Bull. Here I am. See me, Bull, see me,*' jerked him from slumber so rudely that he projected himself out through the door of the shed and went reeling down, dazed, into the long pasture to the right of the gate.

Hobbled by his trousers, but still managing to cling to the bottle, Ronan moved faster than he had moved in years. With pernickety little steps, bare-bummed and bare-thighed, he minced towards the gate, lured, like the bull, by the flash of Vassie's white tablecloth.

The Highland bull stopped dead in his tracks.

'Oh, God!' Quig murmured under his breath. 'Oh, God, no!' then, beginning to run, shouted, '*Get him away from there, Vassie. Get him away.*'

It was already too late.

What Ronan imagined he saw by the open gate or why Lear thought that Ronan posed a threat remained mysterious, but the forces that locked drunkard and bull were ineluctable. So Ronan continued to mince across the home field while Lear found focus and, steaming like a locomotive, drew a bead upon him. Then, he, the bull, lowered his head and dug up divots from the track by the gate; one, two, three and then, for luck, a fourth, tossing the clods right and left and behind him in as many seconds. Time enough for Vassie to spin round and flap the cloth wildly and shout and, when that failed, to take a skitter of steps back towards the Highland.

Ronan pressed on regardless. Bottle hugged to his chest, he tripped down the slope, yelling unintelligible cries, as if dreaming that he was a warrior from the golden age who had been wakened from timeless sleep to battle the horned monster that challenged his kingdom. He fumbled, raised the bottle like a club, might have toddled straight into the points of the horns if his trousers had not finally snagged about his ankles and brought him crashing down.

The whisky bottle, half full, leapt from his grasp and shattered. His cries turned at once to wails. He rose to his knees and groped for the bottle but, just as Lear reached him, fell full length, not on to the horns but under them. The animal's muzzle slicked a parting from his brow to his nape and the hoofs – quite dainty hoofs but sharp as spears – trod upon him, flattened him and went away. And Ronan lay face down, twitching, twitching and insensible while inches from his lips the last of his precious *usquebaugh* trickled stealthily into the earth.

Although they had left the lodge early it was a fair distance to the path that led to the north beat and it was after ten o'clock before Mr Carbery's party emerged from the shadow of the glen and found itself in sunshine on the rim of Coire Coilichan.

Party was probably too grand a word for it now that the ponies and dogs had been left below, out of sight and earshot of the desolate ground where according to the stalker, Johncy Thomson, good stags were often to be found. It was the smallest group on the hill. In his present mood, however, Iain wished that it was smaller still; not one stalker, Johncy, one ghillie, McCallum, and another gun, Biddy, but absolutely nobody at all, so that he might be alone to commune with rugged nature and rid himself of the unpleasant sensations that plagued him, most of which were associated with Biddy.

It was not that she was a trial on the hill. Far from it. She was as sturdy and competent as he could wish for. She knew not to drink too often from the mountain streams, not to let her spying-glass clink, to keep her rifle covered so that the sunlight would not glint on the metal. She even knew too how to tumble when – rarely – she missed a step, how she must drop on one knee or down flat and not, like some idiots, flail with her arms, scaring every deer for miles around. She spoke hardly at all and then only beneath her breath and obeyed every signal that Johncy Thomson gave without question or complaint. She had obviously taken to heart everything that he – and McCallum too probably – had taught her and, on the hillside, was more asset than liability.

Iain tried not to look at her, though, for the sight of her made him feel weak and rather helpless. She seemed so strong, so much in control of herself that he felt quite slack and feeble by comparison.

He had not slept with her last night, had made no attempt to visit her bedroom. Consequently, he could not help but wonder if Fennimore had made a move and if that move had been welcomed or rejected.

After a communal but not too convivial dinner during which Fennimore had paid her no more attention than he paid to the other ladies at the table, Biddy had gone early to bed. Iain, though, had sat up late, watching for some telltale sign that his Lordship had more to look forward to upstairs than a good night's sleep. But there had been nothing at all to go on. Fennimore had retired just before midnight with no sly comments or self-satisfied smiles, just Shane, his valet, waiting in the hall outside the drawing-room to follow his master upstairs and help him disrobe.

And at breakfast in the dining-room there had been no special exchanges or accidental touchings to hint that Biddy and his Lordship had been in any way intimate. Iain, therefore, had nothing more tangible to contend with than lingering suspicions as he trudged behind Biddy and the stalker on to the rim of the corrie.

It was not a deep depression but, rather, a wide, shallow bowl that tilted down from the ridge that linked the summits. Big grey boulders, mottled with lichen, were perched on the far side amid tiers of grass split and ribbed by heather-hag. The texture of the landscape was rich, not muted, and the wind, slithering around the bowl, had the taste of harvest to it, though there was not a cultivated field within ten miles.

Iain kept himself low and breathed deep of the wheaty wind, while Biddy and McCallum waited back a bit for Johncy to complete a preliminary reconnaissance.

The stalker was a small, quick-witted man with sharp features and curly black hair. He seemed too youthful to be so experienced but Iain and Biddy had been on the hill with him before and knew that he had a high reputation among his peers. There were few days when Johncy Thomson could not find a stag for you or, failing that, a hind or two just begging to be shot. It was said that he could read the wind better than any other man on Tormont and that if you were patient and followed Johncy's instructions he could sometimes get you a shot of a hundred yards or less.

Under Johncy's eagle eye Biddy had taken her first stag; also her best, the result of a long sporting shot from an awkward position in a flurry of sleet. She had practised hard to improve her marksmanship before the start of last season, Iain knew, plugging away at the iron target she had set up in the scrub behind An Fhearann Cáirdeil – before the Browns came to spoil it. He doubted if her aim would be so accurate this year for the distractions that she had gathered around her back on Fetternish would surely affect her concentration, no matter how Johncy Thomson coddled her.

Iain experienced a little wave of bitterness, tempered by the knowledge that nothing, not even love-sickness, would affect *his* aim when the horns were in his sights. Shaking off the dull, dragging sensation that, for once, strenuous exercise had not worked off, he crawled to the stalker's shoulder and whispered, 'What do you see there, Johncy?'

'Nothin', sir.' The stalker answered without taking the telescope from his eye. 'The herd that was here last week for Mr Ormiston seems to have moved away. We are on the right side for spottin' them, though, Mr Carbery.' He spoke in a soft voice out of the side of his mouth. 'We've got wind an' sun in our favour an' if there is a stag on the floor we'll get the beast within range, I promise you.'

Iain leaned his shoulder against the stalker's buttocks and looked back at Biddy and her ghillie, the pair of them seated, knees drawn up, beneath the sight line of the corrie rim. Biddy had peeled an orange and was splitting the leaves with McCallum. With McCallum, Iain thought, not with me. Why not with me? Why has she not offered to share with me? Even as the thought entered his mind, Biddy glanced up and, digging in her pocket, produced a second orange and offered to toss it to him. He was on the point of accepting when he felt little Johncy Thomson stiffen.

Iain was beside him, cheek by jowl, in an instant. 'What is it?'

'Hinds,' Johncy answered.

'Only hinds?'

'Aye, but they are dotted about an' feedin', sir, so there will be a stag in the vicinity, like as not.' Johncy did not wait for Iain to untie the leather cylinder in which he kept his glass, but handed a brass telescope back to him and, pointing, said, 'If you will be lookin' to the side of the third ledge of heather by the three stones you will be seein' the hinds for yourself.'

'How many?' Iain said.

'Six or eight.'

Iain leaned across the stalker's back and adjusted his angle. He lifted the stout brass spy-glass, fiddled with the lens and brought the great gaudy blanket of the corrie swooping suddenly into focus, heather clumps and spills of scree and big isolated boulders all individualised. He scanned slowly, looking for the landmarks – then he saw them; not six or eight, but eight or ten hinds, not clustered, not moving, not alarmed but quietly feeding on the ribbons of grass between the heather. Iain's heart thudded. His breathing became quick as he tracked the lens left and right in tight circles, seeking the stag that must be lying up somewhere in the vicinity.

Even when Biddy eased herself against him, soft and bulky in her tweed jacket and skirts, he was not distracted. He felt hale and complete again. With the stalker, the woman and he all bundled together, like a giant cocoon, his uncertainty left him, and, putting an arm about Biddy, he drew her closer. He slipped Johncy's glass into her hand and held it steady. He could see the hinds with the naked eye now, a quarter of a mile away across undulating and exposed terrain.

Biddy said. '*Is* there a stag?'

'He is out of sight, Mistress Baverstock, but he will be there.'

'Iain?'

'Aye, I think Johncy's right. He'll be lying down, perhaps in the rocks.'

McCallum had come up too, now. He kept himself apart from the huddle, lay belly down, a khaki handkerchief draped over the barrel of his telescope to kill the glint. He was a good man with guns and knew much about the habits of game but he was not a trained stalker and would defer to Johncy Thomson when it came to making decisions.

'Do you see anythin', Macky?' Johncy asked.

'Only the hinds.'

'He'll be in the rocks, man,' Iain said, with more emphasis.

'Then, surely, we must try to get closer,' said Biddy.

'Easier to say than to be doing, Mrs Baverstock,' McCallum told her.

'Aye, ma'am,' Johncy agreed. 'The ground is too open. We will need to be goin' higher, to come at him from above – if he is there at all.'

'Down wind?' Iain enquired.

'It is a cross-wind, mostly,' Johncy said. 'It will not be so easy even at that, though, for the hinds might pick us up an' give the old chap the signal.'

'What's the ground like at the top of the corrie?' Iain said.

'Broken.'

'Scree?'

'No, but it is broken enough for to be givin' us cover.'

'Then that's what we'll do,' said Iain, decisively and, feeling much better, rolled away from the stalker and helped Biddy to her feet.

*   *   *

168

'What is this that you are telling me, Vassie Campbell?' Andrew Kirkhope said, after he had finished attending to the patient. 'Are you telling me that your husband was gored by that great, hairy brute out there?'

'He was not gored. He was trampled upon.'

'Why did you not bring him straight to my house? Surely Biddy would have lent you a conveyance.'

'Biddy is not at home,' Vassie said. 'She has gone away to the shooting. Besides, it did not seem wise to be transporting Ronan far in his condition.'

'Hmm, well, perhaps you have a point there,' the doctor admitted. 'Or could it just be that you did not want to be showing your face in town?'

'Whatever it was,' said Vassie, thinly, 'you have done your work now and no doubt you will be telling me he will not last out the week.'

'I will be telling you nothing of the kind,' Dr Kirkhope said. 'I will be telling you what I have been telling you for years, that what you have here is not a man but a damned miracle.'

'Do you mean that he is not dying?'

'What made you think that he was dying?' the doctor said. 'What makes you think that he will ever die? Oh, no, no, Vassie Campbell, it will be taking more than a mere attack by a bull to do your husband in.'

'What?'

'I am sorry to have to disappoint you,' Kirkhope said, 'but as far as I can make out he has sustained nothing worse than a broken bone in his wrist and some contusions on his shoulders and back that will be giving him gyp – or should I be saying would give gyp to a normal man but will probably pass unnoticed by your husband.'

'In other words . . .'

'In other words, Vassie, he has been thrashed a bit but he is in no danger of succumbing to his injuries. It seems you will have to be putting up with him for a while longer, unless you can fetch in another bull – one with better eyesight – to make a better job of it.'

'If you are suggesting that I would deliberately . . .'

'I am suggesting nothing of the sort,' the doctor interrupted. 'I am telling you plain and straight that Ronan should have been dead years ago. By all the laws of medical science the whisky should have killed him by now. But perhaps, this time, it was the whisky that saved him. He has a bruise in the region of his liver that should have crushed a stone but, given the hardened state of that organ, I am just surprised that the bull did not break a leg on it.'

They were standing in the main room of Pennypol. The curtains that separated the bed neuks from the kitchen were open to allow air to circulate but even at that the smell in the cottage was unwholesome and Dr Kirkhope did not wish to linger in it. He could see the patient out of the corner of his eye, the plaster bandage that he had applied to the broken bone in the left wrist very white in the gloom. But the rest of the man, naked beneath a blanket, was indistinct, his skin a strange orangey-brown colour, the like of which Kirkhope had never seen before and would probably never see again.

It was not jaundice as such but rather, he supposed, a radiant decay of the cells; another bizarre manifestation of the break- down that alcohol had wrought on Campbell's flesh. Now and then, the good doctor even looked forward to cutting the old drunkard open just to see what odd hues his organs exhibited after a lifetime on the bottle.

He snapped his bag shut.

He said, 'Do you want me to take a look at the bull now?'

Vassie hesitated then, seeing the joke, emitted a little sniff that may, or may not, have been laughter.

'The bull is fine. Quig lured it away before it could turn on Ronan again. But,' she said, 'you could be taking a look at our outhouse if you wish. It got itself knocked over and is badly damaged.'

It was Kirkhope's turn to chuckle. He lifted his tweed cap from the table and stuck it on his head then, taking Vassie by the arm, led her out into the fresh air. He glanced behind him, just once, to make sure that Campbell had not been visited by another miracle and had suddenly recovered his wits, then he said, 'Do you still have a good supply of the medicine I gave you?'

'Yes.'

'If he is in pain, you may increase the dosage. Double it, in fact.'

'Aye,' Vassie said. 'And for his bruises I will be using an arnica solution mixed with some butterfat to make a cream.'

'That will help him heal as well as anything,' Kirkhope said. 'If there is any serious swelling around his middle or in his groin or if he passes blood . . .'

'He often passes blood.'

'God! Well, if there is more than usual, send for me at once.'

'When will I be taking off the bandage?'

'I will come back to see him in a day or two,' Kirkhope said. 'And when the time comes, in three or four weeks, I will snip away the bandage.'

'I can be doing it myself.'

'Come now, Vassie, would you be denying me my fee?'

She stood motionless, not looking at him but out to sea, her features not pinched but sagging, her eyes narrowed to membranous slits. Kirkhope saw her throat bob and wondered what emotion, if any, the little spasm signified; grief, relief, anxiety, or disappointment that she was not shot of her husband yet?

Vassie said, 'It is not the fee. I can be paying your fee. I am the one who will look after him, though, without . . .'

'Without what?' the doctor said. 'Without my intervention?'

'He is my husband. He is my fault.'

'That is a queer way of putting it, Vassie,' Kirkhope said, gently. He touched her shoulder and turned her to face him, looked down into her eyes. 'What about you? Are you well enough yourself?'

'Yes, I am well. I am never anything else.'

'You could send him away, you know.'

'I will not be doing that.'

'I know of a place that would take him in,' Kirkhope persisted. 'He would be well cared for there. He would receive treatment for his condition. It would cost money, true, but your daughters might be prepared . . .'

'Treatment?'

'To free him from his dependence on spirits.'

'To cure him? To make him as he used to be?'

'I doubt if that is possible. He is too far gone.'

'Then why would I be wanting to send him away?'

'For your own sake, Vassie, to make things easier on yourself.'

'That is no reason,' Vassie said. 'I do not hanker for an easy life. I have what I have, Andrew Kirkhope, and I will be seeing it through without your interference – aye, or your pity, for that matter.'

'He cannot last much longer.'

'So you have been telling me for ten years.'

'That is so,' the doctor admitted. He shrugged. 'But he is so – I do not know what he is – so defiant, perhaps, or stubborn.'

'Are you saying that he will outlast me?'

'No, no, of course I am not.'

'For if that is your opinion I will tell you that you are wrong. Ronan will not outlast me. I will see him in his grave before I go to mine. Have no fear that it will be otherwise.'

'Well,' Kirkhope sighed, 'considering the state that he is in I would not in all seriousness be making a wager against it. Have you informed your daughters of the accident?'

'Why should I be bothering them with my troubles?'

'He is their father, after all.'

'They have enough to concern them without having to wring their hands and rush down here every time Ronan Campbell takes a tumble.'

'Being trampled upon by a Highland bull is a bit more than a tumble, Vassie,' Kirkhope told her. 'I ask only because I will be going back round by Pennymain and will drop in the news to Innis if you wish it.'

'I do not wish it,' Vassie said. 'I will be taking care of him myself.' She paused, then said, 'Besides, Innis will already know what has happened. Someone will have seen Quig at your house and it will be all round the north part of the island already that something has happened at Pennypol.'

'So that's where Quigley has gone, is it?' Kirkhope said. 'To tell Innis? What of Biddy? Where is she shooting?'

'On Tormont, with her fancy friends.'

'Indeed?' said Kirkhope. 'That will be with Lord Fennimore's party. Ah, Vassie, how proud you must be to have your daughter mixing in such august company.'

'She may mix with who she likes,' Vassie said. 'It is none of my doing.'

He studied her closely, searching for some sign of the pride that must surely be in her that a crofter's daughter had risen so high in society that she was invited to shoot with a peer of the realm. But Vassie Campbell was resolute and unyielding and, he thought, it really would not matter to her if Biddy was taking tea with the Queen at Balmoral, the sour old woman would still refuse to be impressed.

In her perverse way, Vassie Campbell was just as arrogant and ignorant as her husband had been in his heyday and perhaps, Kirkhope thought, she deserved no better fate than the one she had forged for herself. He blinked and cleared his throat, ashamed of such an awful heresy, for he knew that he was supposed to be on her side and subscribe willy-nilly to the fallacy that she and her like were the salt of the earth when, in fact, they were nothing of the kind.

'Are you waiting for your fee?' Vassie asked. 'I will be paying you now if that is what you are waiting for.'

'What? No,' Andrew Kirkhope said, 'of course I am not waiting for my fee. I will be sending you my bill in the usual manner only when the patient is fully recovered.'

'And what if he dies?'

'Vassie, he will not . . .'

'Will it cost me more if he dies?'

The doctor was tempted to ask her if that was what she really required of him – to see her husband off once and for all. Then he thought better of it and, forcing a bedside smile, gave her a courteous little bow instead.

'I will call again on Friday forenoon,' he said. 'If Ronan's condition worsens, however, and you feel he needs my attention before then . . .'

'He won't,' said Vassie, and, with a curt nod, turned on her heel and went indoors again, leaving Andrew Kirkhope to find

173

his own way back to the burn-side where he had tethered his pony.

It was a long, arduous stalk; interesting too, though, and filled with the sort of tensions that drew Biddy back to the hills in spite of herself.

She had no particular addiction to the act of killing and once the shot was fired, once the bullet was on its way, felt a strange sadness at what she had done and a fear for the victim that was quite out of keeping with the occasion. She could not deny her pleasure in the results of her marksmanship, however; her sadness was fleeting, a little shadow on the soul that danced away in an explosion of triumph when the rabbit or the hare rolled over, or the grouse fell from the sky or, as now, when a stag or a hind in the hinterland beyond her rifle sights slumped to the ground, shot clean through the lungs or the heart.

Up on the high tops in breezy autumn sunshine, the stealth of the approach was all and she could put out of her mind not only its ultimate purpose but most of her other problems too.

As she moved along behind Johncy Thomson on the shoulder behind the ridge she felt lithe, almost fluid, inside her casing of woollens and tweeds. She carried nothing, of course. McCallum, a few yards behind, toted her rifle, her cartridges, even the packet of sandwiches that would constitute lunch. Iain, on the other hand, would not relinquish his gun to anyone. He was inordinately fond of the weapon and, even if there had been a spare ghillie, would have carried the Mauser himself.

Iain was not himself today, not himself at all. He was red-faced and puffing quite badly by the time they reached the knob of rock where the ridge dipped away behind the corrie. He did not complain, though, and forged on like a trooper as Johncy led them in single file on to the bare, wind-groomed shoulder south-east of the Tormont glens.

All of Mull, all of Morven seemed to be spread out before them. The Sound was a deep, dark greeny-blue, flecked with crisp little waves and dotted with yachts and steamers and the black, locust-like lighters that chugged the inshore waters carrying parcels of cattle or sheep or cargoes of coal and timber from one island to the next, or hoving away to Oban or down the fretwork coast and around Kintyre to Greenock, Glasgow and the Clyde; and the mountains, all the mountains, that were never as purple as English visitors supposed they would be, were gathered under colours much less royal, a mingling of blues and browns and soft, pale yellows distilled out of mist and cloud.

In the heather an old cock-grouse crowed raucously.

McCallum wriggled to the edge of the corrie to see if the hinds had been put to flight by the alarm signal. The animals' heads were turned in every direction but they did not appear to be unduly disturbed. At Johncy's suggestion, however, the members of the party rested on the backside of the ridge for five minutes to give the deer a chance to settle then, crawling on knees and hands, slipped down one by one into the corrie.

Although they were still three or four hundred yards away, Biddy could see the hinds distinctly; also the cluster of large boulders that rose from the heather-hag. She was tempted to fish out her spy-glass but Johncy signalled her to get down on her belly like a snake and Biddy sank down on to her stomach and propelled herself forward with her elbows.

She did not care about the wetness that seeped through her skirts; a minor discomfort compared to her mounting excitement. She did not know if, in fact, a stag was hidden among the boulders but she was tense with expectation. She glanced along the line of her body and saw Iain's red face and glowering eyes a yard or two behind her. He was concentrating on keeping low and seemed oblivious to her scrutiny but McCallum gave her a wink and a grin to indicate that he at least was enjoying himself.

Cautiously, Biddy crawled out of the heather roots on to rank grass. The wind streamed directly across her and the sun, veiled by a wisp of light cloud, hung high on her left.

Johncy put a finger to his lips and nodded towards the boulders and Biddy, even without the 'scope, soon picked out the shape of a stag propped in the dry wallow between the boulders. Johncy was less interested in the stag than in the behaviour of the hinds. The females were the sentinels, guardians of his majesty's rest; the final leg of the approach must be made without alerting them to danger. Then, as they watched, a second stag rose from behind the first, a magnificent brute, heavily antlered, wet muzzled, with a great deep belly to him. He posed for a moment, sniffing the wind, head turning this way and that, slowly, so slowly, his coarse flanks glossy as silk in the autumn sunshine. They heard him grunt and sigh, heard the click of his hoofs as he moved around the hard ground by the boulders and vanished.

Johncy's signs were very easy to interpret. Thumb cocked and finger triggered he pointed towards an old oak stump that protruded from the ground left and ahead of them. Biddy nodded. Iain too. McCallum, lying flat on his back, silently unsheathed Biddy's rifle and loaded it. He passed it carefully to her, butt first. She took it, her heart thudding twenty to the dozen but her hands steady. She watched Iain uncover the Mauser and, with a cartridge from his pocket, load it, too. The faint whisper of canvas, a fainter whisper of cloth, the tiny *sneck* of the bolt lug seemed deafening in the wispy silence.

Another sign from Johncy: McCallum must wait here. Then the stalker was on the move again, crawling away so slowly that he hardly seemed to be making ground at all.

Biddy tucked her skirts between her thighs, cradled the rifle between elbow and hip, and set off after him, wriggling into the heather.

She heard Iain scuffle after her but kept her nose down and followed Johncy's trail without glancing round. She could see nothing of the stalker except the heels of his boots as he traversed the strip of heather and headed towards the half-buried tree stump. She followed him blindly, stopping when he stopped, moving on when he moved on. The rifle grew heavier as the minutes passed and she was relieved when, at last, she saw Johncy just ahead of her, lifted slightly on his elbow, waiting.

The ground under the arch of the stump was as soft and black as blood pudding. Trunk and broken branch had been rubbed bare and tufts of coarse red hair clung to them. The smell of deer was strong. There were droppings and deer slots everywhere. Sweating in her tweeds and panting with exertion, Biddy drew herself up alongside the stalker. Seconds later, Iain levered himself out of the heather. His face was rivered with sweat and his eyes bulged.

Grinning, Johncy put a finger to his lips again and raised himself just enough to peer beneath the arch of the stump. His mouth formed a soft, pursed O of surprise. He signalled to Biddy and Iain to come up to him and, with a soundless laugh, pointed with his trigger finger.

Both stags were lying in a grassy bay among the boulders. The first beast had the charred-looking hide that age brings and a head that was less than perfect. Brown, broken antlers gave him a ferocious appearance, though, and he was no less massive than his younger rival. The younger stag was full-horned, a sixteen-point royal and, gralloched and bled, would weigh out heavier, Biddy reckoned. She was puzzled as to why the old stag and the young would share the same covert, for the rutting season had begun and rivalry between males was notoriously fierce and bitter.

She glanced to her left and saw that the hinds had stopped grazing. They had lifted their heads, not spooked yet but inclined to be wary. She touched Johncy's sleeve. He had already noticed the hinds' restlessness, how they stepped and pawed, how their ears twitched and nostrils flared. They, the guns, were closer to the stags than to the hinds, however, and as soon as the stags lifted would have a clear broadside shot or, better yet, a quarter on at each of them at a range of not much more than a hundred yards.

Johncy would not be hurried, would not allow his clients to rush their shots. On the other hand, he too had been puzzled by the sight of two stags in consort and, with the cock-grouse starting to croak again, knew that the opportunity for a clean shot might be limited. His little brown hands flew, gesturing first to Iain to take up his stance, then to Biddy. He held them poised, calmed them with his palms and then, like the conductor of an orchestra, swiftly raised them up.

As soon as the heads appeared above the stump the hinds

were off like the wind. The younger stag raised himself instantly. He was short in the leg, long in the body, his horns white tipped. He took the route up the shank of the boulder, hoofs clicking frantically, and then he leapt and went – and Iain fired.

When Biddy heard the thud she immediately readjusted her sights and fixed her attention on the remaining beast. She breathed. Steadied. Took deliberate aim not at the whole animal but a spot six inches behind the fore-leg and half-way up the body. He was slow. He was sick. He was confused. She could see his eye roll towards her, full of fear, as he scrambled to find the strength to run. His hoofs scraped the boulder, his shoulder leaned into it, then he thrust out, lifting his head, showing her the full broadside.

She pressed the trigger. Heard the thud.

He ran, ran as if he was young again, the long, dark-haired body riding out of the covert, mouth agape, breath sawing, eyes wild.

She knew enough not to leap to her feet at once, for the younger stag had gone charging off and, if wounded, might well lie down. Last season she had witnessed one beast, bruised along the spine, drag himself out of standstill and before Iain could place a second shot he had been off downhill and lost. She remembered that vividly. She did not even glance at the old stag. She knew while the bullet was still in the air that she had taken him cleanly. She was vaguely aware that he was dropping, kneeling in thin air, head dipping, then rolling over, shot through the heart.

She felt no triumph, no excitement. Almost mechanically she turned, reloaded and searched for another target.

The younger stag had not fallen. Iain was on his knees, the barrel of the Mauser braced in a vee of the tree stump. Biddy was not sure where Johncy had got to. She darted her eyes, spotted him crouched safe by the stump. She heard Iain fire a second shot. Saw the young deer reach for the hillside and charge into the heather-hag, confused by the sound. The hinds, in groups, had fled away. The stag crashed on, blood on his haunches, vivid as paint. She saw him crash through the heather against the slope, then come around again, quarter on.

She aimed well forward and pressed the trigger.

'And then,' Fennimore declared, as if he had been an eye-witness to the event, 'the damned thing fell. One bullet was enough. A heart shot, Johncy informs me, at the best part of two hundred yards.'

'The range increases with every telling,' Iain said. 'I knew it would.'

'Come now, Carbery, you cannot begrudge the lady her triumph. Two shots in thirty seconds, both of them target perfect.'

'I don't grudge her anything,' Iain said. 'I'm just pointing out . . .'

'An almost perfect head, too. Forty inches at the beam.'

'Aye, but the other one was trash.'

'Twenty stones, dead weight, is not trash,' said Clarence Parker. 'He may have been knocking on but he was still in prime condition. I would have been proud to have claimed that stag for myself. Pay no heed to Carbery, Mrs Baverstock. He's probably jealous.'

'Nothing of the kind,' Iain said. 'But facts are facts. It was my first shot that wounded the creature. Don't forget that.'

'A score along the flank,' said Fennimore, scornfully.

'Why, man, you practically missed,' said Parker.

'At fifty yards,' said Fennimore.

'Fifty!' Iain yelled. 'One hundred and fifty, more like.'

He leaned his elbows on the dining-table, scowling. He had already drunk too much; champagne to celebrate Bridget's feat, whisky before dinner, Spanish and French wines with dinner and now brandy.

The long day on the hill had taken its toll on most of the guests. They had crawled off early to bed or, since manners were not at a premium, nodded in their chairs at the dining-table. Lord Fennimore would have none of it. He was a man who loved carousal and needed no more excuse for a celebration than Biddy's claim to two fine stags. He had had the corpses dragged into the front hall and spread on a tarpaulin for all to admire. He had had Biddy – who would have preferred to lie down – pose beside them for Mr Parker's camera; had, in short, made such a fuss of the widow of Fetternish that there was hardly a man or woman in the company who was not sick of hearing her praises sung.

Other stags had been taken, two to be precise, and a couple of hinds shot for the pot. There had been other alarms and adventures on the tops that day and a multitude of tales worth telling, but Fennimore would not entertain them, and admiration for Biddy's marksmanship swiftly turned to envy and envy to boredom with, in Iain Carbery's case, more than a dash of anger.

'How could you miss a beast that size, Carbery?'

'Had you been at the tipple, uh?'

'Been at the nipple, perhaps.'

'Enough of that sort of talk, gentlemen. There is still a lady present.'

'Biddy,' Iain said. 'Why don't you tell them the truth?'

'I – I was fortunate, that's all.' Biddy repeated the modest phrase for the fifth or sixth time since dinner began.

'Ah, but what *was* the range? Tell us that, if you will, Mrs B.'

'According to Thomson,' Biddy shrugged, reluctantly, 'just under two hundred yards.'

'And Carbery missed at fifty. Good God!'

'*It wasn't bloody fifty.*'

'Oh, was it only forty? Sorry.'

Laughter erupted around the table.

Lord Fennimore was on his feet. The strenuous day on the hill had apparently invigorated him. He had a brandy glass in one hand and a cigar in the other and he waved them about as he spoke. His high spirits owed more to anticipation than to liquour. He had been swift to grasp the implications of Bridget Baverstock's achievement and had immediately set about alienating her from Carbery, that hearty little nobody. He enjoyed making Carbery squirm. Later, he would make Biddy Baverstock squirm too, but in a different way.

Biddy watched him warily. She was well aware that Lord

Fennimore's intentions were less than honourable and that he had misjudged the effects that the killings had had on her.

She was not possessed of the passion of the hunter. If anything she regretted her accuracy with the rifle, her two remarkable shots. She acknowledged that her coolness, as well as her aim, had been impressive and had accepted Johncy's congratulations, and McCallum's, as her due. For a little while she had been strutting and arrogant, preening herself before Iain. Then the stags had been dragged together and bled, and had not looked so magnificent any longer, old and young in apposition, both equally dim and sad with the ropes about them and their guts spilled out on the reeking grass.

She could not put that image out of her mind, try as she might.

Iain struggled to his feet and tried unsuccessfully to assume an air of dignity. 'I have had enough of this,' he said. 'I am going to my bed.'

'Sure you can find it, old man?'

'Must be all of forty yards away, you know.'

'Perhaps Mrs Baverstock can find it for you.'

'Please,' Biddy said, 'that's enough.'

'Oh, let him go,' said Fennimore. 'If he falls down in the passageway I'll have Shane pick him up in the morning.'

'I – will – will not – fall down,' said Iain and, without so much as a passing glance at Biddy, steered himself to the dining-room door and went out.

Out of politeness Biddy remained at the table for another ten minutes, then, weary in body and soul, excused herself and went upstairs to her room where, to her chagrin, she found Iain seated dolefully on the side of the bed.

'Oh, no, no,' Biddy said, sighing. 'Iain, I am really not . . .'

'No more am I,' he interrupted. 'I haven't come for that. I'm here for an answer. Now. Tonight.'

She plucked at her jewellery, removed the items and put them into a plush-lined box on the top of the dressing-table. She unpinned her hair and released it and, because it was Iain and she had no secrets from him, she unhooked the back of her gown and eased it away from her bodice. It had been hot in the dining-room but the bedroom was chilly. The promised maid had still not materialised. The fire in the little grate had almost gone out and Biddy's hunting outfit lay on the chair where she had discarded it. The room had a dishevelled air to which Iain, unfortunately, contributed.

'Are you inebriated?' Biddy asked.

'Sober enough to hear your answer.'

The velvet gown felt suddenly heavy. Everything felt suddenly heavy. Biddy did not have to force herself to speak softly; she was too exhausted even to raise her voice. Iain fixed his gaze on the globe of the oil lamp while she tugged and wriggled and stepped out of the gown. She wore neither corset nor knitted stays over her petticoat for, an island girl, she cared little about nipped waists and the infinitesimal measurements demanded by high fashion.

She stood by the chair, shaking out the dress, clad only in a slip-bodice, frilled petticoats and gartered stockings. She said, 'I am thinking that it is not wise for you to be here tonight, Iain.'

'Why? Am I intruding?'

'I am tired, that's all.'

'Are you waiting for him, for Fennimore?'

'No. I am only trying to get to my bed.'

'Give me your answer then and we can both get to bed.'

'My answer?'

He swung his head, ponderous with fatigue, and stared at her, heavy-lidded and lugubrious. 'It's no, isn't it?'

She sighed and threw the gown over the chair on top of her tweed skirt. She seated herself beside him, nudging his buttocks to make him give way. The bed was large but spongy at the edges and she was thrown against him, closer than she would have wished. He did not touch her, though, made no movement that might express tenderness or desire. Backs to the door, they stared into the depths of the oil lamp together.

Biddy said, 'I do not want to marry you, Iain.'

'Why not?'

'I cannot marry now – not at this time, I mean,' Biddy said. 'I have the boy to be thinking of.'

Iain started and turned his head. 'The boy? What boy?'

'Donald, my nephew.'

'What the devil does he have to do with it?'

'I am his guardian.'

'Nonsense!' Iain's anger showed. 'The truth, Biddy – why won't you have me? Am I not exciting enough for you? Or do you think I'm just after your money like some damned adventurer?'

'I do not think that at all.'

'Naismith told you, didn't he?'

'Told me what?'

'That I am acquainted with your brother-in-law.'

'Willy told me nothing of the sort.'

'Oh!' Iain was only momentarily nonplussed. He paused, then said, 'Well, I am – acquainted with Walter Baverstock, I mean.'

'How long have you know him?'

'Years.'

'Does he know that you have visited me at Fetternish?'

'Yes.'

'And that we have slept together?'

'Yes, that too.'

'He is more than a passing acquaintance then?'

'Yes, I suppose he is.'

'And the rest of the family?' Biddy said. 'Agnes, for instance?'

'I am acquainted with them all. I knew your husband, too, when we were boys together and then again in Edinburgh.'

'I assume that Walter and Agnes put you up to it, to courting me. What did you hope to gain by it?'

'I think they are after a hold on Fetternish.'

If she had been less exhausted Biddy might have flared up at Iain's confession but she felt oddly unmoved by the knowledge that he had plotted against her with her in-laws. It was typical of the Sangster Baverstocks to underestimate her intelligence and to suppose that she would sign away Fetternish to any man, even a husband. Grasping at straws, they were, just grasping at straws. As, she suddenly realised, she had been doing too.

'Is that why you took me to bed?' Biddy said.

'Unfair, Biddy,' Iain told her. 'You took me to bed, if you recall.'

'That is not a very gallant thing to be saying.'

'You want a child. Do you not still want a child – and, no, I do not mean a nephew, a substitute; I mean a child of your own?'

'You know that I do.'

'Marry me, then, and we will . . .'

'Iain, I have already given you my answer.'

'I love you, Biddy.'

'Is that also part of the plan, a last desperate measure?'

'Of course it isn't,' Iain said. 'I love you. I do. I love you.'

She was very still beside him on the bed. She experienced no particular animosity towards him and no bitterness that he had been in cahoots with the Baverstocks all along. He was, she thought, too uncomplicated a man to be a catspaw for a family as greedy and devious as the Baverstocks.

In one sense, it was she who had betrayed *him* by not being able to conceive. She had flouted every taboo by sleeping with men out of marriage, and Iain was her victim just as much as she was his. She thought again of the old stag and the young lying side by side, empty and ugly on the tarpaulin in the hall and felt a strange hollowness within herself, as if she had also been emptied of substance and touched by death.

'I wish I had not come here,' Biddy said, almost to herself.

'I will take you home first thing tomorrow.'

'That would hardly be polite. What would Lord Fennimore think of us if we left so soon?'

'I do not care what Fennimore thinks, or Walter Baverstock, or any of them,' Iain said. He took her hand. 'I only care about you. Marry me, Biddy.'

'Iain,' Biddy said, 'I cannot.'

'Because I haven't been able to give you a child?'

'Because I do not love you.'

'That did not seem to matter to you before.'

'It matters to me now,' Biddy said.

'Look, if it's Fetternish that concerns you, I'll sign a waiver, a prenuptial agreement, anything you care to put before me.

The Baverstocks have no claim on me and will have no claim on you through me. Any decent lawyer will be able to draw up such a document.'

'I do not need such a document,' Biddy said. 'Fetternish is mine.'

'And will always be yours.'

'Until I die.'

'Oh, Biddy, don't say that.'

She pushed herself up from the spongy mattress. 'I am tired, Iain, dog-tired. I always get morbid when I am tired. Would you go now, please?'

For a moment it seemed he would balk. He looked, Biddy thought, even more weary than she was, with a crumpled stoop to his broad shoulders and odd dark rings about his eyes that reminded her of a badger. But he did not look sly; Iain was, she thought, incapable of looking sly. He continued to sit on the bed, big hands loose, neck bent and brow thrust out as if he had been hypnotised by the glow of the oil lamp.

He uttered a sound, not quite a whimper, then said, 'If you knew how much I love you, Biddy, you would not send me away like this.'

'We will go shooting again tomorrow, Iain. Perhaps you will have better luck then.' Even to herself she did not sound convincing. 'Surely we can remain friends.'

'Friends?' Iain hoisted himself wearily to his feet. 'No, Biddy, I doubt if we will remain friends.'

'Iain . . .'

'What?'

'Please go now,' Biddy said.

'Yes, I think that's the best thing,' Iain Carbery said.

He stepped around the bed and paused to look back at her in the gentle light of the oil lamp.

At that moment, a light-hearted little tapping sounded upon the door and Edgar, Lord Fennimore, too impatient to be courteous, eagerly entered the room. Peer and commoner stared at each other blankly for perhaps half a second then Iain, swelling with fury, shouted, '*Swine!*' and with a single hefty blow, an uppercut, felled his Lordship on the spot.

Carbery was gone from Coilichan before breakfast.

Biddy left not long after.

For both of them the Highland game was over, with nothing much to show for it but two dead stags, a dislocated jaw and, in poor Iain Carbery's case, a badly broken heart.

BOOK TWO

INNIS

SEVEN

A Leap in the Dark

It was early afternoon before Innis got over to Pennypol to visit her father, an hour or so after Quig had brought her news of the accident. It had disconcerted Innis to see how it had affected the man she thought of as her cousin. Quig had not been amused. There had been no down-playing of the incident, none of the callous humour at her father's encounter with the bull that would so amuse the denizens of the McKinnon Arms when word of it percolated down to the village.

Although he had not been seen in Crove for many years, Ronan Campbell was still the butt of village jokes. Hector Thrale would cobble up an exaggerated account of what had taken place at Pennypol and Skipper Morrison would be thoroughly grilled next time he put in at Tobermory. The Campbells would become laughing-stocks again, which, Innis knew, would please many of the locals, for there was still much animosity towards a family that was perceived as having grown too big for its boots.

Innis did not need Quig to point out how serious the matter could have been, however, and what sort of repercussions might have accrued if her father had been killed. The precarious balance of the Fetternish community would have been thoroughly upset. Lear would have had to be shot, Biddy summoned back from Tormont, official enquiries set in motion, her mother's future at Pennypol put in jeopardy – all because one useless old drunkard had been stupid enough to be in the wrong place at the wrong time.

It was not so much a visit as a viewing.

Dead to the world, her father was propped up on two grubby bolsters, blankets squared across his chest, his mouth open. The plaster-of-Paris bandage on his arm was anomalously white and pure in the smoke-browned interior of the cottage. As usual, Innis felt like an intruder; the kitchen held few pleasant memories and her mother was not welcoming. She left Becky outside with her mother and spent only two or three minutes alone with her father, just long enough to clasp her rosary and offer up a vague sort of prayer, not for her father's soul but for the healing of his body, a gesture of compassion that would surely have wrung scorn from Vassie.

Her mother was in a strange mood, smug, almost exultant at her part in the farce that had so nearly become a tragedy. Her sole concern seemed to be that the bull had suffered no lasting trauma and would still be able to perform to his full ability.

Irritated, Innis gathered Becky up and left as soon as she could.

She headed back to Pennymain then on to Fetternish House where Quig had gone to wait for Donnie at the end of the school day. It did not occur to Innis to seek out her husband, to inform him what had taken place. Somehow, when it came to dealing with Campbell family crises Michael was the last person she wished to involve. She was pleased to see Willy Naismith, though, for his concern for her father's welfare seemed genuine.

Willy took Becky into his arms, escorted Innis into the kitchen by the side door, seated her at the table and told Queenie to pour her a cup of tea.

Quig was already at table, polishing off a second helping of ham and eggs. Mopping his plate with a pinch of bread, he looked up at Innis and said, 'He will live, I take it?'

'Yes,' Innis answered. 'Doctor Kirkhope says that there is no serious damage. He has broken a bone in his wrist but it has been bandaged and, when I saw him, he was fast asleep and not in pain.'

Quig nodded, popped the bread into his mouth and chewed.

'I thought as much,' he said.

Innis sipped tea and felt soothed to be in the company of men she respected. Perched on Willy's arm, Becky munched on a shortcake biscuit and scattered crumbs liberally over the steward's lapels.

Innis said, 'I notice that Mr Morrison has sailed without you, Quig. Will you not be going back to Foss tonight?'

'No, I will be staying at least until tomorrow.'

'He can sleep here,' Willy said. 'I'm sure the mistress wouldn't object. We've plenty of spare beds.'

'I am needing to talk to Donnie,' Quig said.

'And Mr Brown, the schoolmaster, is wanting to talk to you,' Innis said.

'Sounds ominous,' said Willy to Becky. 'What do you think, wee lamb? Is Donnie in for a telling-off?'

'Aye,' Becky agreed. 'He will be getting a lickin', so he will.'

'Do you really think so?' said Willy. 'Is Donnie not a nice boy?'

'Aye,' Becky declared, amiably fickle. 'Donnie's a nice boy.'

Fights were common in the Glasgow schools in which Gillies Brown had taught. Most were mere scraps, violent little outbursts that flared up like sulphur matches and burned out just as quickly – a kick, a couple of wild punches, a retreat from further engagement, a few tears perhaps, and that was that. Others were more calculated and sometimes became quite vicious. Gillies had learned by experience to read the mood of a class and he could usually predict when conflict was in the offing. Then he would corner the antagonists before trouble started and – rough justice, this – give them both a strapping to take their minds off their differences and unite them in hatred of higher authority.

If he had been a little less enamoured of Gavin's mother he might have identified the boy's predisposition to violence. If he had been a little more objective in his attitude to Donnie Campbell he might not have confused politeness with passivity – which was all very well in hindsight. As it happened, neither he nor Janetta were sharp enough to notice that the cousins had become not just rivals but enemies.

In fact, there were no clues in the behaviour of the class to indicate that Gavin and Donnie were about to come to blows, none of the usual trading of insults, no preliminary shoves and nudges to alert fellow pupils. Even those who had been with Gavin Tarrant in Dervaig school and had seen him lose his temper before, could not believe that he would be daft enough to square up to his older and larger cousin. Donnie himself had no warning that Gavin, whom he thought of as a cold wee fish, nursed a grudge against him and that the grudge had curdled into hatred.

It was all Gavin's fault, all Gavin's doing. He could not have chosen a worse day to provoke a fight. The reason for it remained an enigma, however, something that Gavin could not explain to himself, let alone to Mr Brown or, later, to his father. It just seemed to steal upon him, a mean, swelling rage that grew worse as the morning progressed.

He was thinking, vaguely, of Mr McCallum and Mrs Baverstock, his aunt, how they had gone away somewhere down the island to shoot at deer with rifles; how Donnie Campbell lived in his aunt's house and how Donnie Campbell would have a gun of his own soon; how he might never have a gun of his own, for a rifle was not the sort of thing that a shepherd ever needed, not on Mull at any rate, and it was not a luxury that a shepherd could afford to buy. If Donnie Campbell wanted a gun, though, he could be having one just for the asking, for Mrs Baverstock was rich and could buy anything she wanted for anyone she liked. If she had liked him better than Donnie Campbell then she would have bought him a gun, except that he was not the one who lived in her house and called her 'Auntee Biddee,' and she would never buy him anything because she did not like him.

'Gavin Tarrant, have you any idea what I've been talking about?'

'What?'

'I hope you haven't been day-dreaming again.'

'No, Mr Brown.'

'In that case perhaps you'll be kind enough to tell the class the name of the man who built the Suez Canal.'

'Pardon?'

'The Suez Canal,' said Mr Brown, patiently. 'What was the name of the engineer who planned and built the Suez Canal?'

Gavin did not glance desperately around for help, nor did he scan the ceiling for inspiration. He stared straight at the blackboard upon which were written certain words. If rage had not already begun to consume his reason he might have found some clue upon the board to help him bridge the gap between ignorance and humiliation.

'Let's give Gavin a hint, shall we?' said Mr Brown. 'Charlie, what was the engineer's nationality?'

'He was a Frenchman, Mr Brown.'

'Good. Kristin, where is the Suez Canal?'

'In – in Africa.'

'Which particular part of Africa?'

'The Egyptian part.'

'Correct. Now, Gavin – the Frenchman's name, if you please?'

He sat in stone cold silence for several seconds then, because he had to say something, answered, 'Napoleon Bonnypart.'

Mr Brown was beside him, hands flat on the desk, leaning as if to shield him from the laughter that swirled about the classroom.

Gavin continued to stare at the blackboard.

The written words had no form, no meaning. They were as incomprehensible as the scribbles of lugworms on sand. He blinked. He saw a whole shoal of silvery little fish dart and whisk away, there and then gone.

He blinked once more.

'Well, I just hope that answer demonstrates ignorance and not impudence,' Mr Brown said. 'I'll put your stupidity down to the fact that you've been sitting there with your head in the clouds for the past half-hour, for we have just finished hearing about – about who, Donald?'

'Ferdinand de Lesseps, sir.'

'Do you hear, Gavin? Ferdinand de Lesseps. Not Napoleon Bonaparte who, by-the-bye, had been dead for forty years before the Canal was opened.' Mr Brown pushed himself upright. 'Now, for your benefit and the benefit of any other idlers who may not been listening, I'll ask Donald to put the lesson into summary. Sit up, Gavin. Pay attention.'

Gavin stared straight ahead.

'Donald, what two seas does the Canal unite?' Mr Brown said.

'The Red Sea and the Mediterranean.'

'When was the Canal opened?'

'Eighteen hundred and sixty-nine.'

'How long is it?'

'One hundred and one miles.'

'Who originally owned it?'

'The French.'

'How did Britain acquire it?'

'By the purchase of a controlling interest sixteen years ago.'

'Good, very good. Why do you think the French gave up control of the Canal to Great Britain?'

'I think it was because we have charge of Egypt.'

'That's right, Donald. Now, why is this Canal so important?'

'Because it links Europe to Asia without the ships having to sail all the way down and around the Cape of Africa. It is the key to trade with . . .'

Gavin heard hardly a word that issued from his cousin's mouth. He could see his cousin's profile, chin tilted up, lips moving. He could sense Mr Brown standing approvingly nearby. But the realities of the classroom flickered and darted away like the vision of the little silver fish.

His limbs became stiff. His throat closed. He could not blink. Strange swooning sensations, not unpleasant, gripped him. He felt as if he were swaying from side to side like an empty boat. He might even have fallen from the bench to the floor if Miss Janetta had not rung the dinner-time bell and Mr Brown, after reprimanding him again for his lack of attention, had not dismissed the class and sent them milling out into the yard, with Campbell there among them.

They were laughing. They were laughing at him. He imagined that they were patting Donnie Campbell on the back. He could hear their laughter ringing back from the yard, from the field. He started blinking again, very rapidly. He could feel his eyes grow wet, not with tears, certainly not with tears, but with an oily, phlegmy substance.

Mr Brown was saying, 'You'll have to do better than this, Gavin. I don't know what's wrong with you but your mother...'

He rose from the bench and walked past the teacher. He seemed to be drawn to the squares of daylight, to move into and through them as if they were made of glass, or not glass but jelly, a clear and yielding jelly. He glimpsed his sister, Rachel, who called out his name. He glimpsed Miss Janetta, the bell still in her hand, her long, severe face angled in his direction. He walked out of the classroom, out of the school-house into the daylight.

There was sunlight, blinking, on the side of the hill across the river. He could see sheep there, tiny, tiny, tiny sheep, like tufts of bog-cotton, like tiny silver fish swimming in a sea of daylight.

He walked across the corner of the yard, and then he ran.

He ran the last few steps and hurled himself on to his cousin's back. It was not impulse but compulsion. He could no more have prevented himself than he could have taken wing and, like a gull or a crow, have flown up over the sunlit hillside, the flocks and the bracken. He locked his hands about his cousin's neck, pinched his legs around his cousin's waist and flung himself backward, screaming. But it was not enough, not enough to release the rage that was in him. He screamed furiously again and grappled for a better hold. And then he *was* flying, flying high and wide, mouth wide open so that when he struck the grass all the breath – all the rage – came whooshing out and the back of his skull struck the ground hard.

Silvery fishes fled across his vision, turning scarlet as they disappeared. He heard a great ringing sound, more like an organ than a bell, coupled with the bray that he uttered as the breath was knocked from his lungs. He had been thrown, thrown and turned like a ewe lamb and before he could breathe again his cousin was upon him, seated upon his chest.

'You should not have been doing that, Gavin,' his cousin said. 'Do you hear what I am telling you? You should not have been doing that.'

Gavin gathered oily saliva into his mouth and spat.

He saw his cousin's face jerk away. Then it came back again, ringed by classmates, by the whole school, it seemed. He saw his sister's face, Charlie McEachern's face, Kristin Dugald's face, all the others, like the sea closing over a hole in the daylight. He strained to free himself. He heaved and wriggled between Donnie's thighs, but Donnie would not let him go.

'Aye, you should not have been doing that either,' Donnie said and, with three or four calm little strokings of the wrist, patted then slapped Gavin's cheeks, back and forth, back and forth, until they glowed like coals.

'No, Donnie,' his sister cried. 'Do not hit my brother.'

'You are right, Rachel. I am sorry.' The cousin sighed, swung his legs away then he, Gavin, felt his shirt grow tight about his throat as Donnie gathered his clothing into his fist and pulled him upright. 'God, but are you not a sorry sight, Gavin Tarrant?' Donnie dropped him and gave him a push that sent him staggering across the grass. 'Go away and wash your face or there will be more trouble when Mr Brown sees you.'

Too late: Miss Janetta and Mr Brown were there already.

'What is this, Donald? Pray tell me, what's going on here?'

'It was – a – a misunderstanding, Mr Brown,' Donald answered.

'Did you strike this boy?'

'I had to. He was – yes sir, I did.'

'Look at his face, for Heaven's sake. What have you done to him?'

'What came over you, Donnie?' Janetta said.

'I will not have bullying in my school, Campbell,' Mr Brown snapped. 'There can be no excuse for a boy of your age picking on a younger lad. Six strokes of the cane should teach you to be less free with your fists in future. Into the classroom. Now.'

'Dad . . .' Janetta began.

'*Now*,' Mr Brown thundered, then hesitated. Hiding his bewilderment behind a mask of anger, he peered into Gavin Tarrant's smudged little face in search of an explanation. None was forthcoming.

Quite deliberately, Gavin began to sob.

And watched, triumphantly, as his cousin was led away.

The situation was bound to lead to awkwardness between them but Gillies was optimistic that Innis would listen to his account of the incident before she passed judgement. In fact, he respected Donald for coping with the punishment with resignation and not resentment. Gillies had had to force himself not to hold back, not to vary the rhythm or weight of the strokes and knew that Donald's hands would smart throughout the afternoon. Resentment would have been a natural reaction but Donald seemed to harbour no grudge and had shrugged off the strapping as if it had been no more than he deserved.

'Why did you do it, son? Why did you hit him?'

A shake of the head. 'I do not know, Mr Brown.'

'Did he start it?'

Another shake of the head.

'Did Gavin say something offensive?'

More shaking of the head.

'Are you telling me that it was entirely your fault?'

'Aye, Mr Brown. All my fault.'

'Then I've no option but to punish you.'

'I know.'

There had been no display of silly adolescent martyrdom that some pupils affected after they had had their hands warmed. Donald had simply winced and tucked his fiery fingers into his mouth and then with a nod – a nod, indeed – had gone out of the empty classroom again into the yard. He had passed throughout the silent throng and had gone across the field not, Gillies reckoned, to weep but to bathe his hands in the cold water of the burn, which was a sensible thing to do to avoid swelling. Later, he had noticed Donald quietly eating his dinner as if nothing at all had happened.

Of the Tarrant boy there had been no sign. It was not until the bell had rung and the class had assembled in the yard that Gillies had spotted him again; a blotchy, petulant little face, avoiding everyone's eye, as if he were the wrong-doer and not the wronged which Gillies reckoned might very well be the truth.

That afternoon Donald had walked home to Fetternish with only Rachel for company. The schoolmaster's children had not known quite what to do, whose side to take. They had loitered, waiting for Janetta who, in turn, had waited for her father so that they had gone along the road together, saying very little or nothing at all. Later, when the youngsters had gone to bed, he would talk it over with Janetta. Until then he decided he would act as if nothing out of the ordinary had happened and hope that Innis would understand that he had his duty to do and must protect the principle of good order.

It was not Innis who was waiting at the crossroads, however, but Willy Naismith. Gillies's heart sank. He had never found the Fetternish steward anything but friendly. But now, in the waning light of an autumn afternoon, he realised just how daunting the fellow could be. He stood with arms folded and beard bristling. Gillies felt Janetta draw close. He glanced at her, saw her raise a questioning eyebrow.

'Now you're for it,' Janetta said.

'Mr Brown?'

'Ah, Mr Naismith. Good afternoon to you.'

'I want a word, sir, if you please.'

'If it's about Donnie, I assure you . . .'

'It is about Donnie.' Willy Naismith wrapped his arms about his chest and swayed ominously. 'Donnie's – er – guardian has arrived from Foss. There's been a bit of a stramash with the Foss bull down at Pennypol and Ronan Campbell has been injured – slightly, just slightly.'

'I'm sorry to hear it,' said Gillies. 'What does that have to do with me?'

'Quig – Robert Quigley – would like a word with you. Innis is with him in the house right now so if you can spare a half-hour of your valuable time to talk with him he would be much obliged.'

Gillies glanced at Janetta again but she looked away.

'May I ask what Mr Quigley wishes to talk to me about?' Gillies said.

'Donnie's future.'

'Is that all?'

'Isn't that enough?' said Willy.

Aileen could smell winter in the offing, that period of brittle seaweed and hard sand and the sharp odours of cattle dung with the softness gone. She had no knowledge of what winter meant or why the seasons changed. She moved through time as though it had no more meaning than air. She harboured only faint memories of what happened when daylight faded and the wind grew teeth. Even so, she thought she could feel storms rising far out at sea, the lift of the waves away beyond the marker stones, further out than the sails of the herring boats, further out than the sky.

Without Quig to look out for her, without Donnie, she had taken to the shore again and to the rocks above the shore. She felt as if she had slipped back into an old time, though she could not recall what time that had been or what it had signified. She had a vague sensation of guilt – though that word too was meaningless for Aileen Campbell – of naughtiness, of doing something that was somehow wrong. She had not lain out above the sea and listened for the fairy music for a long time, a long, long time – and thought of him again, raising him up out of the hard-limbed hilltop as if he were a cloud that lay upon her like the clouds that lay on the mountains of the land across the water.

With Quig and Donnie both gone and Mairi busy with the cattle and the old man nodding in the bed or in the chair in the room by the fire, she was free to roam the isle, to skip and stumble, to chant to the gulls and the seals, to drape her hair with bladderwrack and the husks of sea-pinks, to paddle in pools and crack open limpet shells and the shells of little blue mussels and the shells of the little crabs that scuttled away from her almost as quick as thought.

She carried the offerings in cupped hands to the flat stones on the point of the island where Quig had told her that the Mothers were buried and where the old man would be buried and where she would be buried too when the time came for her spirit to fly away too, so Quig said. She did not understand what Quig meant, though he had told her the tale often enough, for he came often to that place when he was not busy with the cattle or with the old man.

She thought of it as Quig's place, as the fort of Dun Fidra and the standing stone of Caliach had once been her places. She could only remember those secret places when she let her mind empty of everything else and she could never remember their names.

Because she could not find her secret place no matter how hard she tried, she took the husks of the sea-pinks to Quig's place; took the cracked limpets and mussels and soft-shelled crabs and spread them upon the flat stones, laid them in careful little patterns following the whorls of lichen or the lines of the graven letters, straight and crooked, that distinguished the stones; then she lay down on the flattest stone and looked up at the sky and sang the little song that he had sung to her, the man who had smelled like her father but who had come up out of the earth in the harvest twilights to reap his reward.

And the longing was in her again, the pain that was not pain. But it was not the same now, now that the song was gone and the man lost and the home hills were far away. There was nothing but the smell of the sea beyond her knees, and the cold smell of winter in the offing. The song she sang to summon him was lost in the crumple of the waves on the rocks and the bark of seals and the wind coming down not from the hills but the sky.

She got up at last, shivering, and ran.

When she came around the corner of the hillock she saw the house and the smoke rising from it like cloud, a pale, pale wraith of smoke against the cold sky and she felt the grip of sickness in her belly, like a cramp. She fell down, fists pressed into her belly. She wondered if she had brought him to her after all, if the shape by the shore, the shape that drifted with the smoke was the man she remembered or if he, it, had come and gone again, returned without her to the people under the hill.

Crouched low, hands still pressed between her thighs, she

crawled through the spiky grasses until she could see the house. The light from the west was almost gone and the shadows were long and on the home hills darkness had gathered and it was already night. A lantern had been hung from the hook on the post of the verandah and the old man had been brought out in his chair. Mairi had brought him outside, though there was no sunshine to warm him and the air was cold, so cold now that there were no moths fluttering in the beam of the lantern and the woman's breath hung white in the air.

She was bare-legged but with a shawl about her shoulders. She sat the way a man sits, knees spread and her hands on her knees. She sat on the top step of the verandah with the chair behind her, the tall chair in which the old man sat. He was not nodding. His head was not down. He was the way she remembered him from a long time ago, upright, chin out, staring across the waters to the home hills. His hair was wispy in the lantern-light but his breath was not white. She could see the last little trail of smoke curl away across the sand as the wind shifted with the tide and then it was clear to her, and she knew that she had not brought him but had sent him away.

At once the fear went out of her. She got up. She brushed her skirts clean and walked jauntily down the path that led from the rocks around the stoop of the thorns and came at the house from the side.

Mairi glanced up, not startled. Her breath was grey. She was smoking a cigar, one of the old man's cigars and she had a glass on the step between her feet. She bent forward, took up the glass and, still looking at Aileen, emptied it and put it down again.

Aileen climbed the steps.

Her grandfather did not turn his head. The blankets had fallen away and she could see his wrinkled bare arms resting on the arms of the chair and his eyes, not dark at all, staring out at the sea and the hills. He looked as he had not looked since she could not remember. He looked tall again and keen, as if he might leap up eagerly to greet her as she skipped out of the darkness.

'Not cold?' Aileen said.

The woman sucked on the cigar, making the tip glow. She let grey smoke drift from her mouth and roll away into nothingness in the cold air.

'No, dearest, he's not cold.'

'Put his blanket on.'

'He doesn't need his blanket now.'

Aileen squatted by the chair leg, looking up. She could see his fingers, like crab claws, gripping the chair and the broad strip of canvas across his chest and the thin, twisted strip of linen about his neck, the knot tight and hard behind the chairback.

'Aileen,' Mairi told her, 'your grandfather is dead.'

'No?' Aileen said, giggling. 'No?'

She got up and leaned on his knees, thrust her face close to his and in the little poll-parrot voice that he had once so liked, said, 'Kiss, kiss, give us a kiss.'

The woman drew her back.

'Go inside now, Aileen.' Mairi's voice was thick and smoke had made her eyes water. 'I will be sitting with him for a little while longer.'

Aileen moved uncertainly towards the door. It was dark in the house and the lamps were unlit. She thought that if she went into the bedroom at the back of the house he would still be there, just as he has been when she had left him. He would still be there, nodding in the bed and yet he would be out here too, not as he was but as he had once been, head up and chin out, looking out across the bay to the hills.

'Tell Quig,' she said, firmly.

'No need, dearest,' the woman said, her fingers busy with the knot behind the chair. 'I think that Quig already knows.'

It was too early for the genteel ladies of Edinburgh to be settling down to tea. On Mull, however, capital manners had no relevance; not to Willy or, it seemed, to the visitors who were doing full justice to the bread-and-butter, to the scones and yellow sponge-cake that Margaret had laid out in the drawing-room. Willy himself brought in the teapot and jugs, then, with a bow, left his mistress's sister to attend to the serving. He had already shooed Donnie and Innis's girls downstairs to the kitchen and had learned – from Rachel, not the lad – what had occurred in the school field that dinner-time. He did not commiserate with Donnie, did not take the boy's side. He had too much respect for Gillies Brown to undermine the schoolmaster's authority but he did wonder what Innis would make of it and how Mr Brown would explain his actions.

Gillies too had given the matter some thought. In the end, he was perfectly frank. He did not make light of the punishment; on the other hand, he gave it no more weight than it deserved. He confessed that he did not know who was responsible for starting the 'scrap' and for that reason had chosen to make an example of the elder boy. His explanation certainly sounded plausible – particularly through a mouthful of bread-and-butter – and to Gillies's relief Innis and Quigley soon let the subject drop in favour of other topics.

Although the schoolmaster was impressed by Robert Quigley, he could not deny that he felt twinges of envy at the ease with which Quigley and Innis conversed. Quigley was younger than his 'cousin' by a year or so but he had one of those plain, blunt faces that made him appear more mature than his age and, Gillies was pipped to notice, he still had a full head of hair.

He listened to Quigley's story of the bull and the drunkard and noticed that neither Quigley nor Innis were amused by the incident. He kept silent, ate a scone with raspberry jam and drank tea while the couple discussed other pieces of family business, mainly concerning Innis's grandfather. He was, it seemed, close to death and, according to Quigley, would be fortunate to survive the week, let alone the winter.

'I am sorry for my rudeness, Mr Brown,' Quigley said, at length. 'As you may have gathered Innis and I do not see each other very often and have therefore much catching up to do.'

'Please do not apologise, Mr Quigley,' Gillies said. 'It's obviously a distressing time for you both. I believe, however, you had a wish to discuss Donald's future with me?'

'That is true,' Quigley said.

Listening to him was like listening to Donnie. Man and boy

spoke with identical inflexions, neither Lowland nor Highland but something between, not so slow as the local dialect but nonetheless considered, as if every utterance was preceded by careful thought.

'I take it you've heard that I have a high opinion of your – of Donald's intelligence?' Gillies said.

'I did hear something of the sort, yes.'

'Well, it is not exaggerated,' Gillies said. 'Oh, perhaps Mrs Baverstock does lay it on a bit thick but she's fond of the boy and doesn't have much experience of youngsters.'

'Whereas,' said Quigley, 'you do.'

'I do, indeed,' said Gillies Brown.

'How far will Donnie's learning carry him?' Quigley asked.

Gillies hesitated. The question was more direct than he had anticipated. He put down his tea-cup, prodded his spectacles with his forefinger and glanced at Innis who, as if to encourage him, smiled and nodded.

'Before I answer,' Gillies said, 'may I ask how Donald was educated?'

'From textbooks listed on the Perth Academy curriculum that his great-grandfather ordered for him.'

'Who led him through his first lessons?'

'My mother.'

'Your mother?' Gillies could not hide his surprise.

'She raised Donald in much the same manner as she raised me,' Quigley said. 'She herself was taught to read and write at Sabbath school and, after that, learned counting and natural science from borrowed books. She was also a poorhouse teacher for a short time before she took to the road and joined up with her people – before she had me, of course.'

At what point in the process of selection that governed the wandering tribes had fecklessness given way to ambition, Gillies wondered. Perhaps it was survival not ambition that had changed the pattern for Quigley's mother, and her learning skills had been acquired randomly, not by trial and error.

'When Donnie grew older,' Quigley went on, 'his great-grandfather spent time with him at his books, until he grew too frail. After that – well, I imparted what little knowledge I could to the boy.'

'You have done a fine job with him,' Gillies said. 'He will certainly be ready to move on come the end of the summer term. Is that what you wanted to hear from me, Mr Quigley?'

'Are you telling me that his education has been adequate, Mr Brown?'

'More than adequate,' Gillies said.

'For what, though?' Robert Quigley said.

'What do you have in mind for him?' Gillies said. 'I think I would be prepared to stick out my neck and say that he is capable of attaining the highest sort of honours in medicine or the law or, if you wished it, to enter upon a career in the Kirk.'

'No,' Quigley said. 'No, it would not be the Kirk.'

'What then?'

'Agriculture.'

'That is a two-year course,' said Gillies. 'Given that Donald has practical experience as well as a good head on his shoulders I reckon he would be accepted by any of the three colleges that carry the subject.'

'And after that,' Quigley said. 'Surveying, perhaps?'

'Ah!' Gillies said. 'The examination of the Institute of Surveyors is not so easy a target. He would need to work in the profession as an apprentice and continue his studies for some years before he could apply for his charter.'

'It would be worth having, though, would it not?'

'Absolutely,' Gillies said.

'Is this what Donald wants to do?' Innis asked.

'He is young enough to need guidance and direction,' Quigley said.

'Towards a career in estate management, you mean?' said Gillies.

There was a moment's silence and Gillies noticed that Quigley seemed nonplussed. His lips pursed and he assumed the same defensive look that Donald had worn when the strap came down upon his palms.

Innis's mouth had opened just a little but when Gillies glanced at her she closed it with an odd popping sound. He was surprised that she had not already deduced what was on her cousin's mind. But perhaps she had not suspected Quigley of such deviousness, if, of course, that's what it was.

Gillies said, 'Mr Thrale will not live forever.'

'I do not know what you mean,' Quigley said.

'Aye, Quig, but I am thinking that you do,' said Innis.

It was Robert Quigley's turn to give a little *tut* of annoyance but then his expression turned rueful. He shrugged his shoulders. 'Is it wicked of me, Innis, to be looking out for the lad's future?'

'I should have guessed,' said Innis.

'It is nothing that is cut and dried,' Quigley said. 'But Thrale will *not* be living forever, not even Thrale. In five or six years at an estimate Fetternish will be needing a new manager, a more efficient manager than Thrale ever was.'

'You are as bad as all the rest, Quig,' Innis said, without any sign of rancour. 'Foss will become too small for you and you have an eye on Fetternish.'

'Foss is too small as it is,' Quig interrupted. 'There was a substantial living to be made there when Evander was in his prime but times have changed. A few acres of grazing ground far from a railhead will hardly be supporting one family, let alone several.'

'Is that why you sent the others away?' Innis said.

'Part of the reason,' Quig admitted.

'And the other part?'

'It will not be my land to dispose of when the old man passes on.'

'Surely my grandfather will not leave you penniless, not after what you have done for him?' Innis said.

'I have not witnessed the will,' Quig said. 'It is lodged with the lawyers in Perth. I am not blood kin, however, and I doubt if he will leave Foss to me.'

'Whereas Donnie is blood kin?'

'Aye, that is so,' said Quig. 'But I would not be having the lad stuck offshore with just fifty head of cattle and tariffs on transportation that will shear away most of his profits. It is one thing to live frugally in a frugal world but it is quite another to wish such a thing upon your children, especially when the world is improving so fast that it takes your breath away.'

'Donnie is not your child, Quig.'

'No, but he is as close to a son as I am ever liable to have,' Quig said. 'I am not prepared to let his future take care of itself. I was fortunate – or should I be saying that my mother was fortunate – to be cared for by a generous man like your grandfather. I owe it to him and his family to look to the future. I have a debt to pay to Evander McIver and I am not one for forgetting it. Mr Brown?'

'Yes, Mr Quigley?'

'Will you be good enough to find out exactly what it will take to put Donald through a diploma course at a college of agriculture and to back an application for admission on his behalf?'

'I will,' Gillies said. 'Do you have a preference?'

'A preference?'

'Glasgow, Edinburgh or Aberdeen?'

'All things being equal – Glasgow.'

'Very well.'

'When the time comes,' Innis said, 'will you be doing the same sort of thing for my son, Mr Brown?'

'Your son?'

'Gavin,' Innis reminded him.

'If . . .' He hesitated. 'Certainly, if he's up to it.'

'Up to managing Fetternish, do you mean?' Innis said.

'I meant,' said Gillies Brown, desperately trying to retrieve the situation, 'if you and your husband feel that Gavin would benefit from a scientific training when the time comes.'

'And when will that time be?' Innis said.

'When he is old enough,' said Gillies, lamely.

He watched Quigley touch her, the brown-skinned hand upon hers, and noted how the fretfulness went out of her at once. He had never had that sort of power over anyone, the quiet, charismatic authority that needed no words to embellish it. He felt unjustifiably upset by the gesture, by the little wedge that Robert Quigley had unwittingly driven between him and the woman from Pennypol. He had no right to be envious of

Quigley and felt like a fool for nurturing such emotions. But he could not help himself. He had no claim upon Innis Tarrant who was married to another man and who, he had come to realise, was the product of a culture that he did not yet understand.

'I know, Quig, I know,' Innis said, softly. 'You are only doing what is best for Aileen's son and I should not be holding it against you. Gavin will be a shepherd like his father and will be happy enough with that, I expect. We have no right to ask Biddy for anything other than paid employment. After all, we did not have the burden of bringing up Aileen's son or of looking after grandfather in his old age.'

'That was no burden, Innis,' Quigley said. 'Besides, it is not what is done that I have to be thinking about now but what will happen when Evander's suffering is finally at an end and we are left to fend for ourselves.'

'And will that be soon?' said Innis.

'Very soon,' said Robert Quigley. 'I promise you, very, very soon.'

At last the wind had begun to pick up. The blow had been threatening all afternoon. The rams had first become aware of it, then the ewes. There had been no great fuss among them, no moaning and roaring in the way that sometimes affected cattle, just vague restlessness and a turning of tails towards the sea.

He had been out by the point of Olaf's Ridge when the gulls had come wheeling inland in a great screaming flock. He wondered if they had been blown off course by a storm far out to sea or if there was nothing to their flight but random chance. Of course his wife would have seen God in the passage of the herring gulls, God lurking behind the incident, just as her idiot sister Aileen had seen the interfering hand of sprites and fairy folk in every gnarled bush and ominous thunderhead.

Michael did not believe in God; or, rather, refused to believe that God had any time for the little creatures of the earth; that He had scattered them here and forgotten them so that they were condemned to live out their days in obedience to no law but that of the society that harboured them and had no obligation but to endure. Michael did not fear the darkness or what lay beyond. He left such morbid speculations to his brother, the priest, and to his convert wife. He had trouble enough struggling with the dark urges that made his stomach knot and his brain ache, with the desire to reclaim that which was rightfully his and to bring Biddy Baverstock to heel again.

Now it was night and he could hear the wind beating against the gable and growling in the chimney. When he placed a piece of driftwood on top of the coals the wood caught and sparked instantly and was soon burning fiercely. Fruarch, who had not seen enough weather yet to be stoical, lay in his basket on the far side of the hearth, whining slightly, muzzle tucked under paws, watching the thin sliver of carpet by the door waver and rise in the draught.

The children, even Gavin, had been restless. It had taken Innis the best part of half an hour to see the girls off to sleep and she had left the tiny, bowl-shaped oil lamp lit to comfort them. She sat now on a chair at the table with the big, flute-shaped lamp to light her mending, her box of threads, jar of buttons and card of needles spread to hand, a shirt lifted up to her breast while her fingers worked at repairing a tear in the sleeve.

He watched her in silence. She had told him what had happened that day, about her father, about Donnie and Gavin's scrap, what Quigley had said to the schoolmaster up at the house. She had not mentioned Biddy, not one word about Biddy who, Michael knew, was shooting at Tormont with her fancy friends. Biddy would not be shooting at this hour, though. She would be dressed up in all her finery, in the black velvet dress that showed off her bosom, jewels glittering at her throat, her shoulders bare, and she would be laughing. He imagined her laughing, laughing the way she had laughed at him once, and flirting with all the gentlemen.

In the oil-lamp light Innis looked so neat and wholesome that he was almost afraid of her – as he had been afraid of the nuns who had come to the door of his mother's house in the

Ettrick Pen to collect cast-off clothes for the orphanage; something so contained, so virginal and untouchable about them that he was rendered bloodless and bodiless by their presence and would run through the house and hide in the hayloft until they had gone. He could not run from Innis, however, from his marriage to Innis, from the knowledge that he had entered her and could, if he wished, enter her again at any time; knowing, though, that even as he entered her so she would enter him and he would be one with her, no matter how he tried to dominate.

It was not that she did not respond to him, not that she was cold. If there was coldness then the coldness was in him. What he received from Innis was a pervasive warmth that was in itself too gentle to be satisfying. It disturbed him that Innis could bring sanctity even into the marriage bed. What he really wanted was a taste of the sort of wantonness that Biddy had brought to love-making when he was young and wild.

He watched her, thinking of Biddy, and listened to the wind growl.

Then he said, 'If this wind gets much worse Quigley will not be getting back to his island tomorrow.'

She lifted her head, startled not by what he had said but by the fact that he had spoken at all. She said, 'He will be wanting to get back, I am sure. He has arranged to take Dr Kirkhope with him.'

'Kirkhope? Why?'

'To see if anything can be done for my grandfather.'

'Like what? A miracle?'

Innis nodded. 'Yes, it would be merciful if the Lord took him. He is long past his time.'

'How old is he?'

'Eighty, I think, or older.'

She waited for him to continue but Michael gazed mutely at the piece of driftwood in the grate, at the salty blue sparks it gave off as the draft sucked it into shapeless ash. He rubbed his hands on his thighs and thought what to say next. When he looked up again Innis had gone back to her sewing.

'If he dies in the next day or two,' Michael said, 'it will spoil your sister's fun and games. She'll have to come back for the funeral.'

'If it does happen,' Innis said, 'Willy will be dispatching a telegraph from Dervaig to the post office at Salen and they will send someone out to Coilichan with the news.'

'Did Willy think of that?'

'No. Quig.'

'Quig seems to have thought of everything,' Michael said. 'The doctor, the telegraph – the will too, I suppose.'

'The will is lodged with lawyers in Perth.'

'What does it say, I wonder?'

'I have not the slightest idea,' Innis said.

'Quigley will know.'

'He says that he does not.'

'Oh, he will know. Quig knows everything. He's ready for it. Prepared for it,' Michael said. 'It wouldn't even surprise me if he had trained that damned bull to trample on your father.'

Innis put down the half-mended shirt. 'Why would he be doing that?'

'To get rid of the old tosspot,' Michael said.

'Get rid of my father? Why?'

'Why? Why? You're asking me when you should be asking Quigley.'

Innis laid the shirt to one side. Head cocked a little, frowning, she said, 'Is it that you are thinking Quig is after something that he should not have?'

'Oh, he's after *something*, your precious Quig, but I can't work out what it is just yet.'

'He only wants to send Donnie to college.'

'Is that what the fight was about?'

'I do not know what the fight was about.'

'Did Gavin not tell you?' Michael said.

'No, I thought that he might have told you.'

Michael laughed. 'Perhaps Gavin was just thinking how nice it would be if someone was to send him to college too, to learn all about the pigs and cows.'

'If that is what he wants . . .'

'What? You'll talk to your sister, scrounge from your sister?'

211

'I will be scrounging from no one, Michael.'

'Perhaps by that time Quigley will have more money than any of us, and you can go to him and smile your wee smile.'

Innis ignored the jibe. 'If you are wanting Gavin to go to the mainland for his education then we will pay for it ourselves.'

'Will we? With what? Buttons?'

'Is it only money that you are thinking about? Is it the prospect of money that has put you into this mood? You have no reason to be jealous of Robert Quigley. I doubt if there will be much coming his way when my grandfather dies. But if there is,' Innis said, 'if Quig inherits everything then it is no more than he deserves after what he has done for us.'

Turning in his chair, Michael said, 'How much is there?'

'I do not know.'

'There's the island itself, and the herd – and Pennypol.'

'Pennypol belongs to my mother, as well you know.' Then she paused and stared at him. 'Is it owning Pennypol that you have set your heart on, Michael?'

'I could make something out of that tract of ground,' Michael said. 'I wouldn't hire the grazings out to your sister for next to nothing, though. No, I would not. She wouldn't be having me as her lackey, at her beck and call, not if I had a piece of ground of my own.'

'What is this?' Innis said. 'You know that Pennypol will never be yours.'

'It may be yours, though, when they've both gone.' He laughed again. 'Aye, and if Quig had trained that bull a wee bit better then he might have had them both away with it this morning and we would all have been better off.'

She moved her hand, not suddenly or violently, and dragged the string of fifty-five beads from behind the bobbin box. He had not known that her rosary was there. He felt himself tense imperceptibly as she took the beads into her palm. He wondered where she had hidden her crucifix and if he was going to have to contend with that too if the Aves and Paternosters and Glorias failed her.

'Is that what you are wishing?' Innis said. 'That they would

212

all pass on and let us benefit from what they have worked so hard to get?'

'I'm not thinking of me,' Michael said. 'I'm thinking of Gavin.'

'And the girls?'

'Oh, the girls. Yes, the girls too,' he said. 'For all it is – a few miserable acres of land and a cottage by the shore.'

'Is that why you married me?' Innis seemed more curious than offended. 'Did you marry me just to stake a claim to Pennypol?'

'No,' Michael said. 'That is your father's history.'

'And you are not like him.'

'Thank God, no. I wouldn't go lounging about in a boat all damned day, sucking on a whisky bottle while my women did my work for me. I'd make that stinking cottage fit to live in for a start, then I'd scour off Biddy's cattle and get a decent flock of my own up from the Borders and . . .'

'For Gavin, all for Gavin?'

'This is the life he knows. The best life for him.'

'And for me?'

'You?'

'What do you want for me, Michael?'

The question brought him up short. He did not understand what she meant by it, especially as she had used the word *for*, not *from*. What did he want *for* her? He wanted nothing *for* her. He had already given her everything that an island wife could need. He felt a little stir of anger at her ingratitude.

'What I do, Innis, I do for all of us,' he said.

'No matter what tomorrow may bring?'

'I don't pretend to know what tomorrow will bring, but I will be ready to take advantage of it,' he said, pretentiously. 'There's no more you can ask of me than that, is there?'

Innis shook her head.

'Is there?' he insisted.

'No more than that,' Innis agreed and, leaving her mending on the table, went through to the back room to be alone for a while.

Biddy and news of Evander McIver's passing reached Fetternish House almost simultaneously. She had hardly had time to take off her hat and arrange her wind-tousled hair before Dr Kirkhope arrived hot-foot from the pier at Croig to inform her that her grandfather had passed away. Word was sent immediately to Pennymain, and Campbells and Tarrants were propelled into a state of activity that seemed almost as blustery as the weather.

There was no time for grieving and, Biddy said, no need for it. Had they not all been praying for grandfather to die? Was it not a mercy that his sufferings were over? According to Dr Kirkhope the end had been peaceful, a matter of falling asleep in a chair on the verandah and not waking up again. Mairi Quigley had found him, had taken him indoors and had laid him out to await Quig's return from Mull. It had been entirely fortuitous that Quig was accompanied by the doctor, for Kirkhope had been able to make his examination, issue a certificate on the spot and return within the hour to Croig. Being a decent sort, the doctor had notified the family, alerted the undertaker, and officially registered the death in the council office in Tobermory.

He also brought letters for Biddy and Innis, not hastily scribbled notes but detailed instructions from Quig concerning the funeral arrangements. Mr Prole, the undertaker in Salen, had already been briefed as to what McIver would require of him and a launch had been hired to convey mourners to the island if, that is, the weather did not make the crossing too hazardous.

Quig also forwarded a sealed letter for delivery to Tom Ewing. It was addressed in Evander McIver's spidery handwriting, sight of which made Innis feel as if she was holding a piece of history in her hand. She considered taking the letter personally to the manse but decided that that would be imprudent and asked Gillies if he would drop it in on his way to school the following morning. She had a notion that in writing to Reverend Ewing her grandfather would be calling in a debt from beyond the grave. She seemed to remember that

Tom Ewing had promised that he would conduct the funeral service on Foss in spite of the fact that Evander belonged to no church. How long ago the letter had been written Innis could only surmise for it had been several years since her grandfather had been able to construct a sentence, let alone hold a pen.

Everything seemed too carefully planned, too cut-and-dried, as if Evander and Quig between them had plotted to fulfil some ancient prophecy but had been so thorough in the doing thereof that all the mystery, all the authenticity had been removed. Innis did not share her doubts with anyone; not with Michael, who would not have understood and certainly not with Biddy who, after her unexplained return from Tormont, was so brusque and haughty as to be almost unapproachable.

In Vassie too there had been no outward signs of sorrow.

'Hah!' she had said, when Innis had brought her the news. 'So he has gone at last, has he? Well, it is not as if it was before his time.' Then she had stalked into the cottage, into the gloomy bed-neuk and, loudly enough for Innis to hear, had shouted, 'Do you hear what Innis tells me, Ronan Campbell? My father is dead and you will be having what you have waited for all these years. It is too late for you now, though, is it not? Hah? Do not pretend that you cannot hear me. My father is dead, and I only wish that it was you who had gone instead of him since you were never half, never a quarter of the man he was.' Vassie abruptly reappeared in the doorway. 'When is the burial to be?'

'On Friday. On Foss. A boat will leave Croig at noon.'

'Will the women be there?'

'Not at the interment, I'm thinking,' Innis had answered. 'That would not be proper. But Quig has invited us to the house beforehand.'

'I mean *his* women?'

'I do not know who will be there.'

'And the reading?'

'Reading?'

'The will and last testament?'

'I have no information about that,' Innis had said, stiffly. 'Will you be coming with us on the boat or will you not?'

'Aye, I suppose that I had better turn up.'

'Then I'll see to it that you are collected in the dogcart in plenty of time.'

'Who will look after him – your father? He cannot be left by himself.'

'I will see to that, too. Willy or Maggie will do it.'

'Good,' Vassie had said; then, to Innis's astonishment, had stepped back into the cottage and deliberately slammed the door.

If Evander McIver had thought to be buried on the mainland or even upon Mull then the turn-out would have been magnificent. Curiosity, if not respect, would have drawn crowds to the graveside and women and children to the kirkyard wall and there would have been a great wake, marked by lamentation and strong drink, and no shortage of hands to help carry the coffin of such a grand old man, such a legend, from the house to the church.

There would probably even have been a piper drafted in for the occasion and work would have stopped for miles around as the strains of the bagpipe, solitary and sad, drifted up from the village and rolled away across the hills.

But there was none of that nonsense. There were only the black, foamy channels between one island and the next, and a bitter north wind cutting at your cheeks and numbing your brow, and spray shooting up over the bow of the *Gannet* and splattering on the canvas awning that kept the passengers from drowning altogether. And the line of the horizon and the slithering skerries and the dark, looming crags of uninhabited islands heaving up and down, see-sawing up and down, and the sound of Minister Ewing retching over the rail with his buttocks in the air while Donnie Campbell held on to one arm and Michael Tarrant held on to the other to prevent him vanishing entirely over the side.

Biddy too was pea-green about the gills and even Vassie had turned an unusual shade of grey beneath her granite tan. But they were resolute women, one of them a lady, and they had the will to keep their mouths shut and eyes closed and, aided by a little prayer from Innis now and then, just managed to reach the bay below the house of Foss without disgorging their breakfasts.

If there had been a piper on hand – which there wasn't – surely he would have been moved to tune his chanter and wail away with *Little White Lily* or *Land o' the Leal*, or some other solemn bardic tribute as the minister of Crove was carried ashore by four stalwart young men in thigh-boots and propped more or less upright on the beach.

The fact that he had been redeemed by four of Evander McIver's bastard sons and was assisted up to the house by two of McIver's bastard daughters did not seem to matter, morally, to Reverend Ewing. He hardly knew whose hand it was that offered him a posset of whisky and strong black coffee. He accepted it and drank, and coughed, and drank again and, with the cure-all racing down into his stomach, managed to lift his right hand, remove his salt-stained hat and shake the hand of the man before him who, he vaguely realised, was Robert Quigley. Who the others were he did not know nor did he much care, for an aroma of cooked meats and baked fish wafted out of the house and it was all he could do to swallow the rest of the restorative medicine and, bracing himself, draw in a queasy breath.

'It is good of you to be making the crossing on such a morning as this,' Quig said. 'We will be doing the thing, the honours as quickly as is possible, however, for I think that this wind will be veering to the west soon and we would not be wanting you to be marooned on Foss, not when you have a parish to be looking after over on the bigger island. Would you care to have a bite to eat first, or afterwards?'

'A–a – afterwards, I think,' Tom Ewing said and, still hanging on to the posset cup, let Quigley guide him into the room where the body lay.

In the past dozen years Innis had visited Foss on only a handful of occasions. Now, though, she realised that the place that had always seemed so changeless had in fact changed; unless, she thought, the changes were in her.

The unfortunate crossing, with the *Gannet* pitching and Tom Ewing being violently sick, had robbed the trip of sentiment, of the melancholy that she had hoped would compensate for grief. She had tried, had tried very hard, had even prayed about it, but she could not grieve for her grandfather who, she knew, had gone to a better place, a place that *was* changeless and eternal.

When she reached the beach, however, and counted the strangers – McIver's clan – and recognised hardly a one of them, when she saw how tattered the wooden dwelling had become and how the little green isle itself seemed to have shrunk, she experienced a twinge of regret; not grief, not profound and resonating sorrow, just the wistful acknowledgement that her grandfather and her girlhood were both gone now, and that no amount of wishing would ever bring them back. She recognised Mairi, of course, and a woman called Katrin but the girls and boys were men and women now and had attained an individuality that separated them each from the other and all from her.

The padded chair – empty – still stood upon the verandah. The young men who leaned on the rail nearby seemed almost callously indifferent to it, and the young women, two of whom were so like Innis physically that they, not Biddy, might have been her sisters, gathered in a group by the steps, whispering in that sly, critical manner that strangers so often mistook for arrogance. They would, Innis reckoned, be discussing Biddy and what Biddy was wearing and, if they were true-blue islanders, would be estimating what the mourning rig-out had cost and what she, the lady of Fetternish, would do with it afterwards.

Only the family came into the book-lined parlour where Grandfather McIver was laid out in his coffin. The coffin was raised on two stout trestles above the India-pattern carpet that had once seemed so expensive but that now looked not only threadbare but cheap. The house smelled of dampness and cigar smoke. The aroma of cooking from the open hearth in the back room was overpoweringly corporeal. The lid of the coffin had been left aslant, her grandfather's face exposed. Mairi, or possibly Mr Prole, the undertaker, had dressed him in Jacobite costume, in a frilled shirt and a jacket with little silver thistles instead of buttons. His hair, what was left of it, had been scraped back into a pigtail and fastened with a loop of silver thread.

It was the first corpse that Innis had ever seen. Her drowned brother Donnie had been so long in the water that his coffin, at Dad's insistence, had been sealed up tight. She approached with trepidation, expecting fear or revulsion or a sudden flux of grief to overwhelm her. Her mother stood to one side of her, Michael on the other. On the nether side of the coffin, like partners in a game of chance, were young Donnie and Mairi and Quig. Out of the corner of her eye Innis noticed Aileen leaning against the oak post that separated the parlour from the kitchen and munching casually on a sticky piece of ginger-bread as if all the activity bored her and she had no kinship with the strangers who had invaded the house.

Innis looked down and felt – nothing. She was surprised at this absence of feeling. The man in the coffin was certainly her grandfather; but by exactly the same token it was not her grandfather at all. And he was not sleeping; he was dead. Papery features, the delicate line of the lips and his feathery lashes were all far too refined to seem authentic. He looked, Innis thought, like a poor copy of himself. She gave a little sigh of disappointment and flicked the beads of the rosary in her jacket pocket: ten of this and ten of that. She heard one of the young men on the verandah guffaw, a mutter of voices, the murmur of the waves and, behind that, stretching out and out, more sea sounds and wind sounds.

'There is nothing we can be doing for him now,' Vassie declared. 'By God, though, he was a handsome devil in his day.' She tutted as if that was another thing to be held against her father, then she stepped back to make room for Biddy who, though she had hardly known her grandfather, was the only one among them who wept.

The house service was short and, Tom was ashamed to admit, fairly perfunctory. Although his stomach had settled and his head had stopped spinning, he had not quite recovered from his ordeal on the *Gannet* and felt, not unnaturally, drained of enthusiasm as well as energy. In fact, he regretted having made promises to McIver; he supposed that the magic of Foss had influenced him to cast caution to the winds when he and Innis were young all those years ago. There was no magic left on McIver's isle now. It was a dreich, drenched, decaying sort of place and, as he intoned a prayer for the soul of the deceased and uttered a few words about redemption, he doubted if the Presbytery would be in the least put out by his agreement to accord the libidinous old sinner a decent Christian burial.

At the root of Tom's disenchantment lay recollections of that day long ago when Innis had first brought him to Foss. In addition to agreeing to see that McIver was buried like a Christian he had also promised to take care of Innis. In the keeping of *that* promise he had failed miserably. Not only had he lost Innis to a dour incomer, he had lost her to the Church of Rome, which was far, far worse. If McIver was looking down on him now from some grassy corner of heaven surely he would realise that it was not his but Innis's fault that the promise could not be kept.

Tom was relieved to get out of the low-beamed living-room, to escape from the house and the women, several of whom bore a remarkable resemblance to the girl he had once known, had once loved. It would have been easier on him if they had resembled Biddy, had been striking, red-haired beauties, for Biddy was still accessible and he could still sustain a faint hope that one day, before it was too late, she might have a fit, fall in love with him and replace Innis at the centre of his affections.

He followed after the coffin. It was carried by six pallbearers, the same four stalwarts who had lifted him from the boat, aided by Quig and young Donnie. They moved fast and sure-footed and the slope of the little hillock soon put the beach and the boat out of sight. The lads were still in their thigh-boots, Quig and Donnie wrapped in oilskins and he, the

Reverend Thomas Ewing, had a black topcoat flapping over his robes and his hat tied on with a crape ribband that the woman, Mairi, had found for him. Behind him, all in black, stalked Mr Prole the undertaker, who seemed determined to give value for money and would supervise not only the filling of the grave but, in due course, the setting down of the marker stone that McIver had purchased many years ago from the quarrymaster at Tormore.

It was not until he came over the crown of the hill and in sight of the open sea, however, that Tom was gripped by the solemnity of the occasion. Until then it had been a chore, a duty, a disappointment; too planned and pretentious to be other than lackluster and lacking that arrogance that he thought of as inimically Highland; that pride, that stubborn refusal to be reduced to inconsequential dust by anything, even death.

And then the wind caught him, the wind from the north. It was filled with salt spray from the waves upon the shore; thunderous waves and a pearly haze of spume and the line of the sea lying out black and fretful to a sky that was darker than the grave; a long, low line of cloud, broken-backed and bow-shaped, without a blink of sunlight to grace the mutinous Atlantic or the sour stramash of breakers that rolled over the skerries, that rolled in upon the point of Foss and seethed like milk over the potholes and rockpools that ringed the rough pasture.

Tom watched the coffin slant and twist. He caught his breath as Evander's sons and grandsons staggered beneath its weight. They braced themselves and, leaning forward, trudged on again with rain and spray all about them, forged on as remorselessly as the sea itself, as if their intention was to march straight into the breakers and cast the coffin into the deep.

They had reached the farthest point of dry land on the island, and the most exposed; a horseshoe of turf fringed with heather and withered bracken, the markers so discreet as to be almost invisible. Only a mound of brown earth and a canvas tent pinned down with stones told what the place was and why they were here. Ancient graves of slate and schist, Pictish or Irish or Norse – not even McIver had known which – and three slabs of pinkish granite, two flat and one prised upright by the earth-mound: Evander's wives and two dead babies waited patiently for him to come to them again, to be snug and warm again, beneath the turf, beneath the stones.

Tom felt the blood stir within him, the fierce melancholy pride that linked him with the elements and the sentimental dead. He watched the young men lower the coffin to the grass and saw Prole strip away the canvas that covered the grave. He did not crouch now, did not tuck his chin down into his chest. He pulled off his topcoat, wrapped his hat in it and pushed them down into the heather. He could taste the salt spray stinging on his lips, and the rain. This was just the sort of day, he thought, that McIver would have chosen for his funeral, not some summery afternoon, with the sea shimmering meekly, the Treshnish Isles reduced to pastel, and Mull a faded silhouette. He watched young Donnie wrestle with the ropes and Quig, on one knee, clear debris from the graveside and wipe the coffin lid with a sweep of his arm.

The others, the bastard sons and grandsons, stood with their backs to the wind; Michael Tarrant with them, Prole too, then Donnie, then Quig, each with a rope in his hand, ready to lift the old man and lower him away.

Tom took out his Testament and opened it. He held it in both fists, rice-paper pages fluttering like tiny wings against his thumbs, rain spotting the pages and puckering the words. He read in a loud voice, flinging his words into the wind. Then, at the appropriate moment, they let the coffin down, sinking it into the ground, and drew the ropes away.

Off to his left, huddled in the salt haze above the heather, Tom noticed the women, shawled and shrouded, watching from a distance, Vassie and Innis and Aileen, and the one called Mairi; like echoes, like ghosts of the women who had been here before and who waited now with infinite patience in the warm brown earth beneath the stones.

'*Dadda-eee*,' he thought he heard the child-woman cry. '*Dadda-eee*.'

But then he could have been wrong.

EIGHT

The Feeding Box

Even before the reading of Evander McIver's will Innis realised that it was going to be the same old story, the same greedy scratching for advantage that affected all families when inheritance was at stake. In the Campbells' case the possession of land was the factor that would excite and divide them.

In Michael's eyes, for instance, Fetternish, Pennypol and Foss seemed to have become linked, not so much by deed of ownership as by fabrication and desire. In the days following the funeral he spoke incessantly about the will. Sparked by the foolish belief that McIver had left a fortune for disposal, he was convinced that Innis, her grandfather's favourite, would come in for the lion's share and that he, her husband, would be elevated at a stroke to landowner and without effort or experience become a gentleman of equivalent rank to Bridget Baverstock.

He was more loquacious than Innis would have believed possible. Even in bed, he droned on, lying in the darkness with his hands behind his head, talking less to her than to himself, speculating on what might be in store for them when McIver's legacies were doled out, going on and on until his flat, Lowland voice began to seem like that of a stranger, and Innis would try desperately to close her ears to his foolishness.

She had grown so used to his coldness that she could not cope with this new, insinuating warmth. It was as if her husband had been lost in the salt-sea mists of Foss, had been spirited away and replaced by a substitute whose features were exactly the same but whose character was entirely altered. His sudden concern for her happiness seemed both obsequious and clumsy. He would bound into the cottage of an evening in search of a welcoming kiss, would twine an arm about her waist as she served supper and pull her to him and hug her. He repaired the leaky roof of the outhouse at last and cleaned and trimmed all the lamps. He even went so far as to teach Fruarch a few tricks, or tried to, until the dog grew bored and went and hid under Rachel's bed.

At night, late, he would take Innis's hand and put it to him and, when she did not recoil, would roll on to her and enter her.

He was willing to do even that to please her.

During the day he would discuss matters with Barrett, his one and only confidant, for Barrett never seemed to tire of the subject.

'Are you sure there will be something in it for you?' Barrett said. 'It is not as if there are not enough children of his own in need of a share.'

'Quigley claims that it'll all come to blood kin,' Michael said.

'Are they not blood kin?'

'They are not legitimate.'

'I hear that he fathered dozens.'

'I don't know how many he fathered,' Michael said. 'All I know is that they've been sent packing. There were hardly more than a dozen, all told, at the funeral. That doesn't seem to me like much of a tribe.'

'Enough to thin the pickings, however,' Barrett said. 'Besides, there may not be so much as you imagine. My father says that old man McIver was never so well-off as folk said he was. My father remembers him when he was still travelling about the games trying to earn a few shillings in prize money and a few pounds in wagers. McIver would be in his fifties by then and if my father is to be believed he was well past his prime and would be losing as much as he would be winning.'

'Didn't he win the island in a wager?'

'The Duke was glad to be rid of it, so I have heard.'

'Are you telling me,' Michael said, 'that the island is worth nothing? I can't believe that. It looked like prime grazing to me.'

'For bull-breeding, perhaps,' Barrett said, 'but it would hardly be the sort of place that a shepherd would be wanting to put a flock. I know that I would not be wanting to take myself out there eight or ten times in the year just to see what the storms had left me. No, and I would not be enthusiastic about paying through the nose to ferry the fat lambs away to Oban. And I would not be living there. Oh, God, no, not for all the tea in China.'

'It's a fine big house, you know,' Michael said.

'It could be the palace at Scone for all I would be caring.' Barrett shook his head. 'It will not be in that direction that I would move my family if moving was on my mind at all, which it is not.'

'Nonetheless, if it comes my wife's way . . .'

'What? Will you be going out there to farm it yourself?'

'Well, that remains to be seen.'

'Now, if it was Pennypol,' Barrett said, grinning, 'I would be glad to be having that patch for my own. Aye, I could be setting myself up there fine.'

'So could I,' Michael said. 'So, indeed, could I.'

'She will be owning it outright now. Vassie, I mean.'

'She will.'

Barrett laughed and shook his head. 'She will not be selling it to you, not when it is making money in rent.'

'That's true,' Michael agreed.

Barrett wiped rain from his eyebrows with his forefingers and laughed again, a wee bit less certainly this time. 'You are thinking of Pennypol, are you now? And how will that be done? How will you persuade Vassie Campbell to let you have what she has hung on to for thirty years and more? Will you be giving her Foss in exchange, if Foss comes your way at all?'

'I might do that,' said Michael.

'Aye, then she would need to be hiring a boat every week, a boat with a deep hold to ferry in his lordship's supply of whisky.'

'Anyway, anyway,' Michael said. 'It's all up in the air until the lawyer comes from Perth to gather the legatees and tell us exactly what's what.'

'When will that be happening?'

'Soon, I'm told, soon.'

'But not soon enough for you, I am thinking.'

'No, not soon enough for me.'

Michael Tarrant was not the only one to be affected by the prospect of an imminent inheritance. Unknown to Vassie, intelligence regarding the old man's passing had seeped down into a most unexpected place, into a region so obscure that she could not possibly have guessed what was going on there.

To say that she was astonished by her husband's reaction would be a severe understatement. What she found in the cottage at Pennypol upon her return from Foss shocked her; not Ronan in a moaning stupor, not Ronan roaring for more whisky, but Ronan up out of bed, clean-shaven and dressed in a musty serge suit that he had not worn in ten years. The suit hung on his skinny frame like a rag on a scarecrow and his head protruded from the shirt collar like a turkey looking out of a bucket. He was red-eyed and his jowls were a little bit bloody where the razor had wavered but somehow he had dragged himself from the slough of drunken incompetence and sat at the table with a mug of tea before him and not a bottle in sight, watching the cottage door and waiting, waiting like something ready to pounce.

'Where is Margaret?' Vassie said.

'I sent her home,' Ronan croaked. 'I am not needing a woman to be looking after me, not some chit of a girl, anyroads.'

'She is not a chit of a girl. She is a married woman.'

'Is she?' Ronan frowned. 'I do not think I knew that.'

'She is married to Naismith, Biddy's steward.'

'Aye,' Ronan said. 'Well, be that as it may, Vassie, will you not be telling me how much you have brought back with you? Is it so much that it has to be kept secret even from your own husband?'

He spoke, or imagined he spoke, with the old wheedling

softness, that sly, cajoling charm that once-upon-a-time had taken in folk, including Vassie, and had tricked them into believing that Ronan Campbell was just an honest fisherman with a tender heart. The voice, like the rest of him, was gone now, reduced by age and illness to a grating whisper. But the fact that he managed to speak at all, to string together not just one or two words but several coherent sentences filled Vassie with horror. Whatever molecule was active in the scent of money, it seemed that its effect upon the males of the Campbell clan was not just invigorating but miraculous.

Dressed in her shabby weeds, a black straw hat tethered to her hair, stockings soaked from the walk down from the track-end, Vassie for once found herself speechless.

She tried but could not form words in her mouth.

She had answered him initially out of habit. But when she stared at him again and realised that he really was propped there with his arm in its white plaster-cast resting on the table, drinking *tea* and talking, talking to her as if he had never been away she turned giddy with horror, and all the strength, spunk and gumption that had kept her going week after week, year after year drained away completely.

She experienced a little flash, not across her vision but deep inside her skull and then a strangely soothing warmth spread down her neck like hot oil. She fell sideways, caught herself with one hand on the table, bent her knees and, while Ronan watched dispassionately, laboured to hoist herself upright.

She must not show weakness.

She knew what he would do to her if she showed weakness.

Her jaws moved, chewing on the words, papping them down to a sort of mush so that she, not he, sounded intoxicated.

'What is wrong with you, woman?'

'Alve bun ta mal Dal's funnel.'

'Aye, and by the sound of you, you have been disposing of what was left of his brandy.' Ronan pushed the tea-mug towards her, nudging it with the plastered arm. 'Here, take some of this. It will help sober you up.'

Vassie swallowed the mush on her tongue. The giddiness was passing off. Tilting her head she stared at the rafters, at the lantern's flickering flame, then, groping, scraped out a chair and seated herself. She mewed a little, closed her fists, and by an effort of will managed to find her voice.

'Ma faller's – my father is dead.'

'Do you think I am deaf to all that has been going on?' Ronan said. 'I heard you plotting to go away to the funeral, leaving me here with just that bitch of a girl to look after me.'

'Your alm – arm?'

Ronan glanced at the white plaster and patted it as if it was a pet. Both hands trembled, though, and his head bobbed like a thistle on a stalk. He was barely more composed and coherent than she was, and conversation between them occurred in fits and starts as first the husband and then the wife strove to pretend that they were in full command of their faculties.

Vassie said, 'Do you remember what happened to your arm?'

'Bull. I fell – and Quig sent the bull at me?'

'Is it hlut – hurting you?'

'Where is his money, Vassie? What have you done with his money?'

'Hah! Did you think it would be buried on the beach and we would dig it up and share it out and be bringing it home in sacks like clams?'

'How much have we got?'

'We have got nothing.'

'Are you lying to me again?'

'I am not lying to you,' Vassie said. 'There is no money for any of us because he left a will and it will not be proven before the end of the month.'

'Proven?'

'It has to be doing with the law.'

'What law?'

'I do not know what law,' Vassie said. 'It is what I have been told and that is all I know about it. The lawyer will be coming to Biddy's house as soon as the will has been proven and we will be told all together what is to come to us.'

'What has to be proved? That you are McIver's daughter?'

'He has other children who may have a claim.'

'Who told you all this? Was it Quig?'

'It was not Quig. It is the law of property, Ronan.'

'We are being cheated.'

'No.'

'It is as well for you, Vassie McIver, that I am here to see you are not cheated out of your due. By God, I will be seeing that it comes to us at last.'

The tea had wetted his lips but the moisture had been instantly absorbed as if by sand or blotting-paper. His mouth looked dry and sticky. He ran his tongue around his teeth then licked his lips again, again and again. Head lowered, he flicked his eyes this way and that as if he could not quite believe that he was upright at a table, without a bottle close to hand.

His right hand shook violently now and he had sense enough to plant the plaster upon it and pin it down.

'Are you not wanting a drink, Ronan?' Vassie said.

'I-I have drink. I have – tea.'

'Whisky is what I am meaning.'

'Is there a bottle?'

'Six bottles, hidden away.'

'Ah, ah-nah!'

'Will I not be getting one for you?' she wheedled.

'Jesus!' His voice was so faint and grainy that Vassie could only just make out the question. 'How long will we have to wait for this bloody lawyer?'

'Weeks,' Vassie said. 'Months, for all I can be telling.'

'Jesus! Jesus!'

'Are you sick again, Ronan? Are you going to vomit?'

'Then Pennypol will be yours and you can sell it.'

She was shaking slightly, a faint, timid tremor of shoulders, neck and head that made it seem as if everything was agreeable to her.

She said, 'If I wish to.'

'Sell it to . . .' He strained for the name. 'To Biddy.'

'There will be no gain in that, Ronan. In selling, I mean.'

'Aye, but there is. I could be buying another boat with the money.'

'Another boat? And who would you be drowning this time?'

'Drowning?'

'Would you be drowning our second Donnie like you drowned the first?'

He scowled. 'Are you telling me Donnie is not dead?'

'Donnie. Aileen's son. Your son.'

'We could go away – with the money – go to . . .'

'I cannot hear what you are saying.'

'Weeks,' he said, shaking violently now.

'Uh-huh,' Vassie told him. 'Or months, perhaps.'

'I cannot . . .'

'If you are going to be up and about again I will need to be having that suit cleaned,' she said. 'And it would be doing no harm to have Angus Bell sharpen your cut-throat while we are about it.'

He dragged the plastered forearm from the table and drove it into the pit of his stomach, rocking back and forth, back and forth, his mouth agape and his eyes broad as saucers.

Vassie had no knowledge of how long her husband had been without alcohol or what effect deprivation would eventually have upon his wasted organs. She had listened with only half an ear to all the things that Dr Kirkhope had told her and had not stored them in her memory. Even if she had, she doubted if she would be able to recall them now for it seemed that her brain had become addled with the shock of finding Ronan Campbell up and about and lucid enough to know what was going on.

All these years, lost in drink, he had managed to cling to one futile aim and desire, to see Pennypol sold and to live a life of ease on the proceeds. It did not seem to have occurred to him that the pattern of his life had been set in stone and could never be altered, that the little turf-roofed, smoke-blackened cottage on the shore of Pennypol Bay had always been the best place for him and his demons.

'Are you sick? Do you want me to fetch you whisky?' she said.

'No,' he growled, still rocking. 'No, I do not.'

'You will die without it, Ronan.'

His tongue flickered like an adder's. He peered at her, his face grotesquely contorted, as if his muscles had already begun to adjust themselves to new, inflexible, whiskyless shapes. Sticky little hinges of phlegm whitened the corners of his lips. 'Where is the stuff, the stuff you give me when I hurt?' he said.

'Whisky?'

'The doctor's stuff. Give me the doctor's stuff.'

'Oh, we have none of that left.' Vassie said.

She pushed herself up from the chair, the room spinning. She held on to the table, focused on the lamp, crossed the kitchen to the cupboard above the dresser, opened it and took down a bottle of Old Caledonia and a glass. She crabbed back to the table and placed the bottle and glass before him.

'We have this, however,' she said.

He continued to peer at her, arms pressed into his belly, hands locked out of sight. He would not give in, not while she was there. He had just enough manliness, enough stubborn pride left not to capitulate while she watched.

'Drink up, dear,' Vassie said, smiling, and went outside to feed the dogs.

What a spell of weather ushered November in. Gales and heavy rains kept the Fetternish folk skulking indoors save when necessity drove them out to tend stock, draw water or rifle the peat stack.

Innis was eager to attend mass in the chapel in Glenarray and say prayers for her grandfather, but Sunday was so wild that she decided to leave the children at home with Michael and, in a borrowed cart, went alone to the evening celebration in Tobermory. To her disappointment she found that Father Gunnion had been struck down with a quinsy throat and Father Rosmire, the young priest who had been sent in his stead, had been so overwhelmed by the voyage from Oban that he had not recovered even by Sunday evening and had fumbled through the mass in a distracted way that had pleased none of the parishioners who had scuttled through the rain to receive blessing.

Throughout the week Gillies Brown and most of the Fetternish children were conveyed to and from school in a big, covered wagonette drawn by a strong horse and driven by no less a personage than old Mr Bell. Each dark morning Michael escorted Rachel and Gavin to the crossroads to be picked up and each afternoon, in driving rain, they came racing down the track and over the bridge at the Solitudes by themselves and Innis, indoors, saw nothing of her sister, her mother or her friend, Gillies Brown.

Cut off from company for the whole of the week and pinned, pining, on Pennymain by the unrelenting rain, come Sunday she almost wished that she was a Protestant again so that she might join her sister and the Brown family at morning service in Crove. Tom Ewing would not object if she turned up to hear him preach, of course, but she had experienced too much prejudice in the village to risk creating trouble for the minister. Besides, her sole reason for wishing to join the congregation in Crove was selfish and had nothing to do with a desire to worship God. She missed Gillies Brown; that was the long and short of it. She longed to see his cheerful, none-too-handsome face again, to hear his voice, to note the pleasure in his eyes when he greeted her.

She had been trapped on Pennymain with Michael and the children for what seemed like an eternity and had seen nothing of Gillies since the day before her grandfather's funeral. Her isolation felt more acute – almost ridiculously acute – than ever before for even with Michael going on at her about the will, even with his new-found attentiveness and his spurious attempts at affection, she was not comforted.

At any time she might have wrapped herself up and forged across the hill to Pennypol to exchange words with her mother, might have battled up the familiar track to Fetternish House to take tea with Biddy or, failing that, to sit in the warm basement kitchen and chat with Willy and his wife. But such excursions held no appeal and, she knew, would not soothe the hurt within her, that strange, intricate tangle of emotions in which grief and guilt were no longer as dominant as they should have been.

While Michael waited impatiently for word of the reading of the will, Innis waited only for that time when she would see Gillies Brown again, that moment when he would raise his brows and smile at her and she would feel wanted, valued, in a way that defied rational explanation.

In the lowering hours of late afternoon, when dampness and cold made everything so miserable, she would think of the Browns and wonder what they did with themselves in the long dark evenings, wonder what sort of a home they had fashioned out on the point of An Fhearann Cáirdeil. She had never been inside their cottage, had never had the temerity to 'drop in' uninvited, as she believed Biddy did from time to time.

In the weeks after the Foss funeral, however, she was sorely tempted to start out with a lantern for the lonely headland, to knock upon the cottage door and surprise them, to be brought in and made welcome by the schoolmaster's children, fussed over by the schoolmaster himself. But she could not do it. She could not bring herself to lie to Michael, to betray him by yielding to the inexplicable urge to share with Gillies Brown all the doubts that had come upon her lately and to acknowledge, through him, that she was not truly loved.

It was not so far to Tobermory as it was to Glenarray nor was the road quite so wild and inhospitable. It was still a far piece, however, with several steep hills to negotiate, the wind so fierce off the moors that even the sturdy Fetternish pony laboured and Innis now and then would draw in by the roadside to give it a breather. There were no oil-filled lamps upon the dogcart, only two hurricane lanterns stuck out on stout poles, the candle-power too weak to illumine more than a yard or two of the road surface and the night too dark for the pony to make any speed at all.

Crofts and cottages passed at a snail's pace, bridges and rushing streams. Innis could see little against the dense, starless sky and the blobs of rain that fell, whirling, out of the lantern light. She was dry enough in the dogcart with the stiff canvas hood cowled, shuddering, about her, warm enough too with a couple of shawls and a blanket wrapped around her knees. Even so, she knew that she had erred in making a late trip to the distant town and vowed that, come what may, next month would see her back at Glenarray.

It was well after eight o'clock before Innis glimpsed the lights of Crove below her, too wan and scattered to give much cheer. Besides, she still had another three miles to go before she reached home. She would not leave the dogcart at the stables tonight. She would ask Michael to stable the pony in the lambing shed at Pennymain and return the rig to Fetternish first thing tomorrow. She passed the first of Crove's churches, Tom Ewing's charge, and entered the deserted main street. Evening service was over, the congregation dispersed. There was a light in the manse window and she was teased by a notion that she might call in upon the minister, surprise her old friend and cadge supper from him. But although she liked to think of herself as bold, like Biddy, she was by nature too conservative to surrender to that impulse.

She rode on past the ill-lit cottages, past the McKinnon Arms, Sabbath-shuttered and dismally dark, past the iron gate of the Free Church, barred and padlocked as if in fear that someone would want to break in. The pony found a second wind and increased its pace. And if he had been another fifty or a hundred yards along the Fetternish road she might have missed him altogether, might have driven past him in the dark. Then nothing would have happened, and their friendship might simply have petered out before spring came round again.

'Gillies?' Innis called out in astonishment. 'Mr Brown?'

Apparently he had been walking homeward when the approach of the dogcart had brought him to a halt by the very last of the cottages. His greeny-yellow oilskin was just visible against the whitewashed wall. He had a bag on a strap across one shoulder. When he pushed back the hood of the cape she saw that he was wearing his Sunday-best hat, a rather silly little bowler that sat just too snugly on his head. He had button boots on his feet and had tucked his trouser-legs into his stockings so that he looked, Innis thought, like a travelling player costumed for Shakespeare.

She reined the pony to a halt.

Gillies swept off the bowler and gave her a bow. 'Madam,' he said. 'You're a Godsend, if ever I saw one.'

'Fetternish, sir?'

'Aye, the crossroads, if you please.'

He climbed up beside her, close beside her, and settled the bag on his lap.

'What on earth are you doing here at this time of night?' Innis said.

'I might ask the same thing of you.'

'I have been to chapel in Tobermory.'

'Well, I've been to church in Crove – twice, as a matter of fact. So there!'

The pony stood motionless in the shafts, sawing a little. Innis did not rush to start it forward. The pines that marked the tail of the Fetternish road tossed strenuously in the wind. She knew this road, every step of it, and the pony did too. She might, if she wished, snuff out the lanterns and let the little animal carry them home in darkness, snug and secure, as if, Innis thought, they were tucked up in a bed together, a travelling bed, and their meeting was more dream than reality.

'Actually,' Gillies said, 'I've been in Crove all day. I attended the morning service with the children, then Janetta took them home while I did some work in the schoolroom.'

'Was it not cold?'

'I lit the stove.'

'What sort of work?'

'Oh, this and that. Bringing the school log up to date. Preparing questions for the first of the Merit Certificate examinations.'

'Could you not be doing that at home?'

'It's not so easy at home, not with the youngsters milling about.'

'And a dog,' said Innis.

'Oh, yes, and a dog.' Gillies said. 'The minister was kind enough to give me tea. He's a good man, is Tom Ewing – but I expect you know that already?'

'I do,' said Innis. 'What did you talk about? Religion?'

The tops of the pine trees raged in the wind. The pony snorted and stamped, not impatiently. Innis could see herself reflected in the oval lenses of the schoolmaster's eye-glasses, tiny and pale, like a faded miniature. She felt oddly breathless, oddly afraid.

Something is about to happen to me, she thought. *Wait. Wait.*

'We talked about you,' Gillies said.

She did not flutter, did not pretend that she was flattered, did not cry out, 'Me? What could you possibly have to say about me?' She watched him. He was frowning too now, as puzzled as she was, perhaps, by a coincidence that may not have been a coincidence at all but might have been decreed by someone or something that neither of them understood.

'I see,' she said, softly. 'Did Tom tell you?'

'That he was in love with you and wanted to marry you? Yes.'

'Did he tell you why he did not marry me?'

'He thought you were too young for him,' Gillies said. 'No, that's not the whole truth, Innis. I believe he thought that he wasn't good enough for you.'

'Until I married a shepherd, until I married Michael.'

'Tom isn't in love with you now, if that's what you mean.' Gillies said. 'Well, perhaps that's another white lie. Perhaps he is but just won't admit it.'

'Why are you telling me these things?'

'I'm just answering your question.'

'No,' Innis said. 'Men do not talk about their feelings in such a free and easy manner. I think, Mr Brown, that you are making it up.'

'Why would I do that?' Gillies asked.

'I do not know.'

He leaned his forearms on the book-bag, took off his eye-glasses and wiped them assiduously on a clean cotton hand-kerchief. He put the glasses on again and the handkerchief away in his pocket. In the minute or so that it took to perform these actions Innis remained silent. She waited for him to hint that she should move on, that he was anxious to be home, to see his children, to eat the supper that Janetta would have cooking, but he did not. He sighed.

'There's no pulling the wool over your eyes, is there, Innis?'

he said, at length. 'Tom and I did talk about you, for whatever you may think to the contrary, men do discuss their feelings now and then.'

Innis said, 'I am married. Tom knows that, and he would not do anything to insult or offend me. He would not . . .' At a loss, she shook her head.

'Certainly not. Tom wouldn't forget himself,' Gillies said.

'Do you mean that *you* would?'

'I don't mean that at all. I admit, though, that I have had you on my mind. In fact, I was thinking about you when I heard the wheels come up the street behind me. For a minute there I wondered if I'd conjured you up out of thin air just by wishing.'

'What *did* Tom tell you about me?'

'He warned me to be careful.'

'Careful of me?' said Innis.

'Careful of myself, of becoming too – too enamoured.'

Innis said, 'Did he not think to warn you about my sister?'

'No, no, no. That would've been quite unnecessary.'

'Biddy is all the things that I am not,' Innis said. 'And what is more she is free and unencumbered and – did Tom not tell you? – would not be averse to marrying again if the right man came along.'

'Aye, Tom told me all that too.'

'I fancy Tom may have half a mind to propose to Biddy himself.'

'Don't you listen, Innis?' the schoolmaster said. 'Don't you hear what I'm saying? What I'm saying has nothing to do with Biddy, whether she's pretty, whether she's wealthy, whether she's after a husband or whether she's not. I'm not attracted to your sister, Innis. I'm attracted to you.'

'I think we should be going on now,' Innis said.

'I think perhaps we should,' said Gillies.

He had no notion of time, no awareness that it was growing late and that his mother had not returned from Tobermory. He had not lifted himself from the blanket by the hearth since the supper dishes had been cleared, at least not high enough to see the brass-faced clock on the mantel. He could hear the quick little tick-tick-tick of the mechanism, like a hurrying heartbeat, when he thought to listen for it but it seemed to do no more than add to the cosiness of the kitchen.

He had lain belly down on the blanket that his father had tossed him while his sisters had whined and snivelled and, even after they had washed at the basin and had gone and put on their night-gowns and had come out again, still whimpering and whining, he had refused to stir himself and they had been forced to step over him to badger Dad to give them hugs and sit with them because, being girls, they were afraid of the dark back room and, so they said, just wanted Mammy to come home again.

Gavin did not care if Mammy never came home. He was content to lie by the hearth at his Dad's feet, enveloped in the smell of the peat smoke, the smell of the whisky that his father had poured for himself and tobacco from the pipe that his father smoked. Content to hear his sisters still whimpering in the back room and the whine of the dog, the soft-bodied, floppy, useless pup, that Dad had lifted on to the bed to shut them up.

He had spent most of Sunday out of doors, not with Dad, though, for Dad had done nothing but tour the ewe field and come home again. He had been out all day despite the weather. He liked the rain and the wind. Bare-legged, with a coat tied over his head and shoulders, he had gone as far as An Fhearann Cáirdeil and had lain up in the gorse to see if he could see any of them. But they had not been there and the cottage had been deserted. So he had gone back to the ridge that looked down on his aunt's house and had seen the wagonette come back from Crove and Donnie Campbell and Mrs Baverstock and the Browns go into the house by the front door, and he had lain for a long time in the bracken, watching, until he was sure that the Browns were not coming out again.

Then he had run home to Pennymain. He had eaten his dinner quickly and had gone hurrying out again, although his Mammy had shouted, 'No, Gavin, no. Have you not had enough for one day?' He had gone down to the top of the shore but no further. He hated the sea when it ran at him all white and clawing. He had checked the snares he'd set a week ago and found a rabbit caught by the leg. It was dead, though, and something had eaten away half its head. He had thrown the corpse on to the beach and had watched the gulls come in off the waves and feed on it. If he'd had a gun he could easily have picked off the big, grey-winged birds by sighting on their eyes.

Then, in the dusk, he had come home again, had found Mammy gone, and the girls girning. He'd dried himself with his Dad's shaving towel and had eaten his supper. Then he'd taken out the pile of tattered journals that Barrett had loaned him and had started leafing through them, reading a bit here, a bit there, looking at the pictures mainly, pictures of pirates with curved pistols, buffalo hunters with long, spindly rifles, African explorers potting at lions.

Gavin had no grasp of the continuity of narrative, however thrilling, and did not understand the rooftop escapades in which men hung from ropes and other men in capes shouted at them. He was grateful to Barrett for lending him the hoard of cheap magazines, though. Grateful to his mother for not being there so that he might read them without her disapproval. Grateful for his father's presence in the chair, glass in hand, pipe in mouth. Grateful for the rush and roar of the wind and peat glowing hot in the hearth; the luxury of enjoying a languor that was not sleepiness but another sort of pleasure that came upon him when he contemplated the depictions of the guns.

'Gavin,' his father said.

He rolled over on to an elbow and looked up at his Dad; a huge foot in a woollen stocking, a calf, a knee and then, beyond it, his father's face. The unfamiliar angle made his father seem larger than life. He lowered the copy of the *Argyll Advertiser* that he had been reading. The newspaper made more planes and angles across his knees.

'Do you know what time it is?' his Dad said.

'No.'

'Past your bedtime.'

He blinked. 'Where's Mammy?'

The enormous foot waggled and his father's head turned. He looked up at the shelf above the fireplace, at the clock. 'I don't know where she is. It's late and she should have been home an hour ago.'

Gavin, uninterested, turned on to his stomach and drew the last of Barrett's adventure magazines from the bundle.

'Did you not hear me, Gavin? Bed.'

Gavin said, 'She could be at the house.'

'Were you at the house today?'

'Aye.'

His father rustled the newspaper and leaned down, leaning over his knees so that his face and the broad sole of the stocking seemed to be on the same level.

'Did you see Bid – Mrs Baverstock?'

'I did. Her, and the others.'

'What others?'

'Browns.'

'Back from church?'

'In the long waggon, aye.'

'Who brought the dogcart down for your mother?'

'Nobody that I was seeing. I think she went to the stables to collect it.'

Dad slipped from the chair, discarded the newspaper and, kneeling, stroked a hand across Gavin's hair as if he was a collie or a cat. Gavin shivered. He did not like being touched, not even by his father. He shifted away. Drawing his legs up, he turned on the pivot of his hip. His cheeks were flushed with the heat of the fire and sweat prickled his back and legs.

He said, 'They all went into the big house and did not come out again.'

'Who went into the big house, son?'

'Aunt Baverstock, Donnie Campbell, Miss Janetta and the others.'

'Mr Brown too?'

'Not Mr Brown. Mr Brown was not with them.'

His father rested his shoulder against the edge of the chair. It did not seem a manly sort of position, more like one his mother would take when she was drying Becky after a bath, or when she thought she was alone. Gavin did not know why but he did not like having his father on the same level as himself. He got up. He looked down on his Dad.

He said, 'Perhaps Mammy is at the house too.'

'Maybe that's where she is, yes.'

'Perhaps Mammy is with Mr Brown.'

'What makes you say that, Gavin?'

'Because she meets him after the school.'

'In Crove?'

It was untrue and Gavin knew that it was untrue. He did not pause to consider the implications of his answer, though, nor was there malice or mischief behind it, only an innocent need to please his father.

'Yes, in Crove.'

'Do you not mean at the crossroads when she meets Rachel?'

'No, in Crove,' said Gavin, nodding.

His father gazed into the heart of the peat-fire for a moment then picked the pipe from the arm of the chair and tapped his teeth with it. He was still hunched in a unseemly position, knees drawn in, one shoulder resting against the chair. 'Is it not Aunt Baverstock who goes to Crove to meet Mr Brown?'

'No.'

'Are you sure, Gavin?'

'I have never seen Aunt Baverstock there.'

'Rachel and Becky, what does Mammy do with them?'

'They go with Miss Janetta,' Gavin said. 'She takes them away.'

He was dimly aware that he was being drawn into a lie, a lie that had become more complicated than he had intended. He did not look at his father's face now but down at the journals strewn at his feet, yellowing paper curling in the heat from the fire. He could see a picture of a man with a rifle, a slender-barrelled rifle, longer than Mr McCallum's. The stock was pressed against the man's shoulder and in the bushes ahead of him was a black man wearing nothing but a cloth at his waist and a string of beads. A little spurt of smoke hung on the barrel of the rifle and the direction of the bullet darting through the air was traced out by tiny broken lines.

'Were you out at the farm today too?' his father asked.

'Yes, in the forenoon.'

'Mr Brown, was he there?'

Gavin shook his head.

His father placed the pipe in the hearth and got up.

He moved slowly, almost stiffly. Gavin wondered if he had caught something from one of the sheep, the staggering disease that knobbled them and made them fall to their knees. Then his father was upright, not sick after all, not angry but quite himself again and back on his proper level.

'Go to bed,' he said. 'Take your books if you like. I'll light the wee lamp and you can read until your mother comes home.'

'Where is she?' said Gavin. 'Is she lost?'

'I doubt it, son,' his father said and, stooping, helped Gavin gather up the lurid journals from the floor.

By the time Michael had made space in the lambing shed, had put down straw, groomed and fed the pony and had covered Biddy's dogcart with a tarpaulin, Innis had settled the girls to sleep at last and was warming up stew for her supper. She had taken off her hat and put it away in the box, had hung her travelling coat on the rack and had removed her shoes and stockings and placed the shoes neatly side by side on the edge of the hearth.

She padded about the kitchen barefoot like a child, a stealthy child, making almost no noise with the pans, spoons and crockery.

Michael did not resent being asked to put up the pony.

Innis had done the sensible thing, riding down the long track to Pennymain instead of walking in from the stables. Innis always did the sensible thing, the intelligent thing. It was one of the facets of her character that he most disliked. She had even carried the dog, Fruarch, out from the back room and had put him into his basket with a little hank of mutton to keep him chewing until he too fell asleep.

Michael seated himself by the fire and took up the newspaper.

She ladled stew, steaming and savoury, into a bowl, cut bread into thick slices and, seated at the table, began to eat hungrily, mopping up the gravy with the bread. Mid-way through her meal she got up, took the kettle from its hook, poured boiling water into the teapot and brought the pot to the table.

'Do you want some, Michael?' she asked.

He lowered the newspaper and stared at her as if she had just crept out of the wainscot. 'I'll take a cup, to keep you company.'

'Let it infuse for a bit first.' Innis went back to eating from the bowl.

He waited, then said, 'Did you go to Glenarray after all?'

'Why would I be going to Glenarray when there is no service there in the evening? I went to Tobermory.'

'You were gone for a long time.'

'Father Gunnion is ill.'

'What? Taken ill at the service?'

'No, he was too ill to make the crossing, poor man. The mass was conducted by another priest; Father Rosmire.'

'Did he hear your confession?'

She ate, then said, 'Yes.'

'Is that what took you so long – making your confession?'

He expected her to turn and frown, to be puzzled by the question and the barb in it. Instead she kept her back towards him and said, quickly, 'I do not know what you mean.'

'Did you call in at the house then?'

'House?'

'Call in on Biddy on your way home?'

'No.'

'On someone else?'

'Who would I be calling on after mass on a Sunday night?'

'We thought you'd got lost, Gavin and I.'

'I – no, I did not get lost. I had to rest the pony, however, for the wind was so big against us coming up past the Mishnish Lochs that . . .'

'Did you also rest the pony in Crove?'

'Michael, what . . .'

'I thought you might have met someone you knew, that's all.'

'Now who would I be meeting in Crove on a Sunday night?'

'Tom Ewing, perhaps.'

'Well, I did not.'

'Or Gillies Brown.'

'Gillies Brown?' Innis said. 'No. No one.'

And Michael knew that she was lying to him yet again and wondered, without passion, why.

The reading of Evander McIver's will would take place at half-past two o'clock in Fetternish House on the second Saturday in the month of November. Relative parties were notified by letter from the offices of Dollan, Forsythe and Aitchinson, solicitors, in Perth. The letters were very flowery, rendered in a legal language that had Innis scratching her head and that Vassie could not decipher at all without her daughter's aid. What it boiled down to, however, was simple enough: turn up at the feeding box and see what was in it for you.

Down at Pennypol Ronan Campbell climbed out of his stupor once more and began the process of drying himself out to be ready for the great occasion. On Pennymain Michael Tarrant went quiet again, retreating not into surliness or suspicion, however, but into a smug and confident mood that worried Innis considerably. At Fetternish House there was too much going on for Biddy to fret about the disbursement of her esteemed grandfather's bit-and-bobs or who might benefit most from the bequests. Fortunately she had Willy's shoulder to lean on when it came to making arrangements. And she had also received by post a certain item of information that excited her more than the reading of the will but which she kept, mischievously, to herself.

On Foss Robert Quigley prepared himself to act as nominated executor by battening down the hatches on the old wooden house and driving all the remaining cattle into the sheltered pastures under the crown of the hill. On Saturday morning, early, a hired ferryboat would come out from Ulva and carry the Quigleys, mother and son, and Aileen Campbell across to Mull, and for the first time in almost half a century Foss would be without a herdsman and the cattle, and the ghosts, would have the island all to themselves.

Saturday morning was grey and scudding, with spits of rain on the wind and snow already dusting the heights of the Cuillins and the summit of Ben More but the hired boat from Ulva ferry made the crossings to and from Foss without a hitch. Steamer passage up the sheltered Sound of Mull to Tobermory was equally comfortable for Mr Forsythe who, as it happened, was no wispy old man but a burly little chap in his thirties with a manner so brisk and pugnacious that he might have made a career in the boxing ring rather than the law.

He had spent Friday night in Oban's most salubrious hotel on the Corran Esplanade, no more than a hundred yards from the dingy little boarding-house in which one of his clients reposed. And he had climbed the gangplank of the *Dalriada* directly in front of the man without recognising him, though there was no reason why he should since Neil Campbell, Glasgow shipwright, and Stephen Forsythe, Perth solicitor, had never met before and, after that day was over, would never meet again.

If it had not been for the size of the man it is doubtful if Willy Naismith would have recognised Innis's brother either, for years of labour in the yards had marked Neil indelibly. He was still tall and bulky but no longer the fresh-faced youth that Willy recalled and the innocence, the daftness, had gone from him, buffed away by the responsibilities of marriage and fatherhood and earning his daily bread. He had a firm, dour mouth and a guarded look in his blue eyes that indicated that he was no longer a fool and would not be taken in by sentiment. He was here only because it might profit him and for no other reason. He would take what he was given and ask for no more, but he would give nothing of himself in return.

He shook hands with Willy, shook hands with the solicitor, and climbed into the back of the Fetternish dogcart with an air of resignation as if he would rather be anywhere but back on Mull.

'Did Biddy get my letter?' he asked, after a while.

'She did,' Willy answered. 'She's looking forward to seeing you again after – what is it? – twelve . . .'

'Thirteen.'

'Thirteen years.'

'Will my mother be at the house?'

'Certainly, she will,' Willy told him.

'And him – my father?'

'No, he's far too ill to go anywhere.'

'Good,' Neil said, nodding curtly; then said again, 'That's good.'

There were tears, of course, copious tears, first from Biddy and then from Innis, but none at all from Neil who seemed more irritated than embarrassed by such shows of emotion. He was encased in black serge, in the three-piece suit that he wore to St Anne's church most Sunday mornings and to meetings of the Greenfield Orange Lodge throughout the week.

The suit was his most prized possession, along with a Masonic pocket-watch and a silver-plated cigarette case that his father-in-law had given him to celebrate his Third Degree. Brushed and pressed by his wife, the formal black suit lent him dignity and, he believed, separated him from the callous ruck with whom, day in, day out, he worked. It was the suit that held him together now, that stiffened his backbone and kept his temper and his tears in check while he sat at his sister's table and ate his sister's food and, later, loitered by the fireplace in the hall drinking his sister's whisky while he waited tensely for his mother to arrive. But she did not, as Naismith had predicted, come alone.

He was with her.

He too wore a black suit, but it was stained and rumpled and hung on his bones like a rag.

They were watching, all watching. Both his sisters, Tarrant the shepherd, the young man who had his brother's name but was not his brother's son.

Neil put down the whisky glass and walked forward to greet her. He did not know what she saw, and did not much care. He was not out to impress anyone, not even his mother. What he saw, however, ripped into his heart like a hook. She was old now, old and withered. He realised that while he had been growing up she had been growing old. He had expected her to be the same, small and quick and severe and he had prepared himself to deal with her on those terms. But those terms, he saw at once, were obsolete and he resented the change in his mother almost as much as he resented Biddy's high-falutin' manner and improved circumstances. He felt – disappointed in her.

She swayed, squinted at him, and uttered his name.

'Neil?'

'Aye, Mam, it's me.'

'Neil, is it you?' She spoke differently too, not sharply but hesitantly and with the trace of a slur.

Crowding behind her, his father said, 'Who is it?'

'It is Neil. Do you not see, it is our Neil.'

'What is he doing here?'

Neil put his arm about the woman. He could smell Pennypol, that rich, sour smell of cattle and cooking, of peat and dogs and whisky, and the odour of her body too, dry and arid as old straw. He hugged her with one arm and felt her sag against him, limp at first and then, in an instant, stiffening. He was not moved by anything much except shame, and a certain rage that it had come to this, that she had been so soon reduced to this caricature.

He felt his father paw at him, groping for recognition.

His father should not have been here at all. His father should have been lying dormant in the bed on Pennypol, passive as a kipper in a box. Everything that Biddy had written him about his father was true. He was a man more dead than alive. Nothing about him seemed to be alive, nothing except the fiery, calculating eyes in the cadaverous face. Greed in a man never dies, Neil thought as he stepped hastily away, even up to the last pitiful, pathetic gasp.

He saw the hand groping for his, the crooked smile, the rotted teeth and hollow cheeks and he stepped away again, back to the table, lifted the whisky glass and drank from it while his father, shuffling after him, stared now not at his long-lost son but at the liquor, stared at it greedily, tongue flicking in and out like an adder's, his scrawny throat working on a dry swallow.

Vassie said, 'Did you not know that he was coming, Biddy?'

'Yes, but I thought that it would be a nice surprise for you.'

'I should have been told,' Vassie said.

Innis had taken her by the arm and led her across the hall to one of the big leather chairs, helped her down. She, Vassie, moved slowly, her head turning to stare at Neil, never letting Neil out of her sight.

'Innis, did you know?'

'No, Mam,' Innis said. 'I was surprised too. Is it not good to see him again, though, and how well he looks?'

'Where is he?' Vassie said, peering.

'I am here,' Neil said.

'I am meaning – where is *he*?'

Ronan grunted and swung from the waist and waved his fist. He had leaned the plastered wrist upon the long table as if the decanters there were magnetic and he was drawn to them like a piece of rusty iron.

'I am here too, old woman, never fear. You will not be getting rid of me so easily,' Ronan said. 'I have come to hear for myself what is going on and what you will be getting out of all this.'

'Oh,' Biddy said. 'Is that the reason, Dada?'

'I will not be letting her cheat me,' Ronan said.

'No one is trying to cheat you,' Neil said.

'What would you be knowing about it?' Ronan said, with a little snarl that gave his voice strength. 'You who ran away and deserted us in our time of need. Do think that I have forgotten how you left us grieving for your brother, and him just dead and buried? How it was that you – you abandoned me to . . .' He took in breath and let it out again. 'To . . .' He shook his head, wiped his lips on his sleeve. '. . . without – without even a boat to be calling my own.'

Neil said, 'I did not lose your boat for you. I was not the one who drowned Donnie.' He seemed about to say more, to be lured into accusation and denial. Then he stopped himself. He tugged at the waistcoat, adjusting it over his lean belly and deftly extracted his pocket-watch. He stared at the engraving, the Masonic emblems, for a moment and then clicked open the case, consulted the dial. 'It is nearly half-past two o'clock now,' he said. 'I'm hoping this will not be taking too long for I have to be on the steamer at half-past five.'

'Are you going back tonight?' said Innis.

'There is a train out of Oban at twenty minutes past seven.'

'I thought – we thought,' Biddy said, 'that you would be staying.'

'Well, I'm not,' Neil said. 'I've a family to take care of and it's bad enough that I had to forgo two days' work just to come here. I am not for staying any longer than I can help. So where is that lawyer mannie and why can we not get on with it?'

'We are waiting for Quig,' said Biddy.

'Quig?' Neil frowned. 'From Foss?'

'He has to be here,' Mr Forsythe said. 'He is, after all, the appointed executor of Mr McIver's will and, according to documents drawn up some years since, he is legally empowered to act on behalf of Aileen Campbell and her son, Donald, although only in financial matters since the woman's parents are both still extant.'

'Extant?' said Ronan.

'Alive,' said young Mr Forsythe, with an apologetic shrug as if the matter was perhaps open to interpretation.

At that moment Quig and Aileen appeared from the direction of the kitchen stairs. The young woman was dressed in an old-fashioned, close-fitting dolman with, incongruously, a tam-o'-shanter on her head. She had a cheek full of currants and Quig, with the corner of a handkerchief, wiped a trickle of juicy dribble from her chin an instant before she darted, beaming, into the great hall and ran straight to her brother, crying out his name like a little gull, 'Neil, Neil, Neil, Neil,' and flung herself into his arms.

All business and quite oblivious to the affecting scene before him, Mr Forsythe plucked his document case from the table and, gesturing towards the drawing-room, said, 'Well now, ladies and gentlemen, I think we are about ready to begin.'

It was not unusual for the minister to drop into Miss Fergusson's shop at the nether end of the main street from time to time for, in the absence of a village pump, there was no better place in Crove to meet his parishioners.

In addition to a fondness for dessert wines and small cigars Tom Ewing had lately developed quite a partiality to strongly-flavoured sweetmeats and would sniff away at the sample jars that Miss Fergusson laid out for him before he made his purchase of clove candy, Parma Violets and a fire-proof tin of Uncle Stan's Hot Cinnamon Balls. Who 'Uncle Stan' was or what grudge he harboured against the human race Tom Ewing had no idea. But the balls were hot all right, so hot that just one tucked under the tongue would send a seismic shockwave through the system and flavour one's disposition for the rest of the day.

Freda Thrale, the estate manager's wife, accepted one from the minister's tin but as soon as she left the shop spat it out on to the grass. Elsie MacDonald, the Clarks' housekeeper, was not so prudent. She decided that swallowing the ball whole would be the safest way of protecting her mucous membranes and was consequently in process of being revived with sips of soda water and pats on the back when Mairi Quigley entered the shop.

She made no fuss, no grand entrance. Even so the sight of her there in the narrow doorway was enough to arrest Elsie's choking fit at once and distract Miss Fergusson and Tom Ewing from their healing ministrations.

She was dressed to the nines in a blouse, bolero and flared skirt, with a flat boa around her neck, gauntlet gloves and a hat, not a bonnet, so ornate and supple that it quivered with every little movement of her head. She wore her hair short to show her ears and her ear-rings. Anything less like a cattleman's mother would have been hard to imagine. She looked – Tom groped for a comparison – like a Spanish gypsy, not the kind who sold fortunes in the Dundee market or travelled on the back of onion-sellers' donkeys round the streets of Oban but the kind who danced on tables clicking castanets and brought brave bullfighters to their knees with their wild and fickle ways.

Admittedly Mairi Quigley did not behave as if she were wild or fickle. She was as demure in manner as she was garish in appearance and waited quietly by the door while Elsie was hoisted back on to her feet and, with a final pat from the pastor, sent outside for a breath of air.

'Ah, Miss – Mrs . . .' Tom began.

'I think you may be calling me Mairi, Mr Ewing,' the woman said.

Miss Fergusson drew in her breath in a little hiss that signified shock and disapproval and scuttled to safety behind the counter. She was, Tom thought, probably appalled that he even knew the gypsy woman let alone had the temerity to accept an invitation to call her by name.

'And what are you doing in Crove, if I may ask?' he said.

'I have come with Robert who is at the big house for the reading of the old man's will,' Mairi answered. 'But it is not for me to intrude upon the family and so I have come down to the village instead to buy ribbon and pass the time.'

'We have no ribbon here,' said Miss Fergusson from behind the scales. 'It will have to be Tobermory if it is ribbon you are after.'

'Miss Fergusson,' Tom said, finally remembering his manners, 'may I introduce Mrs Quigley from the island of Foss. She is, I believe, a distant cousin of Mrs Baverstock's.'

Miss Fergusson sniffed and, if he had not been a man of the cloth, might have accused him of fabricating the truth. 'Even so,' she said, 'we have no ribbon here, none as would be suiting the likes of – of this person.'

Mairi smiled. She had painted her lips and her teeth seemed very white and strong against the rosy colouring. Tom could not tear his gaze from her, from the painted lips and dark glittering eyes that – did he imagine it? – were sizing him up with equal interest.

She was nothing like Biddy, nothing remotely like Innis, yet he felt something of the same rapport with her that he had with Vassie Campbell's daughters whom he had known for

251

half a lifetime. But she, Mairi Quigley, was everything that a respectable, set-in-his-ways parish minister should have abhorred – gay, garish, vulgar and irresistibly confident. Most important of all, she was no chick, no gosling, but a woman almost as mature as he was himself, a factor that he could not ignore.

'Mairi,' he said, 'would you like a sweetie?'

'I'd love a sweetie,' Mairi Quigley said.

'They are very strong.'

'My favourite kind.'

Tom prised open the lid of the tin and offered it to her. She shook her head and held up her gloved hands.

'You give me one,' she said.

She opened her mouth and closed her eyes. Tom placed a cinnamon ball on her plump tongue and, with his heart beating faster than it had done in years, watched the sweet disappear. She sucked noisily.

'Good?' Tom asked.

'Very, very good,' Mairi answered, and stuck out her tongue for more.

Willy had had Maggie trim his hair and beard before breakfast, had dressed in his tartan trews and military-style cutaway and had donned with them his best butler manner to add a touch of distinction to the gathering in the house. Guest bedrooms had been aired and fired and preparations for dinner had been put under way, very early by Cook, and so by the time the mistress and her guests repaired to the drawing-room for the main event Willy was ready to sit down for half an hour and put his feet up.

Maggie had made coffee, a large pot, and she, Cook and Donnie were with Willy in the kitchen, drinking coffee and munching Dundee cake when suddenly the bell on the board above the door jangled.

It had been months since the automatic bell had stirred into life, for Biddy preferred to summon her servants personally or, if that was not convenient, by using a little handbell that seemed less distant and imperious than the wired contraption that connected public rooms to servants' quarters. But it was the automatic bell that rang that afternoon, jerking and twitching, fast and furious, so that Willy was up out of his chair, Maggie with him, and the pair of them were off upstairs *tout de suite*.

'What can they be wanting now?' Queenie said, thrusting herself up from her chair and heading for the pans that were steaming on the stove. 'I just hope it is not their dinners. Donald, will you be going upstairs to see what the commotion is all about and to let me know what is going on?'

'Perhaps they have finished their business?'

'In less than twenty minutes?' the Cook said. 'Never,' and, gesturing with a wooden spoon, sent the boy trotting off upstairs in Willy's wake.

Ronan was first out. Blind with rage, he barged through the doors of the drawing-room with a show of force that Lear might have envied. Behind him the rest of the legatees remained frozen in astonishment at his sudden, furious outburst. Only Biddy had the sense to leap from her chair and tug on the bell pull to summon assistance from below.

Roused by his shouting the dogs, who had been locked in the gun-room, began to bay mournfully and by the time Willy and Maggie arrived in the hall the scene was one of confusion. Ronan had hurled himself against the Jacobean table, scattering glasses and decanters in every direction. He was sick, mad with rage, and howling like a hound. He danced up and down among the shards of broken glass, jabbering, 'Nothing. We have got nothing. He has given us nothing. I have waited thirty years for nothing. Wasted. Wasted. Wasted my life on her for nothing.' And then went off into a great skirl in Gaelic that no one, not even Vassie, could understand.

'What is it? What's happened?' Willy asked.

Biddy told him, 'He thought there would be money, and there is none.'

'None for him, you mean,' Willy said.

'None for him,' Michael Tarrant said. 'And precious little for any of us.'

'Mrs Baverstock,' the solicitor said, 'I think perhaps the gentleman should be restrained before he does himself harm.'

'He left us the bull,' Vassie said, shaking with laughter. 'My Dada left us the bull.' She came forward, moving like a shadow, lifted the last whole bottle of whisky from the tray on the table and approached the prancing man with it. 'Never mind, Ronan, my dearest, you still have me and you still have your family and you still have this to see you out.'

He was raving, foam at the corners of his mouth, eyes watering, brow beaded with sweat. He beat upon the table with the plastered arm and then, spinning round, snatched the bottle from his wife's grasp, clutched it possessively to his chest for a moment before he pulled the cork with his teeth and drank from the neck. He poured the contents into his open mouth, drenching chin, throat and chest.

'There now, do you see?' Vassie said. 'That is all he wants.'

He struck her a sudden swinging blow with the hand that held the bottle. She fell to her knees among the broken glass. He kicked her once, would have kicked her again if Neil had not intervened. Willy and Quig, even Michael, all moved towards him but Neil reached him first, pinned him in a bear-hug and dragged him, still screaming, towards the front door.

'Madam?' Willy said, urgently.

'Yes, open it,' said Biddy.

Willy hastened to throw open the door and then stood to one side while Neil carried his father through the little hall and out into the smirr of rain that had blown in from the west. He carried him, struggling in his embrace, across the gravel and on to the lawn and dropped him, threw him down upon his back and, while the family watched from the doorway, placed his foot upon his father's chest and, stooping, spoke to him awhile, quite softly and earnestly, and then came back.

They made way for him as he strode back into the house.

Innis had helped her mother to her feet and had brushed the broken glass from her skirts. There was no sign of blood, no visible wound at all where Ronan had struck her. She seemed entirely unperturbed by the violence that had been done to her, stoical almost to the point of stupidity. In fact, she was still chuckling and pushed Innis away as soon as she had found her balance.

'What a fool I have for a husband. Pennypol was always mine and he did not know it or would not accept it. I could not be rid of it, though, any more than I can be rid of him,' Vassie said, to no one in particular. 'What have you done with my coat, Willy Naismith?'

'Mam, you cannot go now, like this,' Innis said.

'We have a lot to discuss – about Foss, about everything,' Biddy said.

'Aye, well, I have never been much of a one for discussion,' Vassie said. 'Besides, I will have to be getting my husband home.'

'You cannot be going on your own,' Biddy said. 'I will send for the cart. Willy will take you down to Pennypol and help you with him.'

'I am wanting no help.'

'I will come with you, if you wish,' said Donnie. 'If he falls I can lift him.'

Vassie looked at the young man in silence, then nodded. She put her coat about her shoulders. She beckoned to Neil and invited him to kiss her on the cheek. She gave him a little pat upon the shoulder then, with Donnie at her elbow, went outside to hoist her husband to his feet and steer him down the track that led to Pennypol.

One by one the others drifted back into the drawing-room.

All except Aileen who, kneeling on a chair by the window in the hall, peered out into the rain as pale and frightened as if she had seen a ghost.

'I haven't much time,' Neil said. 'I've no intention of staying on Mull until Monday and being docked another full day's pay. Besides, it all seems pretty cut and dried to me. Quarter share in everything for my sisters and myself, isn't that what your rigmarole means, Mr Forsythe?'

'Boiled down, Mr Campbell, that is the essence of it.'

'Had McIver no legal obligation to take care of his – his other dependants?' Michael asked.

'None of which I am aware,' said the solicitor. 'My father drew up the original will. He was an exceedingly meticulous man who obeyed Evander McIver's instructions to the letter. I think you may take it that the disposition of the heritable property will stand. There appear to be no claims against the estate and no debts outstanding for which, I think, we must thank Mr Quigley who has been so diligent in managing Evander McIver's affairs.'

'I am sure we are all grateful to Mr Quigley,' Neil said. 'I'm just wondering, though, why he got nothing for his pains?'

'Mr Quigley will act as a trustee for the quarter share that falls jointly to Aileen Campbell and her son.'

'Does that mean he gets his hands on Aileen's money?' said Neil.

'It means Grandfather trusted him,' Innis put in. 'But is it not time that we asked Quig what *he* wants us to do?'

'About what?' said Michael.

'About Foss,' said Innis.

'Mrs Tarrant has a valid point,' Forsythe said. 'Some financial settlement – a wage or profit-sharing arrangement – will have to be agreed between the three of you and Mr Quigley here if the McIver herd is to be maintained.'

Neil said, 'I thought the herd was ours now?'

'It is,' said Biddy.

'What about Pennypol?' Neil said. 'Can the herd not be grazed on Pennypol after we sell the island?

'Pennypol belongs to mother,' Innis said. 'Do you not remember? It was given to her before we were born on condition that she did not sell it.'

'She can sell it now, can't she?' Michael said.

'Yes,' said Mr Forsythe. 'I have checked the original deed. If she wishes to do so your mother may put Pennypol up for sale at any time.'

'I'm not bothered about bloody Pennypol,' said Neil. 'All I

want to know is how much cash I'm going to get when every-thing's finally settled.'

'Surely the sensible thing to do is to hold on to Foss and the herd and each of us take our share of the profits as an annual dividend,' said Biddy.

'No,' Neil said. 'I want my quarter share paid to me in cash as soon as possible. I've four children to raise and the money will give them a start in life, a better start than I ever had. If the three of you want to buy me out then that's up to you. But I'm having none of your dividend nonsense.'

'If we are selling the island, though,' Innis said, 'what will Quig do?'

Up until now Quig had taken no part in the discussion. He looked up and shrugged. 'I will not be staying on Foss now that Evander's gone. If you wish to keep hold of the place then you will have to pay Aileen her share too and either lease out the grass or employ someone else to tend the herd.'

'Is that what you think is best for Aileen?' Michael said.

'It is what I think is best for Donnie,' Quig answered. 'I will be making sure that Donnie is educated and has *his* chance in life and it is to that end that I will be using Aileen's money. Mr Forsythe will not disapprove, I take it.'

'On the contrary,' Forsythe said. 'I think that is an admirable plan and one which Mr McIver would have been delighted to endorse.'

'I am sure he would,' Quig said, 'since it was his idea in the first place.'

'Are you telling us that Grandfather wanted Foss sold?' said Biddy. 'Innis, did he ever say anything to you about selling Foss?'

Innis shook her head. She was watching Quig carefully now. He had lost his suavity all of a sudden. There was a certain tension in his manner, a caution that made her wonder if her cousin was more devious than she had given him credit for. He was, she knew, a shrewd negotiator when it came to selling cattle and that he had been ruthless in sending his other 'cousins' away. It suddenly occurred to her that perhaps Foss had been deliberately run down and that it was Quig's intention to purchase it cheaply for himself; though where he would find the money to do so was another mystery.

'How do we know what Grandfather wanted?' Biddy said.

'If he had wanted Foss kept as it was then he would have left it to me,' Quig said. 'It is a thing we talked about often, before his mind went away from him. He has given you, his grandchildren, a choice . . .'

'Some choice!' said Michael.

'. . . and it is all there in the will if you look at it closely enough,' Quig continued. 'If the three of you wish to keep Foss as it is then you may do so but you must act in harmony, all be together and in agreement. And that, from what I gather, is not the case.'

'And you, I suppose, speak for Aileen?' said Michael.

'I am entitled to speak for Aileen, am I not?' Quig said.

'Yes, you are,' Biddy said. 'Of course you are.'

'I say that Foss should be offered for sale. With your permission I will arrange for the sale of the cattle, including the breeding bulls, and will put the household articles to auction. I will be keeping a stern accounting, of course, and Mr Forsythe will have sight of all the receipts so that an exact division of what is there can be made to each of you, including Aileen.'

'But – but the graves?' said Innis. 'My grandmother is buried there, and I had always thought . . .'

'What?' Biddy interrupted. 'That we would be buried there too? Do not be so damned fanciful, Innis. Foss was not *our* home, thank God. I have no intention of having my bones lie there. Quig, how much is the herd worth?'

'At rough estimate,' Quig answered, 'not far short of two thousand.'

'And the land?' said Biddy.

'Seventy-seven acres of old arable, three hundred and ninety acres of good pasture, with spring water, a sheltered harbour, a habitable dwelling house and no crofters – in all I would say about fourteen hundred pounds.'

'What would it fetch in annual rent?' Biddy went on.

'Miles out in the Atlantic,' Michael put in. 'Not much.'

'Thirty pounds a year would be more than reasonable,' Quig said.

'I might be prepared to rent it,' Biddy said, 'just to keep you there.'

'I do not want to be kept there,' Quig said.

'And I'm not waiting for my money,' said Neil. 'If what you say is right, Quigley, then Grandad McIver knew fine I wouldn't stand on sentiment. I want my eight or nine hundred pounds, not a quarter share in an island that I'll never see again and never wanted to see in the first place.'

'But, Quig,' Innis said, 'if Foss is sold, if the cattle go – what will you do?'

'Look for work elsewhere.'

'And Aileen?'

'I will take her – and my mother – with me.'

'And Donnie?' Biddy said.

'And Donnie too, of course,' said Quig.

NINE

A Sorrowful Sinner

The kiss had cost her dearly. She could not meet Gillies now without guilt or look upon her husband without fear that he might guess what was going on within her head, within her heart, as if she had become as transparent as a preserving-jar. Even so, she thought of the kiss almost every minute of every day, reliving that moment in the Sabbath darkness when Gillies had drawn her to him and, without a word of warning or apology, had pressed his lips to hers and she had responded willingly by not thrusting him away.

Closeness, intimacy, breath upon breath; the memory itself was addictive. If she had not been a woman of conscience she might have plotted how to deceive Michael and be alone with Gillies Brown, to feel his arms about her, his mouth on her mouth once more. Biddy would not be so hesitant. Biddy would not forgo the pleasure of fulfilment. Biddy would accept it courageously. But her sister had not given herself to the Church of Rome, had not promised to be virtuous and obedient. She envied her sister more than ever, coveted the selfishness that brought Biddy whatever she wanted and, for all its contradictions, showered her with blessings in abundance.

In the night, when Michael and the children were asleep, Innis would kneel before a candle and pray to the Blessed Lady for release from temptation, pray until her knees hurt and her neck ached, for in the act of praying she was at liberty to think of Gillies and lavish upon the memory of the kiss all the wilful enjoyment that remorse denied her.

She might have made the journey to Glenarray to ask Father

Gunnion's advice, except that it was three weeks before the father's next visit and she was not even sure that he would understand. In spite of her devotion Innis was sceptical enough to wonder if a celibate gentleman of mature years would be able to ease her burden and suspected that all she wanted from him was an assurance that the kiss had done no lasting harm to her soul.

For a time, half a day, family affairs had taken her mind off Gillies.

She wondered what difference the money would make, if her grandfather had foreseen the trouble it would cause and if, in some strange way, he had intended his legacy to be a small act of revenge for the family's neglect. He had left Quig nothing, after all: Quig, who had cared for him, who had loved him with almost biblical devotion, had not been materially rewarded for his years of service, yet Quig did not seem dismayed. It was as if, somehow, he had been liberated and that liberation was, perhaps, reward enough.

She had been disturbed by her brother Neil's abruptness, how coarse and inconsiderate he had become. She had tried to remind herself that he had a wife and four children to consider and that what he did, he did for them. She did not think much of what her share would mean or what she might do with it. She had been more affected by her father's outburst, however; shocked to see him there at all, to hear the soft, reedy snarl in his voice as if he still believed that he was a force to be reckoned with and might control not only his own but Vassie's destiny. And Quig, the saintly Quig? Had she really detected in him an element of mendacity that made him less than dependable? And Michael, her Michael, still going on about the inheritance as if he had lived in poverty and had had to beg for his bread. She no longer knew what any of them wanted or, for that matter, what she wanted – apart from the love of Gillies Brown.

'Do you think she knows?' Janetta said.

Gillies put down the book, a volume of Hugh Miller's geological essays that he had carried up from Glasgow in his pack. He had not been particularly engrossed in the history of fossils and eased himself back in the chair, crossed his long legs and sighed. He had taken to wearing two pairs of woollen stockings, one long and one short, for the draught along the stone floor could catch your ankles like a scythe and he had always been prone to chilling.

Fortunately, his children had grown used to airiness and had become quite hardy, running about barefoot even now that winter had set in and the cottage often shook with the gales that came in from the Atlantic. He envied his son and daughters their adaptability and was grateful that they still regarded living on Mull as an adventure and the lonely dwelling at the end of a mud track as more homely than a cluttered apartment in a Glasgow tenement.

They were all asleep now, even Tricia, who still, now and then, shed a few tears for her mother just before bed.

Gillies adjusted his glasses, peered up at Janetta and said, 'Do I think that who knows what?'

'That you have a fancy for her sister?'

'Pardon?'

'Do you think that's why she's been avoiding us?'

Gillies shifted uncomfortably in the low-slung wooden armchair.

Janetta was perched in one of the straight-backed chairs that Biddy Baverstock had found to furnish the rented cottage. She had mending on the table and Pepper, snoring, lay at her feet like a footstool.

'I don't think anything of the sort,' Gillies said. 'Mainly, I admit, because I have not the foggiest what you're talking about.' He cleared his throat. 'There is, dearest, a certain confusion in your grammatical construction, particularly in respect of pronouns. Who am I supposed to fancy and who is avoiding us?'

She looked very severe, his eldest, with her straight nose and straight hair and those candid slate-blue eyes that reminded him so much of Clara's. She had a way of pursing her lips too, as if she was holding a needle in her teeth.

'If you're going to pretend that you don't know then there's

263

very little point in continuing the conversation,' Janetta said.

'Very well,' Gillies conceded. 'You've been holding your disapproval in for most of the week, therefore I assume that you assume that I've been making sheep's eyes at Mrs Baverstock and she's taken the huff. Correct?'

'Not correct,' said Janetta. 'Not Mrs Baverstock.'

'Oh!'

'Innis Tarrant.'

'Innis is a friend, that's all.'

'Nonsense!'

'She's a married woman, for Heaven's sake, and a staunch Catholic.'

'I know she is,' Janetta said. 'I'm just wondering what you think you're playing at going soft on a married woman.'

'Going soft? Is that what you think?'

'What happened that Sunday night two weeks ago?'

'Mrs Tarrant gave me a lift from Crove. Glad I was of it, too.'

'There's more to it than gratitude,' Janetta said. 'You haven't been the same since. Does she think you're an easy target because you're a widower?'

'That's a dreadful thing to say, Janetta.'

'Is it truth, though?'

'Firstly, I am not an "easy target", as you put it. Secondly, Innis Tarrant is no flirt. So it isn't the truth or anything like it.'

'You do like her, though?'

'Of course I like her.'

Janetta leaned forward, mending neglected. She placed one large foot on each side of the dog and braced her elbows on her knees. In that pose, in this mood, she seemed too aggressive to be his darling daughter. Gillies prodded at his glasses and strove to appear jocular, to humour her as if she were still a child.

'You know what her boy's like?' Janetta said.

'Gavin? Well . . .'

'Didn't it occur to you that her husband might have the same violent streak in him as his son, the same hot temper?'

'I wouldn't call Gavin violent, not exactly.'

'You brought us here in all good faith, Dad,' Janetta said,

'and it is no bad place for us now that Mama . . .'

'Wait,' Gillies said. 'Are you suggesting that out of respect for Mama's memory I shouldn't make a friend of the opposite sex?'

'I'm suggesting that you might choose your lady friends more carefully,' Janetta said. 'You *are* soft on Innis Tarrant, aren't you?'

Jocularity wouldn't work, Gillies realised; the subject was far too delicate for levity. He also suspected that somehow she knew about the kiss.

He said, 'What if I am?'

'We are incomers here,' Janetta said. 'If there's a scandal we'd lose this house and our teaching posts and be back where we started. It would not be so easy to find another position, not with a blemished record.'

'A scandal?' Gillies said. 'There isn't going to be a scandal. Do you think I'd do anything to harm you or the children, or Mrs Tarrant for that matter? I'm not some dastardly villain from one of your *People's Friend* stories.'

'Perhaps you can't help yourself.'

'Oh, no!' Gillies told her. 'I *can* help myself. I'm not a pimply boy, you know. One of the advantages of becoming an adult is that you learn that you *can* help yourself. Only self-indulgent weaklings will tell you otherwise. I'm as settled here as you are and I'll do nothing to upset you or the children. My family comes first as far as I'm concerned. And I'm sure it's just the same with Mrs Tarrant.'

Janetta hesitated, then said, 'Now if it had been the other one . . .'

'What other one?'

'The sister.'

'Mrs Baverstock?' Gillies was unable to hide his surprise.

'If you'd been smitten by Mrs Baverstock I'd have understood it.'

Gillies cocked his head. 'Why?'

'For one thing, she's a widow.'

'And I'm a widower,' Gillies said. 'Do you think that love and affection work like arithmetical calculations, Netta? No, no. There's nothing neat about them, or any sort of human emotion.'

'Do you not find Mrs Baverstock attractive?'

'Dear God, girl!' Gillies exclaimed. 'Are you trying to marry me off?'

'I'll not always be here to look after you.'

'Believe it or not, I'm quite capable of looking after myself.'

'I know you aren't young any more. I worry about you.'

'Thank you,' Gillies said. 'I appreciate your concern.'

'I'm not a child, Dad. I realise that a man has certain needs, and Mrs Baverstock . . .'

'Happens to have a fine big house that would accommodate us all in comfort.' Gillies was amused at his daughter's naïveté. 'So it would really be quite convenient if I went "soft", as you put it, on her. You'd approve of that match, would you?'

'She likes you, you know.'

'She likes you too, you and the children. She enjoys young company.'

'Because she's lonely.'

'Probably.'

'All the more reason . . .' Janetta said.

'Janetta,' Gillies said, 'I'm not setting my cap at Biddy Baverstock just because she rattles about in a big empty house and happens to be unmarried.'

He got up, not too hurriedly. He was not irked by his daughter's concern for his well-being or her clumsy attempts at match-making. In a sense he was flattered by it. He was aware that she considered herself a woman of the world, although her experience of life was still very limited. He had, perhaps, a little more respect for her than she had for him now but that was just part and parcel of the process of growing up and he had never put her down, and never would.

That, however, did not prevent him from telling her a little white lie now and then, strictly for her own good.

He stretched and yawned. 'I'm not setting my cap at anyone.'

'What about Innis Tarrant?'

'No,' he said, 'not even at Innis Tarrant.'

Biddy had been weeping quietly to herself, on and off, for days.

It was her time, of course. Nature had again reminded her that the months were mounting into years, that change was inevitable and decay just around the corner. Foss and her grandfather, Pennypol and her father, Quig threatening to take Donnie away; in spite of what her family and friends thought she too was a victim of circumstances over which she had no control. She might buy this, purchase that, sack this person or employ that one, but none of it counted when it came to the bit and responsibility only added to the burden of her loneliness. She was perceived as a practical person, down-to-earth, determined and forceful. Underneath, though, she was all weakness and tears.

Neil came, and Neil went. She had not been sorry to see him go.

Quig and Aileen had stayed one night and had left again for Foss.

Even Michael Tarrant, with his hungry eye, had refused to stop and sup with her and by Sunday afternoon she had been left high and dry with Donnie, whom she loved like a son but would surely lose once Quig and Foss were gone.

In the week following the reading of her grandfather's will she crept about so quiet and miserable that even young Donnie was moved to ask if she was coming down with something.

Two weeks ago, on Sunday afternoon, Fetternish House had been filled with young people. At her invitation the Browns and Donnie had assembled at the dining-table after church. They had devoured every scrap of food in sight and then had gathered, impromptu, around the piano in the drawing-room and had sung their hearts out, all the old Scotch songs that any of them could remember and the guttural songs of the Glasgow streets that brought a gruff kind of humour to the party.

Oh, how much fun they had all had. How they had applauded her for her playing and thanked her for her hospitality. Then they had gone home again in the gloaming, trailing away out of sight and earshot, leaving nothing in the gaunt old house but echoes, echoes, and Donnie, still buoyed up, humming

Johnny Cope or *The Couper o' Fife*, ate his supper and climbed the staircase to his bed.

Contrast between that carefree Sunday afternoon and the events of the following Saturday had been just too much for Biddy. She had slipped swiftly into a state of melancholy that nothing, not even a morning's shooting with McCallum, could lift. She almost wished that Iain Carbery would turn up to entertain her with his clumsy wit and, when she was right again, to carry her off to bed, not to make babies but just to hold in his arms. Iain would not return to Fetternish, though, for she knew that she had treated him shabbily and that even a buffoon like Carbery had some shreds of pride.

Over all, however, hung Quig's hint that he might take Donnie away.

She might wrestle for the boy, of course, might take the question of custody to a court of law. She knew little of such matters, however, or what the cost might be. And the prospect of her sister Aileen being drawn into the limelight was quite appalling. She could not do that, not to Aileen, not to Donnie, not even to Quig. If Quig chose to leave Mull, she must reconcile herself to losing Donnie forever, to see him drift off into that same realm where her brother Neil now dwelled, alive and thriving, certainly, but as lost to her as one of the dead.

The weather suited her blue mood, days of grey billowing rain without much force behind it, the sea hazed out and the air more dank than chill. She walked the dogs, drank more brandy than was good for her and, huddled in the Georgian wing-chair by the fire in the hall, brooded about her empty future. And, when the tears welled up in her, she would creep off upstairs to bury her face in a pillow or stand in the bare sewing-room at the top of the house and stare, weeping, from the window at the turbid acres of her estate.

'What, in God's name, is wrong with you?' Willy said. 'I can't believe you're grieving over the old man of Foss.' He put the brandy glass into her hand and, without invitation, poured a glass for himself and seated himself on the horsehair sofa. 'What it is, Mrs Baverstock? What's ailing you, lass?'

She cowered in the wing-chair, knees drawn up, and hugged

the glass to her breast. She did not meet Willy's enquiring gaze but stared at the splutter of flame that crept along the pine logs in the grate. Ever since dinner she had been filling up with tears and with Donnie gone – not into the wide world yet but only upstairs to bed – she had been on the point of stealing off to weep in privacy when Willy had stalked out of the corridor and caught her off guard.

'I – I do not know what's wrong with me.' Tears ran down her not-so-pale cheeks. She groped for the handkerchief that she kept tucked in her sleeve and, juggling the glass, dabbed delicately at her lashes. 'Oh, Willy, Willy. I'm so unhappy.'

Willy was tempted to put his arm about her for it moved him more than he cared to admit to see his mistress so distressed. But there was a point at which decorum put the hems on sympathy and Maggie had already warned him not to overstep the mark. He made murmuring, curmudgeonly noises for a moment or two to give Biddy time to compose herself, then he drank his brandy in a swallow and said, 'If it isn't the men – and it can't be the men – it must be you.'

She blinked, and the tears dried up a little.

She said, 'Beg pardon?'

'It's high time you saw a doctor, a proper doctor, a woman's doctor.'

She sat up straight from the waist and asked, in alarm, 'Oh, Willy, do you really think I'm ill?'

'Of course I don't think you're ill. But I think you might make yourself ill if you don't find out soon why you can't bear children.'

'I can't bear children because – because I'm not married.'

'Dear Heaven!' Willy said. 'It'll be garlic on the bedposts and dead herrings under the pillow next. Being married is not what makes you fertile. Being married won't automatically guarantee a pregnancy. In fact, if my own painful experiences are anything to go by – well, never mind all that. I've said enough as it is.'

'No,' Biddy said, sitting up even straighter. 'Go on. Go on.'

'What of these men that you've had here?' Willy said. 'Mr Carbery, for instance? What would it have been like if you'd married him and *hadn't* had a child? Would having a husband like Carbery be enough for you?'

'No – not that I do not like Iain . . .'

'He had no money,' Willy said. 'Not a penny to call his own, except a few shares in the Baverstocks' factory which, as we know only too well, are not bringing in as much as they used to do. But would that be enough?'

'What?' said Biddy. 'The shares?'

'No, not the shares,' said Willy patiently. 'The man.'

'I am not sure I understand, Willy?'

'All right,' the steward said. 'Let me put it this way, if you marry for love and remain childless then you will still have a loving husband to call your own. If you marry for money then at least you will have security and someone to look after Fetternish and its affairs and that too would be compensation. But if you marry just to have children, and find out that you can't . . .' He shrugged.

Biddy nodded. 'That is all very well, Willy, but I'm not in love with anyone. At least I don't think I am.'

'Then find out if you can have children,' Willy said, 'for if you can't then you won't be living in hope and will be looking for a different kind of man.'

'That seems very – very calculating.'

'Of course it's calculating,' Willy said. 'It's also common sense.'

'How do I – you know – find out if there's something wrong with me?'

'Consult a doctor who specialises in woman's troubles.'

'Are there such doctors?'

'Of course there are,' Willy said. 'Their plates are all over Edinburgh. Very reputable men, most of them. Ask Kirkhope. He's bound to know of a good one and if he doesn't then he can find out. A consultation will not come cheaply but it would be money well spent, wouldn't it?'

Biddy frowned. 'What if – if the doctor finds something wrong?'

'Then he may be able to put it right.'

'Do you think so, Willy. Is that possible.'

'More than possible.'

'But if he cannot?'

'Then at least you will know where you stand.'

'Aye, and it will not be on the side of the angels,' Biddy said. 'I will do it, though, William. You are right, as usual. Will you come with me?'

'I think it would be more suitable if you took Maggie.'

'Yes, yes, of course.'

For the first time in days Biddy smiled. He had given her something positive to think about and however much she might fear the findings Willy knew that she had the courage to go on with it, to discover the truth. He got up and took the brandy glasses to the table and put them on to a tray to carry downstairs.

'Willy?'

He looked round. She was no longer hunched up in the chair. She had spread herself out, one arm over her head and her legs stretched out before her with an air of sensuous languor that would have driven most men wild.

'Yes, ma'am?' Willy said.

'Why could I not have married you?' Biddy said.

Willy laughed. 'Because Maggie got there first.'

'Very well,' Biddy said. 'I will call on Doctor Kirkhope on Monday.'

'First thing?' Willy said.

'First thing,' said Biddy.

They met at last, apparently by chance, where the path dipped into a hollow of brambles and wild raspberry canes, withered now and wet with the week's rain.

The weather had improved a little towards evening and Innis had brought Becky and Fruarch out for a short walk before the cold blue darkness closed in. She had headed across the bridge and up the old sheep path to a track that led to the back of the walled garden and intended to go no further than the knoll that gave a view of Fetternish House and the headland of An Fhearann Cáirdeil.

Becky and Rachel had been at loggerheads, unusual for sisters who normally rubbed along so well. Winter and long nights were already taking a toll on tempers, however, and the little one had been uncharacteristically fractious and out of sorts all day. When Innis had put on her coat and suggested a walk Rachel had stubbornly refused to budge from the fireside and had stayed behind with her father, pleased to have him all to herself for once. Gavin had been gone all afternoon. He had the knack of vanishing with the same thoroughness as Aileen had vanished when she was his age, a fact that had not escaped Innis's notice and that worried her a little now and then, though she knew that boys were different and that Gavin, like his father, could not bear to be cooped up indoors for long.

Although the light was melancholy and metallic, Innis was relieved to be out of Pennymain with just her little daughter and the dog for company. The path dipped into the bramble hollow and rose to the shoulder of the hillock from which she would be able to see the headland and, if she were lucky, smoke from the Brown's cottage thin and distant against the clouds that layered the mountains of Ardnamurchan. It was the one spot on the entire estate from which both dwellings were visible, not walls and windows, but only the chimney of one and smoke from the other in vague and harmless conjunction.

And then they were there, strolling down the slope towards her, as if she had conjured them up out of clear air simply by thinking of them: Evie and Pepper and, a step or two behind, Gillies himself. She was startled, then alarmed, and, as if the little family group somehow posed a threat, reached out for Becky's hand and drew her daughter towards her. The dogs were already dancing about, tails wagging, sniffing, each taking the measure of the other.

'Ah, Innis,' Gillies said, hiding his pleasure and his embarrassment. 'Are you back from your church service already?'

'There is no service on this day,' Innis said. 'The father only visits Mull once in each month. What are you doing so far from the farm?'

'Just taking the air. And you?'

'The same,' said Innis.

Becky tugged at her hand and Innis let her go.

Gillies's jacket was draped over his shoulders, a muffler wound around his neck. He was hatless and did not seem to feel the cold. He was not a handsome man but his height gave him presence and the spectacles made him seem benign and quizzical at one and the same time. He glanced at the children who had followed the dogs into the verge of the bramble patch and were giggling at the antics of the animals as the pair scurried about in the undergrowth and popped up all sleek and soaked to ensure that they had not been abandoned. Then he looked at Innis, still benign but not smiling.

'I have seen nothing of you lately,' he said, 'or of your sister.'

'My sister?'

'Since the lawyer's visit,' Gillies said. 'Did it go smoothly?'

She felt safe with him, safe too with a question which, so far as she could tell, was no more than politeness. She wanted to confide in him, to confess, to have him kiss her again there in the afternoon light but she would not give in. She felt stronger now that she was with him, as if there was less to fear than she had imagined. Even so, she kept her distance.

'I would not be saying that it went smoothly,' she told him. 'The matter appears to have resolved itself, however. Foss will be sold, along with the cattle. The proceeds will be divided equally between us.'

'So some money will be coming your way?'

'Yes,' Innis answered. 'It is not much.' She paused. 'I am telling you a lie. It is more money than any of us have ever had in our lives, any of us except Bridget, that is.'

'What will you do with your windfall?'

'I have no idea,' said Innis. 'There is nothing that I want.'

'Nothing?'

'Nothing that money can buy.'

'Your husband will find a use for it, no doubt.'

'Probably.'

'Will he buy sheep?' Gillies said.

'Why would he be buying sheep?' Innis said. 'He has no grass upon which to graze them.'

'There's nothing but grass, as far as I can see.'

273

'Biddy's grass,' Innis said. 'Michael would not be permitted to put his own sheep upon Fetternish ground.'

'I see,' Gillies said. 'I hope you don't think I'm being too inquisitive?'

She did not think that at all. She wanted to answer all his questions, to tell him the truth; that the sum of money that her grandfather had left mattered hardly at all compared to what she had discovered about herself in the course of the last two or three weeks. She did not want to go back to Pennymain, at least not to Michael. If she had inherited a magical wand instead of mere money from Evander McIver she would have spirited herself and her children to An Fhearann Cáirdeil with it and brought down upon her husband the blessing of forgetfulness. She could not say it, though, could not take the next step, although she did not regret the first.

'Not at all,' she said.

'Well, then,' Gillies said, 'might I ask about Donnie, if provision has been made for his education?'

'He is Quig's responsibility.'

'Oh, I thought that your sister . . .'

'Quig will look after him,' Innis said.

'Who will look after you, Innis?' Gillies Brown said.

She felt her heart beat against her breast-bone; no romantic metaphor but a physical manifestation of emotions that she dared not acknowledge, dare not define. She gasped a little, like a fish pulled out of water, struggling to breathe in the strange new element in which she found herself. She felt as if the girls were watching her, though a glance told her that they were still busily occupied in playing with the dogs. Gillies watched her, however, his expression alert and attentive, not teasing.

'My – my husband looks after me,' Innis stammered.

'I know he does,' Gillies said, softly.

He slipped fingers and thumb under his glasses and lightly massaged his eye-sockets. For a moment Innis wondered if he was wiping away tears. But, of course, he was not. He was as strong and sensible as she was and would not weep over what he could not have, what could never be.

He gave a rueful shrug of the shoulders. 'It won't happen again, Innis.'

She did not pretend that she did not know what he was talking about, did not flirt and cajole, did not tease, the way Biddy might have done.

'No,' Innis said. 'I am not sorry that it did, however.'

'I'm not going to apologise either,' Gillies said. 'I don't regret it, not for a minute. But it can't happen again. It can't happen again because I don't want us to become suspicious of each other, to be sorry that we ever met. There's enough distrust in the world as it is and not nearly enough of – of the other thing.'

'Affinity?' Innis said.

'Affinity will do,' said Gillies.

'It is the reasonable and rational thing to do,' Innis said. 'Although I do not feel reasonable and rational right now. Do you?'

'God, no!' he said.

She touched his sleeve; a little, almost shy, dabbing touch.

'Thank you, Gillies,' she said. 'Thank you,' then, calling to Becky, turned back towards Pennymain which, she suddenly realised, was no great distance at all from the cottage at Friendship Farm.

Maggie had never been in Edinburgh before. Indeed, she had never set foot on the mainland until that morning. Her excitement at travelling on a steamer then a railway train and the shock of arriving in the brusque, bustling heart of the capital was almost too much for her.

If she had been with Willy – wife and not lady's-maid – she might have swooned away at her first sight of Princes Street's fairyland of lighted shops and salons. Under the circumstances, however, she could not allow herself to weaken.

She steeled herself not to gawk, to ensure that the hired porter did not shed any of Mrs Baverstock's luggage in the course of the cab ride to the Wellington Hotel.

The hotel was monumentally grand. Even Biddy could not disguise her awe. In spite of her association with peers of the realm, she was not much more sophisticated than her maid when it came to it. She was also extremely agitated at the prospect of her appointment with Sir Archibald Petty who knew more about the functions of the female than any other man in the kingdom and, according to Dr Kirkhope, had even treated several members of the Queen's own court.

Maggie's excitement served to soften Biddy's anxiety slightly. The pair ate dinner together at a discreet corner table in the vaulted dining-room. Dressed in a new black tea-gown, Maggie was passed off as a 'companion' since maids and other members of the servant class were not permitted to set foot in the Wellington's public rooms let alone sup on fare that was considered far too good for them.

Maggie slept like a top that night. Biddy hardly slept at all and managed no more by way of breakfast than a bowl of milky porridge and a couple of grilled herring. Agitation had become fear, fear of exposing herself to a total stranger, fear that Mr Petty might discover some dreadful malady lurking in the warm, damp darkness of her insides. The fact that she had never been ill and was seldom even mildly under the weather did not console her and, as the morning progressed towards the eleven o'clock appointment, she began to feel increasingly queasy and to suffer strange stitching pains in her lower abdomen.

The cab ride to Sir Archibald's consulting-rooms in Melvin Crescent was a nightmare. Every shoogle and shake of the conveyance's wheels on the capital's cobbles seemed to increase the impression that a great wobbling, ectoplasmic ball was rolling about in her stomach. She wished now that she had brought Willy with her for he would have calmed her down, reassured her, and taken heed of her last wishes. Maggie was far too entranced by the sights that flitted past the cab window to do more than pat her mistress's hand occasionally, and murmur. 'There, there, Mrs Baverstock. The doctor will soon put you right.'

As it turned out the doctor had the air of a man who might subvert an uprising in India or subdue a warlike tribe in Afghanistan without breaking sweat. His brooding brown eyes, Biddy thought, had seen everything and were impressed by nothing. He was certainly not impressed by her stammered attempts at name-dropping.

'Are you acquainted with Lord Fennimore?' Biddy would enquire at one point early in the conversation.

'That Irishman!' the doctor would exclaim in a tone that conveyed less dislike than disgust, as if she had claimed a chatty friendship with Jack the Ripper.

The doctor's house was similar to Austin and Walter Baverstock's, except that it was twice the size and seemed to have been decorated by industrial engineers, all marble and parquet and wrought-iron, like a municipal art gallery. Everything inside was dark, forbidding and glossy, even the house-keeper who showed them into the waiting-room. Within seconds, she escorted Biddy out of it again, across the echoing hallway and through another door into a room so pale and cold that it seemed as if the very air itself had been etherized.

Sir Archibald Petty wore a morning-coat, pearl-grey waist-coat, striped trousers, and the sort of high collar and cravat that even Biddy considered old-fashioned. His shirt had long starched cuffs out of which his hands appeared, small and shy and pinky-white, like pet mice. In other respects he was a large man, broad-shouldered and barrel-chested, with a corona of grey-brown hair and a grey-brown beard that seemed to have been specially trimmed to display his pretty little red-lipped mouth.

He stood by an ornate desk that was flanked by two spidery iron stands from each of which dangled an arrangement of pelvic bones, chained as if to prevent their escape. Behind Biddy, like something breathing on the nape of her neck, was an examination table complete with straggling leather straps. Beside it she glimpsed a rack of porcelain basins topped by a tray of ugly steel instruments.

She shook Sir Archibald's ice-cold hand, accepted a chair, collapsed on to it and stared into the sheet of grey-white light from the tall windows. She could see the backs of the terraces, windows and chimneys and closes outside and – an enviable spark of life – a young housemaid vigorously beating dust from a carpet.

The surgeon asked her a solemn but innocuous question about the weather on Mull.

Eager to impress, she answered him at considerable length.

He asked about her journey.

She answered that question too.

He asked about her menstrual cycle.

Biddy's cheeks grew hot. She strove unsuccessfully to be bold and enlightened but felt her shoulders sag and head droop until she was looking, as if for inspiration, down into her lap.

She mumbled an answer, brief but honest.

Sir Archibald Petty offered no help, no words of comfort.

Biddy wondered if he treated the ladies of the court in this manner or if he considered a mere landowner from the Inner Hebrides as being so deficient in modesty that he did not require to be tactful. A faint prickle of annoyance stirred within her. She lifted her head, squared her shoulders.

He was writing on a thick white pad with a graphite pencil.

He said, 'Is intercourse painful to you, Mrs Baverstock?'

'Not in the least.'

'Do you find the act abhorrent?'

'Pardon?'

'Distasteful. Unpleasant.'

'No, I do not.'

'How often does the act of intercourse take place?'

She was tempted to answer, 'Not often enough', but she was not sufficiently angry to be impertinent just yet.

She said, 'Not regularly.'

'Once a week, once a month?'

'Not so often, no.'

'Is this because of reluctance on your part, or upon your husband's?'

'Oh!' Biddy said. 'I thought – did Dr Kirkhope not explain?'

'Explain?' Sir Archibald said.

'That I have been a widow for twelve years.'

'Am I to take it then that you have not participated in an act of intercourse in all that time?'

'Of course I have,' said Biddy. 'I am from farming stock, Mr Petty. I know what has to be done to make babies.'

'Do you have a common – a partner, a regular partner?'

'Regular enough,' Biddy said.

She was no longer afraid of him. He had already demon-strated so much disapproval that another sniff, another hesita-tion or raising of the eyebrow hardly mattered. Suddenly she felt released from the terror that had plagued her all morning. In spite of his fancy language the surgeon was only doing his job and she could hardly blame him for disapproving of her morals.

'If you are prone to cohabit with a single partner then the fault may lie with him,' Sir Archibald said. 'It will perhaps be necessary to ensure that the gentleman is not at fault.'

'Well, they cannot all be at fault,' Biddy said.

'All? How many have there been?'

'Five, all told.'

'I see.' He made a note on the writing-pad, a very brief note. 'Five – in how many years?'

'Seven or eight years. None of them have made me pregnant.'

'These – these liaisons, are they fleeting?'

'On the contrary,' Biddy said.

'Are they . . .' He tapped the pencil against his pretty red lips then said, 'I think I must ask you, Mrs Baverstock, if these cohabitings are casual?'

'Certainly not, sir,' Biddy answered. 'They are anything but casual. They are undertaken in the hope and with the intention that I will conceive.'

'Really? Out of wedlock?'

'Wedlock will come after.'

'After what?'

'After one of them makes me pregnant.'

The surgeon put his hand to his mouth as if to stifle a gasp. He coughed, then said, 'I take it, Mrs Baverstock, that you regard yourself as a liberated woman?'

'Well, sir,' Biddy said, 'I have no intention of marrying a man who cannot give me what I want.'

'Children?'

'One would do,' Biddy said. 'Several would be better.'

'But this has not happened? By which I mean that you have

not conceived with any of the – the gentlemen in question?'

'If I had I would not be here.'

'True,' Sir Archibald conceded. 'Pain?'

'No.'

'Sickness? Vomiting? Cramp?'

'No.'

He asked her a dozen more questions, each more intimate than the last. But the flush had gone from Biddy's cheeks. She was almost beginning to relax. The surgeon's manner had changed too, as if her candour had blunted the edge of his haughtiness. In due course he rang a little bell on the desk and a middle-aged woman, not the housekeeper, appeared from a side room. She wore a spotless white apron and a huge floppy muslin cap.

'This is Miss Chapman,' the surgeon said. 'If you are ready, Mrs Baverstock, she will see to it that you are prepared for examination.'

'Do I have to take my clothes off?'

'You will be given a gown,' the surgeon said. 'Would you prefer your maid to help you undress?'

'I think I can manage,' Biddy said.

The side room had a screen and a chair and a plain wardrobe in it and the woman, Miss Chapman, was very meticulous in putting away Biddy's clothes. She was given a white linen gown to wear and, when it was settled over her, she was ushered out into the consulting-room once more.

Mr Petty had lighted a pair of portable gas-lamps. They hissed fiercely and shed a weird white light upon the examination table. A clean sheet had been stretched over the table and taped down. Two of the basins on the rack had been filled with warm water and released faint clouds of steam into the chill air.

The surgeon had removed his morning-coat and had hung it on one of the spidery stands as if to given protection to the pelvis there. He had also removed the elongated shirt-cuffs and they stood upright on the desk, like paper vases. He too wore a gown, tight about his shoulders and middle, collar and cravat showing above the round lapels. Four large cotton towels were piled on a knee-high stool at the table's end, adjacent to the padded stool upon which, Biddy reckoned, the surgeon would sit.

Fear was back with her again; not embarrassment but raw terror at what the examination might uncover. She felt herself shrink and cower and, as the woman led her forward, shivered uncontrollably.

Sir Archibald looked at her, not noticeably impressed by the mass of auburn hair, by the full breasts and sea-green eyes that had turned so many male heads.

Biddy swayed a little, knock-kneed, arms folded across her stomach. When he touched her she leapt back. He touched her again, the small soft white hand upon her shoulder. She felt the authority in him and a strange, unsexual tenderness flow through his fingers.

He led her to the edge of the table.

'Now, Mrs Baverstock,' the surgeon said. 'Hop up, if you please.'

And Biddy, unresisting, did.

Only Willy knew why Biddy had gone to Edinburgh. And Willy was saying nothing. Innis suspected that it might have to do with selling Foss or, just possibly, with dwindling returns from Biddy's holding in the Baverstocks' tweed mill. On the other hand, if business had been on the agenda then Willy, not Maggie, would surely have accompanied her sister to the capital. For whatever reason, Biddy had gone without a word, traipsing off with a pile of luggage and Maggie at her side to catch the early morning boat from Tobermory.

News of Mrs Baverstock's departure did not remain secret for long. By dinner-time half the folk on the estate were speculating on what the widow of Fetternish might be up to on the mainland and how it would affect them and by the following morning a rumour had begun to circulate that it was Fetternish that was to be sold, not Foss, and that, come Ladyday, they would all be turned out of their homes and left to fend for themselves. The rumour was without foundation, of course, was, in fact, plain silly but that did not prevent the tenants scaring themselves with tales of doom and gloom or that old devil, Hector Thrale, from stoking the fires of uncertainty as he made his rounds.

Barrett raised the matter with Michael soon after they met for their morning pow-wow. 'I have been hearing that the mistress is for selling Fetternish,' he began. 'I do not suppose there is much truth in the rumour?'

'None,' Michael said.

'Has she not gone to Edinburgh, then?'

'She has gone somewhere,' said Michael.

'But not to Edinburgh?'

'I don't know where she's gone. I'm not in her confidence.'

'I was thinking that perhaps Innis . . .'

'Fetternish is not going to be sold,' Michael said. 'She will have gone to see some man or other.'

'The shooting gentleman?' said Barrett, who had promised his wife that he would try to find out what was going on. 'What is his name now? Carbery – yes, Mr Carbery. Has she gone to visit with him, do you think?'

'It wouldn't surprise me,' Michael said.

'I hope that she does not come back with a wedding-band.'

The same thought had drifted through Michael's mind. It was no more reasonable than the speculation that Biddy had gone to Edinburgh to put Fetternish on the market but it fed Michael's own peculiar fantasies. He had already begun to plan what he would do with the eight or nine hundred pounds that Innis had been promised as her portion of her grandfather's legacy and he waited impatiently for the isle and its cattle herd to be sold and a final figure arrived at. But his schemes did not include the possibility that Biddy would remarry in the near future and her mysterious trip to the mainland had disturbed him too. He had questioned Innis carefully but his wife seemed as ignorant as everyone else as to Biddy's purpose and intentions.

'Biddy Baverstock will not rush into anything,' Michael said. 'She's waited this long to take another husband. She's not going to jump at the first man that comes along.'

'Mr Carbery would hardly be the first man, now would he?'

Barrett said. 'What if she is expecting? Would that not be reason enough to send her skimming off in search of a husband?'

With a little buzz of anger ringing his head, he realised that Barrett might have stumbled on the truth, or a version of it. There was no way of knowing what other man or men Biddy might have given herself to for he, Michael Tarrant, was only too well aware that she was more hot-blooded than a woman should be and that if she had not been the lady of Fetternish she would undoubtedly have been branded a whore.

'It might be,' Michael conceded.

'I will tell you who will be knowing,' Barrett said, his moon-face glowing with eagerness. 'Naismith will be knowing for sure.'

'That tight-lipped bastard will not betray his mistress's secrets.'

'Is Willy Naismith not a special friend of your wife's? Can Innis not wheedle it out of him,' Barrett said, 'if you ask her to?'

Michael glanced at the young shepherd in dismay. In all the years that they had worked together he had never suspected that Barrett was just as devious as his kith and kin and just as keen on hearsay. He remembered again Innis's denials, remembered too how she had lied to him about her meetings with Gillies Brown, aye, and other matters too. In his mind one calumny began to run into another, to mingle and mate like ewes in season.

It had not occurred to him before that he might lose his hold on Innis as, once long ago, he had lost his hold on Biddy. He was incapable of understanding how that might happen or how Biddy's marriage – if there was one – would affect his marriage to Innis, his job or his status in the family but fear came over him with the same irrational persistence as his daughters' fear of the dark. He did not experience it as fear, even as threat, but as a sudden bleakness of spirit that he could not explain to himself, let alone to the moon-faced young man who hovered eagerly at his side.

'Ask her,' Barrett said. 'Tell her.'

'I will do no such thing,' Michael said, flatly. 'If things are as you think they might be then we will find out soon enough.'

'Aye, when we are all sent packing.'

'We will not be sent packing. Why would we be sent packing?'

'To make way for deer,' Barrett said. 'If the mistress was to marry Carbery would he not be for turning Fetternish into a shooting estate?'

'Never.' Michael shook his head. 'Never in a million years.'

'Will you not be asking Innis to . . .'

'I will not be asking Innis anything,' Michael said.

'Are you afraid she will not tell you the truth either?' said Barrett then, realising that he had pushed his boss a step too far, suddenly slapped his hands together and cried, 'Well, we will be leaving all that silly sort of tattle to the women. It is not a thing that grown men should be bothering about. It is beneath contempt what these stupid women get up to.'

'Stupid women?' Michael said. 'I hope you don't mean my wife?'

'Not at all, not at all,' said Barrett. 'No, no, I am not meaning to say a word against Innis.' Then, to avoid further gaffes, he clambered swiftly over the fence and with one of the dogs trotting at his heel, set off towards the winter grazings at twice his normal speed.

Falling in love with a man who was not her husband was a selfish business but that morning Innis's thoughts were not focused entirely upon herself.

It had been the best part of two weeks since she had last seen her mother and her conscience had been pricking her. Her father's appearance at the reading of the will had alarmed her. The sight of him, smug and arrogant as always, even if he was but a husk of his former self, had made her wary. She worried that she would find him not just recovered but restored and that he too would become a factor in the complicated equation of her life on the low shore. She had avoided Pennypol for that reason.

It was a streaming blue-black morning with rain held back

284

only by the strength of the north-west wind. The sea heaved against the jetty and made long relentless rushes on to the sand. On Olaf's Ridge the pines creaked and bristled, tugging against the anchoring earth. The coastal headlands dropped away as far as the eye could see and Old Caliach, the standing stone, stood out stark upon the point, keeping her watch upon the west.

Becky held tightly to her hand as they came down the path from the wall at the top of the calf park. She wore a round-eyed, attentive expression that might turn to apprehension and even to tears at any moment. Innis recalled how it had been with her when she was a child of Becky's age, how certain shades of wind and weather and the very colour of the air itself had seemed threatening, almost malevolent. She kept her daughter close against her skirts and did not, not for an instant, let her grip on the little hand slacken.

'Are we going to be seeing Gran?'

'Yes, dearest.' Innis said.

'Will he be there too?'

'I expect Grandpa will be asleep.'

'Will he not see me then?'

'Oh, he might,' said Innis, and let it go at that.

Smoke rose from the hole in the cottage's thatch then, thickening, stripped away in a pungent brown coil that dipped over the bull-pen and shore pasture where Lear and the bullocks roared at each other across the fences and the dogs, loose for once, streaked back towards the house, barking ferociously. Innis hoisted Becky into her arms.

'We should have been bringing Fruarch with us,' Becky whispered. 'Fruarch would be sortin' them out.'

Nose to tail, Vassie's cattle dogs sprinted along the base of the big wall and leapt the dike at the bottom of the cattle park. They were on her almost before she knew it, snarling and slavering, darting in, crouching down, creeping forward to snap at her skirts. Innis held Becky high against her chest, little boots and stocking legs tucked neatly in against her body. She walked on, no stutter in her step, pretending to ignore the dogs that snarled around her, refusing to let them see how much she feared their yellow teeth and their ferocity.

She allowed herself to be herded over the little dike and escorted towards the cottage, while Becky clung to her and whispered in her ear, 'Bad doggies, bad, bad doggies.'

The door of the old byre hung open. In the new byre, down by the jetty, cattle milled about, nuzzling and champing on a litter of straw and dung that spread like curds across the track towards the heavy gate. Even upwind, Innis could taste the peat smoke on her tongue. And, of course, the cattle dogs were running loose among the pieces of the herd, driving Lear to distraction with their barking. Innis realised that something was seriously wrong.

When she approached the front of the cottage the dogs dropped behind, circling, sniffing and whining about the entrance to the shed where as a rule they were kept locked up. On the stones outside the cottage door were bones, old soup bones browned in the boiling, so scant of meat that not even the gulls bothered to examine them. Glass too, glass broken into shards, glass pulverised into ashy patches. The neck of a bottle, a bottle bottom's stout round heel. Plates and cups, smashed willy-nilly, spilled away from the threshold in a pattern that suggested not chaos but rage.

Still carrying Becky, Innis stepped cautiously around the debris and standing ten or twelve yards from the cottage door called out to her mother.

There was no answer.

Peering into the gloom Innis could make out firelight on the walls, no little smoulder this but a blaze of peat and driftwood fanned by the wind. Destruction had affected the kitchen too. Chairs had been thrown about, the dresser toppled, the bed curtain ripped from its strings and hurled towards the door, clothing strewn everywhere. In the midst of the wreckage, propped against the table-leg, was her father, drunk as a lord.

Whisky bottles were all about him, some half filled, some almost empty. If he had not been so shrivelled he would have resembled a bear who had found the honey store. Rocking gently forward and back, he crooned contentedly to himself while whisky trickled down his chest and drenched his thighs.

'Oh! Oh! He is not asleep,' murmured Becky. 'He will see me, Mammy.'

Innis glanced towards the byre then, shifting the child's weight in her arms, turned towards the vegetable garden, turned again to peer along the foreshore. Her mother was nowhere to be seen. She braced herself then, with a grippe of pure fear in the pit of her stomach, stepped over the broken glass and entered the cottage.

Vassie was lying face down upon the stones by the hearth. Her skirts were hitched up and her skinny legs crooked as if she had been struck down while attempting to crawl away from someone or some thing. One bare arm was extended towards the ladder that led to the loft. Her head was cocked at a peculiar angle, thrown up a little by the hump of her shoulder-blade. Her cheek was bruised and her forehead, bleeding a little, was grazed. Milky spittle at the side of her mouth, like the blood on her brow, had dried in the heat from the fire.

Innis swung Becky round and sat her on the end of the table.

'Gran is sleepin' on the floor,' Becky said.

'Stay there, dearest,' Innis said. 'Gran is sick.'

She stepped over the whisky bottles, over her father's out-stretched legs and knelt on the floor by her mother's side. The heat from the heaped hearth was fierce. One side of her mother's body was baking hot, the other cold as frost. Innis cradled her mother's head in both hands, eased her shoulder down flat then, lifting the fragile body, drew her gently back from the blaze. She was breathing, but only just, a shallow, uneven rhythm, so weak and thready that Innis expected it to cease at any moment. One eye, the right, was closed, the other half-open, a silvery glitter showing under the unblinking lid.

'Mam?' Innis said. 'Mama, what has happened to you?'

Vassie gave no sign that she had heard, no sign of recognition or comprehension save a slight twitch of the right arm and a flexing of the fingers that may, or may not, have been involuntary.

Still holding her mother against her, Innis reached out and plucked an old coat from the clothing on the floor. She folded it as best she could and tucked it under her mother's head, turning her so that she lay on her back. She tugged down the skirts, straightened the limbs, legs and arms, made her mother neat rather than comfortable then, fighting back her tears, got up.

Becky was still seated on the table, her thumb in her mouth. She showed no sign of tears but her little face was white. Innis went to her and put her hands to her daughter's shoulders and held her quite still. This was the sign between them that Mammy required obedience. Even before Innis spoke, her daughter was nodding solemnly.

'Gran is sick,' Innis said. 'We will have to go and find Daddy so that he can send for Doctor Kirkhope. We will be going in a minute but until then I want you to sit still and do not move. Do you understand, Rebecca?'

'Aye.'

Innis found a blanket and put the blanket over her mother, tucked it tightly beneath her feet and hips. Vassie was still motionless, as limp and helpless as a corn-doll. She was still breathing, however, her upper chest lifting and sagging again, and the glitter in the unblinking eye had not dulled.

Innis got to her feet and turned to her father.

He was not insensible. He had been watching her, watching her with that faint arrogant grin on his lips. As she approached him he lifted the bottle and supped from the neck and put the bottle down gently on the floor beside him and braced himself for what he knew would come.

She caught him by the hair and dragged his head forward. He could not resist her moderate strength any more than he had been able to resist Neil. He had nothing left, nothing but a voice and even that, this day, was feeble. He tried to laugh but had no heart for it and lay there while Innis shook him, shook him until his head waggled and his shoulders lurched, while she shouted, 'What have you done to her? What have you done to my Mam?'

'She fell down,' Ronan said. 'She just fell down upon the floor.'

'When? When did she fall down?'

'Last – last night, would it be?'

'And you left her there?'

'She left me – left me without – without – whisky. She would not – not even tell me where she had put the whisky.'

Innis let him go. He sagged back against the table-leg and adopted a pathetic pose. His chin bristled with grey stubble. He smelled of urine as well as the whisky, but his helplessness, she knew, was pure sham.

'Yes,' Innis said in the quiet unruffled voice that he had always hated. 'But you found your whisky, did you not? You had enough gumption to find the bottles but not enough to even put a blanket over your wife.'

Innis lifted Becky from the table and held her in her arms.

'Where are you going?' Ronan said, showing alarm for the first time. He struggled, elbowed himself up. 'Surely you are not going to leave me here with – with her?'

'I am going to fetch the doctor,' Innis said.

'So it is serious then, is it?'

'Very serious.'

'She will not be dying on me, will she?' Ronan said. 'If she dies who will take care of me then?'

But by that time Innis had hurried away.

The tenement was burly enough to withstand the winds that arched uphill from the Port of Leith and the wide expanses of the Forth. But it was not new nor even middle-aged. Gables shored by timber, stairs by unmortared brick, it had the appearance of a medieval fortress fretted by sundry half-forgotten wars and catastrophes. It was not a foul slum like the slums of the Grassmarket or those that hid in the vennels off the Royal Mile. It was heading in that direction, though. In five years or ten weather and neglect would surely strip the last tarnished pretension from its walls and the building, like its inhabitants, would quietly give up the ghost.

Biddy had no knowledge of Edinburgh's underclass or its intricate social distinctions. Even so, she had not anticipated that Iain Carbery would live in such a shabby building and, walking up the street with Maggie at her side, checked the address carefully before she finally tackled the dark inside staircase that did not even have a gas-mantle to light up the gloom or a window to let air in and the smell of the closets out.

It was early afternoon, not long after midday. Biddy had not really expected to find her lover resting at home at that hour and when the door of the apartment opened in answer to her knocking she did not immediately recognise the man who opened it as the robust and hardy sportsman who had so often shared her bed.

'Iain?' she said. 'Iain Carbery?'

'Oh, God! Dear God!' he said. 'What are you doing here?'

He wore a lumpy old dressing-gown and a night-shirt so patched and threadbare that she could see his body hair through the material. He was barefoot, tousled and unwashed and carried with him the musty odour of an unmade bed. He had lost his summer sun-tan and appeared pale and thin.

'I seem to have called at an inconvenient time,' Biddy said.

'What? No. What *are* you doing here? Are you – are you with child?'

'Do not be ridiculous. How could I possibly be with child after what you have done to me.'

'What I have . . .'

Biddy had promised herself that she would remain calm. Seated in the hackney cab she had ranted away to Maggie and nursed her anger all the way from Melvin Crescent to Leith Road. She had confided more than was prudent to a servant, perhaps, even if the servant was Willy Naismith's wife. Dismayed by Sir Archibald's diagnosis, by his cautiously-phrased suggestion that she might be no more than a victim of her own promiscuity she headed straight for Carbery's chambers which had turned out not to be 'chambers' at all but a grisly tenement in a down-at-heel neighbourhood.

'What have you done, Iain? You know what you have done.'

Her voice echoed down the narrow stone staircase. She had a sudden vision of the denizens of the tenement gathered at the close-mouth, sniggering. Nothing people of that class liked better than to see a lady brought low.

She said, 'Are we to be kept standing here on the – the . . .'

'Landing,' Iain said. 'No, you had better come in.'

'Both of us,' Biddy stated as she stepped over the worn threshold. 'I have no intention of being alone with you, Mr Carbery, not after the way you have treated me. My maid can wait in the drawing-room while we converse.'

'Drawing-room? There is no drawing-room,' Ian said. 'She may wait here in the hall, if you wish.'

The hall was no more than a tiny cubby with a coal-box in one corner and a coat-rack from which Iain's shooting-jacket and ulster hung like a gamekeeper's trophies. With the landing door closed there was barely room to breathe and Iain had no choice but to usher the ladies into his living quarters, a cramped square-shaped apartment with only a scullery and bed-neuk to give it dimension.

The furniture, such as it was, was too heavy for the size of the room; an ancient sofa and a deep-buttoned leather chair, a copy of a Carlton House table that had seen better days more or less summed it up. Propped and pinned on walls and shelves, however, were mementoes of Iain's glorious days in the field; a stuffed salmon swam in a glass display case, a fox's head leered cheerfully from a wooden shield; a wild-fowler's piece was arrayed above the mantel under a shelf of staghorns. Plaques and prints galore depicted pheasants on the nest, quail snuggled in the heather or, unbelievably, a fox cub curled asleep in a welter of chicken bones.

Iain hastily removed a pair of breeches from the chair, a grubby shirt from the sofa and tossed them into the bed-neuk.

'Please be seated.'

The ladies sat.

'May I offer you something? Tea, bread, a boiled egg, perhaps?'

Biddy glanced around. 'You do not seem to do yourself very well, Iain.'

Iain sighed and tweaked the untrimmed moustache that hung like a ragged pelmet over his lips. 'I do the best I can on what I have, Bridget. Now what will it be? I may have some bottled beer somewhere.'

'I want nothing, thank you,' Biddy said, 'nothing but an explanation.'

Maggie occupied the sofa, Biddy the one and only chair. Iain leaned against the table, drew the dressing-gown over his midriff and tied the cord tight.

'Things have not been right with me, Biddy,' he said. 'After the incident at the lodge – my unfortunate contretempts with Fennimore – I appear to have been cut adrift by all my former friends.' He paused, giving Biddy an opportunity to contradict him, which she did not do. He went on, 'In addition to which I did not receive the impression that we parted on the best of terms or that a communication from me to you would be welcome.'

'That,' Biddy said, 'is not what I meant by an explanation.'

'Oh. I see,' Iain said. 'It's the Baverstocks, isn't it?'

'The Baverstocks?'

'Are you angry with me because I know the Baverstocks? I never could fathom what your in-laws hoped to gain by advancing our friendship. Let me assure you, however, that I'm not responsible for falling income from the manufactory. I'm suffering considerable financial strain myself because of the drop in the market for woollens and tweeds.'

'Margaret,' Biddy said, suddenly, 'please be good enough to step out into the hallway for a few moments. I wish to speak with Mr Carbery in private.'

Maggie promptly made herself scarce.

Although the sofa was vacant now Iain made no move towards it. He remained at the rickety table, resting his weight on hip and elbow. He looked haggard, Biddy thought, haggard and ill.

She glanced towards the door then, speaking low, said, 'I have just come from a consultation with a surgeon, Iain.'

'Good God! A surgeon? Are you ill, Biddy?' he asked in alarm.

'He suggests that I may have harboured a contagion. That, however, is not the reason that I have not conceived.' Biddy spoke to him in a whisper. If she had been furious he could have dealt with it but he could not cope with her control. 'Is it you, Iain?' she said. 'It is you, is it not?'

'Yes, yes,' Iain blurted out. 'It's me.'

'How long have you had this loathsome disease?'

'Once, I only did it once, Biddy. I wouldn't want you to suppose that I prowl the streets looking for other women.' He threw up his hands in despair. 'I love you, Biddy. I wouldn't hurt you for worlds.'

'How long?'

'Not long enough,' Iain Carbery said.

'Explain.'

'I have not lain with you since I became infected.'

'Is that the truth?'

'It happened after we were together last time.'

'This girl, this woman . . .'

'Nobody, nobody of any consequence,' Ian said, desperately, then added, 'The only thing to be said for her was that she reminded me of you.'

'I see.' Biddy clenched her teeth.

'Red hair. She had red . . .' He cupped his hands to his cheeks, appalled at his own crassness. 'I was lonely, Biddy. I was so horribly lonely.'

'I think that you deserve to be.' Biddy gathered her skirts and rose to her feet. 'There is no more to be said. Goodbye.'

'Wait, Bridget. Please wait.'

He reached out to touch her then stopped, arm frozen in mid-air.

She regarded him with such coldness that he felt the organs inside his body turn hard with shame and a terrible sense of loss.

He had lost his physique, his health, had aged ten years in half as many weeks. He knew that he would never be the same again. It was not the fault of infection or the red-haired trollop whom he had picked up behind the quays. It was the fault of this woman, this Biddy Baverstock who had lured him into seduction and through seduction into love, a contagion that would not surrender to simple cures.

He hated her and loved her at one and the same time.

Helplessly he watched her step around the furniture to the door.

'Don't go,' he whispered. 'Don't leave me like this.'
But Biddy had already gone.

Doctor Andrew Kirkhope was not well pleased at having his authority challenged by a house steward but Innis Tarrant was on the steward's side and he, the doctor, was obliged to yield to the daughter's wishes.

He could see some sense in Naismith's suggestion, though, for however risky it was to move the patient in her present state it would probably be even more dangerous to leave her at the mercy of her drunken husband. So, after a brief, heated argument with Innis Tarrant, he agreed to allow Vassie to be transported to Fetternish House in the back of a long cart. In any case there was little enough he could do for the poor woman and her fate was more in the lap of the Gods than in his hands.

An apoplectic seizure had affected Vassie's brain and brought on a degree of paralysis. How much damage had been done was a matter of conjecture but Kirkhope's experience led him to suspect that Vassie's stroke was mild. If nature had decreed that the woman's time was up, though, surely it would be better for her to pass away in the peace and quiet of a bedroom or, for that matter, in the back of a cart than in the stench and the debris of the place that she called home.

Vassie had no say in the matter. No protest was possible, no sound from her lips, not even a twitch of the hand. Only the thin sliver of pupil that showed beneath her eyelid seemed alive and it, to Dr Kirkhope's astonishment, still burned with fierce hatred.

'Very well,' the doctor said. 'But I'll not be held responsible for what might happen while she is being carried to the house.'

'I cannot nurse her here,' Innis said.

'You mean you will not?' the doctor said.

'I will not become his slave,' Innis said. 'Make no mistake, Dr Kirkhope, that is what will happen if I try to nurse my Mam here.'

'Where is he, by the way?'

'Locked in the byre with his bottle,' Michael Tarrant said.

'Do you think he knows what's going on?'

'Oh, yes,' Innis answered. 'He knows what's going on.'

'Well, you can't just abandon him,' Kirkhope said. 'He will starve to death in a week without Vassie to look after him.'

'I will feed him. I will bring him food.'

'Even if your mother recovers,' Kirkhope said, 'she'll be an invalid. Frankly I doubt if she'll ever be able to farm this patch again.'

Michael said, 'If Ronan wants to starve himself to death then that's his affair. Get the old woman away from here first and we'll argue about what to do with the old man later.'

'Doctor Kirkhope, will you ride with her in the cart, please?' Innis said.

'Of course,' Kirkhope said. 'We will need a firm mattress, a narrow pillow and plenty of blankets. We will also need someone to hold her steady to prevent further shocks to the brain.'

'I will do that,' said Innis. 'Michael, please go over to Muriel Barrett's house and collect Becky and see to it that Gavin and Rachel get something to eat when they come home from school. I will stay with my mother.'

'If she survives,' Michael said.

'She'll survive,' Innis said. 'Believe me, she will survive.'

Innis could not recall ever having seen her mother naked before and she felt embarrassed by what she had to do now, without modesty or fastidiousness to protect her. Vassie had soiled herself like an infant and, like an infant, required to be sponged and carefully dried. She lay upon towels, on a sheet on the bed, as motionless as a corpse, and as she laved her mother's intimate flesh with the big creamy sponge Innis became breathless with anxiety, with the fear that Mam had passed on without a sound and that she, somehow, was to blame for it.

Innis wore an apron that Willy had brought up from the kitchen, a clean garment of lightweight cotton. Across the end of the bed Willy had draped two pairs of Biddy's underdrawers, a flannel night-gown and a woollen robe. He had lighted the fire in the upstairs bedroom and had lit two lamps. He had also brought in a tray with lemon water in a jug and one of the dining-room's big silver soup spoons and, just before he had departed, Doctor Kirkhope had administered a calming remedy to the patient, trickling it into the corner of her mouth with great care.

There was no more that medicine could do for Vassie Campbell, not that night at least. Innis and Willy Naismith would supply all the nursing that was required until such time as the extent of Vassie's paralysis could be properly determined and, if possible, relieved.

They whispered together at the door, doctor and steward, but Innis was too occupied with undressing her mother to eavesdrop.

Each movement she was required to make seemed fraught with the risk that it would damage her mother, who was limp and pliant as seaweed in her hands. She rolled in Innis's arms without a murmur, unprotesting at the loss of dignity, utterly dependent, drifting in and out of consciousness, aware then not aware, yet, Innis believed, still clinging tenaciously to whatever was left within, whatever spirit remained.

It took an hour to make her clean. Her skin was smooth beneath the tidelines of her dress. So smooth and lily-white that Innis was astonished by it, as if it was a secret that her mother had kept from all of them, hidden beneath a walnut face, leathery forearms and hands like crow claws. Only the visible parts of her had aged. Labour and labouring, the bruising business of the years had laid not a glove on her belly and breast which were still so like a girl's, so delicate and pure that the sight of them all exposed made Innis cry.

'Oh, Mam. Oh, Mammy, what have we done to you?' she sobbed.

And her tears fell on the white sheet, on the white flesh that had given her birth while her mother, uncomforted and uncomforting, lay as still and light as a thistledown that might at any moment be lifted away by the wind.

Willy said, 'Is she sleeping?'

'I think so,' Innis said. 'She is just lying there, so quiet and unnatural.'

'Did you pray for her soul?' said Willy.

'I prayed for her recovery,' Innis said.

'To the Blessed Lady?' Willy said.

'Yes, and to Saint Joseph, and to Saint Jude.'

'Surely that should do the trick,' Willy said.

She had heard such remarks before but she had not expected them from Willy Naismith. In fact, she had prayed intensely at her mother's bedside, offering her own repentance as a sign of faith, promising that she would put temptation behind her and would renounce her love for Gillies Brown if only God saw fit to spare her mother. She knew from the Catechism and from Father Gunnion's sermons that you could not negotiate with God, that He was no horse trader, no ethereal cattle dealer, but she did not know what else to do, what she could offer in exchange except love and guilt and piety.

'I didn't intend to be disrespectful, Innis,' Willy said. 'If there *is* going to be a bit of a miracle on Fetternish then it certainly will be due to you and not the rest of us sorrowful sinners.' He put an arm about her shoulders and gave her a hug. 'Go on home to your husband and children. Queenie and I will take turns to sit with your mother throughout the night. If there's any change for the worse then I'll come down and fetch you myself.'

'Biddy must be told,' Innis said.

'I suppose we could send her word by the telegraph.'

'So you do know where she is?'

'Of course I know where she is,' said Willy.

'In Edinburgh?'

'In the Wellington Hotel in Edinburgh,' Willy said.

'What is she doing there?' Innis asked.

Willy shook his head.

'Will you not tell me?' Innis said.

'She'll tell you herself, I expect,' Willy said. 'I'll despatch a telegraph message to the Wellington first thing tomorrow if you wish, Innis, but, all being well, your sister and my wife should be catching an early train to Oban and will arrive in Tobermory in the mid-afternoon. That was certainly Biddy's plan.'

'I wish she were here, now,' said Innis, sighing. 'Biddy always knows what to do about things.'

'You mean your father?'

'Yes.'

'She won't take him in,' Willy said. 'I'm stone-cold sure of that, Innis. She'll not have him in this house, not for any reason or at any price.'

'If it were not for the children I would take him.'

'Aye, and that would be more than he deserves,' Willy said. 'God, even thinking about taking him in is more than he deserves.'

'I cannot just be leaving him on Pennypol.'

'No, not when there are the dogs to be fed and the cattle to be looked after and that big bruiser of a pedigree bull to be coddled through the winter. If it were up to me I know what I'd do.'

'What would you do?'

'It isn't up to me, though,' Willy said.

'Stop being so coy, Willy Naismith,' said Innis, heatedly. 'Tell me, what would you do?'

'Send for Robert Quigley.'

And Innis said, 'Of course.'

If you had been enjoying a dish of hot chocolate in the conservatory of the Wellington Hotel that cold December afternoon you might have noticed a tall, auburn-haired lady and her rather gauche companion tucking into sandwiches and scones and, after a whispered confabulation on the conflict of greed with good manners, putting away between them two meringues and a gigantic creamy eclair. Starch and sugar seemed to have a soothing effect upon the pair, particularly upon the strikingly good-looking woman with the red hair. In the course of the mid-afternoon repast her manner changed from one of gesticulative restlessness to rather broody sobriety so that the last of the meringue was forked away with an air that could only be described as distant.

Several of the more mature gentlemen in the room, wives notwithstanding, were probably tempted to saunter to the corner table amid the palm fronds to cheer the young lady up and charm her out of fretting about the choice of this hat over that or this shade of material in preference to another. The companion, however, seemed to have found her voice and, leaning over empty plates and silver tea-pots, was doing a bit of cajoling on her own account while the lady with the red hair continued to scowl and shake her head.

Eavesdropping, even by the waiters, was impossible, for the pair communicated in fits and starts, sitting back every time someone came near, so that to the less than casual observer the conversation soon ceased to appear trivial but became intense and conspiratorial and – dare one say it – charged with a genuine, unfeminine emotion.

'If Willy were here, Mrs Baverstock, he would be telling you exactly the same thing as I am telling you,' Maggie said.

'It is not your place to be telling me anything.'

'Are you not going to tell Willy then?'

Biddy did not reply.

Her anger had finally diminished and, in spite of the scones and cream cakes, she felt quite hollow inside. Her confrontation with Iain had not gone at all as expected. His confession had done nothing at all to alleviate her shame.

It was not Sir Archibald Petty's probing of her intimate parts that had left her burning with embarrassment but his suggestion that she was to blame for her own woes and that the application of a little moral rectitude would benefit her more than an hour under the surgeon's knife. As far as the eminent gentleman could discover there was nothing wrong with her, nothing that needed adjustment or repair. He had not called her foolish, not in so many words, but his warnings had been firm enough to frighten her.

In many ways she would have preferred Sir Archibald to have 'found something', some growth or obstruction that an operation could have safely removed. What ailed and galled her was the fact that the body she had so often contemplated in the bath and in the mirror, was just as it appeared to be – sturdy and sound and ripe for motherhood. Even her mild infection – so mild that it caused her no pain and only marginal discomfort – was no excuse for her inability to bear children and, with science no longer her ally, she had already begun to wonder if the whole barren business was really some sort of divine judgement and a punishment for her sexual incontinence.

How could she explain that to Margaret, or to Willy, or to anyone?

Only her dear, devoted Catholic sister, Innis, would understand. And Innis would surely put on that prissy little prune-mouthed expression that she, Biddy, had always hated and would offer to pray for her, as if fertility was something that could be ordered up like ham hocks or a sack of oats.

Then Margaret was back, pecking at her across the pots.

'Are you not going to tell *anyone* what the doctor said?'

'No, I am not,' said Biddy.

'He told you that you were healthy, did he not?'

'What if he did?'

'If that is the case why are you so down about it?'

'Margaret,' Biddy said, threateningly, 'may I remind you that I am your employer and I am under no obligation to tell you anything.'

'Are we not also your friends?'

'Do not be ridiculous.'

'Who else cares about you as much as we do, Mrs Baverstock? Your sister Innis, perhaps. But she has her own life to lead. You just have us, just as we have you, and since you were one of us at one time . . .'

'Margaret, stop blathering.'

To Biddy's relief Margaret sat back.

A young waiter passed the table bearing a great tray of pots and jugs. He was handsome in a doltish sort of way, with a spray of black hair that bobbed across his forehead, and sly, curious eyes that slid admiringly in her direction. He looked neat and lithe in his tight black trousers and waist-nipping maroon jacket and Biddy, with a shocking little spurt of desire, wondered if he, a complete stranger and far, far too young for her, might be capable of launching her on the path to motherhood. And then he went away. And she felt hot, hot and tearful again at the recognition of her own promiscuity, those damnable, untidy passions that she could not put from her, even here, even now.

'He looks like Donnie.' Margaret followed the waiter with her gaze. 'Is that what you were thinking?'

'I was thinking nothing of the sort,' said Biddy, turning crimson. 'And he does not look in the least like Donnie. Donnie is much more . . . Oh, I have had enough of your questions, Margaret, and your impertinent comments. I am going to my room.'

'Do you want me to come with you?'

'No, I do not.'

'What will I . . .'

'Go and walk about the streets, see the sights, buy something to take home to Willy. Just leave me in peace.'

'Until when, Mrs Baverstock?'

And Biddy, sighing, said, 'Dinner-time.'

It was long after nightfall before Iain thought to stir himself and light the gas globe that flanked the mantelpiece. He was stiff and cold, for the coals in the grate had burned down to ash and he had been so wrapped in misery that he had failed to notice that the room had grown dark.

Still clad only in his dressing-gown he knelt before the hearth and raked listlessly at the clinker but it, like his future, was without warmth, without spark. He leaned forward until his head touched the iron canopy and peered down at his belly and thighs. His body seemed wasted, no longer muscular, no longer virile as if, drained of vital fluids, it had begun to collapse in on itself like the cheeks of a toothless old man. He shivered. He, who had never felt the cold before, shivered and drew the dressing-gown about him.

Outside, the street was busier than ever in the hour after dusk. He could hear vendors crying their wares, the rumble of cart wheels on cobbles, feet tapping on pavements, young girls shrieking with laughter. He could smell fish fries, beef stews, the cloying odour of the corner pub yeasty in the night air, horse manure and coal smoke and the rancid seepage of the tenement itself. And in the mix, overriding it, a faint lingering whiff of Biddy's perfume, that musk, that soft, sharp fragrance that reminded him of heather bells and thyme, sea-wrack and bracken, of Fetternish and Mull, and Biddy's clean warm bed.

Still hunkered by the fireplace, he put his head in his hands, covered his face with his fingers and moaned at his foolishness in losing all that he had, in giving everything up for love of a woman.

He had never been in love before, would never be in love again. He had underestimated the honesty that love demanded, its discipline, its rigour. He had loved her and he had lost her. He had not been man enough to keep her. Now there was only guilt and sorrow left, nothing else. He had lost her and had lost himself in her. He must live with that loss for the rest of his life for he knew that he would never see Biddy again.

He got up, pushing himself up, and shuffled into the bed closet.

He knelt on the floor-boards and groped beneath the bed. He brought out the gun-case, placed it on the bed, groped again and found the wooden chest in which he stored his cartridges. He fished inside the chest and picked out two cartridges. He held them lightly in his palm, his face over the chest. He could smell the exudations from the wood, powder grains, acrid and lovely, a fresh smell, open and manly.

Standing, he took the Anson from its case and loaded it.

He hefted the gun in both hands and pondered about technique. There would be a correct technique for this too, he supposed, but he had never studied it, had never had instruction. He gave a little grunt, almost a chuckle, at the thought that all the most reliable teachers on the subject must be dead.

He put down the gun and untied his dressing-gown.

It fell open, baring not just his chest but his belly and thighs.

That did not feel right, not right at all. There was something too defenceless, too immodest in nakedness. He was no one's sacrifice, no one's victim. He needed a touch of dignity to see him out, a Roman sort of gesture, bare-chested but not exposed. He tied the dressing-gown again and, with the shotgun crooked in his arm, tugged down the vee of the collar, and laid the barrels of the gun lightly against his breast. He let out a little 'Oooo' as cold metal touched his flesh.

He tried out a position, gun butt braced against the mattress, right arm extended, chin settled over the hard round holes. He could just reach the triggers with his forefinger. But it didn't feel right to do it there in the bed closet in the half dark. It felt furtive. He wanted it to be the opposite of furtive. He wanted it to be frank and open and somehow definitive. He carried the loaded shotgun into the living-room and turned up the gas.

Antlers cast tangled shadows across the ceiling. The salmon's glassy eye shone brightly in its case. The pert little fox head leered down at him, smiling with shining teeth. He seated himself on the sofa and settled back. He placed the gun butt between his feet and clasped it with his ankles. He adjusted the slope of the barrels. He stretched down an arm and laid his forefinger over the triggers, then he changed the angle of his hand and cocked out his thumb instead.

Thumb or forefinger? Forefinger or thumb?

Left hand, or right?

He tried it one way, then the other.

He leaned forward and pressed the metal against his throat, against the point of his chin, laid the barrels on his under lip, under his nose and, drooping, against his forehead. Each position had its advantages, each its disadvantages.

'God!' he thought, sitting back. 'What if I miss? How humiliating not to be able to make a clean shot at short range. I'll never live it down.'

He tried again, but his confidence had waned.

Chest, throat, mouth or brow? Lung, heart, larynx or brain? All very confusing, really, when the shot had to be perfect and absolutely fatal.

He laid the Anson across his knees and sat back.

Ten minutes ago his choices had seemed simple but now they had become manifold and complex.

Biddy, or nothing? Grief, or nothing?

He looked up at the stuffed salmon, the fox head, the array of antlers and experienced again their wildness, their innocence, their infinite indifference to his fate. He could smell – or thought he could – the river, the stubble fields, the bracken, and, coming in through the stale smoke of the city, a taste of the wind from the hills.

'Hell and damnation, Biddy!' he shouted. 'Hell and damnation!'

Then, laying the shotgun aside, he stalked into his little kitchen to scramble himself an egg.

TEN

The Higher Learning

Once the danger was past and it became clear that Vassie would recover most of her faculties, her convalescence brought a certain tranquillity to Fetternish.

The days were ordered about the invalid's needs and the quiet bedroom at the end of the first-floor corridor became, for Innis as well as Biddy, a haven from the flux of change that seemed to be sweeping in around them. With New Year just around the corner there was a feeling of optimism in the big house and a closeness between the sisters that had never existed before. Strange that a minute seepage of blood inside their mother's skull could have so affected them, could have defined with such awful clarity the line between life and death, between future and past, and caused them to examine their own needs so much more closely.

At first Vassie herself was unaware of the seriousness of her condition. She lay calm and clean in the white bed and smiled at her daughters, at Donnie, Maggie and Willy, at Mr Ewing, at anyone who came into the room to sit with her for an hour or so. She smiled and even winked at Dr Kirkhope when he took her blood pressure and examined her pupils and, within a week, encouraged her to sit up and then to stand, well supported, and test her balance. She slept a great deal, quite peacefully, did not converse and did not seem entirely connected with the folk who came to call or those who served her needs. And when asked what she recalled of 'her accident' she just smiled and smiled and wagged her head sagaciously.

Vassie's gentleness was no more real than the hiatus that her illness caused in Fetternish affairs. It was simply, the girls concluded, a form of forgetfulness, a complete, unwitting shedding of the past; all memory of who she was and what she had done wiped away by the pressure of loose blood upon her brain cells, all bitterness, all enmity, all sense of responsibility erased. She had become sweet and acquiescent at last, released by a thumbprint of bruised tissue from the dark self-loathing that had marred her character and fuelled her cantankerous autocracy throughout the years.

She was not fey like Aileen. She did not hallucinate like Ronan. In spite of her lack of communication even from the first she seemed to know vaguely who everyone was and, if she had wished it, to be capable of framing the question, 'Where is Ronan? Who is looking after Ronan?' But she did not ask that question, did not breathe his name and, it seemed, had finally abrogated all responsibility for her husband's welfare.

'Should we not tell her?' Innis said.

'Tell her what?' said Biddy.

'That Dada is all right. That we are looking after him.'

'If she wished to know, she would have asked.'

'She has not asked about anyone or anything,' Innis said.

'Perhaps that's why she is as she is,' said Biddy.

'What do you mean?'

'Happy,' Biddy said.

'Is she happy?' said Innis.

'Of course she is,' said Biddy. 'She has nothing to worry about except getting well again. She knows that I – that we will take care of her. I think she has given in to the inevitable and rather enjoys the feeling.'

'But she is ill, Biddy.'

'No, she is mending.'

'And when she is well again, will it all come rushing back?' Innis said. 'Is that the price she will have to be paying for a full recovery?'

'Not if I can help it,' Biddy said.

'How can you prevent it?'

'By keeping her here with me.'

'What if she does not want that? What if she wants to go back?'

'Back to what?' Biddy said. 'By the time Mam is fit to go anywhere there will be nothing of the old life for her to go back to.'

'You cannot sell Pennypol without her permission.'

'No, but as owner of the lease I *can* arrange to have it properly managed.'

'Quig?' Innis said.

'Yes, Quig. That was your bright idea, was it not?'

'Will he take it on?'

'He will be a fool if he does not.'

'And Dada?'

'Yes,' Biddy said. 'Yes, Dada is the one fly in the ointment. We cannot expect Quig to take care of him too.'

'Or to have Aileen living in the same house as him again.'

'That is the truth,' said Biddy.

'What will we do?'

'Get rid of him,' Biddy said. 'Get rid of him once and for all.'

Biddy's secret did not remain a secret for long. Although she trusted Margaret to keep her mouth shut, Biddy elected to tell her sister the reason for her visit to Edinburgh and its surprising outcome. Innis, in due course, informed Michael and within a day or two word had spread far and wide that Mrs Baverstock had been examined by a famous Edinburgh doctor who had once treated the Queen.

The honour conferred upon the good folk of Fetternish by this tenuous royal connection diffused interest in precisely why Biddy had gone to consult the eminent physician. It was generally agreed, in muted but not unsympathetic tones, that she suffered from 'a woman's problem' connected with her age and her fondness for consorting with incomers; a guess rather nearer the mark than even the most ardent gossips would have believed possible.

'There is nothing wrong with me,' Biddy told Innis, three or four days after she returned to Fetternish and after the shock of finding her mother so ill had subsided a little. 'According to the best physician in the country I am as fit to bear children as you are.'

'Then why hasn't she borne any?' Michael enquired when Innis passed on the information. 'Perhaps she hasn't found a man who can service her properly. God knows, she's been trying hard enough for the past few years.'

'Michael!'

'Well, is it not true? Do you think she has been having these strangers to stay at her house just because she is keen on shooting?'

'Michael, you should not be saying that about my sister.'

'Now that she has had herself poked and probed and has been given a clean bill of health, what your sister will be seeking is a man who has already proven himself capable of fathering children.'

'Why do you say these things, Michael?'

'Because it is a plain fact. Biddy knows that her breeding season will soon be over and that Fetternish is lying there waiting for an heir. She won't want her precious estate to fall into other hands.'

'Other hands?'

'To come down to Gavin, for instance,'

'If she leaves it to anyone it is more liable to be Donnie.'

'Look at the mess your grandfather made of his legacy,' Michael said. 'No, it'll be better for all of us in the long run if Biddy finds some man to suit her.'

'Some man like you, do you mean?'

'Aye.' He hesitated, smirking. 'I could be making a fine job of it, I tell you, if I was not otherwise encumbered.'

'Encumbered?'

'I already have a family. I already have a wife. It is your sister we are talking about, Innis, not you – or me for that matter.'

'Perhaps you should have married Biddy when you had the chance.'

'Biddy wouldn't have me because I was a Roman Catholic. But you,' he smirked again, 'you were less fussy and a deal more determined. There was no escaping from you, Innis, once you had me in your clutches.'

He had never voiced his disappointment so openly before, though the gist of it had hung between them for six or eight years, a faint hint of accusation that she had somehow cheated him out of the chance to better himself. She no longer knew what Michael wanted, what he expected from her. For years she had meekly accepted all the blame for the weakening of feeling between them, for the loss of whatever bond had brought them together. She could not reasonably deny, however, that she had fallen in love with him and had set out to steal him away from Biddy. She knew that he had been Biddy's first lover and no matter how she had tried she could never quite rid herself of the suspicion that she did not compare well with her sister and that Michael, if he had his chance again, would choose Biddy, not her, to be his wife.

She had gained from selfishness, however, had gained immeasurably from her conversion to the Roman Church whose Professions and Sacraments had enriched her life in ways that not even Michael could imagine, and had somehow justified her initial calculating deceptions in forcing Michael into marriage, in believing that he would come to love her as much as she loved him. In that supposition she had been wrong, had been naïve, for neither prayer nor punishment could bring about a change of heart in Michael Tarrant who had, she now saw, resented her love from the first.

If he could discuss Biddy, whom he loved and had always loved, as callously as if she were a breeding ewe then how did he think of her, of a woman who had trapped him into marriage and to whom he owed nothing but responsibility, and certainly no love?

'Do you still want her?' Innis said quietly.

'Whether I want her or not is immaterial,' Michael said. 'I can't be having her and that's the end of it. But there are other men around here who do want her and who can be having her and all I'm saying is that she would be advised to pick up one of them instead of some stranger from the mainland who'll steal control of Fetternish while Biddy is busy suckling her bairns.'

'Who,' Innis said, shaking her head at his callousness, 'who would you find acceptable as a substitute for yourself? Tom Ewing?'

'Hah! The minister would not know what to do with Biddy. In any case, he is too old and set in his ways to take her on.'

'Who then?'

'How about the schoolmaster?' Michael said. 'How about the famous Mr Gillies Brown? Would he not make Biddy a fine husband?'

'Would he?'

'I'm sure he would like to try,' Michael said. 'I'm sure he would see the advantages for himself and that family of his in marrying a woman who owned a big house and who could provide for his future. He would carry on with his schoolmastering and Biddy would run Fetternish just as she had always done.'

'And what would Biddy get out of it?'

'Bairns, children, babies.' Michael's voice had gone flat again. There was no teasing note in it now, no trace of hard humour. He was testing her. 'Aye, Brown is a sturdy sort of ram, I'd guess, and would be very dependable when it comes to the servicing. He has a right hefty brood to prove it, doesn't he? No saying how many more would have come off his stem if his poor wife had not been called away to her rest.'

'But – but she does not love him,' Innis said, and immediately regretted it.

'Love?' said Michael. 'Is it still a case of love? How do you know that she does not love him or will not come around to loving him? Are you saying, Innis, that the famous Mr Gillies Brown does not love Biddy?'

'I – I do not . . .'

'He'd be a queer chap indeed if he did not want to bed her.'

'Michael, please do not . . .'

'Unless there is another that he wants to bed more.'

'I do not know what Gillies wants.'

'Do you not now?' Michael said.

'No. No, I do not.'

'Then perhaps he does want Biddy? Perhaps he wants

nothing other than to have your sister in his bed, and his family set up in comfort in her house.'

'He is not that kind of man.'

'What sort of man is that?'

'Calculating,' Innis said.

'Do you mean he would not scheme to get what he wants?' Michael said. 'Whatever that may be. I mean, do you think that you'd be able to see what he's up to, a clever man like that? I mean, if he wanted *you*, for instance, do you think that you'd be able to see just what he was up to and resist?'

'I thought we were talking about Biddy's future, not mine.'

'You're right, Innis, right as usual. It's Biddy's future that should concern us, not yours. Your future is set and settled. Your future is here with me, with your husband and children and the fate you picked for yourself. And,' he pointed his finger, straight and firm, 'don't you forget it either. Don't you forget that you aren't the measure of your sister and never have been.'

'Is that what you really think of me, Michael?'

'It's not what I think that matters.'

'No. No, I do not suppose it is,' Innis said and then, because he had hurt her enough for one evening, got up and went through to bed.

It was a raw and scouring morning close to the shortest day of the year. Only the coldness of the wind kept the rain at bay and the sea was big and wrathful, swollen with wintry tides. It seemed to be lying at his very door that daybreak and he felt almost afraid of it in a way that he had never been afraid of it before.

The sight of it troubled him and flying spray, carried wild on the wind, came whirling up over the new byre and changed into little globs of salt that flecked the earth of the potato patch, clouding the cottage's beady little windows. He urinated hurriedly against the gable wall, crabbed indoors again, shut the rattling door with his shoulder and, fumbling, bolted it.

He looked helplessly around the kitchen. Two full bottles of Old Caledonia had been placed on the table but he had a half bottle left from last night and he would not need to start on today's ration before someone arrived to feed him.

The man, Innis's husband, had come down yesterday evening and had howked the coal out of the pile for him and had brought in a board of peat. Peat and coal were heaped along the wall under the loft ladder where all he had to do was reach out for them. He had been cold enough to do it, to keep the fire alight. The man had brought him a jug of stew with three or four boiled potatoes bobbing it in and had poured the stew into a pan and had heated it for him on the fire and had put it out into a bowl and had put the bowl and a spoon on the table, and had left again. He had made himself eat some of the stew. What he had not eaten was still in the bowl, coagulated under a skin of mutton fat. He was hungry. His belly and bowels ached. If nobody came to feed him in an hour or so he would eat what was left of the cold stew.

He stood in the kitchen, thinking what he would do and what sort of order he would do it in. He could hear the wind screeching in the empty loft and the howling of the dogs, who were hungry too. They were not his dogs. They were cattle dogs, Vassie's dogs. They would not be right until she came back to look after them. His feet and legs were cold. He took the half-empty bottle carefully from the dresser cupboard where he had hidden it. He had to be careful with his drink. He could not be sure that someone would come to feed him and if he broke or lost one of the bottles he would have to go out into the weather and try to walk over the ridge to Innis's house or to Biddy's house where they had taken Vassie.

If he was careful with the whisky, however, he would not need to go out for two or three days, even if they forgot about him.

There was fresh water in the big bucket and he had made him a brew of tea last night and had put some of the whisky into the tea, and sugar. He would not run out of sugar, not if he was careful. The tea had been warming, very warming and he had even sweated a little after he drank it, and had lain by the fire with his head on his arm with the sweat on him and would have lain there all night long if the candles had not gone out.

He did not like the sound of the winter's morning, the sound of the wintry sea. He did not like Vassie being away. He was a patient man, though. He had always been famous for his patience. He would lie where they had put him, would lie where he was safe, until Vassie came back to look after him. Vassie would make the sound of the sea go away.

He left the bottles on the table where he could see them. He slunk to the wall under the ladder to the loft where he felt safe. He sat down and leaned against the peats. He still liked the smell of the peats. He stretched out his feet to the fire, crossed his hands over his chest and rocked and rocked, trying to ease the grippe in his belly and his hunger. If he took drink then the hunger would go away. If he took drink now and no one came to look after him . . . He could hear the sea buffeting the door, pounding on the door like a great, angry fist.

'*Rooow-nan,*' it seemed to be shouting at him. '*Rooow-nan.*'

'Go away,' he shouted. Shouting made him dizzy. 'It was not me. I did you no harm. I took nothing away from you.'

'*Rooow-nan. Rooow-nan. Rooow-nan. Are you in there?*'

'Go away. Go away.'

'*In the name of God, Ronan, will you open the damned door.*'

'Vassie will be back. You had better not be letting Vassie catch you. I will be telling Vassie on you and then you will catch it.' He rolled on to his hands and knees and crawled on all fours past the hearth stones to hide under the table. 'Do you not know that this is Vassie Campbell's place? She will be back, I am telling you. She will be back. She – will – be – back.'

The pain in his belly and bowels became unendurable. His head ached with the effort of shouting. When he tried to force himself to stand upright his legs would not work. He got himself on to his knees and, braced on the knuckles of one hand let himself empty. He could not help it. It was not his fault. It was all Vassie's fault for not being there.

He let out a long cry, half pain and half relief.

The door rattled.

He saw a line of salty white daylight. He saw a white thing, like a worm, in the crack of the door. He heard voices, the clack of the bolt. Then the door burst open. He sat back in the baggy mess that he had made, and gaped.

There was a man with a creature in his arms, a woman behind him.

He saw the man with the creature in his arms turn away.

The woman came forward. She was dark against the daylight, a stranger who was not quite a stranger. She had a hat on her head and her hair was tangled like eels in a net. She wore earrings of fine gold wire and rings on the fingers of each hand. She wore a silk dress and brown button boots and a tasselled shawl, ornate as a peacock's tail, pinned at her breast with a golden brooch as big as a clam shell.

She towered over him, her painted lips curled in disgust.

She shook her head.

'No,' she said. 'No. Not this.'

'Take Aileen outside, Mam. I will be dealing with it.'

'No, Quig,' she said. 'Many things I have done for you, but not this.'

'What do you mean, Mam?'

'I mean,' said Mairi Quigley, 'that before we come to stay here this animal must go.'

'My God! I've never seen so many books in one room before.' Gillies moved around the dining-room table examining the volumes that Willy and Innis had set out so neatly. He eased out a heavy folio and opened it carefully. 'Look at this. Gould's *Birds of Britain*. What wonderful hand-tinted plates.' He glanced up at Innis. 'Did they all come from your grandfather's collection?'

'Yes,' Innis said. 'And seven big baskets out in the hall have still to be unpacked. Quig brought them over on the puffer yesterday. He decided not to risk the little sailing boat.'

'I should think not.' Gillies wrinkled his nose at the very idea of such a precious cargo being damaged by sea-water. He slotted the Gould carefully back into its place in the row and picked out another volume. 'What's this? McNair's *Travels in Mexico*. The original edition too by the look of it.'

'They are valuable, are they not?' Innis said.

'I'm no expert,' Gillies said, 'but I reckon there's material on this table that any Edinburgh bookseller would give his eye-teeth to possess. You must put them to auction.'

'Biddy wants to keep them.'

'What for?'

'For Donnie.'

'Is Biddy entitled to hang on to them?' Gillies said. 'I was under the impression that your brother in Glasgow had to have his share.'

'Biddy says that what Neil does not know will not harm him.'

'That hardly seems fair.'

'Well – some of the books are stained by mould and dampness.'

'Mould will brush off and if the volumes are stored in a dry atmosphere for a while the dampness tends to come out of the pages,' Gillies said. 'I used to toddle round the Glasgow book-shops when I had time. I bought an odd item here and there, as much as my purse would allow but, no, I'm no antiquarian.'

'As executor, it will be up to Quig to account to the lawyers for all the heritable property, including the books.'

'Does Quigley have any idea of their worth?'

'Quig is nobody's fool,' Innis said. 'He knows they have value.'

'You want to keep them too, don't you?'

'There is not enough space in Pennymain to store them.'

'Surely nobody would grudge you your pick of the lot?'

'Neil would,' Innis said. 'Of course, he will have his quarter share of the sale of the cattle and whatever the island fetches, if we can find a buyer for it. But books,' she laid her hand on books on the table, fingers spread not acquisitively but tenderly, 'are somehow different. They are what my grandfather *was*, if you take my meaning, more part of him than the land he owned. Does that sound foolish?'

'No, oh, not foolish at all,' Gillies said. 'Is it to foster Donnie's education that Biddy wants to keep the library here?'

'Mainly I think it is to keep my brother from getting his hands on it.'

'I doubt if the lawyers will accept that argument.'

'There is something that my grandfather could not have foreseen, something he could not have known about when he drafted his will.'

'You mean your mother's illness?'

'No, I mean my father.'

'Is he sick again too?'

'He is a drunkard, you know.'

'Yes, I know,' Gillies said.

He had come close to her now, the big brown leather-bound volume of Mexican travels still tucked under one arm. The dining-room curtains had been drawn, though there was still a trace of daylight in the afternoon sky and, in spite of Gillies's presence, it did not seem like a Saturday. It seemed, Innis thought, like no time, no time that clock or calendar could properly record, a floating time because of its strangeness, here in her sister's house with the books all around her and Gillies Brown beside her.

She felt kinship with him because of the books, because he understood what they meant to her, not as objects to be sold but as pieces of history, the route to a higher learning. She had the same sense of rapport with Willy, with young Donnie too, because of the books. But she was not in love with Willy Naismith and her feelings for Donnie were of quite a different order from her feelings for the Glasgow schoolmaster. And she was safe with him, quite safe, here in her sister's house, far from the cold shore of Pennypol and the dark dell of the Solitudes.

He was very close, almost touching her.

She leaned against him, her shoulder resting lightly against his arm.

'We do not talk of these things,' Innis said. 'We are supposed to keep them to ourselves; family secrets.'

'Everyone knows what your father is.'

'But not what he has done.'

'What has he done, Innis?'

'Wicked things, vile things.'

He did not ask, did not probe. He said, softly, 'I see.'

'I cannot forgive him,' Innis said. 'I try. I do try. But I cannot find it in my heart to forgive him, even when I pray.' She sighed. 'They say that it is an illness, that he is possessed by drink. They say that he cannot live without it. But I think it is a weakness, part of the weakness that my father and men like him give in to.' She leaned closer, pressing against his shoulder more firmly as if she needed his support to stand upright at all. 'I did not ask you to come here just to look at my grandfather's books, Gillies.'

'No,' he said. 'I know.'

'I need to talk to someone, someone who will not say to me "Be rid of him. Toss him out", just because they have something to gain by it.'

He put the book down and placed an arm about her waist. There was no cupidity in the gesture, only caring. He led her from the table, through the columns of books that lay on the carpet to a chair by the fireplace and, as if he had danced with her and now the dance was over, waited until she was seated before he moved away. He leaned on the high-backed chair opposite her, looking at her out of the tops of his spectacles in a manner that she might have found comical if he had intended it to be so, and if he had smiled.

'Talk to me then, Innis,' Gillies said. 'Tell me what's wrong.'

She sighed again. She wished that he would come close to her, would - or could - hold her and give her comfort. But to have him there at all was blessing enough. She said, 'They want to send him away.'

'Who are "they"?' Gillies said.

'My sister, my husband, Quig and his mother. All of them.'

'Send him where?'

'To a place called Redwing which is near Perth.'

'A hospital?'

'Doctor Kirkhope says that it is a hospital, a place where my father's condition will be properly treated. But I think that is not the truth.'

'Surely Andrew Kirkhope would not lie to you, Innis?'

'I think that it is an asylum.'

'Even if it is,' Gillies said, 'that doesn't mean he won't be

317

well cared for or that there's no possibility of him being let out again.'

Innis looked down at the carpet between her feet. 'I do not want him let out again. I do not want him cured and to come swaggering back to Mull as he was ten or fifteen years since.' She paused, still not meeting Gillies's eye, then continued, 'If my father is gone, if Quig takes over Pennypol then my mother will be obliged to stay here with Biddy and will not have to work again. She will have time to heal, and she will be happy, as happy as she can ever be, for the rest of her days. But if my father is still here or if he returns he will claim her and she will go with him and he will kill her with his demands.'

'Is your mother well enough to understand what's happening?'

'No, not yet. It is our decision to make. Biddy's decision – and mine.'

'Could you not wait . . .'

'The last of the Foss cattle will be sold next week and my grandfather's house will be empty. Advertisements for the sale of the isle will appear soon after New Year. Besides, Quig is needed on Pennypol to take charge of the Fetternish herd. He will not come while my father is there. He cannot. He cannot bring Aileen back to Pennypol while my father is there, and he will not abandon her.'

'And you can't take your father to live with you?'

'I have two young daughters.'

'I see. And Biddy won't?'

'No, Biddy won't. For my mother's sake she wants him gone.'

'Only for your mother's sake?'

'No,' Innis said. 'She wants to punish him.'

Still he did not enquire, did not pry. He waited, leaning on his arms on the chair back, watching her. After a moment, he said, 'And you, Innis? Do you want to punish him too?'

'Yes.'

'For what he did to your mother?'

'For what he did to all of us.'

'Who will pay the bills for Redwing?'

'I will pay a portion from the money that will come to me

after Grandfather's affairs are settled. Biddy will pay the rest. She would pay it all but that would not be fair.'

'Do you think that's wrong? Do you think that's blood money?' Gillies shook his head. 'It seems to me to be no more than your father deserves.'

'Although I cannot forgive him,' Innis said, 'it is not up to me to judge him or say what he deserves.'

'You can't always be on the side of the angels, Innis,' Gillies said. 'What would be best for you right now? What do you want to do with him?'

'Put him away.'

'Then do it,' the schoolmaster said. 'No tears, no lamentations, Innis, just have him put away.'

Naturally it fell to Willy to organise the ousting of Ronan Campbell from the black house by the shore. Being a touch more cynical than either of Ronan's grown-up daughters he had taken the precaution of enlisting the assistance of Michael Tarrant for, however much drink had undermined Ronan's strength, Willy suspected that the little fisherman would not leave without a struggle.

Innis had explained to her father that he had been booked into an hotel in Perth for a short holiday, that change would do him good. He had scoffed at the very idea, of course, had refused even to consider it. 'Vassie will be back for me,' he had shouted. 'She will be back here any day. I must have the place warm for her and be here when she arrives.' Innis had asked her father if he knew where Mam was. He had blustered, had puffed, had drunk whisky to refresh his faculties and, because his memory was so vague and raddled, had eventually declared that he thought she had gone to stay with Evander McIver on Foss.

Innis had crossed herself and asked pardon for her lies.

Then she had informed him that Vassie was not on Foss but in a hospital in Perth and that he would be taken there to visit her and then brought back.

He had looked at her slyly and had shaken his head. 'You are trying to be rid of me, girl, are you not now?' he had said, and had laughed that smart, croaking laugh that had raised the hair on the nape of her neck. 'I know what you are doing. You are taking me up to that damned big house of Biddy's to live there like some idle lord. I will not go. I will not go.'

He had watched her sort out and take away his soiled clothing. He had watched her bring back his clothing, laundered and ironed. He had watched her pack his clothing, what there was of it, into a small wicker hamper, and, because he had no awareness of the passage of time, had sniggered at her stupidity in thinking that she could catch him out, and, sprawled on the bed or on the floor or lolling across the table, had laughed at her and had told her confidently over and over again, 'I am going nowhere. My place is here.'

At Willy's suggestion Innis had furnished her father with a single bottle of malt whisky each day for the nine days that it had taken Dr Kirkhope to finalise arrangements. She had placed one bottle upon the table each morning and had told him that there would be no more. He had grasped that piece of arithmetic well enough and had doggedly eked out his ration; had shouted at Innis, though, called her cruel, called her other names too, names so offensive that Innis's heart should have been hardened against him but, oddly, was not. The more he'd insulted her the more she'd felt like a Judas, and the more she dreaded the day when the attendant from Redwing would arrive to accompany Willy and her father away from Pennypol on a journey from which only Willy would return.

In Biddy's house behind Olaf's Ridge Vassie lay in a soft white bed, smiling her soft smile, quite oblivious to the decisions that her daughters had made on her behalf and the manoeuvres that were necessary to sever her from her husband and to bring to all – all save Ronan, that is – a modicum of peace and harmony.

On the pastures around Pennymain sheep continued to graze on the sparse winter pick and in the fields near to Pennypol the cattle roved just as they had always done. Morning and evening Innis milked the four cows and fed the autumn calves. As she carried the milk to the trays in the dairy at the back of the new byre she would think to herself how little had changed – and how much. She would look towards the cottage with its ragged thatch and unwashed stoup and wonder how long it would last, how long any of it would last, and, bad though it had been, would long for it all to come back so that she – they – might begin it all again.

Barrett took care of the cattle. Michael took care of the sheep. Biddy took care of Vassie and Donnie. Willy, as always, looked after Biddy and ran the big house on the headland as easily as he might wind a clock. She, Innis Tarrant, cared for her daughters, her son and husband. But in the lost acres behind the drystone wall that Vassie had built to keep out strangers, her father, unloved and uncared for, wallowed in his own dirt and muttered and smirked as if nothing for him had ever changed and nothing possibly could.

'I will not go,' he screamed. 'I will not go. What are you doing to me? Where are you taking me? Innis, oh, dear Lord Jesus, Innis, Innis. What is it that is happening to me? Why are you letting them do this to me.'

The children were at school. Maggie had taken Becky up to Fetternish to look in upon her grandmother. But all the rest of them were there, all those who had known Ronan Campbell before drink had claimed him, when he had been more than half alive. He had not been bathed, he had not been shaved. In fact, it had taken Willy and Michael a half-hour just to force him into clean clothes, to button him into his greatcoat, wrap a muffler about his throat and stick gloves on his hands while feeding him just enough whisky to keep him malleable.

He had realised by that time that something that Innis had told him was the truth or an approximation of the truth or all the truth that he was going to get, that she had meant what she had said about taking him away.

It dawned on him fully only when he saw the men. What it meant, though, what the great, raw, tearing change to his idle routine signified was beyond him. Initially he jabbered only out of pique at being disturbed. Then the Fetternish cart arrived from Tobermory with Hector Thrale, black as an undertaker and old, sitting gaily on the driver's board; the man, the stranger, sitting behind him, upright as a fence-post and huge, bigger than Evander McIver, bigger than Neil, a swollen-shouldered man in a brown serge suit with a neat little brown trilby hat perched on his head and a neat little brown leather attaché case perched on his massive knees.

Ronan was ready in spite of himself, dressed for the voyage, his wicker hamper roped and ready by the door. The dogs had been fed and locked up again and the gulls had come in on the rising tide and screeched overhead and the cattle, Vassie's cattle, roared down on the foreshore. And the man, the stranger in the brown serge suit with the dainty little trilby hat on his head stood unsmiling in the doorway and said, 'Come along then, Mr Campbell. It's time we were on our way.'

He screamed, *'Innis, Innis. What is happening to me? Why are you letting them do this to me?'* and, when Innis did not answer, flung himself backward on to the floor and clutched at the hearth stones, at the base of the ladder, at the peat-hod and the table-legs, while first Willy then Michael and, finally, the stranger tried to persuade him to stand up of his own free will and, when that failed, caught him by the arms and hoisted him to his feet.

'Do not hurt him,' Innis cried.

'No, Miss, he'll not be hurted,' said the stranger.

A little host of spectators had gathered outside to see the last of Ronan; Biddy and Innis together, Barrett standing back, Hector Thrale by the cart, then up on the hill, pretending not to be curious, Mr McCallum, Mr Clark from the Ards and six or eight tenants and field-hands.

The event might have inspired a bag-piper to invent a new lament if Ronan's departure from Pennypol had been more solemn and dignified. But slung between Michael Tarrant and the officer from Redwing, his arms pinned back like chicken wings, he was dragged from the cottage on his knees, his boots ploughing two straggling furrows on the wet earth. He did not have the strength to struggle and before the path was reached the officer jerked him upright and the pair held him swagged between them as if he weighed no more than a rabbit-skin.

Willy, more sedate than anyone, followed on behind, Ronan's

little wicker hamper swinging pathetically from one hand.

Innis might have gone after them, might have run uphill to the track and, like a bewildered child, have trailed the cart along the track to the crossroads, crying after it and waving until it was out of sight. But Biddy held her tightly. Elbow locked into elbow, Biddy would not let her go until their father was bundled into the cart and Thrale, with a vigour, a relish that belied his age, cracked the whip over the horse's head and the cart moved away.

The sisters saw it lurch over the crest of the moor ground and, very swiftly, disappear. Michael stood with his hands on his hips staring after it. On the hillside the spectators turned their heads to watch it out of sight.

Biddy drew in a deep, stiff breath.

'Good riddance,' she said.

And Innis, though affected, did not disagree.

In the lull between noon and early evening milking the fishing boat appeared out of nowhere. It followed the coastline closely, tacking this way and that under shortened sail. The boat, the *Walrus*, was undecked and laden, the sea brisk enough to make it wallow in the currents that sucked around the little isles and out of the mouths of Mull's long sea-lochs.

The boat was Quig's, bought and paid for. He would not leave it behind. He was the son of a drover, though, no more competent with tiller and sail than an islander had to be. With the tide on the rise and the wind from the shore he navigated a prudent course around Caliach Point and followed the line of the bay with bows nudging into the waves that strode in from the Atlantic. Before the jetty was reached he trod down all the canvas, put his mother to the oars and told her when to pull and when to ship and, with Aileen kneeling in the prow, steered the craft smoothly in against the stone.

Leaping ashore, he moored the boat fore and aft. Then, stepping down again, he lifted Aileen up on to the jetty, watching her all the while. He wondered if she even noticed how the place had changed, the big new byre close at hand, the jetty itself lengthened out and squared with mortar, the fields that stretched into the heart of Fetternish all fenced and trim. The house itself was the same, though, the cottage in which she had been born and raised and from which she had been dispatched into exile over a dozen years ago.

He watched her closely as she stood above him on the jetty. He could tell nothing from her eyes, those corn-flower blue eyes whose terrible vacancy veiled all thought and feeling. He noted how she moved, though, for he had learned to interpret those subtle little motions of her body, the way she cocked her head or lifted her arm or, as now, stood stock still, staring vacantly up at the vegetable plots and the turf-roofed cottage, dark and deserted under the lip of the moor.

'Aileen,' he said, quite sharply. 'Aileen.'

'Hah?' She turned, her arms stuck out from her sides. 'Dada?'

'Take the boxes that I will be handing up to you and put them safe behind you, away from the water's edge. Do you understand me?'

Her saw her lips move, thin lips, paler than seemed natural in the tight, weathered little face. Her eyelids fluttered. She glanced away from him again towards the dwelling.

'Aileen. Do you hear what I am saying?'

'Aye,' she answered in a tone that signified neither comprehension nor the lack of it, in that sweet, weak little voice that came out of her mouth when past and present, fact and fantasy swirled higgledy-piggledy in her damaged brain. 'Aye, Quig, aye.'

The boat was rolling under him. He balanced himself with spread legs before he lifted one of the wooden crates and slid it on to the jetty. Aileen looked down at it and then, with a jerky movement that indicated obedience, lifted it, turned and put it down behind her. By that time Quig had replaced it with another and Aileen, comfortable with repetition, did the same. He was constantly surprised at her strength. She seemed fragile, almost brittle, as if she had been fashioned out of the same stuff as a scallop shell. She would work now until the boat was empty of everything but oars and sails and mast. He would not order her to help the transfer of all their goods and chattels from the jetty to the cottage. He would find a barrow or a little cart and do that while his mother and Aileen got the feel of the house.

He had about three hours until full dark. Donnie would come down at the end of the school day and there would be just enough light for Donnie to help him drag the boat ashore. He did not like to leave the craft against the jetty for he knew what a squall could do to timber laid against stone and he would feel safer with the *Walrus* high and dry. He would not be needing the use of the boat again, not before summer and perhaps not even then.

He unloaded more boxes. He watched Aileen and his mother too now stoop and turn. He worked faster, in rhythm with the lift and fall of the sea. There was no one to see them arrive. No one to greet them. Only the cattle, stout Foss-bred stock. He took comfort in the sight of them plodding curiously along the shore towards the byre, as if to give him a welcome. He would be glad to see Donnie, to have Donnie close to him again. But he would not take Donnie to stay in the cottage. Of course, he would inform Biddy Baverstock that he wanted the lad back with him, that it was only proper that he should be with his mother. Biddy would protest, would suggest that Donnie be left to enjoy the comforts of the big house and, at the last moment, he would reluctantly agree. He wanted Donnie to stay at the big house. He needed Donnie to keep a hold on Biddy.

'Is that the last of them?' his mother said.

'It is,' Quig said and clambered up on to the jetty.

'Are you sure that he has gone?' Mairi said.

'Do you not hear the dogs?'

'Doggies,' Aileen said. 'Fingal's here.'

'No, Fingal's gone. It is other dogs now.' Quig took her hand. 'If something had gone amiss with the arrangements, Mother, then the dogs would not be locked up. Someone will be down to feed them before nightfall and to see to the milking. If you want to be sure that Campbell is no longer in residence then we will walk up to the cottage now and I will bring in the stuff later.'

'I'll be needing my own saucepans,' Mairi Quigley said. 'I'm not cooking in anything he's left behind.'

'You'll have your own pots, and dishes too,' Quig said. 'I'll bring them up first, then you can make us a bite of supper. We'll be ready for it by then.'

'I'm ready for it now.' His mother took his arm and started up the path to the cottage, Aileen hanging on to his other hand. 'I don't like this miserable place, son. I hope we don't have to stay here too long.'

'No, not one minute longer than we have to,' Quig said. 'I promise you, Mother, our next step will carry us up in the world.'

'In which direction, Quig?'

'In that direction,' Robert Quigley said and, disengaging his hand from Aileen's, pointed northward, towards Fetternish.

Michael said, 'So Quigley's installed in Pennypol, is he? That didn't take long. He must have arrived before your father was out of Tobermory.'

'There is nothing for Quig to do on Foss now the last of the bulls has been sold,' Innis said.

'Who bought it and what sort of price did it fetch?'

'It went to the Duke of Montrose, I believe, for four hundred guineas.'

'And the fat stock?'

'Gone weeks ago.'

'So there's a chance we'll be seeing our money soon?'

'Cheques and banker's drafts have been lodged in a special account with the lawyers in Perth,' Innis said. 'You seem very eager to receive this money.'

'Even if Foss does not attract a buyer, it's a substantial sum and it could be earning a healthy rate of interest for us.'

Innis said, 'It will provide a nice nest-egg for Gavin and the girls.'

'The girls?' said Michael. 'What do the girls need with money?'

'It will pay for their education.'

'Will your Mr Brown not give them all the education they need?'

'They may not wish to stay on Mull,' Innis said. 'They may wish to go to a university on the mainland and now we will be able to afford to send them. But if that is not for them then the money will provide a dowry if and when they choose to marry.'

'You have it all cut and dried, I see,' Michael said. 'What if I've plans of my own for how it should be used? Is it not my money as much as yours?'

'Of course it is,' said Innis.

'Well then,' Michael said, 'we could buy a piece of land and fifty ewes to start with and set up on our own. Then we'd be free of your sister.'

'I do not feel that I am dependent upon Biddy.'

'No? Well, I do,' said Michael.

'Where would you be looking for this piece of land?'

'Where ever I could find it.'

'In the Borders?' Innis said.

'Not necessarily.'

'I would not want to be leaving Mull at this time,' Innis said, 'with my mother ill and – and so many other things going on.'

'Other things?' Michael said.

'Changes,' Innis said.

'If things fall right, perhaps we would not even have to leave Fetternish,' Michael said. 'I mean, there is land in plenty round here.'

'Biddy's property, all of it.'

'Not all of it,' Michael said. 'Pennypol doesn't belong to Biddy.'

'What?' Innis said. 'Would you have us live in that dismal cottage?'

'I'll live in any house that's mine,' said Michael. 'It isn't the house that matters, it's the grazing. Pennypol has good grass and with cattle off and sheep brought on I could be raising a flock for our profit and not your sister's.'

'But Quig . . .'

'Quig's only a worker, an employee like the rest of us. Biddy will find something else for him,' Michael said. 'Will you talk to your mother about it when she's feeling better? I mean, what can she want with the place now that she's too weak to work it, now that your father is off her hands for good and all?'

'She draws rent on the grazing,' Innis said. 'It is her income.'

'Some income!' Michael said. 'In any case, she'll have a lump sum to invest if she still wants to draw an income – though I can't see the need now she's got her feet under Biddy's table. Biddy's not going to turn her out.'

'No, but Biddy will have to be paid for the improvements.'

'What? A new byre, a jetty and some fancy fencing?'

'I had no idea that you wanted a place of your own.'

'I do, though,' Michael said. 'I want something to hold on to, whether it's a house or a flock or a wife. Something to hand on to Gavin, not just a job on his aunt's estate. Will you talk to your mother? After all, she can't live forever. Sooner or later you'll inherit some of those shore acres and you may as well have it now while there's still something left of it. If she'll sell the place to anyone she'll sell it up to you.'

'I do not want to live there, Michael. I do not want to go back to my father's house and start out all over again.'

'Would you rather we left Mull?' Michael said. 'Would you rather I rented a small holding on the mainland, away from your sister, your mother and all your other so-called friends?'

'No.'

'Then talk to her,' he said. 'Find out what she wants for the place.'

'What if Mam will not sell?'

'Persuade her,' Michael said.

'I doubt if Biddy will stand for it.'

'By that time,' Michael said, ominously, 'Biddy may have no choice.'

He came in by the side door from the gardens, slipping into the corridor quiet as a mouse. He took off his overcoat and hat and hung them on the peg and laid his little overnight bag where no one would trip over it. He came into the kitchen without a word and seated himself on the chair at the deal-topped table, head cradled on one hand as if his jaw ached.

The kitchen was only temporarily deserted, not abandoned. Vegetables had been peeled and chopped and arranged in colourful little piles ready to be put into the pot and a big, crispy, beef pie that Mrs McQueen had made earlier in the afternoon was baking in the side oven. A tray of oat bread cooled on the shelf by the larder and a milky-pink blancmange quivered on a floral plate on the dresser waiting to be decorated with little spears of angelica or florets of crystallised ginger. It was all very pat, all very ship-shape and Willy should have been relieved to be home again, safe from the perils of travel by rail and boat in the gloom of the mid-winter day.

But he was not. He was subdued, so uncommonly grey and quiet that even when Margaret came bustling into the kitchen he did not rise to greet her with a kiss and a cuddle and a word of cheer but remained where he was, watching her, until after a moment she noticed him and, startled, stepped back from him as if he was an unwelcome intruder.

'Willy!' she exclaimed. 'What are you doing just sitting here? I did not hear you come in.'

He forced a smile of sorts and, shifting position, held out his hand. She frowned, hesitated, then came to him and took his hand on hers. She leaned against the table and studied him cautiously. 'What is it, dear? What's wrong? Was it a stormy crossing?'

'No, no, the crossing was fine.'

'You were not sick?'

'No.'

'You are looking very pale, though. Are you cold?'

'I'm all right.' He sighed, glanced at her and tightened his grip on her hand. 'It was a mistake,' he said. 'They shouldn't have sent him to that place. Aye, I know: he's no better than a selfish old drunkard who can cause trouble in an empty house – but . . .' He shook his head. 'Not that. Not there.'

She knelt by his knees. 'Oh, Willy, was it that awful?'

'I had no idea . . .'

'You're home now, with us.'

'Aye, but he's not. He's stuck in that place for the rest of his days. Ronan Campbell will not come home again.'

'I thought you did not like the man?'

'I don't. I detest him. But that doesn't prevent me . . . God, Maggie, you should have seen how those helpless old men staggered and stumbled about the corridors, bumping into each other, lifting their fists as if to ward off ghosts. Others, like Campbell, were locked away in quilted rooms. Clean enough, tidy enough, yes, but not - not *alive* any more, just stored away out of sight as if they'd never had any worth.'

'Willy, Willy. Oh, I'm sorry you had to see it.'

He drew her against him, nuzzled his nose into her hair and inhaled the fragrance of it, no fancy perfume this but the soft, female smell of the woman he loved and who, he hoped, loved him. 'Please, Maggie,' he murmured. 'Please promise me, whatever happens, whatever befalls me, whatever age does to me in the end, do not, please, put me away.'

She gave a sob and drew him to her, both arms about his waist as if to hold him safe against the threat of the shadows that stalked him and of which he had been made aware. Through him she could feel the grimness of the place to which Ronan Campbell had been taken, the cruelty in the care, the unlovingness; that institute of shameful secrets, where men who through negligence or self-indulgence or even no fault of their own had become mere empty encumbrances and had been cast aside because of it.

'No, no, Willy.' She stroked his white hair. 'It will not happen to you. Never, I swear. I will not let it.'

'How can you stop it, Maggie?'

'I can. I will not let them take . . .'

'No,' he said. 'Growing old, I mean.'

'Ah, William, you are back, I see.'

'Yes, ma'am.'

'How was the trip?'

'Quite comfortable, thank you.'

'Did he give you any trouble on the boat?'

'None at all.'

330

'Tell me about Redwing,' Biddy said. 'I should have gone to inspect it in advance, I suppose, but – well – I have been rather pressed of late. Is it suitable for a man in my father's condition?'

'It's all that Doctor Kirkhope said it would be.'

'I take it he'll be well looked after there?'

'I'm sure he'll have the best of attention,' said Willy, stiffly.

'I should hope so,' Biddy said, 'considering what they charge in fees.'

'I hear that Quigley has already taken over at Pennypol.'

'Oh, yes,' said Biddy. 'That was the arrangement and, fortunately, there were no hitches. I admit that I will be glad to have someone responsible to take care of the cattle.'

'And Donnie, too?' Willy said.

'Donnie?'

'I assume that Donnie has gone home to be with his mother?'

'This is Donnie's home now,' Biddy said.

'What does Donnie, let alone his mother, have to say about that?' said Willy, in no mood to be placatory.

'In fact, Donnie is in the dining-room arranging the books from my grandfather's library. He seems perfectly happy to stay where he is.'

'What have you decided to do with the books?' Willy said. 'Are you going to send them away too?'

'No,' Biddy said. 'My grandfather cherished that library of his and books are such an asset in a house this size. I've decided to keep the whole library. I'll have the long wall in the drawing-room properly shelved and, of course, I'll pay my brother Neil a reasonable sum in lieu of his share.'

'On whose valuation?' said Willy.

Biddy sat up, ruffled by his tone. 'What *is* wrong with you, Willy?'

'You seem to be having everything your own way.'

'My own way?' said Biddy. 'Nothing of the damned kind. And don't, pray, be impertinent. I did not ask for any of this to happen, for my grandfather to die and my mother to fall ill and . . .'

'No, but then you pick and choose, don't you?'

'What is *that* supposed to mean?'

'Keep Mama. Keep Donnie. Keep whatever you fancy. Toss out all the rest, all the nasty things you don't want to take responsibility for.'

'For instance?'

'Aileen. Your father . . .'

'May I remind you, Willy, that you agreed that my father would be better off in an institution.'

'Aye,' said Willy. 'So I did.'

'And it's no damned business of yours what I do.'

'If you wish my resignation . . .'

'For God's sake, Willy! Your resignation? Where would you go? What would you do? You'll never find another position like this one, not at your age.'

'I take it then,' Willy said, 'that I'm not considered *quite* useless, even if I am tottering on the verge of the grave?'

Biddy had no clear idea of why her strong right hand had suddenly developed a tremor, though, given the timing, she had a vague suspicion that it might have to do with the trip to Redwing. She had been feeling good about herself, about her prospects, about the manner in which she had coped with all the family crises and had squared everything – almost everything – away to everyone's satisfaction. She had not antici-pated that she would have to cope with a tantrum from her stalwart steward.

She got up and placed herself before him.

Willy was one of only a handful of men of her acquaintance who was taller than she was and to whom she had to look up. She did not mind that. In fact, it pleased her. She stood on tiptoe, her hands on her hips and stared him straight in the eye.

'You will not resign, Willy, because Margaret will not let you,' she said. 'You are a prisoner here, old chap, in case you had not realised it. That is the price you will have to pay for making yourself indispensable to far too many people, most of them female. Now, will you kindly trot downstairs, waken Cook from her forty winks and have the table set for dinner – dinner for two.'

'What's wrong with eating here?' said Willy, grumpily. 'Since the dining-room is still littered with your newly-acquired library. Donnie won't object to having his supper in front of the fire.'

'Donnie will be taking his supper in the kitchen with you before he goes upstairs to sit with my mother for an hour or so.'

'And what will you be doing?'

'Entertaining a guest, William.'

'A guest?' Willy frowned. 'Your cousin Quig?'

'No,' Biddy said, with an unavoidable arching of the brow. 'Gillies Brown, if you must know; tête-à-tête in the dining-room.'

'*Tête-à-tête?*' said Willy, shrilly.

'Hmmm,' Biddy said. 'In the dining-room.'

Christmas was Tom Ewing's favourite time of the year. In this, in Crove, he was more or less out on a limb for Nativity celebrations, with cribs, carols and holly wreaths, were regarded as a mite too close to Catholic idolatry for die-hard Presbyterians. Indeed, in the 'other church' in Crove the Lord's birthday was hardly acknowledged at all and Barclay Boag, minister of that church, and Tom Ewing had not exchanged a civil word in years. This was not Tom's doing, of course. He would have preferred to debate differences with his counter-part but knew by experience that rational discussion was impossible; that Saint Peter himself would have a hard time convincing Mr Boag that he was worthy of being let through the iron gate at the top end of the main street let alone that Christmas was, or should be, a season of rejoicing.

Tom's elders, Hector Thrale among them, were hardly better disposed to indulge in all the falderals that surrounded Christmas in more southerly realms like Tobermory where, so they believed, an influx of incomers was already undermining dour centuries of tradition.

They, the elders, were generous men, however. They granted their soft-hearted minister a certain leeway when it came to selecting hymns and readings for the Christmas service but drew a firm line at exchanging gifts or cards with him. Such tokens of friendship and esteem were reserved for New Year's Day which, in the quaint, unmodified calendar of Protestant isles, was still accepted as the best time for sentimental indulgence.

Changes, though, were definitely in the wind. They blew not from an obvious centre of corruption like Tobermory but from Fetternish, where Mrs Bridget Baverstock had announced that she was giving a grand Christmas party for all her workers and tenants, children included, and that she would not look favourably upon anyone who turned down an invitation.

Tom had no intention of turning down Biddy's invitation, of course. He had already made his December trip to Dundee to visit his ageing mother and buy toys and trinkets in the city's emporium and a few lace-edged cards to send to enlightened friends. He had seen very little of the Campbell sisters of late. They had been much occupied with their own affairs. He had visited Vassie's sickroom to offer prayers for a speedy recovery and had heard from Biddy that Ronan, for his own good, was to be sent into temporary care on the mainland; also that Robert Quigley would be brought in from Foss to tend the Pennypol herd. All of this information – especially the news about Quig – somehow lightened the cloud of melancholy that had settled over the Reverend Ewing in recent years, though he could not pinpoint just when he had begun to feel better, or to fathom the reason for it.

He would certainly have denied that it was connected to that afternoon in Miss Fergusson's shop when Robert Quigley's mother, like a warm, spice-laden breeze from Araby, had first wafted into his life. He might even have denied that the progress of his restoration increased, along with his heart rate, when on entering the pulpit on the morning of Sunday, December 20th he saw the whole conglomeration of Browns in from An Fhearann Cáirdeil, along with Biddy, Donnie and Margaret Naismith – and there, in the third pew from the front, the doll-like figure of Aileen Campbell with Robert Quigley's mother, Mairi, seated by her side.

Tom could hardly bring himself to announce the number of

the opening psalm for looking at her and when she caught his eye, which she did without difficulty, and lifted her gloved hand and gave him a tiny, finger-rippling wave, he felt suddenly so light and fizzy that he almost floated upward to the roof, like a bubble in a glass of gin. And if *that* wasn't quite enough to bring down the walls of Jericho then the events of late Sunday afternoon most certainly were.

He was sprawled in his chair in the library at the back of the manse, feet propped on the desk, a ham sandwich smeared with English mustard in his fist when the knocker on the front door rapped out a merry little tattoo. He had been contemplating Christmas, Biddy's party and Mairi Quigley, all mixed up in a blissful haze that surely had nothing to do with the three glasses of sherry which had smoothed the way for the ham and mustard. For once the minister did not leap guiltily to his feet, stuff the titbit into the ink drawer and hide the glass and decanter in the space behind his concordances. He swung his feet to the carpet, murmured, wryly not irritably, 'Now who the devil . . .' and, with a shrug, padded through the empty house to answer the front door.

He expected a complaining elder or a Sabbath School teacher with a question – common at this time of year – about the racial origins of the three Wise Men, or an outraged Mr Sapsford, his clerk, come to show him the three Irish pennies that someone had dropped into the collection plate. What he did not expect, even in this mellowest of moods, was to discover Mairi Quigley skipping about on his doorstep with a great big wicker hamper at her feet.

'Madam,' Tom said, 'what the devil are *you* doing here?'

'Looking,' she said, 'for a water closet. Do you have one?'

'Why, yes.'

'Inside?'

'Turn left along the passage, and left again.'

'Thank God!' she said. 'Do you mind?'

'No, I . . .'

'That's yours, by the way. The hamper, I mean.'

She was past him before he could prevent it, inside the manse and flurrying away down the darkened passageway towards the water closet that the parish had had installed only last spring and that Tom, embarrassed by such a luxury, wouldn't even let Mrs McCorkindale, his housekeeper, enter let alone clean. He stared incredulously after Mairi Quigley; at the flirt of her skirts, the bob of the feather in her Gainsborough-style hat, at her heels, hob-nobbing on floorboards that hadn't encountered such speed and lightness in three decades.

Fuelled not a little by the wine of Spain, Tom stepped outside on to the path. He peered up the length of main street, across at the church, across at the kirkyard, across the damp, uncritical fields beyond. He stopped and hoisted up the creaking hamper, he paused and glared round once more.

'What?' he said, aloud. 'Well, what's wrong?' and, receiving no answer, strode swiftly back inside the manse and closed the door with his heel.

Biddy nudged her sister forward into the circle of light around the bed.

'Do you know who this is, Mam?' she said.

Vassie was propped up on two firm pillows. Her hair had been washed that morning and formed a feathery little corona over her forehead that gave her an appearance of surprising alertness. She was less brown-skinned than she had been but did not look particularly pale or unhealthy, merely fragile. But the glitter was back in her eyes and, Biddy reckoned, her mother's reluctance to communicate was not due to a damaged mind at all but to some deep change within her, some almost malign need to assess and evaluate her position while she gathered physical strength.

She wore an expensive cotton night-gown, a lemon-yellow bed-jacket with fussy little ribbons and ties and a tiny cotton night-cap that perched on her fluffy grey hair like a golf ball on a tuft of rye grass. The drooping eyelid had developed a nervous strength but she did not seem to have control of it just yet and would blink and wink at incongruous moments while her lips slid just a little into a pout of sheer concentration.

She stared at Aileen who, in what passed for Sunday best on

Foss, was no match for her oldest sister when it came to style. In the grand bedroom she, Aileen, had the appearance of a doll that had been either too well loved or too long neglected. She was very quiet and clung to Donnie's hand and seemed, Biddy thought, less like the lad's mother than a younger sister who had been smitten by a sinister disease. Donnie's gentleness and concern for her made him seem more mature than his years and in this last month or two he had begun to sprout up so that he was a full head taller than the child-woman who stood with him quietly at the side of the big bed.

'It is your daughter, Gran,' said Donnie in the odd sing-song voice he used when he read aloud to the invalid. 'It is Aileen, my mother, come to see how you are.'

Biddy watched the eyes, saw how they moved, how they assessed each of them in turn, travelling jerkily from her to Donnie to Aileen then back to her once more. She waited for a response. There had been words before, polite words, a 'Please' now and then and a 'Thank you', none of them slurred or wayward in her mother's mouth. But there had been very little else, no protests, no complaints and no questions. Now Vassie pursed her lips. Her eyelid twitched and fluttered then opened very wide, so that the pupil seemed as enlarged as if it lay behind a magnifying glass.

'Where is – where is he?'

'What?' Biddy said.

'Where is he?' Vassie said, clear as a bell.

She was utterly still in the bed, arms, thin as straws, stretched out upon the coverlet, head still against the lacy pillow, her little cap just slightly askew.

'Aileen has come to see . . .'

'Ronan? My Ronan?'

'Now that is not very polite, Mother.' Biddy leaned across the coverlet to tidy the cap. The arm moved, hand opened and slapped at her daughter's fussy fingers. Biddy flinched, did not retreat. 'Aileen has come a long way to . . .'

'Where is my Ronan?'

Donnie drew his mother to him, put his hands upon her bony shoulders and held her before him as if she was being set up for a photographic plate. Aileen was smiling now, her teeth showing.

Donnie said, 'Grandfather cannot come to see you because he is drunk and the weather is too wild to fetch him up from Pennypol.'

And Vassie grinned too, like a mirror image of her youngest, showing foxy teeth and the tip of her tongue, reddened by medicines. 'Dead, is he?'

'Of course he's not dead, Mother,' said Biddy, trying once more to adjust the cap. 'It's just as Donnie told you. He's too drunk to . . .'

'All in it,' Vassie interrupted. 'Together.'

Biddy glanced sharply at her nephew. 'What have you been telling her?'

Not intimidated, Donnie answered with a shake of the head.

Aileen put her hands up and stroked her son's wrist as if to show how pleased she was with his honesty.

Biddy said, 'Are you not going to say anything to Aileen, now you have found your voice again, Mam?'

'Hah!' Vassie said. 'Tell the boy not to lie to me.'

'He is not lying to you,' Biddy said. 'Do you want to get up now?'

'No.'

'Do you want us to go away?'

'Yes.'

'Without saying a word to poor Aileen?'

'Goodbye,' said Vassie and to Biddy's astonishment suddenly shut both eyes and ostentatiously began to snore.

'Awww, Mammy is sleepin' again,' said Aileen.

'Oh no she is not,' said Vassie.

Quig said, 'Who is sitting with your mother?'

'No one,' Biddy answered. 'It will do her no harm to be left alone for an hour or two.'

'I take it she knew who Aileen was?'

'Of course she did,' said Biddy. 'I am not so sure that Aileen was too clear on who Mam was, however. Be that as it may, I did not ask you here this afternoon to discuss my mother's health.'

'Is that why you have brought me into the office?' Quig said.

'I suppose it is,' said Biddy. 'Yes, that is the reason.'

She was still dressed in her Sunday best and every inch a lady. But the silks and satins and hair-ribbons did not seem to chime with the old wooden walls of the estate office, the smell of corn sacks and seed samples or sheaves of unfiled bills and merchants' catalogues that were stacked about the place.

The wooden chair was uncomfortable but Quig gave no sign that he was dismayed at being treated rather more like an employee than a family friend. He hitched up his corduroys, crossed his legs and studied Biddy through the smoky halo of an ancient oil lamp.

Biddy settled herself behind the square table that served as a desk. She spread her skirts, pinched her sleeves and planted her elbows on the table between an earthenware bowl of bonemeal and a chemical fire extinguisher.

'You cannot have him, Quig,' she said.

'Who?'

'Donald.'

'So it is Donald we are here to talk about, is it?'

'I know what your game is,' Biddy said, without ire. 'You will try to use my affection for Donald to persuade me to keep him here at the house.'

'The lad's place is with his mother,' Quig said.

'Oh, that is to be your overture, is it?' Biddy said. 'Next you will be telling me that Aileen cannot rub along without the company of her son. Nonsense! She has rubbed along very well without him for years. You raised him, Quig, you and my grandfather between you. Heart-rending stories about motherhood are not going to cut any ice with me now. Besides, you want the best for Donnie and you know I can offer him that.'

'Aye,' Quig said, 'but we do not want him to become an idler, do we?'

'No danger of that,' said Biddy.

'I will be needing him to help with the cattle.'

'Then you may have him to help with the cattle.'

'In which case it would be better if he lived at Pennypol.'

'Quig, Quig,' Biddy said. 'He is a fit young man and can walk – or run – to Pennypol in a quarter of an hour. His schooling must come first. If, that is, you still have it in mind to get him into a university.'

'Agricultural college,' Quig said.

Biddy gave him a smile. She had no dimples – her face was not that shape – even so she could appear fatefully sweet when she chose to be.

She said, 'University.'

Until that moment Quig had been entertained but not daunted by her acuity. He had seen very little of Biddy Campbell Baverstock down through the years. Foss was a long way from Fetternish, not just in miles, and their paths had seldom crossed. The fact that he was her young sister's guardian did not enter into the reckoning. She had seen through his manoeuvrings and had forestalled him. He did not mind that; rather admired it, in fact. But this other thing, this play with words bothered him slightly.

He said, 'It is agriculture that Donnie wishes to study.'

'No, it is not,' Biddy said. 'He has no wish to be a farmer all his life. He wishes to study History and perhaps become a teacher.'

'Did Donnie tell you this himself?'

'Indeed, he did.'

'Was it you who put this notion into his head?'

'No, the notion has always been there,' Biddy said. 'What has been lacking, until now, has been opportunity.'

'But you encouraged him?'

'Of course I encouraged him.'

'That was wrong of you,' Quig said.

'Was it? Why?'

'To give him ideas above his station.'

'His station! His station!' Biddy exclaimed.

She planted her hands on the table now, fingers spread, and cocked her elbows as if she intended to thrust herself to her feet.

Before Quig's astonished gaze she seemed to swell up, to

become more womanly and, at the same time, more masculine. Nothing out of the ordinary, really: anyone in or around Fetternish would have recognised the pose as Biddy exercising her authority. But Quig's view of his 'cousin' had been both romantic and opportunistic, too narrow and constrained to admit that she might have qualities of character that entitled her to be a successful landowner and that luck and good looks were secondary. His cunning was that of the cattle dealer, the islander, an insular, rather arrogant virtue that had been challenged only by his peers, never by his superiors, especially by a woman.

He felt a wee bit shaken by the force of her outrage.

Biddy lowered herself into the wooden chair again and pretended to control herself. She had the poor little chap on toast now. She did not need to sulk, or humour him, or even to throw her weight about. And she most certainly did not need to flirt with him. She had prepared herself in advance for Quig's crafty onslaught on what he perceived to be her weaknesses. He had – as he must be realising now – misjudged her.

'His station is that of a Campbell,' Biddy said. 'He is, may I remind you, my nephew and not just a common tinker who happened to drift on to Foss like a piece of jetsam. My grandfather would understand perfectly the nature of Donald's ambition.'

'Donnie is too young to know what is best for him.'

Even as he spoke Quig realised how lame that sounded. He scrabbled about in his head for another line of argument but, once more, Biddy was there ahead of him.

She said, 'You put him to school. You subjected him to the rigours of education. You have only yourself to blame if Donnie is learning to think for himself. Yes, and to speak up for himself. If you ask him he will tell you what he wants to do. And if you ask Mr Brown, the schoolmaster, he will tell you what is possible. All things are possible, in fact, when you are Donnie's age. He is eager to attend university, to become a degreed teacher. Where is the harm in that?'

'The harm,' said Quig, 'is that he will not come back to Mull.'

'Probably not,' said Biddy.

'And you would let him go?'

'Absolutely,' Biddy said.

'I thought you – you loved him?'

'I do. I admit it,' Biddy said. 'I have tremendous affection for Donald. He is my kinsman and means almost as much as a son to me. But that is no reason to hold him. I thought you were ambitious on his behalf, too.'

'I am. I was.'

'Was?'

'I did not think he would leave us for good.'

'How old are you, Quig?'

'Not thirty yet.'

'When you are my age,' said Biddy, with that fateful little smile on her lips again, 'you will realise that you cannot use people in that way, not even when you think it is for their own good.'

'Use him? I do not understand.'

'Talk to Mr Brown: I have. Talk to Donnie: I have,' Biddy said. 'Lift your eye to the hills, Robert Quigley, from whence cometh the future.'

Quig shook his head. 'My, my, Mrs Baverstock, you are more of a dreamer than your sister Innis. I thought she was the one with the poetic nature and the lyrical turn of phrase.'

'Really?' Biddy said. 'Try this for a lyrical turn of phrase – estate manager. Eee-state Man-a-ger, Quig. Is that not the position you're after?'

It was at this moment in the to-and-fro and bargaining over the price of a bullock or a heifer that the grin would turn to a grimace and that the fist would close and open again, that there would be a spitting into the palm and a shaking of hands and a deal struck with no hard feelings on either side. The bargaining was over, and Biddy Baverstock had won. She had unravelled his entire plan, the programme of insinuation and acquisition that he, and his mother, had knitted up between them in the long wet winter nights on the little isle when there was nothing else to do and no future much beyond spring calving.

'Well, Mr Quigley, is it?' Biddy said. 'Is that what you hoped for Donnie? That he would come back here, not just to Mull but to Fetternish, and I would take him in to replace Hector Thrale who cannot last much longer and is, in any case, long past the age when he should be put to pasture.'

'Manager?' Quig said. 'Manager of Fetternish? I never thought of that.'

'Oh, come, come!' said Biddy. 'You must have thought of it. If you did not think of it and did not tally up the advantages it would bring you then you're not the man you are reputed to be and you are certainly not equipped to manage Fetternish on my behalf.'

'Me?'

'Well, I am not going to employ a schoolteacher, am I?' Biddy said. 'Isn't that what you want, Quig? To be the manager of a well-run highland estate?'

'I do not know if I am capable . . .'

'You will have three years, possibly four to learn all that you need to know. After that I will settle a small pension on Thrale and allow him and his wife free use of their cottage as long as one of them is alive.'

'That is generous.'

'But I *am* generous,' Biddy said. 'Did you not realise that when you were sizing me up? I'm too generous for my own good sometimes.'

'What if I do not want to let Donnie go?'

'You cannot hold him.'

'Can you?'

'Possibly,' Biddy said. 'But I would not dare.'

'What will become of Aileen when Donnie is gone?' Quig said.

'Will there not always be room for her in your house?'

'Yes, there will.'

'And if there is not,' Biddy said, 'I will take care of her.'

'As you take care of everything and everyone,' Quig said. 'I do my best.'

'Who will take care of you, though, Mrs Baverstock?' Quig said. 'Or is that a question that you cannot answer me yet?'

'It is not a question you should even be asking,' Biddy said.

'The answer, though, should be obvious. I can take care of myself.'

'I thought that would be it.'

Quig studied her calmly for a moment, not in the least offended by the fact that she had got the better of him. Then he rose to his feet, opened his palm, spat lightly into it and held it out across the table.

'Deal, Mrs Baverstock?' he said.

'Deal, Mr Quigley,' said Biddy, and pressed her moist hand to his.

ELEVEN

The Bitter Pill

Michael Tarrant was not the only one who thought Biddy mad to waste money on a Christmas party. Others saw in it democratic leanings that few Highland lairds would admit to. But Willy simply thought that the widow woman had bitten off more than she could chew and that, come the day, bedlam would reign within the walls of Fetternish.

Preparing for the feast was half the fun. On the day before Christmas Eve the big house bustled with friends and neighbours all eager to lend a hand. Smells of baking filled the corridors and mingled with the tang of freshly-cut pine logs and with the evergreens that the Browns lugged in to decorate the hall. Evander's books had been moved into the office and the dining-room would be set out with a buffet the like of which Fetternish had not seen since the day of Biddy's wedding.

Austin, in fact, was much on Biddy's mind as she strove to keep reins on the chaotic activities. Her husband had been a charitable man who had taught her that a landowner should not be aloof from servants and tenants, but in Biddy's case it was impossible to determine where 'family' tailed away and who were relatives and who were not. She seemed to have known everyone for so long, everyone except the Browns and they were so out-going and amiable that she felt sometimes as if she had known them for ages too.

The day before the party was marked by many pleasant surprises.

Tom Ewing turned up in the parish gig with eight bottles of

fine old port to add to the communal tub; eight bottles from the dozen that Mairi Quigley had brought to the manse in a hamper to thank him for burying Grandfather McIver. Never one to stand on ceremony, the minister was soon downstairs in the kitchen with his jacket off and sleeves rolled up shaping patties from a gigantic bowl of forced meat while Mairi, gaudy as a Christmas-box, stood at his elbow with a strip of yellow pastry, a cutter and a dish of egg yolk and chivvied him to stir his stumps or it would be New Year before anyone even saw a sausage-roll.

Donnie and Tricia were put in charge of interior decorations and told to keep the more obstreperous elements of the domestic brigade – namely dogs, children and Aileen – out of everyone's way. Much time was spent traipsing in and out of the walled garden with step-ladders and pruning shears until the holly and laurel bushes were almost denuded and Willy, a shade harassed, called out to them to stop before the hall turned into a jungle.

Angus Bell arrived from the stables with a cart-load of logs. He lingered long enough to drink a glass of toddy and demonstrate to a fascinated audience – Evie, Rachel and little Becky – how to make a pocket-watch vanish into your mouth and appear out of your ear and, for an encore, might have made an orange explode in mid-air if Maggie hadn't stormed up from the kitchen and chased him back to work. Then in the grey, calm, cold light of mid-afternoon Mr McCallum came swinging off the moor and down the slope of the lawn with a rod of dead pheasants slung across his shoulders; eight cock birds, hung but not dressed, their cardinal's plumage not quite faded, the blood that had run from their bills bright as new varnish.

Behind the gamekeeper came Gavin, whom no one had expected to see and whom no one, not even Innis, had missed. He toted Mr McCallum's gun.

The weapon was too heavy for him, too cumbersome and he carried it not under one arm like a shooting gentleman but at the port, military-style. The children were outside on the gravel drive with Donnie and Tricia. They stopped what they were doing. Rachel called the dogs to her. Donnie and she held

346

them fast, for even Pepper, who had never seen a hung pheasant before let alone tasted the white tender flesh, had begun to growl and snap.

Donnie knelt by Odin's flank, an arm around the dog's neck, whispering soothingly and not as afraid as he should have been of the hound's bared teeth.

They watched as Mr McCallum gravitated towards the path that led around the house between the garden and the yard, watched Gavin come abreast of them, head high and haughty. With the shotgun carried proudly at the port, he stalked past them without a word and vanished down the path hard on the gamekeeper's heels.

Innis and Gillies Brown were together in the larder, shoulder to shoulder, with cheeses above them and oatmeal sacks at their feet.

They were looking out of the little round window. Deeper into the basement the ice-making machine that Willy so hated ground and grated loudly, almost but not quite drowning out the sounds of merriment from the kitchen where Mr McCallum, a glass in his hand, was regaling Cook and Mrs Quigley with a saucy anecdote about a blind stag and an amorous brown sow.

Outside, in the doorway of the wash-house, young Gavin was seated on a milking-stool plucking a pheasant. He was deft at the task, neat with the feathers, pushing them into the sack that Willy had given him before they could billow all over the yard like snow. His expression was blank, not grim. He held the bird by the legs and plucked downward, tugging at the reluctant wing feathers and, when the flesh was clean, singed away the last stray hairs with the candle that Willy had provided.

'I didn't know he could that,' Gillies Brown said.

'No more did I,' Innis said.

'Hidden talents,' Gillies said.

'Mr McCallum must have taught him how to do it.'

'Does he spend a lot of his time with McCallum then?'

'I suppose he must,' Innis said.

'Perhaps that's what Gavin will be when he is grown.'

'What, a bird-plucker?'

'A gamekeeper, daftie,' Gillies said, giving her a friendly nudge.

'Perhaps,' Innis said. 'You do not think that he will make a scholar then, like his cousin?'

'To be honest, no.'

'I cannot say I'm surprised,' Innis said. She gave a little sigh. 'I sometimes feel that Gavin is not my child at all.'

'What do you mean?'

'Oh, he *is* mine. I gave him birth. But . . .'

'He's not his mammy's big tumshie, is that what you mean?'

'Tumshie?' Innis said. 'What on earth is a "tumshie"?'

'Turnip,' Gillies answered promptly. 'It's a vulgar Glasgow expression. It means that he's not his mother's darling.'

'I would not want you to think that I do not love my son.'

'He's a man's man, Innis,' Gillies said. 'Nothing to worry about.'

They watched Gavin put down the plucked bird and lift another. He held it by the claws and stroked his hand sensuously down its breast, lips pursed. Then he laid the pheasant down on the stone by his feet and, turning, brought out the shotgun that he had leaned against the wash-house door. Still seated he took the gun and broke it open, slanted it toward the sky and looked into the barrels. It was a heavy piece but the boy handled it skilfully. He closed the barrels to the breech and locked them and, raising himself a little, swung the gun and, unaware that he was being watched, aimed at an invisible target overhead and pulled the front trigger and then the back.

'Oh, God!' said Innis, clutching Gillies's arm.

'No, it's not loaded,' Gillies assured her, patting her hand. 'McCallum would not be so daft as to leave it loaded.'

Gavin opened his mouth and let out a small, silent cry of triumph. He held the shotgun poised for a moment then broke the barrels again and blew away imaginary smoke, rubbed the rims with his fingertips, closed the weapon and put it away out of sight behind him. He lifted up the pheasant and held it in his hands as if weighing it then, in a gesture of sheer ecstasy, rubbed the breast feather against his cheek for a moment before he set to work again.

Embarrassed and, for some reason, dismayed, Innis turned away from the window. Inside the kitchen, laughter was raucous. She could hear Tom Ewing's distinctive bray, which was rare enough these days. Gillies continued to look at her, smiling. Gavin's odd behaviour did not seem to have registered with him.

Innis said, 'Why did you close the school today?'

'Because I felt like it.'

'Is that the only reason?'

'No.'

'Because you thought I would be here?'

'Yes. Partly.'

'And the other part?'

'Biddy asked me to,' Gillies said.

'Why?'

'I think she wanted to have the children here today.'

'Do you always do what Biddy asks?'

'It's the first time she has asked me for anything, much.'

'Will it be the last?'

'Innis, for goodness' sake!' Gillies said.

'You had dinner with her, did you not? Just the two of you?'

'Who told you that?'

'On Fetternish few secrets are safe.'

'Particularly as it wasn't a secret in the first place,' Gillies said.

'What did she want with you?'

'Just to talk.'

'About me?' said Innis. 'I mean, about us?'

'What is there to say about us?' Gillies said.

'I thought she might be warning you off.'

'She wanted advice about Donnie.'

'Oh!'

'It seems that the lad doesn't want to go to agricultural college. He wants to get into a university to study for a full degree. To become a teacher,' Gillies said. 'Biddy expects

349

opposition from Quigley and wanted to see what I thought about Donnie's chances as well as his abilities.'

'Oh!' said Innis, again.

'You see,' Gillies said. 'You've nothing to be jealous about.'

'Jealous? I am not . . .'

At this point Mairi Quigley put her head around the larder door and, grinning broadly, said, 'Hey, you two, are you making butter or are you looking for the mistletoe? In either event, perhaps you'd better come out before you create a scandal.'

'Yes,' Gillies said. 'Perhaps we'd better.'

He had set Barrett to check the fences around the lambing pasture. It was early days yet but coarse weather might come in at any time and the drop would be upon them before they knew it. He had taken himself up to the old pasture where hill sheep were fattened, little Scotch half-breeds, robust little grey-faces that seemed to thrive on sparse pick and hard rain and that would fetch a fair price in the market just after New Year when good mutton tended to be at a premium.

The shearing flock was the mainstay of Baverstock income, however, the bread-and-butter of the Fetternish year. Biddy's long-lost in-laws down in Sangster took every scrap of wool that came off the estate for their manufactory and paid a prearranged price that removed some of the gamble out of balancing the books. Even so, Biddy was shrewd enough not to depend entirely upon the wool crop and had instructed Michael to keep some pasture back for fat stock, to ensure that if the income from Sangster suddenly ceased there would be no great financial hiatus in Fetternish affairs. Hence, too, the cattle and, Michael supposed, Biddy's tentative experiments in the rearing of game birds on the wilder parts of the moor, for rents from the small holdings would never be enough to compensate for poor land management or a slump in farm prices.

On that calm, grey afternoon in late December he was alone upon Olaf's Ridge. In fact, with most of the women and children gone from the cottages to help out at the big house, he felt as if he alone was working the long strips of the western coast, though he knew that Barrett and Thrale and Mr Clark's men would be out and about at their duties, for the nonsense of an estate party was an occupation strictly for women who had nothing better to do with themselves, for women and children; and schoolmasters.

He had gone over the Ridge on his own, deliberately separating himself from Barrett and out of sight of all the other cottages. Once the high ground was behind him no habitation presented itself to his view; none, that is, except Pennypol's turf-roofed cottage and the ugly new byre with strings of Foss-bred cattle cropping the oblong acres between the wall, the burn and the shore. He did not like to see cattle on the sand. It seemed somehow careless, as if they had been driven out there as a sacrifice to the monstrous waves, though, that day, the sea was calm as summer, and the beasts seemed content enough.

It took him a minute or two to locate Quigley. The cattleman was not at the sheds behind the cottage or down at the byre. Surprisingly, he was doing what Barrett was doing, checking the boundaries that separated the calf park from the hillside, as if, Michael thought, old Vassie herself had sent him out to secure them against predatory neighbours; a nonsense, of course, since all the ground belonged to Biddy now, if not on paper at least in practice.

He went down the steep slope to the old dike with the sheep dog Roy trotting at his heels. The air was still, so still and cold that you could hear the cattle coughing and even the crackle of their hoofs on the shingle of the tide-line and the bands of dried weed. He could hear Vassie's cattle dogs panting in the hanging bracken too and brought his dog, Roy, close into his side and held him.

Quigley had a stick and a bag over his shoulder but no spools of wire to knit the frayed hedges, no hammer to chisel stones to fit the gaps in the dikes. Like Michael, he wore only a jacket, no coat or oilskin. Like Michael, he did not seem to feel the cold. When he noticed the shepherd, he came up the rise of the calf park, walking fast. The cattle dogs tore after him but when he rounded on them they lay down instantly, already obedient to their new master's signal.

Michael leaned an elbow on the top of the dike.

'You have the place to yourself, I see,' he said.

'Aye, the ladies have gone up to the house,' Quigley answered. 'They will be back before long, I expect, for it will be dark soon.'

'And you will be requiring your supper.'

'Oh, I can wait for my supper,' Quig said. 'Or I can be making it for myself if it comes to the bit.'

'It must be grand to have so little to do,' Michael said, 'that you can manage pots as well as cattle.'

Quig rubbed his nose with his forefinger. 'Is it a quarrel you are wanting, Michael Tarrant? If so, I fear you will be disappointed. I have no reason to quarrel with you.'

'Why would I want to quarrel?'

'Because I am here on Pennypol.'

'What does that have to do with me?'

'They say that cattle and sheep do not mix.'

'Of course they mix. They have been here for years together. Perhaps it is cattlemen and shepherds who do not rub along.' Michael leaned both arms on the wall and looked down upon the cottage. 'Is this enough for you, Quigley?'

'Why would I want more?'

'Because you had more. On Foss, didn't you have more?'

Quig shrugged. 'I have as much as I need.'

'When will I be getting my money?'

'Your money?'

'What is due to my wife?'

'I have put all the papers into the hands of the lawyers,' Quig said. 'I have done what an executor is supposed to do. The rest will be up to them.'

'Will they not pay out until Foss is sold?'

'I doubt if Foss will ever be sold.'

'Is it not good ground?'

'Excellent ground, but it is too far from the markets. It was fine for a man like Evander McIver who liked the solitary life but there are precious few like him left these days,' Quig said. 'It might be doing for a shepherd, though, if he had a bit of money to spend and was looking for a place of his own.'

'It would not be a place like Foss.'

'No, I do not suppose it would be,' Quig said. 'It would be land nearer to his home, would it not? A little patch like Pennypol, perhaps?'

'Pennypol would do nicely,' Michael said, 'if that was what a certain type of shepherd had in mind.'

'What type of shepherd would that be?'

'One who did not much enjoy being at a woman's beck and call.'

'Beck and call?' said Quig. 'I did not think that Biddy Baverstock was such a tyrant.'

'She is your employer too now, so perhaps you'll find out.'

'I doubt it,' Quig said. 'I am not much like you, Tarrant. I do not hold her scx against her.'

'Her sex? Is it her sex that interests you then?'

'That is a very indelicate question,' Quig said. 'I have heard that Biddy turned you down some years ago.'

'She did not turn me down.'

'Then why did you not marry her in preference to Innis?'

'Because in those days she was not worth marrying,' Michael said.

'She is worth marrying now, is she not?'

Michael had kept his tone even until now, had shown nothing of what he felt towards the upstart from Foss, the so-called 'cousin' who had entered his domain and who, as he suspected, had plans to take it over. He knew that he could not compete with Quigley's youth or with the fact that Quigley was free.

'Biddy will not have the likes of you,' Michael said.

'From what I have heard she will have any man who can give her a child.'

'Christ!' Michael exclaimed. 'Is that your game?'

'No,' Quig said. 'It is not "my game". I had not even been thinking of it until you put it into my mind. But it is a suggestion worth considering. Thank you for bringing it to my attention.'

'I suppose you think that the boy will give you a lever in the house.'

'If you are meaning Donnie, she has more right to him than I have. He is not my son, nor my brother either,' Quig said. 'But he will not be Biddy's pet lamb for much longer for he is his own man and will make his own way, regardless of what we have to say about it.'

'Like my boy.'

'I have seen your boy,' Quig said.

'He is just as good as Donnie.'

'I have no doubt of it,' Quig said. 'Are you still looking for a quarrel, Mr Tarrant? I am not going to argue with you about Donnie or your son or what Biddy may or may not want. I am here because I need work and a roof to put over my mother's head and Foss is no longer what it was.'

'What happened to the others?' Michael said. 'That jangling crew the old man had around him, the women, for instance, and the bastards they bore him?'

'He took care of them,' Quig said, 'until he could take care of them no longer, and then they were sent away to find work elsewhere.'

'Who sent them away? You?'

'Yes. It was over, do you not see, that part of it was done.'

'So you could have everything for yourself?' Michael said.

Quig turned and gestured towards the turf-roofed cottage and the bleak pastures that surrounded it. 'Is this what you call "everything"? No, no, Michael Tarrant. I had the best of it, the very best of it. But it was the last of it too. There are few communities like Evander McIver's left, and soon there will be none at all now that the twentieth century is almost upon us.'

'And you, are you what they call – what *do* they call it?'

'An anachronism,' Quig suggested.

'Aye, that.'

'No, I am not an anachronism for I am more than ready to move forward and take what the future offers me without yearning for the past.'

'And what does the future offer you, Quigley? Tell me that?'

'Well, there is the party for a start. Biddy's party.'

'Oh, that!' Michael said and, without even a nod of farewell, turned and headed back up the hill.

*   *   *

354

Willy was right, of course. Biddy's Christmas party was bedlam. She had invited far too many folk. She had put no embargo on anyone, turned no one away. Babes-in-arms, toddlers and gawky adolescents were no respecters of peace and quiet or of the organisation that Willy sought to impose upon them. Good manners were cast aside in the rush into the dining-room.

As Tom Ewing remarked more than once, it was like the Feeding of the Five Thousand. What was left on the tables after the tenants had had their fill would not have filled a thimble let alone a basket, for every bowl, dish, plate and ashet had been scraped clean. There were crumbs on the stairs, orange peel bobbing in the lavatories, candy smeared into the sofas. The smell of spilled beer and tobacco smoke pervaded every aspect of the house.

It lasted the best part of three hours. Biddy's notion of a festive gathering, with songs at the piano and sweet Highland voices raised in Christmas chorus, foundered on sheer weight of numbers and a general ignorance of what the celebration was all about. They came, they ate, they drank; then, like locusts, they rose and left again.

By half-past three o'clock the big house felt empty, though in fact a dozen close friends and relatives still wandered among the debris. They assured Biddy, who was quite tearful with nervous strain, that everything had gone swimmingly, that her tenants and employees had thoroughly enjoyed themselves and had surely learned the true meaning of Christmas.

Willy was a good deal less sanguine about it.

When the last toddler had been found and restored to its mother and the last light-fingered lad had been separated from two crystal glasses and a small silver matchbox and sent packing, he, Willy, declared that he'd had enough, thank you, and locked himself in his room to eat a late lunch and down a glass of brandy in peace and tranquillity.

It was left to Innis to marshal the troops. The same forces who had helped prepare the feast were there to help clear up, wash dishes in the tub or mop the staircase or polish the dining-room furniture with a cloth and a little wax. When that was done, by half-past five, they assembled again in the great hall.

The dogs were let out to be petted and reassured, and Biddy was brought down from her bedroom to be comforted. Sherry was dispensed and the last of the ice used up on cordial for the youngsters, and everyone sat around the fire and went '*Pheeew*' and, after a few awkward moments, laughed.

'Cheer up, Biddy,' Tom Ewing said. 'Next Christmas you'll do better.'

'Over my dead body,' said Biddy.

'Oh,' Innis said. 'I thought you would be asleep.'

'Asleep?' Vassie said, with something of the old growl in her voice. 'How can I be sleeping when that racket is going on? Who were they?'

'Who?'

'Those boys. They came into the room and gaped at me.'

'Is that why you are up and dressed?' Innis said.

'I am not going to be lying here to be gawked at as if I was a freak in a raree show,' Vassie said. 'Is this what she is calling a party? Boys coming in to annoy an old woman?'

'They have gone now, Mam,' Innis said. 'It is just the family that is left, and one or two of our friends.'

'Her friends, I suppose. Her fancy friends, her lords and ladies.'

'No, no,' said Innis, soothingly. 'Our friends. Tom Ewing, Quig and Mairi, the Browns.'

'The Browns?'

'The schoolteacher and his children.'

'Do I remember the Browns?' Vassie said, squinting.

'I do not know. Do you?'

She was delighted to find her mother not only out of bed but dressed in the clothes that Biddy had had brought up from Pennypol; Vassie's Sunday best, cleaned, mended and pressed, and topped off with a spanking new Paisley shawl. It was not Vassie's first venture out of bed but on previous occasions she had had to be helped. Now, apart from a certain lack of assurance in fastening buttons and hooks, she had managed for herself. The effort – if effort it had been – had apparently revived her. There was more than a trace of sharpness in her tone, though her movements were still not certain.

'Yes,' Vassie said. 'The schoolteacher.'

She was seated in a round-sided basket chair that Biddy had had carried down from the sewing-room. The fire in the iron grate crackled with fresh coals and the bedroom was warm and snug. Two big-globed oil lamps lit it admirably and someone, Maggie probably, had drawn the curtains. The light in the room softened Vassie's features and the slight hoity-toity wobble of her head made her seem eccentric but harmless.

For a moment or two, Innis was almost taken in.

'We will be staying for a while yet, Mam,' Innis said. 'But the noise will have gone away. When Biddy plays the piano in the big room can you hear it?'

'Piano?' Vassie considered. 'No, I cannot hear a piano.'

'Willy has saved some roast pheasants and we will be having them for our supper. I will bring you some later. Do you not think that you would be better going back into bed, however? You must not be tiring yourself.'

'I am tired,' Vassie said. 'Tired of lying in that bed.'

'I will sit with you then.'

'You go back to your friends. Send him up.'

'Donnie, do you mean,' Innis said, 'to read to you?'

Her head wobbled, then steadied. The slackness at the corner of her mouth was eliminated by a soft, deliberate swallow. She raised a lace-edged handkerchief in her hand and dabbed at her lips.

'I mean Ronan.'

'Dada is not here,' Innis said.

'Send him up.'

'I cannot.'

'Send him up.'

'Mam . . .'

'Is he dead too?'

'No. He is . . .'

'If he cannot come up, I will come down.'

'Dada is not here,' Innis repeated.

She knelt by the basket chair. She took her mother's left

hand. At first it seemed pliant, almost weightless, then Vassie's fingers closed and Innis experienced the force of her mother's will again, transmitted through fragile bones and tendons.

Stiff-necked, straight-shouldered, head steady, Vassie hissed, 'Where *is* your father, Innis. Where *is* my Ronan? What have you done with him?'

She hesitated. She looked up into the old face, no longer soft and gentle but wicked with determination. She took in a breath, sighed, and said, 'He is in a place called Redwing, in Perthshire, a hospital of sorts where he will be properly cared for. When he is well again, and you are well again, he will come home.'

'No,' Vassie said. 'He will not come home.'

'Mam, he . . .'

'I will not have him back.'

'What? What are you saying?'

'Let him stay there.'

Innis tried to stand but her mother's grip was too strong now, bony fingers locked tightly around her wrist. She struggled a little then, fearful of damage, ceased. She said, 'We could not be taking care of him. He was too much for us, Mam, too sick with the drink. But he did not leave you. He did not just go away and leave you.'

'How much is it costing, this place where he is?'

'Biddy will take care of the cost.'

'I have money. Some money hidden away. I will pay Biddy back.'

'Do not think about money, Mam. The money does not matter.'

'He does not matter.'

'Mam!'

'She is back, is she not?'

Innis said, 'Yes, Aileen is back. She has been to see you. Do you not remember? She came to see you yesterday.'

'From Foss. At Pennypol. At last.'

'Yes, with Quig and Mairi, at Pennypol.'

'And he is not here?'

'No,' Innis said. 'I promise you, he is not here.'

She felt her mother's grip tighten, the wrench of muscles bracing themselves for effort and then, leaning on her, Vassie got to her feet.

'In that case, I will come down now,' she said.

'Are you sure you are strong enough?'

'Aye, dearest,' Vassie said. 'I will come down.'

It was very late now, no longer Christmas Eve but Christmas Day. For Biddy, though, celebrations were over. Tomorrow – today – was bound to seem like an anticlimax. Unlike her sister she had no well of spirituality to draw upon.

She would not spend the day alone, of course. Her mother was up and about again and Quig had finally agreed to let Donnie stay put in Fetternish, so she would not lose her nephew's company just yet. Even so she could not help but dwell on the gathering that she had brought together and of the fun they had had that evening; her mother on the long sofa, with Aileen on one side of her and Donnie on the other, while Mairi Quigley sang sweet songs about lost loves and the love of one's native land, and Tom Ewing stood by the window, wiping a tear from his eye now and then. And the dancing; waltzes, polkas, cavortings that had no steps at all, while she played and Quig or Michael or Gillies Brown turned the pages of the sheet music for her. And the children, Browns, Tarrants and Campbells, dressing for charades, all into the game together, all excited. Tricia Brown kissing Donnie under the sprig of mistletoe that Willy, *joie-de-vivre* restored, had tacked up over the drawing-room door to catch the unwary. Innis dancing with Gillies Brown. Even Michael and Gavin, the boy seated dourly at his father's feet, watching with a supercilious air that no quantity of food or drink could soften or remove.

Then Becky had fallen asleep on the sofa, head resting on her grandmother's shoulder. Aileen had fallen asleep, sitting upright, snoring loudly. Vassie, with a contented little smile on her lips, had closed her eyes too.

It had been quite subdued in the great hall where they had drunk last cups of tea together. And when Innis had lifted

Becky, half asleep, into her arms and Gillies Brown had cradled sleepy little Evie to his chest, and Aileen, her grown-up sister, had taken Quig's hand – she had wanted to cry out, 'No, stay. All of you, stay,' as if, when they had gone, more than just their company would be lost to her.

Later she sat at her dressing-table clad in night-gown and robe, her hair unloosed, the little trinket-box open before her, the little leather trinket-box that she had not thought to open in years, with the brooch that Austin had given her when she was still a girl laid out on a scrap of velvet.

She thought of her husband sometimes, though not often. Usually when she was out on the moor with the dogs or when a particular shade of weather brought him unexpectedly out of the shadows for a moment or two. Then she would recall his eagerness, his extravagance, the courtesy that she had mistaken for weakness. Now, though, she saw it for what it was and, in wistful melancholy, realised that Austin had loved her. It had been the perfect union, a totality into which, given time, all the elements of her person would surely have entered.

She had been too young to appreciate how much Austin loved her, too gauche, too selfish; too much her father's daughter, perhaps, maimed by his cruelty and her own overweening vanity.

At that time she had supposed that she was in love with Michael Tarrant, only because he had dared lead her out of Pennypol to lure her into sexual intimacy, into a knowledge of the body's strange, unguided passions. But she had never loved Michael. She had desired him. Even to this day she cherished a faint, sour longing to have him with her again, to redeem the hardness of her girlhood, to make her sleek and sly and selfish once more. But Austin, not Michael, not Fetternish or money or power, had changed her, though it had taken thirteen years for her to acknowledge that her wealthy Edinburgh gentleman had been a true lover and a true husband and that, in losing him so early, she had lost so much else besides.

Although the house was silent and the weather calm, Biddy did not hear the bedroom door open. She was caught up in sentiment, in longing, the little silver brooch held to her lips as Innis might have held a rosary.

'Are you not for sleeping at all tonight, girl?' the voice said.

Biddy dropped the brooch and, startled, swung round.

Her mother was framed in the doorway, pale as a ghost against the darkness of the corridor. She had thrown the Paisley shawl across her night-gown and had laid the lacy cap on top of her frizzy hair. She stooped into the stick that Donnie had brought up from the gun room to give her support.

'I saw the light under your door,' Vassie said.

Hastily, Biddy dropped Austin's brooch into the leather box, ashamed to be caught with tears in her eyes. She closed the lid of the box and got to her feet, masking her embarrassment with an unctuous sort of solicitude.

'Oh, dear, Mam!' she said. 'Could you not sleep either?'

'I have done enough sleeping these past weeks to last me a lifetime,' Vassie said. Although she walked with the aid of the stick she was not dependent upon it, leaned into it only lightly. She shook her shoulders to prevent Biddy taking hold of her and steering her to a chair. 'What was it that was wrong with me? Was it my heart?'

'No, your head,' Biddy said. 'Did Doctor Kirkhope not explain it to you?'

'If he did I did not hear what he was saying,' Vassie said. 'I was not myself, however, and I am not myself yet either, though I am better than I was.'

'It was a thrombosis of the blood, an apoplexy,' Biddy said, 'but mild, according to the doctor. He is sure that you will recover in due course, if you take care of yourself and do not worry about things.'

'Does Quig have the farm?'

'He does.'

'Quig is a good man. He will look after Pennypol for us,' Vassie said.

'Someone has to look after it, Mother, for I doubt if you . . .'

'Innis tells me that Ronan will not be coming home again,' Vassie said.

'Perhaps, if he is cured . . .'

'Cured of what?' Vassie fumbled the stick into both fists and leaned her weight into it. She seemed to be in control of herself again, complete control. 'I am wanting to see him, Biddy. Will you take me to where you have put him?'

'There is no need, Mam. I assure you he's in the very best of hands.'

'I want to be sure – sure for myself.'

'You're in no state to go anywhere just yet.'

'When I am, as soon as I am, will you be taking me there?'

There were ghosts of all sorts, Biddy thought. Austin, long dead and gone. But not forgotten, after all. Her father still alive, still out there in the broad kingdom that lay beyond the shores of Mull. She understood her mother's anxiety, the need to put him to rest.

'Oh,' she said, 'very well.'

'Do you promise?'

'Yes, Mam. I promise.'

'Good,' Vassie said. 'Now you may help me back to bed.'

New Year came in with a flurry. Along the coast the snowfall was light and soon thawed into rain but on inland hills and the mountains to the north it lay in great swathes, grey and dirty like old flannel.

The third day of January brought a further drop in temperature.

The wind turned arctic. The ground froze hard.

Much against her will, Innis was forced to miss mass on Epiphany Sunday. The track to Glenarray was blocked by drifts and the road to Tobermory was too icy to risk with a horse and cart. She would have walked there and back again, but Michael adamantly refused to let her consider it. Indeed, he painted such a vivid picture of her lying frozen by the roadside that Becky and Rachel wailed in fear for Mammy's life and flung themselves upon her and begged her not to go.

Instead Innis held a little service in Pennymain with candles and prayers read from the Missal. She insisted on Michael and Gavin taking part which, to placate her, they did. Once the praying was over, however, her husband and son, swaddled in their warmest clothes, were off across the pasture to pull hay to fill the feeding troughs before the cold pruned off the weaker ewes.

On Pennypol the story was much the same.

Quig and Mairi drove the cows into the new byre, built Lear a bed in the old byre near the house and strewed the ripe hay along the shore track for the bullocks. Aileen was sick with a cold in the head and spent the day huddled by the fire, moaning to herself and snivelling for attention whenever Quig or Mairi appeared indoors.

On Monday the school closed.

Gillies Brown penned a cryptic note in the log: *Roads blocked or dangerous. Water pipe in classroom burst. Both rooms flooded.*

He didn't add that he, his daughters and son, assisted by Donnie, had spent a miserable forenoon mopping up the mess and that only Mr Ewing's kindness in inviting them all into the manse for hot soup and beef hash had thawed them out enough to make the trek back to An Fhearann Cáirdeil. He did not record that Biddy had dispatched Willy to the crossroads to meet the cart and had taken all the children into Fetternish House to revive them with piping hot chocolate while Gillies jogged home to the cottage to build up the fire and pump water up from the cistern in case it locked in the night.

It was the beginning of the bad spell; not gales and rain, which the islanders were used to, but cold, cold so intense that you half expected to see pack-ice forming in Pennypol Bay or growlers drifting round Caliach Point or polar bears padding about the Solitudes on the look-out for penguins.

Outdoor excursions were limited to breathless dashes to the peat-rack or coal-pile, to the dry closet or water pump, though Donnie appeared at An Fhearann Cáirdeil with a basket of eggs and a canister of fresh milk, and Gillies, guided by Mr McCallum, forged a rough but speedy passage across the moor to Crove to check the condition of the classrooms and arrange with Tom Ewing to have the school board informed that the pipes would need repairing. He returned home in early afternoon, exhausted, face and hands scalded by the horizontal winds that blew across the heather hag and vowed that until the weather improved the school could look after itself.

For eight days the weather held its bitter course. Mull's inhabitants, like most other islanders, huddled in self-imposed isolation, cut off from the mainland not by mountainous seas but by the painful inconvenience of going anywhere and doing anything that did not absolutely have to be done. Then, one afternoon, a blister of sunlight appeared in the layers of slate-grey cloud and that evening snow began to fall again, heavy and moist now, a great soft wall of flakes that moved silently across the bays and headlands to absorb the last of the daylight and turned the darkness white.

Biddy watched the blizzard from the drawing-room. Dining and drawing-rooms had been little used since Christmas for the spacious apartments with their large windows were almost unheatable. Donnie, Vassie and she ate in the great hall where a big fire blazed all day and stout walls kept out the chill. She had entered the drawing-room now, though, to watch snow veil the lawns and terraces and plaster the glass with slippery flakes.

Donnie was in the kitchen, Vassie resting upstairs. Thor and Odin lay lumpily before the hall fire, snorting and shifting position from time to time, but the only sounds were the sounds that the house made; from outside came nothing, nothing at all. And then she heard it, a muffled noise from the front of the house, a dull knocking and, an instant later, the clang of the doorbell.

Automatically she put her hand to her hair to tidy it. She had been so out of society this past week that she had rather let her appearance go. She could not imagine who might have braved the climate to call upon her or what tragedy or disaster the clanging doorbell might presage. She smoothed her dress with one hand and opened the inner door with the other. When she opened the outer door snow swirled so fiercely in upon her that she dipped her head and covered her face with her arm, half blinded by the flurry.

He was white, pure white about the upper parts; a hunchback with a pointed cowl. He carried a long ash pole in one mittened hand and his greatcoat was fastened about his middle with a hempen rope. He might have been a pilgrim, an explorer, a lost traveller, or some vengeful entity that Aileen might have summoned with one of her incoherent spells.

'Me, Biddy. It's me. It's me. Will you please let me in?'

'Iain!'

'Yes, yes. Please.'

She wiped flakes from her hair and brow and, round-eyed with astonishment, took his arm and dragged him into the foyer.

She struggled with the outer door and closed it while Carbery slumped, panting, against the wall. He put his hand up and tugged down the hood, scattering snow everywhere. He was muffled in scarves like a bandit, his features hardly visible save for the buffalo-horn moustaches which seemed to have grown even more fulsome.

He pushed the scarves down with his thumb.

'Sorry to drop in unannounced, Biddy.'

On impulse she put her knuckles to his cheek.

'Good God! You're frozen.'

'Not so bad, not so bad.'

'Come inside to the fire.'

'Must take my boots off.'

'You'll do nothing of the kind.'

'Spoil the carpet.'

'Damn the carpet.'

Iain dunted his heels against the wooden step then, with Biddy leading him, clumped into the hall.

The hounds rose from the hearth-rug and padded curiously about his legs, sniffing his trousers, his sodden woollen stockings and clumsy shooting-boots. Odin sneezed as snow got into his nostrils. Thor let out a single quizzical bark that brought Willy galloping up from the kitchen.

'I thought I heard the bell,' Willy said. 'Who is it?'

'Iain Carbery,' Biddy said.

'*What*? On a night like this?' Willy said. 'What the devil is Carbery doing here in this weather?' He was servant enough, though, to stoop before the traveller and untie the knot holding the rope that kept the visitor's greatcoat fastened. Little crusts of snow, fresh and crumbling, fell to the floor-boards and immediately melted. Odin, still puzzled at the intrusion, licked at one of the puddles and wagged his tail, slashing it this way and that until Willy pushed him away. 'I thought the boats were off.'

'No, the boats are running fine.' He nipped one woollen mitten in his teeth and wrestled it from his numb fingers. Did the other one. Stuffed the gloves into his greatcoat pocket as Willy moved behind him and removed first his pack and then the coat itself, shaking each and putting it down on the long table. 'The boats,' Iain went on, 'are practically empty though, for most of the railway lines are blocked – or were until today. Thaw on now, thank God, or I would still be stuck in Callander, which is not the sort of place in which one wishes to be stuck for long.'

'How did you get here from Tobermory?' Biddy asked.

'Hoof,' said Iain.

'Hoof?'

'I walked,' Iain said, then laughed. 'Quite an adventure, believe me.'

Biddy said, 'I take it, Iain, that you are quite yourself again?'

'Better, all better,' Iain said. 'Inclined to run out of puff, that's all.'

'I'm not surprised,' Biddy said. 'Willy, please be good enough to fetch Mr Carbery a refreshment. What would you like, Iain? Whisky toddy?'

'Perfect,' Iain said. He seated himself on the sofa and stooped to unlace his boots. Only when the steward had gone, did he glance up. 'You look well, Biddy. But then you always look well.'

She leaned an elbow against the stone mantel and watched him struggle with his boots. Then, with an impatient *tut*, knelt before him to ease off his boots and peel off his wet stockings while he reclined. He waggled his toes and, almost casually, brushed her hair with a fingertip.

Biddy sat back on her heels. 'If that's what you're here for,

Iain,' she said, 'I may as well tell you now that you will be disappointed.'

He gave a sharp little sigh and shook his head.

'That's not what I'm here for, Bid.'

'What *are* you here for then?' Biddy said. 'Not even you would traipse half-way across Scotland in the depths of winter just to scrounge a free dinner or two.' She paused, almost smiled. 'Or would you?'

'It ain't pleasure that bring me here, alas,' Iain said. 'It's business.'

'Business? What sort of business?'

'Sangster business,' Iain answered.

'Ah!' Biddy said, then, just as Willy returned from the kitchen with bottle, jug and kettle, gave her lover a shake of the head to warn him to say no more.

Iain appeared to be almost his old self again as he took supper in the hall with Biddy and her relatives. He was easy and affable with Donnie, considerate of Vassie and charming to his hostess. He kept them entertained with tales of the aristocrats with whom he had had acquaintance but, of course, said nothing of his association with Walter Baverstock or the business that had brought him battling through blizzards to Mull.

Biddy was pleased to see him. She had missed his company – and his devotion – more than she cared to admit.

If it had not been for his foolishness she might have taken him into her bed that snowy January night. Might have persuaded him to propose to her. Might even have married him. Iain would have made a decent enough husband and, given a run at it, would probably have managed to father children upon her. But marrying him was no longer an option. He understood that as well as she did. One despairing hour with a red-haired trollop had cost him dearly. He had been tainted. There could be no going back, no forgiving or forgetting.

She showed no impatience to be rid of her mother or Donnie and gave Willy, her moral guardian, no indication that she was eager to be left alone with Iain or that she intended to resume her former intimate relationship with him. Even so, Willy's face was a study in thunder as he cleared away coffee cups and glasses and, fixing Biddy with a magisterial glare, asked if she would require anything more from him that night. Biddy answered that she would not and, about half-past nine o'clock, Willy finally departed.

She lay in the wing-chair, slippers off, feet stretched out to the fire.

Iain sprawled on the sofa, Odin snoozing by his side, Thor at his feet. The snow had eased but the night was blanketed by an uncanny silence. There was no sound but the tick of the clock under the stairs.

'If only it could always be as peaceful as this,' Iain said.

'I hope you're not planning on settling in for the winter.'

'No,' he said. 'No, no. The die is cast, Biddy, and thus it must remain.'

'What are you talking about?'

'I'm off to Africa.' He shrugged as if the statement somehow required an apology. 'I've signed a contract with the United Concession Company. I'll be sailing for the Cape in precisely eleven days.'

Biddy sat up. Tears started into her eyes. It was all she could do to hold them back. She pressed a finger to her lips and swallowed hard before she could trust herself to speak. 'Why are you doing this, Iain? Surely you're not going away just because of – of me?'

'Don't be daft, Bid.' He shrugged again. 'Nothing to do with you. Well, nothing much. I'm in need of a fresh start, that's all. Damn it, I'm not getting any younger and I've had enough of sponging on my betters. Time to make something of myself, and have some fun doing it. Africa is the place for that.'

'But what will you do there?'

'Bit of this, bit of that, I expect.'

'Administration?'

Iain laughed, wheezily. 'Lord, no! They've more than their fair share of clerks and pen-pushers out there already. I'll be shoved up north to a little spot called Mashonaland where, I gather, Rhodes thinks there's a reef of pure gold just waiting to be uncovered. The place is settled – Rhodes has seen to that – but it's still primitive country so I'm told. I'll be a policeman of sorts under the charge of a fellow called Jameson.'

'A solider, in uniform?'

'Mufti. A civilian.'

'What do you know about gold-mining?'

'Not a thing. But I do know rather a lot about guns, which is apparently much in my favour. I was interviewed in Edinburgh by a Mr Todd, the United Concessions agent in Scotland. He seemed satisfied with my credentials and, on his own initiative, signed me to a contract on the spot.'

'Where you do leave from? Leith?'

'No. I sail out of the Port of London on the *Durban Castle* first tide, January twenty-first.'

'So you are here to say goodbye?'

'Sort of,' Iain said. He put his hand into his pocket and bought out a long manila envelope. 'Mainly, I'm here to give you these.' He leaned across the dog and handed the envelope to Biddy. She took it, looked at him, head cocked. 'Go on,' he said. 'Open it.'

She slit the sealing, took out the certificates, held them to the light.

'Shares,' she said. 'Shares in the Baverstock Tweed Manufactory.'

'Only four hundred, I'm afraid. It's all I have.'

'Iain, I can't possibly take these.'

'Why not? It's not a public company, so I can't offer them for sale.' He leaned forward again, his forearm resting lightly on Odin's flank. 'Walter Baverstock would love to reclaim them but after what he did to you, what he did to both of us, I'd burn them first.'

'Walter didn't do anything to me,' Biddy said. 'Oh, yes, I know he'd love to get his hands on Fetternish just to teach me a lesson but that's never been on the cards, not even as a remote possibility. Every ounce of wool we produce goes straight to Sangster and I receive my annual dividends without quibble.'

'Business is not what it was, though,' Iain said.

'I know. But it will surely pick up again.'

'The boys, Agnes's sons, are involved in the management now.'

'Really?' Biddy said. 'I don't see what that has to do with me.'

'You're thirty years younger than either Walter or Agnes. Soon the next generation will take over. When that happens you will probably find yourself out in the cold.'

'If that happens we'll just sell our skins on the open market like everyone else. Walter's little tricks came to nothing, though they did keep me on my toes for a year or two.' Biddy flicked the certificates and offered them back. 'I can't accept these, Iain. I appreciate your generosity, but . . .'

'Hold on a minute, Biddy,' Iain said. 'I'm not *giving* them to you. I want you to *buy* them from me.'

'Buy them?'

'For cash.'

'*Buy* them?'

'Of course,' Iain said. 'What use are Sangster shares to me in Africa? To tell the truth, I'd prefer to purchase a bit of stock in Mashonaland gold.'

'Do you need money for your passage?' Biddy said. 'Is that it?'

'No, no, the company pays my passage. But I'm – well, to be frank, I'm strapped. Absolutely strapped. Not a sou, not a groat to my name. I don't want to turn up on Jameson's doorstep looking like a beggar, now do I?'

'I'll give you money. I'll lend you money,' Biddy said. 'I'm not nearly so well-off as folk imagine, however, so it won't be much, but . . .'

'I didn't come here to scrounge, Bid,' Iain said, firmly. 'Everything's gone. Everything except my guns. All I have left of any value are these certificates and I want you to have them. I'd give them to you if I could, honestly, but I have to raise the wind somehow. They're a bargain, I assure you. Even in a down-market the Sangster tweed mill is a sound investment.'

'All right, Iain.' Biddy tapped the documents thoughtfully against her chin. She felt safer dealing with Iain on a practical level. 'How much do you want for them?'

'One hundred and fifty pounds.'

'You're selling short, Iain.'

'Beggars can't be choosers, Bid,' Iain said. 'Besides, I do want you to have them and one hundred and fifty pounds will see me very tidily equipped. United Concession begins paying my salary from the day I step on to African soil, so that should be all right. And if I'm really stuck for my supper I can always bag a springbok or a lion, I suppose.'

'If the lion doesn't bag you first,' said Biddy, frowning.

'Will you buy the shares at that price?'

'I've never been one to turn down a bargain,' Biddy said.

'Except me,' said Iain. 'I was a bargain, you know. I loved you. Still do, always will. Why did you turn me down, Biddy?'

She laid the certificates on her lap and studied him philosophically. He was right, of course. He *had* been a bargain, the best bargain she would ever be offered, perhaps. But he loved her more than she loved him and that fact frightened her. She had assumed that she could negotiate a marriage contract with the same efficiency as she had arranged a contract for skins, but she had been wrong. Iain had taught her a valuable lesson. She would never make the same mistake again.

'I did not love you,' she said.

'Not at all?'

'Not enough,' said Biddy and, rising, tossed the certificates on to the table. 'Will a banker's draft do, Iain?'

He grinned in relief. 'Made out to Cash?'

'Of course,' said Biddy and, taking a lamp from the table, went off along the corridor to the office to find a pen and ink.

It was a beautiful morning, a spectacular morning, a morning that would live in Biddy's memory for many years to come.

Snow at sea-level was so rare that the island looked new-minted. The moor's soft contours rolled away under a dusting of snow under a sky so clear and blue that Biddy felt she could detect the curve in it. By ten o'clock, of course, the sun would cause the snow to melt and drizzle through the turfs and slide from the eaves. Gnarled tufts of bracken would emerge from its unblemished surfaces, the pines on Olaf's Hill would shake down slush, tracks and cartways would redefine themselves as rich, red muddy scores, and the sheep, her sheep, would pick through the snow and the cattle, her cattle, would trail straw and dung along the shore road. But at half-past seven, when Iain left, it was all still pure.

House, sea and land were enclosed in a dove-grey half-light as the sun rose over the Morven hills. Donnie's breath and the breath of the pony in white wreaths above the hard gravel. Willy had put on an enormous scarf and a ragged, fur-lined balaclava to protect his ears and had insisted on Biddy wearing her quilted ulster cape and hunting-cap, which would have been appropriate, perhaps, if she hadn't had on a dress and a dozen petticoats beneath.

Iain still looked oddly tinkerish, wrapped in his greatcoat with his pack roped to his back. His old heartiness was fully restored, however. Shoulders back and chest out, his gestures were as extravagant, his voice as loud as ever. He had consumed a substantial breakfast and drunk a whole pot of coffee while regaling Willy and Biddy with predictions of how good it would be in Africa and how he intended to make his fortune and come back a rich man. Then, with the banker's draft safe in his pocket, he had shouldered his pack and strode out on to the drive to wait for Donnie to fetch the gig.

He had breathed deeply and performed a few knee-bends, had flung his arms about like a butcher boy and then, for a moment or two, he had been motionless, arrested by the sight of the winter sunlight stealing over the peninsulas, highlighting the little cottages and the blue mountains and the gulls, all the gulls in Christendom it seemed, strung out behind a single brave trawler that was treading toward the isles.

'Oh, God!' He sighed. 'Dear God!', and when the gig arrived and he turned to confront Biddy there were tears in his eyes.

'No swim this morning, Mr Carbery?' Willy said.

'Not this morning, William,' Iain said. 'Next time, though, next time.'

He put one arm round Biddy and kissed her on the lips.

Even through the swaddles of clothing she could feel his

suppleness, his warmth. She clung to him a moment longer than friendship required and when he drew back she felt as if a little portion of herself had been lightly torn away.

'Damn it all,' Iain murmured. He wiped his moustaches with his wrist. 'Must go, old girl. Wouldn't do to miss the boat, would it?'

He shook Willy's hand and climbed up into the gig.

Donnie slapped the reins, the pony eased into the leathers and the gig pulled away uphill.

'Iain,' Biddy shouted. 'Iain.' He looked round. 'Give my regards to Mashonaland.'

He waved. 'I will. I will.'

'And come back safe,' Biddy whispered. 'Please, come back safe,' then, when the gig was gone, let Willy lead her back into the house, shivering in the brittle cold.

February was as unseasonably mild as January had been cold. The Fetternish ewes were plump with lamb and everything was ready for the first of the drop. On Pennypol Quig had a pair of sleek brown calves to cope with and a dwindling store of hay to eke out until the grass came on again. There were many signs that spring had arrived early. But the islanders were not fooled. They knew by experience that winter could come rolling back at any time and, in spite of temptation, wisely put off ploughing and seeding.

Mild weather cheered Biddy and lured her out of doors.

She cleaned her gun, put on her boots and had McCallum guide her round Fetternish's wilder acres. When that palled, she asked him to accompany her to a remote part of the moor where a black iron target in the shape of a stag had been erected. There, on grey, warm, windless afternoons she practised her marksmanship, not because she longed to stalk again or expected a call to join Lord Fennimore that summer – an invitation she would certainly have refused – but just for the satisfaction of improving her aim.

Behind most of the cottages drying-ropes flapped with sheets and blankets. A couple of girls from Coyle were drafted into

Fetternish to help with the wash and assist Maggie with the flat-irons. By the middle of the month domestic chores were well forward for the season. And still the weather held.

Vassie's recovery continued. She was well enough now to toddle round the gardens or up to the top of the drive or, for a bit of devilment, to nag Willy about the poor state of the vegetable plots, which were not even Willy's responsibility in the first place. She still carried a walking-stick but used it less often with each passing day until it seemed like no more than an affectation. When Dr Kirkhope called to examine her, however, she would wait at the top of the hill and wave the stick at him as if he were a stray bullock, would tell him what to do with his opinions, until he barked at her to behave herself or he would lace her medicine with purgatives and she would spend the next week in the water closet.

She did not call on Innis, though she was pleased enough when Innis brought the girls to visit her.

She liked to go out in late afternoon to meet the Browns and Donnie at the crossroads, though, and would watch, sly-eyed, the skittish little flirtations that took place between Innis and the schoolteacher. Vassie had no love for Michael Tarrant, however, and owed him no loyalty, so she said nothing to Innis or to Biddy about what was going on and kept her misgivings to herself. She showed no inclination to venture down to Pennypol nor did she enquire about the cattle herd. When Biddy mentioned Quig or Mairi in the course of conversation, Vassie would deliberately close her eyes as if to indicate that talk of cattle wearied her and the past, *her* past, was best left to take care of itself.

This, of course, was far from the truth.

Vassie had her special confidantes, her tellers of tales and bearers of news, but her manner was so casual, so nodding and drowsy that her informants had no idea that they were being pressed to serve the old woman's curiosity.

'I am hearing, Donald, that your mother's cold is not better yet?'

'No, she has been taking coltsfoot for her cough.'

'Coltsfoot, is it? Who would be recommending that now?'

'Mairi,' Donnie would answer. 'Mairi is good with medicines.'

'Does Mairi put white horehound in the linctus too, I wonder?'

'She does, Gran, and liquorice.'

'Aileen will not be liking the taste of that.'

'She gets honey afterwards or a piece of sugar candy to suck.'

'I see. And what about these calves of yours? Do they thrive without Mairi's medicines?'

'They do, Gran. They are both very greedy on the teat, though.'

'Are they brown or black? I have forgotten what you told me.'

'Brown, Gran.'

With Becky and Rachel she was even more subtle.

'Is Fruarch helping your Dada with the sheep then?' she would ask as she strolled down the track with the girls.

'Fruarch is a naughty dog an' he is kept inside,' Becky would reply.

'Is that so he will not be frightening the ewes?'

'It's so he will not get round Daddy's feet,' Rachel would say.

'Yes, doggies can be such a nuisance to a shepherd at this time of the year,' Vassie would agree. 'You will be having lambs down soon, I expect?'

'Yes, Gran. By the end of next week.'

'That will be why your Dada is in such a temper?'

'He is not shoutin' so much as he used to,' Becky would reveal.

'He is so,' Rachel would say. 'He shouts at Mammy.'

'He does not.'

'He does so. When you are sleepin'.'

'I see. I see,' Vassie would say, and keep that to herself too.

With Willy she was much more direct. She held the house steward in some regard, for Willy was just as sharp as she was and almost as devoted to her daughters. She also had a notion that Willy was not quite deceived by her pretences and had guessed what she was about.

She would begin a conversation about the vegetable plots,

just to ruffle him a little, then, with a distant expression and a little twitch of the eyelids, would say, 'It is the onions that my husband likes, onions straight out of the soil. There will not be many onions where he is staying now, I am thinking.'

'There are onions everywhere, even in Perthshire.'

'Perthshire? Is that far from here?'

'Too far for you, Vassie Campbell,' Willy would tell her.

'How far?'

'Has Biddy not told you how far?'

'I do not like to ask her.'

'Why not?'

'Because it distresses her to be reminded of her father,' Vassie would say, glibly. 'Is it more than a hundred miles to Perth?'

'How would I know?' Willy would answer. 'It's a cart, a boat, a railway train, and another long drive from the station. That's how far it is.'

'Have you been there?'

'I took him there, as well you know.'

'Did you sleep in a hotel?' Vassie would ask next.

'Yes, the Royal, in Perth.'

'Soft beds?'

'Hard as iron.'

'Fine food?'

'Cabbage soup, and gruel for breakfast.'

'Uh-huh,' Vassie would stare vacantly from the drawing-room window or across the garden. 'It is a fine spell of weather we are having, is it not?'

Cagily: 'Is it?'

'Do you think that it will last?'

'Don't ask me,' Willy would say. 'Ask your daughter.'

'About the weather, do you mean?'

'About Redwing,' Willy said. 'And when she intends to take you there.'

It was the first time that Innis had left Mull for the mainland. She had never even been as far as Oban before but, unlike Maggie, she was not dazzled by the sights of the west-coast

port or thrilled by the train ride to Perth. She was concerned –
overly concerned – with her mother and nervous at the
prospect of what they would find at the journey's end. She
would have preferred not to go at all but Biddy had insisted
that she could not cope with Mother on her own and needed
the sort of assistance that only a relative could provide. So,
with Michael's agreement if not his blessing, Innis was hurriedly
co-opted and, with Willy along as porter and guide, set out on
the two-day trip to Redwing before the weather broke and
lambing started in earnest.

When told that Innis would be going away Rachel and
Rebecca wailed and were only appeased by a promise that they
could spend the night at An Fhearann Cáirdeil with the Browns.
Gavin, of course, would stay at Pennymain to help look after
his father and, if some unimaginable disaster struck in Mammy's
absence, Quig and Mairi were not far away on Pennypol.

Even so, Innis left home burdened by feelings of guilt and
dread.

She did not want to see what had become of her father, did
not want to take on responsibility for her mother. Among the
four of them, however, Vassie seemed least flustered by the
vicissitudes of travel. She sat on the deck of the steamer like a
grand lady, flaunting herself in the new clothes that Biddy had
bought her for the trip, and pointed out the sights along the
coast with her stick. She enjoyed the train ride even more. She
loved the hissing white steam, the shriek of the guard's whistle,
the clang of signals, the powerful shudder that ran through the
coaches – the whole rhythm of travel; the same rhythm that
Innis found so queasy and distressing.

'What is wrong with you, girl? Are you not enjoying yourself?'

'Aye, Mam. I'm – I am fine.'

'Look! Look at that castle. What castle is that, Willy?'

'Brander,' said Willy from behind a copy of the *Oban Times*.

'Are you sure?'

'Positive.'

'Well, Innis, there is Castle Brander for you. You are not going
to be seeing a grand sight like that at home, now are you?'

By the time the party reached Perth, however, even Vassie

had lost her enthusiasm and had become enveloped in gloom. She claimed that she was weary and rested in her room in the Royal until the two-in-hand arrived in the hotel yard to collect them for the short drive to Redwing. At the last minute Willy refused to accompany them. He declared that he had no wish to set foot in that dismal institution again and would remain in the Royal to await their return.

It was dusk when the Campbells arrived in Redwing.

Nothing much to the hamlet; a few white-washed cottages, a slovenly sort of inn and, at the road's end, a pair of massive stone gateposts and an iron gate that would not have been out of place in the Tower of London. Beyond it, looming through the pines, were the turrets of the Redwing Institute, its lights not cosy and welcoming but meagre and grim. The women were met on the steps of the main building by Dr Seward. He wore a frock-coat with a high collar. Though polite enough, he was not effusive and somehow managed to convey the impression that visitors were not entirely encouraged.

'How is my father?' Biddy asked.

'He is not quite himself today.'

'Has he been told that we are coming?'

Dr Seward glanced at her in bewilderment. 'Well, no,' he said. 'That would be point . . . would be ill advised.'

'Ill advised?' said Biddy. 'Dr Seward, we are his family.'

'Nonetheless . . .'

He had a trim salt-and-pepper beard and square eyebrows. His frown made Biddy feel inconsequential and she was on the point of reminding him just who was footing the bills when Innis touched her arm to calm her.

Leaning into her stick, Vassie snapped, 'Where is he? Where is my husband?' in a voice so shrill that it echoed in the bleak hallway and away down the dusty corridors that led to the patients' quarters.

Dr Seward lifted his hand – an oddly stiff gesture as if the arm had been jerked up by a string – and made a signal with his fingers. A burly fellow in a striped apron appeared from a closet under the staircase. He was younger by a decade than the doctor but no more friendly or communicative.

'Carson,' the doctor said. 'The keys for number four, if you please. You will accompany us, of course.'

Carson nodded and with a ring of iron keys jangling in his fist led the way down a long ill-lighted corridor. Dr Seward started off after him, leaving the women – huddled, arm-in-arm – to follow in his wake.

The corridor reeked of lamp oil, wax polish and cabbage and, Innis thought, of something else, something sweetish and acrid, like sickness or urine. It was not the smell that disgusted her so much as the noise, a symphony of howls and shrieks that grew louder as they approached the corridor's end.

There, pinned to the wall, was a life-sized crucified Christ carved out of pine-wood and painted in vivid colours, so twisted and grotesque yet so real – down to the very nails – that Innis was repelled by it and, for the first time in her life, flinched from the image of Our Lord. She turned her head away and averted her eyes and if she had not been clinging to Biddy's hand might have covered her ears to muffle the barbaric clamour that came from behind the door.

'Locks?' Carson said.

'Locks, yes,' said Dr Seward. 'Carson, are they feeding?'

'Not yet, sir. Not gone six yet.'

'Good. Open the door, please, and admit the ladies to the side room.'

'Who are we here for, sir?'

'Campbell.'

'Oh, God!' said Carson under his breath, and rotated the key in the lock.

The reception room was adjacent to the patients' suite but quite separate from it. It had a single tall window, barred but un-curtained. It contained no ornaments, no carpets, pictures or decorations, only a table and four chairs screwed firmly to the floor. As soon as her father was brought into the room, Innis saw why. He was not just old, as her grandfather had been old; it was not a weight of years that bore down on him but madness, a raving, almost bestial sort of madness in which all the vigour of youth was evident again but warped and distorted, made frantic by the demons that laid claim to his senses.

She recognised him more by his suit – the worn serge Sunday best that she had sponged for him so often in the past – than by his features. The sly, acquisitive quality was gone and the calculating lust that had been the mark of his character for as long as she could remember was revealed, stamped plainly into his face like a die into tin. His skin was metallic, white and shiny as if he had been polished, not washed, for his appearance before them. His hair had been pomaded and combed in a middle parting but his harried behaviour had caused it to rise again in a spiky corona like, Innis thought, a crown of thorns.

Cinched tight around his waist was a broad leather strap that Mr Carson gripped with all his might as the wizened little creature writhed and pranced before them, chattering like a monkey and, like a monkey, baring his teeth in hatred and rage.

Involuntarily Innis crossed herself.

'Where do you want him put, Dr Seward?' Carson asked.

'At the table, I think. Will he settle?'

'He needs his dinner, that's all,' Carson said. 'He'll be a good boy once he's had his dinner.' A wrench on the strap brought Ronan to his knees. 'Say "How do" to your folks since they've come such a long way to see you. Sit nice at the table, Cammy, and say "How do." '

Dragged upright, Ronan was forced to the chair at the table and thrust down upon it. Still raging, he pumped up and down and hammered his fists upon the table-top like a petulant infant. He was watching them, though, watching his wife and daughters and to her horror Innis detected a glint of recognition in her father's eyes. With it came a sudden cessation of effort.

He sprawled across the table, teeth still bared in a hideous parody of friendliness and charm.

'Ronan,' Vassie shouted. 'Do you not know who I am?'

'Bottle. Bottle,' he said, winningly. 'You have brought me my bottle.'

'No, I did not bring you a bottle,' Vassie said. 'I brought you myself.'

'Bottle. Bottle. Bottle.'

'I don't believe this,' Biddy spoke with considerable force. 'What have you done to him, Dr Seward? Is this what you call a cure?'

'There is no cure for your father's condition.'

'You promised . . .'

'Your father, Madam, is deranged. It is not his addiction to spirits that controls his behaviour now but – but something else.'

'Something else?' Biddy cried. Her father leered up at her and groped at her skirts. She stepped back. 'Can you not even give it a name?'

'Call it the madness of age, if you wish,' Dr Seward said.

'Is he always like this?' Innis put in.

'We use opiates to keep him calm,' Dr Seward said. 'We did not administer any today, however, in the hope that he might recognise you.'

'It appears,' said Biddy, 'that he does not.'

'I believe he does know who you are.'

'Bottle.' Ronan attempted to wriggle over the table. 'Here, lassie, come here to me. I will be giving you bottle.'

'You will be giving her nothing, Ronan,' With an abrupt little snatch of the arm Vassie brought her stick down upon his head. 'You have nothing to give to anyone now and I am thinking that you never did.'

She raised the stick again but Carson drew his patient back into the chair with a tug on the strap. Dazed, Ronan pawed at the air with his fists as if the object of his pain was ethereal.

Vassie put the stick down and leaned into it.

She pressed her breast against the table's edge, peered directly into her husband's face and said quietly, 'Do you not know who I am, Ronan Campbell? Do you not know that I have come here just to tell you that you will never be seeing me again?'

'Mam, do not . . .'

'Ronan? Ronan, tell me who I am.'

'*Bitch!*' he snarled. '*Bitch out of hell!*'

'There!' said Vassie, smiling in satisfaction. 'There now! Do you see? He knows fine well who we are.'

'And then,' said Innis, tearfully, 'my mother told the warder to take him away. He was dragged off into the room where the other patients were hidden. I did not wish to see him in that room for I could hear them and it was not the noise that men make together, not even when they are drunk. I have never heard a sound like it. It was as if they were animals trapped in a pit and knew that they would never get out, would never again see those who loved them.'

'Rage,' Gillies said. 'I think that's what you encountered, Innis.'

'More than that, worse than rage. Despair.'

'They will not be like that all the time, I'm sure,' Gillies said. 'There are bound to be spells when they're quiet and calm and don't know where they are or what's happened to them.'

She leaned into him, nestling against his arm. She had wept for a good five minutes there in the deserted classroom with no one to see or hear her, no one but Gillies Brown. She had held her tears in check for three days. Dry-eyed and hollow, she had discussed her father's condition with Willy, with Biddy, even with Michael, had talked soberly and without obvious compassion about the punishment that had been inflicted upon her father and what it meant. But of that other thing – her mother's glee – she had said nothing, for that was the wound that would not heal, the cut upon her soul.

'He knew who she was, who we were,' Innis said. 'And then, when that was clear to her, she waved her stick and had him taken off.'

'There was nothing else to be done, Innis.'

'She could have – have kissed him, have shed tears. Something.'

'Are you telling me that you didn't know there was no love lost between your parents?' Gillies said. 'Or did you just not want to admit it?'

'He was a detestable man, an ugly man,' Innis said. 'I know

that. But for there to be nothing at all, no trace, no remnant of love . . .' She rubbed her red-rimmed eyes with her knuckle like, Gillies thought, a bewildered child. 'Afterwards, in the hall, Biddy and Dr Seward argued about money while my mother sat quietly on a chair that had been brought for her and smiled and smiled as if she was the daftie and not my father.'

'Do you want to have him home again, Innis?' Gillies asked.

'No.'

'Is that what grieves you?' he said. 'That you can't have him back?'

'No, that he cannot be made well again.'

'Changed is what you really mean, isn't it? You don't just want him cured, Innis, you want him changed, improved and made better than he was.'

Innis nodded. 'Silly, is it not?'

'Not silly,' Gillies said. 'Impossible.'

She was still for a moment then sniffed, sighed and said, 'In the heat of the argument Dr Seward told us that if were not satisfied with the treatment my father was receiving we were at liberty to take him away with us there and then.'

'But you couldn't?'

'How could we possibly care for him in the state he is in? We *had* to leave him. There is simply nowhere else for him to go,' Innis said. 'At that point even Biddy saw sense in what the doctor was saying and that was the end of it. We left him there.'

'Innis, Innis,' Gillies Brown said. 'It's the best place for him, you know.'

'That is what my mother says too. But . . .'

'You don't believe in retribution, do you?' Gillies said.

'Not retribution of that sort,' Innis said. 'I would forgive him if I could but all I can do is pity him.'

'Is that what's making you so unhappy?'

'That,' Innis said, 'and the fact that he never loved us.'

'Are you sure?'

She hesitated. 'Or that we did not love him, not enough at any rate.'

'Enough for what?'

'To save him, I suppose,' Innis said. She shook her head once

383

more. 'What a waste it all seems. What a dreadful waste. It is here, and then it is gone and there's nothing left except regrets.'

'Oh, no,' Gillies said. 'There are happy memories too.'

'Memories of your wife?'

'I could not live without her,' Gillies said. 'She is still as much a part of me as my brain, my breath.'

'Are you not happy here?'

'Yes,' Gillies said. 'But if there were choices, if we could go back to how it was before . . .'

'You would?'

'I would,' he said.

'Perhaps that is the difference between us,' Innis said. 'You see, I would not go back, not for anything.'

The classroom was warm and faintly damp, for though the pipes had been repaired, the flood had left its trail along the wainscot. There were those inimitable schoolroom smells too, musty and chalky and corporeal, that she associated with Gillies and with all that Gillies represented. He had become her harbour, her refuge. She did not have to hide herself or her feelings from him.

'Perhaps he did love you once,' Gillies said.

'Michael?' she said, without thinking. 'No, he . . .'

He moved beside her on the long bench, the same bench that Rachel had occupied barely an hour ago; Rachel, who would be eating scones and drinking chocolate with Becky and Donnie right now, in Aunt Biddy Baverstock's fine big house, and wondering where Mammy had got to. Even when she thought of her children, though, deliberately brought them to mind, like a little talisman, Innis could not resist his comforting arms. She felt no guilt when he held her close. She let her head rest against his shoulder.

'You must put him out of mind,' Gillies said, gently. 'That's all you can do now, Innis. You must put him right out of your thoughts.'

'Michael?' she said again, though this time she knew perfectly well who the teacher meant and what he meant by it.

'Enough,' Gillies said. 'Quite enough.'

He pushed her away, not roughly, and got to his feet.

Hastily, he buttoned his waistcoat and jacket and adjusted his collar. His hair, what there was of it, was ruffled and his spectacles were canted at a comical angle. Innis, in spite of herself, chuckled at his discomfiture. She was no longer confused, no longer uncertain.

'I take it you're feeling better?' Gillies said.

'Yes, much better.'

'Good,' he said, brusquely. 'In that case I'll walk you home.'

'Not home,' she said. 'To Fetternish.'

'Yes, to Fetternish,' Gillies said. 'Come along, woman, we had best be on our way before it gets too dark to find the track.'

'Do you not have a light to guide your faltering steps?' Innis asked.

He looked down at her, not quite smiling.

'Only you,' he said.

TWELVE

Arms and the Man

In the weeks that saw winter tail into spring the little green isle of Foss did not find a buyer. No potential purchasers were tempted out from the mainland to inspect the anchorage or examine the quality of the grass.

Younger members of the New Athenian club teased Walter Baverstock and egged him on to offer for the remote fly-speck of land, to redeem, as they put it, 'your foothold in the Hebrides'. Walter refused to rise to the bait; Iain Carbery's departure had dampened his interest in Mull at last and even Agnes had almost given up hope that one day the great estate of Fetternish would tumble back into her family's possession.

Foss remained deserted. The abandoned house had fallen swiftly into disrepair and dampness and big winds had wreaked havoc upon its timbers.

When Quig went over in early March he found that the verandah had collapsed, a corner of the roof had been blown away and wet rot had infested the main beams. A warm February had brought grass on, though. The pastures were already lush enough to support a small herd or, come to that, a flock of hardy hill sheep that did not need to be coddled from day to day. On the back of the knoll where the old man and his wives were buried nothing had changed, however, except that the new marker's rawness had been weathered away and lichen and moss had already dabbed their paws upon the stone.

Quig did not linger. He, better than anyone, knew what had to be done.

'Rent it? Rent Foss?' Biddy said. 'From whom?'

'Innis and your brother Neil,' Quig said.

'Neil will probably want cash in hand.'

'Has he not just received a cheque for eight hundred pounds?' Quig said.

'You know he has,' said Biddy. 'Notarising payment of the inheritors' shares was your last duty as executor.'

'Not quite,' said Quig. 'There is still the matter of Foss to be settled.'

Biddy and he were conversing out of doors.

The afternoon was blustery and a racing sky threatened more rain. They stood on the snout of Olaf's Ridge, with Fetternish House peeking over the pines and Pennymain, Pennypol and the Treshnish Isles spread out before them, all licked by brawling Atlantic waves. Foss was too low-lying to be visible but both Quig and Biddy knew exactly where it was and stared in that direction as if the sea itself might provide a solution by suddenly swallowing the place up.

'Are you hinting that I should buy it?' Biddy said. 'Do you have such a sentimental attachment to that lump of rock that you cannot bear to see it pass out of the family?'

'I have no sentimental attachment to the place whatsoever,' Quig said. 'I am happier to be here than there. But it is no lump of rock, Biddy. It has good soil and good fat grass and I do not wish to see grazing wasted.'

'You would like me to put cattle on, is that it?'

'Sheep would be better. Greyfaces are very robust.'

'My flockmaster might have something to say about that,' Biddy said. 'What would be the demands upon Michael's time?'

'Lambing, shearing and tupping. Three or four trips in the year,' Quig said. 'Some extra cost in transportation. But you would recover that by the sale of extra skins and mutton. You could be using the old system of feeding up spring lambs. They make wonderful prices, you know. And,' he added, 'I am here or hereabouts if an extra hand is needed to help move them.'

'I thought you were a cattleman?'

'I have no aversion to working with sheep.'

Biddy pushed her hands into the pockets of her ulster and

lifted her shoulders, not because she was cold but because Quig's advice seemed so sound and sensible that she was tempted to take heed of it.

Foss had been extensively advertised and letters had been sent to one or two Mull landowners. So far there had been not so much as a nibble of interest. Chances were that if Foss did not find a buyer soon some eccentric Englishman with a desire to live the life of a hermit might pick it up for a song or, worse, it might go to an amateur farmer who had no notion of what he was getting into.

'Are you thinking about it?' Quig said.

'I am thinking about it,' Biddy admitted.

He was a quiet fellow, Quig, but when something stirred him he could be just as persistent as she was. At times it was hard to forget that he was not blood kin, not really her cousin. She had developed an affinity with him that was difficult to explain. Something to do with Donnie, perhaps, with their mutual affection for the boy. More and more she had come to realise just what a service Quig had done for them by taking Aileen off their hands and raising Donald as if he were a brother or, more likely, his son.

Quig said, 'If you form a little subsidiary company with the island as its only capital asset then you could be paying one third of an annual rent to your brother in Glasgow and one third to Innis.'

'How much would that be?'

'Fifteen or twenty pounds to each of them.'

'I'm already paying for the lease of Pennypol,' Biddy said. 'In spite of what you may think, Quig, my resources are limited. Fetternish does not run itself on thin air, you know.'

'Thirty or forty pounds for four hundred acres of prime grazing is very good value,' Quig said. 'You have your share of Evander's legacy for capital. Tarrant will be able to purchase a few extra hill ewes to get you started and inside two seasons you will have made your money back three or four-fold, and the rest will be jam.'

'If, that is, Neil and Innis agree to rent the island.'

'Innis will,' Quig said.

'Have you discussed the matter with her already?' said Biddy.

'No, but I am sure she will be pleased that Foss is to stay in the family.'

'Perhaps we can persuade Gavin to live there when he is older.'

'Best place for that wee chap,' Quig agreed. 'I think perhaps he has too much Campbell in him.'

'Oh, do you?' said Biddy. 'May I remind you that I am a Campbell too.'

Quig grinned. 'Aye, Ma'am, but there are Campbells and Campbells, just as there are Quigleys and Quigleys. Some are better than others and some, like you, are the very cream.'

He had, Biddy noticed, strong, white even teeth. When he grinned he looked younger, not so much boyish as raffish, as if, in spite of his apparent gravity, there was a bit of the rogue in him after all.

'Quigley,' she said, half laughing, 'are you flirting with me?'

'No, I am only trying to get my own way.'

'Are you now?' she said. 'And do you think you will?'

'I might,' Quig said. 'Aye, with any luck at all, I might.'

It came up out of nowhere, like a storm that had been brewing out of sight of land for weeks. When it broke, though, it did so with a ferocity that took Innis's breath away. Michael had been brooding all through the weeks of lambing. As usual, he had lost weight that he could ill afford to lose, scraped down to skin and bone by long hours out in the fields, by hasty meals and lack of sleep. Although Barrett and he shared the hard work he alone carried the onerous responsibility for the crop that would pay Biddy's bills.

Innis made sure that she kept the girls – Fruarch too – out of her husband's way and did everything that was asked of her without quibble or complaint. She had hot water constantly on the boil, hot food ready to serve at an instant's notice. She also took care of sickly and shivering orphan lambs and saved all those that God intended to be saved, and a few more besides. She was almost as tired as her husband, for extra chores were laid on top of all her other duties, cooking and cleaning and washing and mending, and seeing to it that Gavin and the girls were sent off promptly to school each morning.

Gavin would have played truant if she had be willing to allow it. He was already versed in the mysteries of birthing and, with small strong hands, had been co-opted by his father to help turn tight lambs in the womb and, being his father's son, he endured all the discomforts of shepherding not just stoically but with a kind of delight. He thought of himself as a man, his father's assistant, of the Fetternish ewes as his responsibility; yet each morning he was torn away from them, reduced to what he really was, a small, scowling schoolboy, more sullen and more ignorant than most.

During the lambing she missed two Sunday services at Glenarray.

She learned, though, that Father Gunnion would not be returning to Mull and that his duties had been taken over by a young priest, Father O'Donnell, whom she did not know and to whom she could hardly go for advice. Confession, the sacrament of Penance, was one thing, a matter between her and God. What she really required right now however were definitions, a setting out of the parameters of what was right and what was wrong in the eyes of the Church.

Father Gunnion would have understood her predicament but she doubted if a young priest would. How could she tell a stranger what she had witnessed in Redwing or of the love she felt for Gillies, a love so strong that it could not be denied much longer. If she had been able to confide in Father Gunnion, if the old priest had been able to offer some sort of comfort and, perhaps, some feasible hope of compromise, then it might never have happened.

As it was, she was tired, tired in body and soul, so disillusioned that she made one fateful error of judgement, succumbed to one blinding moment of impulse, after which there was no going back.

He had lambed two difficult ewes by lantern-light late at night in the little paddock near the sheds. It was close to the end of the drop and the fields were brimful of lambs, singles and pairs, and anxious ewes bleating in the darkness. He would be out again before daylight, shaking off sleep, shaking off exhaustion, shaking off her solicitude.

Now, though, he came clumping in through the door, boots and trousers and canvas apron smeared with dirt and a little of the blood of the birthings, hands and arms sticky with the jelly with which he'd smeared them. Earlier that evening he had taken out the last of the orphans and had paired it with a ewe whose lamb had been born dead. He had skinned the dead lamb and tied the orphan in the skin and had coaxed the ewe into accepting it, into letting the wee beast suck at her stiff brown teats. He had them in the pen by the sheds, folded in by straw, and would nudge them out into the field in the morning along with the pair he had just delivered.

He was, or should have been, satisfied.

But he was not.

He went to the basin of hot water that Innis had poured and, stripping off his shirt and apron, washed his upper body thoroughly. Innis picked the soiled shirt from the floor and put it into the basket by the door to wash first thing tomorrow. He turned and, still towelling himself, said, 'I've been thinking what we'll do with the money.'

Innis was caught off guard. For an instant she had no notion what he was talking about. For weeks now his conversation, such as it was, had been confined to sheep, to the progress of the lambing, to telling her what he wanted her to do. Now, abruptly, she glimpsed his real concern; the money, the long, ornate cheque for eight hundred and forty-eight pounds that had arrived, together with an accounting, from the lawyers' offices in Perth.

He said, 'We will buy Pennypol.'

'*What?*'

She was on her knees by the basket sorting out soiled clothing. Her back ached and her eyelids were gritty with the need for sleep. It was now close to midnight and she had been up since before five. She swung round and looked up at him. He was so thin that he appeared almost skeletal.

He towelled himself, saying, 'We'll offer for Pennypol. We

can afford it. It is worth no more than three or four hundred. She can keep the jetty and access rights.'

Stunned, Innis sat back on her heels.

'It is impossible, Michael. What's more, you know it is impossible.'

'Why?'

'My mother will not sell.'

'What's to stop her? Ronan's gone and he's not coming back. You told me so yourself. McIver's dead and buried so there's nothing to prevent a sale. Your mother won't live there again. She's happy up at the big house, being waited on hand and foot.'

Innis drew in a stiff breath. 'Quig has Pennypol now.'

'Quig, is it?' Michael tossed the towel to the floor and put his hands on his hips. The pose was mannered as if he had rehearsed it. 'Is it Quig she'll have, now that she can't have Brown?'

Innis opened her mouth, then closed it again.

'Quigley will get what he wants. Have you not heard? He's persuaded her to hang on to Foss. Any day now you'll be invited to accept ten pounds a year in grazing rents for your share of the island and it, like Pennypol, will gradually become part of your sister's kingdom.'

'I have heard nothing of this.'

'You will. As soon as Robert Quigley wriggles his way into your sister's bed and has no more need of Pennypol.'

'What are you saying, Michael? That Quig and Biddy . . .' Innis got up. She was flushed now and felt a strange fluttering sensation in the pit of her stomach. 'How do you know what Quig's plans are?'

'Biddy told me. Asked me if sheep would do well on Foss.'

'What did you tell her?'

'I told her sheep might do well there but that it wouldn't be my sheep. I told her that if she wanted to keep a flock off-shore then she would have to find herself another shepherd to take care of them.'

'What does that have to do with Quig?'

'It was his idea. She as good as told me so. She told me that if I won't tend her sheep on Foss then Robert Quigley will.'

'Michael, are you suggesting that we buy Foss?'

'Don't be so bloody daft.'

'I am not the one who is acting daft,' Innis declared. 'Do you really *need* to be a landowner, Michael, just to teach Biddy a lesson? Buying Pennypol, even if we could, will not give you *that* much standing.' She came closer, hands raised as if to push him over. 'I will not see my grandfather's money squandered on some whim. That money will provide for Gavin and the girls.' She tried to check herself but she was too weary, too angry. 'Is it Quig you are jealous of now? First it is Mr Carbery, then it is Gillies, and now it is Quig. Buying Pennypol will not get *you* back into my sister's bed. There is not enough money, not enough land in the whole of Mull for that to happen.'

'Is there not?' Michael spoke without emphasis. 'Do you think Biddy wouldn't take *anyone* to her bed if it suited her? She'd have settled on the damned schoolmaster if it hadn't been for you.'

'Me?' Innis said. 'What do I . . .'

'If he hadn't been tupping you. Even your precious sister won't stoop to taking your leavings, Innis.'

'Gillies? You think that Gillies and I . . .'

'What?' Michael said. 'Are you going to hide behind your rosary now? Are you going to tell me that you're far too good, far too "holy" to tup with that Glasgow ram? God, you just have to look at him to know that he's tupped you already, or soon will.'

'Gillies would never do that. Never.'

'Aye, but you would, wouldn't you?'

'Yes,' she shouted. 'Yes.'

'Christ, you're no better than your sister.'

'I *love* him, Michael. Is that what you want to hear? I *love* him.'

'Why?'

'I do not know the reason,' Innis said. 'There *is* no reason.'

'Do you love him more than you love your children?'

'Of course I do not. It is a different sort of . . .'

'More than you love me?'

The word 'love' sounded cruel on his lips. The guilt and regret that had welled up at his questioning suddenly evaporated.

She realised that Michael was not seeking answers or even reassurance. He had never loved her, had never understood just how much she loved him and somehow, without willing it, she had slipped from his circle of influence. She had always been a good, loyal, loving wife and he had treated her as if that were no more than his due. Nothing he could do or say now could compensate for his years of calculated indifference.

'Yes, more than I love you.'

'I thought so,' Michael said. '*Has* he tupped you yet?'

'No.'

'Wait until he does,' Michael said. 'He'll soon change his mind and wish he'd set his sights on Biddy instead of you.'

'I will not . . . No, Michael, I'll not let you spoil it.'

'Spoil what?' Michael slapped a hand against his chest. 'There's nothing much left *to* spoil, is there? Do you think I'm jealous of Gillies Brown? Huh! If only he knew how easy it is to get old Ronan Campbell's daughters to lie down for you he'd be a damned sight less cocky.'

'I will not let you make a fool of him,' Innis said.

'Hasn't he made a fool of me?'

'No, Michael,' Innis said. 'You have done that to yourself.'

'Well now, if that's what you think,' Michael said, fumbling with his belt buckle, 'perhaps I should give you a taste of something that might make you change your mind.' She watched him unfasten the buckle and draw the belt from about his waist. He wrapped the thick, worn leather strap about his fist. 'After what you've admitted to me tonight, Innis, would I not be quite within my rights to give you a taste of this?' She was not afraid of his threat of pain. She tried to think of Gillies, of his tenderness, of his understanding, of the kiss that had meant so much. Michael laid the belt furled upon the table. 'But I won't give you an excuse to go running to your school-master shouting that you're married to a brute. Anyway, I've more to do with my time than browbeat women.' He gave a little grunt of amusement. 'See, Innis, I'm more of a gentleman than you took me for. Or perhaps I just don't care to waste energy on a wife as stupid as you are.'

'I will not stop seeing him.'

'I don't expect you to,' Michael said. 'He'll soon lose interest.'

'What is it you want?' Innis said.

'Only what's mine,' Michael said.

'And what is that?'

'Whatever it is, I can get it for myself.'

'Michael, I . . .'

'Go to bed, Innis,' he said, dismissively. 'Go on, get out of my sight.'

And Innis, without hesitation, did.

No one could quite fathom why Vassie chose Tom Ewing to escort her to Pennypol. Biddy would have arranged a gig to take her there at any time or, now that she was sure on her feet again, would have accompanied her in along the shore track, if that had been her mother's wish.

When Biddy or Innis raised the subject of Pennypol, however, Vassie still appeared to be totally disinterested. She no longer closed her eyes but she would fuss instead with the piece of sewing or knitting with which she occupied her hands and pretend that she had gone deaf; until, that is, a soft March forenoon when the minister dropped by to visit his parishioners at Fetternish.

Vassie was ensconced in the wing-chair in the great hall, her favourite post and one from which she could observe most of what was going on in her daughter's house. Biddy, as it happened, was not at home. She had driven herself over to Coyle to consult Hector Thrale on a matter of repairs to one of the outlying cottages and to rouse the lazy old beggar into doing something about it before the quarter's rent fell due.

Willy admitted Tom, exchanged a few pleasant words, then left the minister to Vassie's tender care while he went down to the kitchen to make a pot of coffee. Like most of her visitors, Tom approached Vassie with caution. He had no clear idea how the illness had affected her or what subtle derangement of clarity and understanding might remain. She was, he knew, a bit of a poseur at times, and did not feel that it was right of her to tease and taunt a minister of the Gospel in the way that she teased and taunted practically everyone else.

Vassie had knitting-needles and two small balls of rose-coloured wool in her lap. She appeared to be fashioning something rather complicated, like a glove, but when he enquired what it was she gave no answer, merely glowered at him for a moment or two, then said, 'I am surprised at you, Tom Ewing.'

'Pardon?'

'I have been hearing about you and the woman from Foss.'

'Pardon?' said Tom again, flushing somewhat.

'Mairi Quigley is her name in case you have forgotten.'

'What have you heard about Mairi – Mrs Quigley – and me?'

'How she visits you. How you meet behind the church. How she drops in at the manse after poor Mrs McCorkindale has gone home. Oh, I have heard all sorts of things about you, Tom Ewing.'

'Who told you these things?'

'Birdies, little birdies,' Vassie said, without the trace of a twitch or, for that matter, a smile. 'There are no secrets in the parish of Crove, and you would be doing well to remember it.'

'Does Biddy – I mean, am I being discussed?' Tom rubbed his chin with his fingertips. There was no whisper of stubble for he'd shaved himself meticulously just before he'd left the manse and had even applied a little of the scented powder that Mairi had given him to prevent rash. 'I mean, has there been gossip, Vassie, and if so what are they saying?'

'There has been a little bit of the gossip, yes, but I do not think that you need be worrying about a scandal just yet.'

'Dear Go . . . Goodness,' Tom said. 'I wonder if my elders know?'

'Of course the elders know. They will be having the most fun they have ever had discussing what you can be up to with a woman like that.'

'A woman like what?' said Tom, bridling. 'I will have you

know, Vassie, that Mairi Quigley always behaves with the utmost propriety.'

'She does not dress with the utmost propriety,' Vassie said. 'She dresses like one of those Spanish women that used come to the Salen Fair every year. But that would be before your time here.'

'Nonsense,' Tom said, a little smugly. 'Of course I remember the gypsy girl. She danced and made predictions.'

'She was hardly a girl,' Vassie said. 'She would be forty if she was a day.'

'I think,' Tom said, 'you're confusing her with her mother.'

'I am confusing her with nobody,' Vassie said. 'It was worth pounds in drink to McKinnon when the gypsy woman danced in Salen, for the heat and the lather she left behind among the men was something terrible.'

'Well,' Tom said, 'I am neither hot nor lathered. And Mairi Quigley is no gypsy girl and does not, to my knowledge, make predictions.'

'I can make predictions, however,' Vassie said. 'I predict, for instance, that you will be making your way to Pennypol as soon as you leave here and will call on Mrs Quigley at the cottage. I predict that Mrs Quigley will smell even sweeter than you do with the lavender water that you gave her last Friday evening.'

'Dear God!'

'I am thinking, however, that it might have been more practical to be presenting her with a new pair of shoes since she has just about worn out her old ones tramping up and down to Crove to throw herself at you.'

'Vassie, how in the name of all that's holy do you know these things?'

'Do you deny it?'

'How can I?' Tom said. 'It wasn't lavender water, though. It was *Peau d'Espagne* and it cost me three shillings and three pence.'

'It seems that Maggie was not paying enough attention.'

'So that's it. That's your source. Maggie Naismith.'

'Are you going on to Pennypol?'

'I am, as soon as I have drunk my coffee.'

'Take me with you,' Vassie said.

'Are you – I mean, should we not wait for Biddy?'

'I do not need Biddy's permission. I want to go now,' Vassie said.

'What if I refuse?'

'*Phew d'Espain*, indeed!' said Vassie, with a little twitch of the eyelid. 'Would the church elders not like to be hearing about that?'

'I will fetch your coat,' Tom Ewing said.

'Do you want to see the calves?' Quig said. 'They are out in the park but I can fetch them in if you've a mind to inspect them.'

'I have seen calves before,' said Vassie. 'I have no need to inspect them.'

'Would you like to lean on my arm?'

'Why would I be leaning on your arm?'

'For balance, if you are tired.'

'I am not tired and I no longer suffer from giddiness.'

'I am pleased to hear it,' Quig said. 'What do you want to see?'

'I did not come to "see" anything,' Vassie told him. 'I came to talk to you. I think it would be best if we strolled out to the wall for our conversation and left your mother to entertain the minister.'

'Oh, yes,' Quig said. 'I would not be wanting to play the gooseberry.'

They moved away from the cottage within which Mairi Quigley was indeed enveloping the minister in a haze of *Peau d'Espagne* while serving him with tea and shortbread. The cattle dogs had been let out. They followed the young man and the old woman at a respectful distance but when Vassie and Quig sat on the grass at the base of the long dike they came and lay beside them, tails wagging.

For a moment or two Vassie gazed out over Pennypol bay, saying nothing. Quig wondered what thoughts were going through the old lady's head, if she was troubled by memories of the family's stormy past or if, perhaps, she loved the place still and was about to reclaim it. She seemed less frail than she had been a year ago, say, for she had lost the sharp edge of restlessness, the driven, almost demented energy that had kept her so lean. She looked relaxed now, still thin but no longer scrawny. She was, he noticed, quite pretty in her way.

'Will your mother be marrying the minister, do you think?'

'I would not be surprised,' Quig replied.

'There will be a bit of groaning and tutting if she does.'

'There is nothing to prevent it,' Quig said. 'My mother is a widow, Mr Ewing a bachelor.'

'She is hardly the picture of a minister's wife.'

'I will admit to that,' Quig said. 'But she could change.'

'Or she could change him?'

'That too.'

'If she does marry and go to live in the manse,' Vassie said, 'what will you be doing with yourself?'

'What I am doing now; staying on here and tending cattle.'

'It would not be proper for Aileen to stay alone with you.'

'Hmmm,' Quig murmured. 'I had not thought of that.'

'She would have to be taken in elsewhere.'

'Who would take her?'

'Biddy, of course.'

'Surely not willingly?'

Vassie didn't answer his question. She said, 'You have been a good friend to our family, Robert. I am thinking it is time you became part of it.'

'Rightly or wrongly, I have always regarded myself as part of it,' Quig said. 'Perhaps in the same way as Donald does.'

'He is kin – and you are not.'

'Is this your way of telling me that I should quit Pennypol?'

'Oh, no, no. That is not my intention at all.' Vassie shifted her weight from buttocks to flank. She leaned against him while she fumbled in her skirt and produced a letter. She handed it to him. 'This is a letter of instruction to my lawyer. I am giving you Pennypol. All of the acres that my father gave to me, from the burn to the dike at the top of the calf park, as far back towards Crove as the old sheep track. I am told that there is a map in Biddy's office that measures the acres and shows the boundaries. The lease has two years to run but in that time you may draw the income from it.'

Cautiously Quig said, 'If you are wanting to be rid of Pennypol then should it not be sold to Biddy and the money divided between the children? Or, if that is not to your liking, then bequeath it to Donnie – or to Gavin, for that matter.'

'What would Donnie be doing with a farm on Mull?' Vassie said. 'It would be nothing but an encumbrance to a clever boy like him. He may choose to come back here to visit his mother and aunts and cousins but he will not be tied. We must not put him under an obligation, not to the land, to Biddy or even to you, Quig, no matter how much he wishes to please you.'

'What about Innis? Should she not have Pennypol?'

'I do not wish Michael Tarrant to get his hands on it.'

'Because he will run sheep on your pastures?' Quig said.

'Sheep!' said Vassie, scornfully. 'That is an old quarrel and not one that moves me any more. It is sound land, Quig. It should really be part of Fetternish.'

'If you make over ownership to me, Vassie, how will Pennypol become part of Fetternish?'

'I will not have you coming to court my daughter without something to offer,' Vassie said. 'Pennypol can be your dowry.'

She was negotiating in the old manner; it was pointless to protest. He must treat her as he would have treated her father, not defensively but with candour. He said, 'I doubt if Pennypol will do the trick. Biddy is no more sure of me than she is sure of herself.'

'Then you must make her sure,' Vassie said.

Quig made a little popping noise with his lips.

Misinterpreting the sound, one of the dogs snuggled close to his knees, tongue lolling and eyes begging. Absently, Quig stroked its ears.

'But I am so much younger than Biddy,' he said.

'That is a nonsense. Five years . . .'

'Six, I think.'

'That is nothing, nothing at all.'

'She still regards me as a boy,' Quig said. 'I question if she has ever thought of me as a suitor.'

Vassie gave a soft chuckle. 'She will notice you, Quig, as soon I tell her that I have made Pennypol over to you. That will be enough to set her thinking – and the rest will be up to you.'

'I take it,' Quig said, 'you have guessed that I am in love with Biddy?'

'I might think that it is because of the spring that everyone is falling in love with everyone else,' Vassie Campbell said, 'but you and I both know that it is the autumn that stirs the loins. It cannot just be a whim of Nature, now can it? How long have you been in love with her?'

'Since about the time Evander and I came over to attend your sick cattle.'

'She was a bonnie lass then . . .'

'She is bonnier now,' said Quig before he could help himself.

Again the soft little laugh: 'You are not the first man to hold that opinion.'

'I cannot help myself,' Quig said. 'Perhaps I would have married Innis, if she had not been so infatuated with Michael Tarrant.' He paused. 'Come to think of it, I was never in love with Innis the way I am in love with Biddy. I have kept it to myself, though, for I did not think it was right.'

'For her, or for yourself?'

'For her.'

'Hah!' Vassie exclaimed, with a trace of irritation. 'Biddy has never known what is good for her. She is wanting children, but not just children. She wants a husband too, a man who can stand up to her. But there are precious few of those in this part of the world.'

'I would still take her even without Fetternish, you know,' Quig said. 'Once Donnie is settled and my mother . . .' He shrugged, apologetically. 'I am here only because of Biddy. If it had not been for Biddy I would have gone to the mainland with the others to look for employment. There are times when I wish that Biddy was a crofter's lass, not a landowner at all.'

'Tell her that.'

'How can I?'

'When she hears that I have given you Pennypol she will begin to pay attention,' Vassie promised. 'And then you will have your opportunity.'

She had slipped on to one elbow, her face very close to his.

She did not resemble her father, but in her eyes, in the shapeliness of her features, Quig glimpsed the Irish beauty from whom she was descended and caught some whisper of an elegance long gone.

'I see that you are determined to make a match for Biddy,' he said.

'And a home for all of us,' Vassie said. 'Do you object to that?'

'You know that I do not,' said Quig.

Below them Mairi Quigley and Tom Ewing appeared, not arm-in-arm, not just yet, but walking so close together that they might already have been husband and wife.

Vassie leaned closer, her mouth an inch from Quig's ear.

'There is one more piece of advice I can offer that might aid you in bringing Biddy to the altar,' Vassie said.

'What might that be?'

She whispered five or six words that made Quig blink at her audacity.

'Do you really think it will work?' he asked.

'I know it will,' said Vassie.

Biddy had been less surprised by her mother's generosity to Robert Quigley than Vassie had supposed she would be. With no more than an arch of the eyebrow and a question or two about the legality of the arrangement, she had accepted Vassie's decision to sign away Pennypol.

In fact, Biddy had known for weeks that her mother was hatching some sort of devious plot, for Vassie had asked Donnie to pen several letters on her behalf and deliver them to the postal office in Crove. Being an honourable young man, though, Donnie had refused to tell Biddy what the letters contained and had kept his promise to his grandmother to say nothing, not even to Quig.

At first Biddy had thought that the letters might be to Ronan. But Vassie had already declared – in so many words – that she preferred her husband to 'Rest in peace'. She had even offered to contribute towards the costs of keeping him locked away in Redwing for she had saved a tidy sum over the years by a combination of hard work and frugality. Biddy and Innis would not hear of it, however, and Vassie did not press the matter.

If Biddy and Innis were not fazed by the transfer of Pennypol to Quig, Michael Tarrant was furious. He had set his heart on owning the place and regarded Vassie's gesture as an act of spite. He took his frustration out on Innis. He ranted and raved as if it was all her doing that Pennypol had been taken from him and given instead to a scheming tinker's brat.

Innis had too much sense to try to placate her husband by explaining that Quig was part of the family and had contributed more to its welfare over the years than he, Michael Tarrant, had ever done.

Besides, she had had enough of Michael's moods. She was bitterly disappointed at his assumption that she was having a love affair with Gillies Brown, even if it was half true. She had taken her vows within a church that allowed no leeway and she had observed those vows to the letter for thirteen years. She had offered Michael love, and her love been rejected. It seemed that all he required was a wife who would obey him.

She no longer felt the need of Father Gunnion's assurance that in falling in love with Gillies she had done no mortal damage to her soul. If she had sinned in thought, she had most certainly not sinned in deed. Thanks to Michael, she had finally come to terms with her feelings for the schoolmaster and found a new source of strength in the relationship that set it once and for all upon an even keel. So, as March gave way to April and the sun shone, Innis had no indication that dark forces were at work in the narrow little community or that before the month was out her life would be changed forever.

It was one of those gruff April days, not as warm outside as the sunshine suggested it might be, and the bay and the broad Atlantic beyond were filled with white-caps.

Ploughing and sowing were underway on Fetternish's arable plots. The lambs had grown independent enough to gallop about the knolls and hide from their mothers so that the pastures were filled with anxious bleating. Up on the moor the curlews cried. It was spring, incontestably spring. Biddy's rents were in. Biddy's fields were being tended. Biddy's calves were being reared on Pennypol just as they had always been. Biddy herself was filled with seasonal stirrings, an alarming sparkiness that drove her to stride about the estate as if she was intent upon measuring every rod and furlong personally.

Sometimes she took the dogs with her but Thor and Odin could hardly keep up with her now for, like Willy Naismith and Hector Thrale, they could not compete with the mistress in litheness and energy. Sometimes she would come upon Mr McCallum as he set traps for weasels or fidgeted near a woodcock already sitting on eggs or a well-camouflaged grouse tucked down into the heather. Sometimes too, at the weekend, she would encounter the Browns out for a stroll and would invite them back to the big house for tea and scones. She was careful never to intrude upon the family at An Fhearann Cáirdeil, however, for that piece of property she no longer regarded as quite her own.

As a rule Biddy went walking alone – though not quite as alone as she believed herself to be. In the evenings and on Saturday afternoons she was often accompanied by her nephew; not Donnie but Gavin. He would trail her at a distance and, like an elf or a sprite, would show not a glimpse of himself no matter how often his aunt paused and, frowning, turned in her tracks as if she sensed that she was being stalked by someone or something.

'So that's where you've been, is it?' Michael would say to his son. 'And what did your Aunt Baverstock do today? Anything interesting?'

'She went round by the headland and back up to the house.'

'Didn't she go down to Pennypol?'

'She looked at it from above the dike then cut away to the shore.'

'Didn't she meet anyone?'

'No one. Mr McCallum is up on the moor.'

'And where is Donnie?'

'I think he has gone to An Fhearann Cáirdeil.'

'Did you see him go there?'

'No. I followed Aunt Baverstock just as you told me to.'

'Good. Good boy,' said Michael.

Four days later, in the early part of the afternoon, he trapped her at the mouth of the Solitudes under the snout of Olaf's Ridge.

He had driven a ewe and a lamb down into the rank undergrowth to furnish himself with a plausible excuse for being there and had tied the dog to a tree to keep it from giving the game away. Then, sitting on his heels in the sere bracken, he waited; waited with slow, churning anger for Biddy to appear.

Innis had taken Becky into Crove to buy groceries. Later she would ride back in the wagonette with Brown and the children. Barrett had gone to the stables on the Sorn road to negotiate the purchase of a little extra feed for the handful of ewes that weren't thriving. Quig's lot would be tucked away on Pennypol. Quig had no reason to stray along the rocky foreshore or venture into the glen. Michael was alone, waiting for Biddy.

He crouched under a shroud of blackthorn. The ewe cropped nearby, the lamb beside her. The dog curled, one eye open, against the stunted alder. Michael could hear nothing but the pounding of the waves on the rocks, the wind funnelling in through the mouth of the glen and, when he listened hard, the fluctuating splash of the stream as it poured from the iron pipe beyond the bridge, sounds so familiar that as a rule he seldom noticed them.

He was sure that she would come.

He willed her to come. He knew what he would say when she came, what he would do to her. He knew that because of Innis and Donnie she would not resist, or not for long; that there would be no repercussions.

He saw the dog's eyes open, ears twitch, the head lift just a little.

'Hush, Roy,' he murmured. 'Hush now.'

He eased his weight forward and peered down the gash towards the shore.

She was standing on the lava shelves that sloped towards the sea.

She had taken off her hat. Her hair in the sunlight was like fire. She wore boots of fine leather, low-heeled. She unbuttoned her hacking-jacket. He could see the pale lemon blouse beneath, the shape of her thighs, spread for balance, within the long skirt. The waves broke behind her, blowing up in creamy white foam. She had sensed his presence, the strength of his willing, as surely as if he had called out her name.

Frowning, she came up towards him.

'Hush, Roy,' he said, in the flat Lowland voice that gave no hint of anger or desire. 'Quiet, boy.'

And then, lazily, swaggeringly, he got to his feet.

On Innis's advice Biddy had avoided contact with her brother-in-law for the best part of the month. Necessary communication had been done through Thrale. She knew that lambing had been successful. She expected no less from her shepherds. She hadn't gone into the pastures around Pennymain to inspect the flock however, for fear that she might meet Michael face to face.

She was only too well aware of what Michael really wanted from her and that possession of Pennypol was a substitute for possession of another sort, a mask for less obvious desires. She was also conscious of the fact that her dislike of the taciturn Lowlander stemmed from a wish to reverse the accepted order of things and summon Michael Tarrant to her bed, to seduce him as once, long ago, he had seduced her. It was not scruple that prevented it, only plain common sense. He had married her sister and had fathered her sister's children and, in all conscience, she could not demand from him that which he had no right to give.

She picked her way cautiously over the rocks to the sheep path that straggled up the bed of the glen.

It had occurred to her on occasion that it might be Michael who was following her and the prospect of being stalked by a man who had been her first lover had brought a strange, haunting sense of *déjà vu*, a sliding back to the days when they were both young and fiery. She had known many men since then, too many. She had sailed so close to the wind that sometimes she longed to be shot of all of them, to be released, cleansed, from the nagging little torments of her sex and, like Innis, to have children to wrap herself up in and a man who would want nothing that was not his due.

He wore a plaid shirt. His sleeves were rolled up over his forearms. His scuffed leather waistcoat was untied. His corduroy breeches were clasped about his belly with a broad leather belt. He was as lean and hard as driftwood, so pared down that even his facial muscles seemed unnaturally taut, as if the skin had been stripped away to reveal only tendon and bone.

'What are you doing here, Michael?'

'I followed the sheep, a stray.'

'Why is the dog tied up?'

'To keep him out of the way.'

'Were you not waiting for me?' Biddy said.

'Some fool I would be to wait for you.'

'I come this way quite often.'

'Do you now?' he said.

'I think you know I do,' Biddy said. 'I think that is why you are here.'

'Why would I wait for you here when I can see you at the house?'

'So that we might be alone,' Biddy said. 'To – to talk undisturbed.'

She came closer. She dared not reveal to him the mixture of fear and eagerness that frothed within her. She might snap at him, deride him, order him away. She might praise him for the lamb crop, ask after Innis, enquire about Gavin and her nieces. None of these things would satisfy him.

'Biddy, you're a bitch,' he said.

'Am I?'

'You knew I wanted Pennypol. You could have got it for me.'

'It was not mine to sell.'

'You could have stopped her giving it to Quig.'

'I did not even know she was giving it to Quig,' Biddy said. 'But, tell me, why do you want Pennypol at all? It is too small to be viable. Even you would not be able to make a go of it.'

'Maybe that's so,' Michael said, 'but I'd have given it one damned good go, I tell you. And at least I'd have been free of you.'

'Is that why you are always so angry?' Biddy said. 'Because I have all the things that you will never have? Because Fetternish fell into my lap and you don't think I deserve it?'

'Bitch!' he said again. 'Who'll be next? Will it be Quigley? Will he be your next playboy?'

'Perhaps,' Biddy said. 'Or perhaps it will be someone else.'

'Are you still hoping to find someone to match up to me?' he said. 'You'll find none half so good, I can tell you. See, I know what you are, Biddy. I've known it since the first time we ever met.' He put his hand out and pressed it to her breast. 'I'll always be here as a reminder of what you turned down, of what you could have had if you hadn't been so damned pigheaded.'

Biddy shook her head. 'I need more than you can give me, Michael, a great deal more.'

'What? More than this?'

She was too strong to fall into his arms but she did not resist when he laid one hand flat against her back and drew her to him. He angled his hips and thrust against her. Even through the layer of tweed she could feel his need of her.

She closed her eyes, tried to induce revulsion; then, when that failed and he began to stroke her, she sought to summon up an image of her sister, to imagine Innis's hurt if she ever found out. For a moment she was balanced on a knife-edge of indecision, weakened by her own autocracy. Then she swayed against him, nuzzling her stomach into him as if she might find protection there; as if this man, whom she did not even like and certainly did not trust, might do for her what all the others had failed to do, might restore the naïve, unlettered ignorance of her girlhood when the only man she had ever known had been her father, her bleak, charming, treacherous beast of a father whose influence she could not shake.

Michael said nothing. He pulled the little buttons from her blouse and, tearing at the silk, parted her bodice and lifted her shift.

She felt cold April air upon her breasts. Her nipples stiffened even before his mouth touched them. It was an all-at-once thing, not calculated pleasure. He sucked her breasts, bruising her flesh with his teeth, his lips and tongue dry. He fumbled with her skirt and the awkward sheaths of underclothing.

'Wait,' she said. 'Wait, Michael.'

He thrust her hand down to him, tilting against her palm. She felt his nakedness and closed her hand upon him.

'Wait, damn you,' she said.

'You want it? You want me to do it again, don't you?'

'Yes.'

She eased her fingers reluctantly from him, watched him, erect and proud, bending and bowing while she fumbled with the buttons and little side buckle and untangled herself from her skirt.

She lay down on the rank grass by the side of the path.

She still wore the tweed jacket, thrown open at the breast, still wore boots, thigh-length stockings, a loose, silky agglomeration of underclothing under which she felt his hands probe and pry.

She stretched out her arms and brought him down, his cheek against her chin, his dry lips parted not to kiss but to suck – while far away, it seemed, far beneath, she felt a sudden stab of penetration and, within seconds, a numbing realisation that he was already ejaculating, that the hot, stabbing fluidity within her was Michael Tarrant's seed.

Chaste kisses were by no means the exclusive property of the middle-aged or, as Donnie regarded them, the practically decrepit. He had no knowledge of what was taking place between his teacher and his Aunt Innis, of course; he was far too concerned with what was happening in his own life to pay much attention to the affairs of his elders. He might be a moderately well educated, sensitive young man but he was no more of a prodigy than any of his cohorts when it came to grappling with matters of the heart, and he had been thoroughly discombobulated by the sensations that had charged through him when Tricia Brown had pressed her lips to his.

It was not those sensations that bothered the lad o' parts, however, so much as the general glow that stole over him when Tricia and he were together. And all he had to do to drive every other thought from his head was conjure up a vision of Miss Patricia Brown and set off hand-in-hand with her, as it were, into the land of dreams.

The hand-in-hand bit was no longer a fantasy. Tricia and he would link fingers at every possible opportunity, a practice that arrested all intellectual process and killed the need for conversation completely. It had been that way since before Easter, since Christmas, in fact. Donnie could not remember when he had not thought of Tricia Brown or, rather, a girl like Tricia Brown, and even he was prone to wonder if she was real at all or if he had invented her the way his daft, rambling, little Mammy had invented fairies.

Tricia Brown was as different from his mother as it was possible to be. She was a tall, willowy, intelligent girl; a pragmatist who still had room in her soul for poetry. Much like himself, really. She was destined to follow him to the city of Edinburgh where he would be put to a crammer's college for six terms to learn Latin & Greek before embarking upon a graduation course in History & Law at the University in October of next year.

Only the prospect of Tricia's eventual elevation to studenthood kept melancholy out of the relationship and soothed the thought that they would soon be parted for a while. Donnie was intelligent but not *that* intelligent; not too intelligent to resist the romantic fallacies that floated in the air of Aunt Biddy's brand-new library whose shelves had mysteriously

411

sprouted a crop of novels that he, like his aunts, devoured uncritically.

At heart he was contented. He did not dwell much on his past, or fret over his ancestry. He knew who his mother was, who his father was supposed to have been and, like Quig, considered that having a rogue in the family tree was really no bad thing. He tended, though, to align himself with his late Uncle Donnie who had drowned in a storm off Caliach Point while bravely trying to save his father and brother; a tragic event, young Donnie liked to believe, that had tilted his Mammy's mind and driven Grandfather Campbell to drink. Nothing that his aunts said, at least in his hearing, did much to disillusion him and in the weeks before hand-holding took over from conversation, Donnie would recount the tale of his courageous namesake as stirringly as if it were a legend.

Now, however, all Tricia and he talked about was their future together, a future so rosy and organised that it almost seemed to have come to pass. When Mr Brown sang his praises in class, therefore, Donnie nodded patiently as if he had heard it all before.

'It is not given to many young men to be accepted on provision by the senate of the University of Edinburgh,' Mr Brown was saying, 'but it is an achievement that is now within the grasp of every child in the realm. Donald, I am happy to say, will take his seat in the halls of learning next year, on the proviso that he attains a modest level of proficiency in Classical languages. Maclean, what do I mean by "Classical languages"?'

'Greeks and Romans.'

'Languages, languages, Maclean.'

A hand shot up; a girl, Elspeth Bowie, aged eleven. 'Latin, Mr Brown. He is meaning the Latin language.'

'Yes, that's right, Elspeth.' Mr Brown smiled. She was a poor wee thing, was Elspeth Bowie; her father was a road-mender with a family too large for his income. 'Would you like to study Latin when you are older, Elspeth?'

'Only if Donnie will be teaching me,' the girl said, but with an innocence that was not shared by the rest of the class who whooped knowingly until Gillies wrapped his wooden pointer on the desk to command silence.

'Donald will be leaving us . . .' he went on.

'Awww!'

'. . . next month to sojourn in Edinburgh and prepare himself for entry to the highest seat of learning.'

'Oooooo!'

Another hand shot up; Maclean's best pal, McClure.

'Yes, Archie,' said Mr Brown, patiently.

'Will Donnie be taught for to speak the Latin by a man from Rome?'

Gillies Brown coughed, turning his head politely to one side. He did not know the answer to that one but years of teaching had taught him how to evade awkward questions.

'A man from Rome,' Mr Brown said, 'is called – what?'

'Brutus.'

'Julias Scissor.'

'Mark.'

'Luke.'

'Second Corinthians.'

Another flail with the pointer: 'Elspeth, is that your hand I see waving in the air again?'

'Aye, Mr Brown.'

'Do you know the correct answer?'

'An Italian, Mr Brown.'

'Well done, well done,' he said. 'Donald?'

He was gone again, far away, hand-in-hand with Tricia who, seated not more than three feet behind him, was admiring the line of his sun-dusted neck and musing on what it would feel like to touch the soft little sprigs of blond hair.

'*Donald!*'

Blinking, much blinking: 'Mr Brown? Yes? Yes, Mr Brown?'

'Out here.'

Donnie rose and stepped around the feet of the younger element. He was dazed but not anxious. Tricia's father plucked a pebble of soft white chalk from the wooden box on the desk and held it out to him.

'On the blackboard, please; an outline map of Italy.'

413

Donald took the chalk. He had a picture of Italy in his head, perfectly safe, but the picture was temporarily clouded by the fact that the Italian leg seemed to have become attached to Tricia Brown and that, try as he might, he could not bring himself to draw *that* on the slate.

He looked at Mr Brown, then at Tricia who smiled and raised an eyebrow as if she had guessed the nature of the naughty thought that had flickered through his head.

'Can't you do it?' Mr Brown asked.

'Yes,' Donald said. 'Yes, I can.'

'Well, what are you waiting for?'

'Do you wish me to be starting with the Alpine borders, sir, or down at the toe off Sicily?'

'Just get – all right, at the toe.'

Donnie put chalk against slate and, spreading his legs, traced the Calabrian peninsula. Following the coastline, he marked first Naples and then Rome while the class stared at their hero with unstinting admiration.

All of the class, save one.

At that precise moment Gavin's envy of his older cousin matured and hatred gave it final shape and form.

He realised that he must kill Donnie.

Soon.

She stretched out full length in the bath, the water up to her nose. Her breasts stung and her loins smarted with the scrubbing she had given them but she could not bear to look at her body beneath the soapy brown surface now and lay sullen and motionless as a salamander, hardly breathing at all.

She had taken no pleasure in love-making, found no relief. Past innocence and past passion had not been restored. Michael had been bent on punishing her in the only way he knew how. She had given in to him, not out of need but in the false belief that she could be just as selfish as he was. And had found to her cost that she could not. She might be the laird of a fine Highland estate but she could not emulate the ruthlessness that separated the sexes.

She was ashamed of herself, deeply, deeply ashamed.

She had betrayed her sister, had betrayed herself. She had belittled her position, had demeaned herself just once too often. For this last selfish folly she would surely be made to pay, not in cash, not in favours, but in suffering. If she had a child by Michael Tarrant, how could she possibly explain to her mother, to Innis how it had come about? If she conceived by Michael Tarrant the whole, vile, stifling thing would start up again, the secrets, deceptions and lies that were the legacy of Pennypol. She might wind up mad like her sister or so tormented that she would have to be shut away like her father.

She had risked everything to prove herself superior to a man who had never cared for her at all.

And it was not over, not yet.

If she bore Michael Tarrant's child he would not let her forget what he had done or what she owed him. He would drag her down into a morass of envy and discontent, of furtive, unfulfilable desires that would stain her life and her child's life forever more. She would never be free of him, or his pettiness, and the one thing that she had wanted more than anything – a child of her own – would become a curse and a burden even before it was born.

Unless . . .

She sat up suddenly.

She was slippery with soap, sleek and shiny as a seal, her hair draped about her shoulders like a cloak.

Unless . . .

She rose from the water, wrapped a bath-towel about her, flung open the door, padded rapidly along the corridor and knocked on the door of her mother's room.

'Who is it?'

'Me.'

'Come.'

It was dark outside now, or almost so, for cloud had blown in on the gruff little wind and big individual spots of rain clung to the window glass, each containing a reflection of the fire, like mustard seed.

Vassie was seated in a chair by the hearth. She wore the new summer shawl that Biddy had bought her and the new pince-nez that Dr Kirkhope had prescribed to improve her vision and – to Biddy's surprise – looked quite plump and benign; almost motherly, in fact.

'Biddy, you are dripping water on my carpet.'

'I know. I am sorry.'

'If you do not put on some clothes you will be catching your death.'

'In a minute, Mam, in a minute.' Holding the towel about her, she knelt at her mother's side. 'I have something I want to ask you.'

'Something that will not wait until you are decently dressed?'

'I'm decent enough,' Biddy said. 'Listen, what would you say if I told you that I had decided to marry again?'

'My opinion would depend on who you have picked for a bridegroom.'

'I was thinking of Robert Quigley,' Biddy said.

'What a good idea that is,' Vassie said and, rather to Biddy's chagrin, uttered a sharp little barking laugh that signified less pleasure than triumph.

Quig contemplated the liquid that Biddy had poured from the big green bottle in the silver ice-bucket. As soon as bucket, bottle and glasses had been delivered to the drawing-room she had sent Willy away. She had wrapped the bottle in a napkin and had popped the cork herself. The cork didn't shoot like a bullet from a gun and there was no loud report, only a faint fizzy hiss.

If Quig was disappointed he gave no sign. He watched Biddy seat herself on the gilt-backed sofa and arrange her skirt about her.

The skirt was gored up to the waist. Her blouse had huge leg-of-mutton sleeves and a loose trimming of lace that cascaded down her front like water in an ornamental fountain. She wore a hat, a muslin thing with spots and a pert little bow that reminded Quig of a swallow on the nest, except that it was pink. She had taken her hair up. He liked that style. It showed off the natural line of her neck, and he preferred things natural.

She observed him cleverly, sipping from the glass in her hand.

Quig sniffed at the bubbles and sipped too. He knew what the stuff was but he also knew what was expected of him. 'Is this champagne, by any chance?'

'It is.'

'Are we celebrating something?'

'Not yet.'

'Do not tell me that you drink champagne every afternoon?'

Biddy frowned slightly. 'Usually it is sherry. Would you prefer sherry?'

'No, this will be fine for me,' Quig said. He drank the stuff, not tossing it back like ale, but sipping it steadily until the shallow glass was empty.

'A little more?' said Biddy.

'Why not?' said Quig.

'Help yourself.'

He went to the bucket and extracted the bottle, carried it to her, did the pouring, returned the bottle to the bucket.

Biddy said, 'Perhaps you are wondering why I invited you here today?'

'I am,' Quig said, 'a wee bit curious, yes.'

Some instinct had warned him that Biddy Baverstock had more in mind than a chat about the Salen Show or the Oban cattle mart. His mother had urged him to tidy himself up, to shave, trim his hair and put on his second-best suit, minus the jockey vest, so that he did not feel too out of place. In fact, he did not feel out of place at all, not with Vassie Campbell lurking out in the hall.

He kept firmly in mind what Vassie had told him.

For once Biddy seemed tongue-tied. Her cheeks glowed like boiled beetroot. She placed her glass on a side table and patted the sofa.

'Will you not be sitting yourself down, Quig?'

'I think,' Quig said, 'I would prefer to stand.'

'Why?'

'To stretch my legs.'

'Do your legs not get enough stretching all day long?' she said, testily.

'Biddy,' he said, 'for Heaven's sake come to the point.'

She bustled, fussed, arranged her skirt, adjusted the tilt of the nesting swallow. The blush spread to her throat now and, Quig imagined, probably even tinted the skin beneath the lace cascades.

He cleared his throat. 'I am sorry. I did not mean to be rude.'

She tightened and visibly took control.

'Quig, what do you think of me? Really think of me, I mean.'

He was tempted to blurt out the truth: *Biddy, I think you're wonderful*. He had been raised by the great Evander McIver, however, and had learned a thing or two about how to treat a demanding woman. He would not allow impetuosity to spoil his chances.

'I think you are very fair,' he said.

'Fair? What do you mean by "fair"?'

'Just, honest, regular in your dealings.'

'You make me sound like a cattle trader,' Biddy complained.

'Honesty *is* a cardinal virtue, you know.'

'Do not patronise me, Quig. I get quite enough of that from my sister.'

Quig appeared to lower his guard. 'I like you, Biddy.'

'Do you not find me attractive?'

'I have always considered the ladies of the Campbell family to be more attractive than most.'

'Damn you, Quigley,' Biddy said.

'And you more attractive than, say, your sister Aileen.'

'Damn you.'

'I think,' Quig said, 'I have somehow managed to offend you.'

'Of course you have managed to offend me.'

'Was it what I said about Aileen?'

'I thought you, of all people, would give me a straight answer.'

He put the glass on the mantel, stepped across the drawing-room to the sofa. He spread his forefinger and thumb, touched them to her chin, lifted up her face and kissed her lips. He

418

released her, returned to the fireplace and retrieved his glass.

'Is that straight enough for you?' he asked.

She sat bolt upright for a moment, then lay back and spread her arms along the back of the sofa, looking, Quig thought, simultaneously flummoxed and smug. 'We-ell . . .' She paused, 'We-ell, why did you not tell me?'

'Tell you what?'

'How you felt.'

'Let us just say that I could not get a word in edgeways.'

'Are you suggesting that I talk too much?'

'Not to me. To other chaps,' Quig said.

'Ah, I see,' Biddy said.

'I doubt if you do,' said Quig.

'Is it having land of your own that has made you more confident?'

'Biddy, Biddy, Biddy,' Quig said. 'You do not understand at all.'

'I understand that you would like to sleep with me.'

'In the middle of the afternoon with a houseful of servants running around and your mother in the hall and Donnie due back from school at any moment?'

'Donnie will have gone to the Browns' house to be with his sweetheart.'

'Even so,' said Quig. 'No.'

'Stay for supper, then, when everyone else has gone to bed . . .'

'No.'

'Tomorrow?'

'Biddy, no.'

'I thought you wanted to sleep with me?'

'I do,' Quig said. 'But I want to be married to you before I do.'

'We can discuss marriage after we . . .'

He put down the glass again, walked over to her, leaned close.

'We are not like cattle or sheep, Biddy,' he told her. 'We do not mate at random. I love you and I would love to be your husband. But I am man enough to expect a commitment first.

It will have to be marriage. I will not settle for anything less.'

She blinked up at him and nodded solemnly.

'Who put you up to this?' she asked. 'Your mother?'

'No,' Quig answered. '*Your* mother.'

'I might have known it,' said Biddy, with a sigh.

That was all the proposal that she would ever have. At that moment the door of the drawing-room burst open and Willy Naismith stood there, panting.

'I'm sorry to disturb you, Ma'am,' he said, 'but there's an urgent matter out here that I think you'll have to attend to.'

'Urgent matter?'

'McCallum's at the door,' said Willy. 'Someone's stolen his shotgun.'

'What does he expect me . . .'

'He thinks it was taken by your nephew Gavin.'

'Was it loaded?' Quig asked.

'Yes.'

'I'll come at once,' said Biddy.

The shotgun had been resting upright against the fence beside the gamekeeper's bag and jacket. Gavin had spied it from the low ridge that dipped from the pasture to the moor. It had not been too easy to get close to it, though, for Mr McCallum had eyes like a hawk. Fortunately, Mr McCallum had been setting traps in the tussocks that grew near the fence and had not been paying too much attention. Gavin had crawled through the grass on his belly.

Aunt Baverstock had ordered the fence. His Dad had gone out, three or four weeks since, to see that it was erected properly. The work had been done by men from the mainland who had brought over the posts and the wire. The wire did not stop the weasels getting at the grouse, though. Mr McCallum had told him that nothing would stop vermin once it had the hunger on it.

He had lain in a dry ditch, close enough to hear Mr McCallum muttering to himself. When he had raised his head he had seen the gamekeeper kneeling on the ground, cutting a mouse in half with his fat-bladed pocket knife, the gun only eight or ten feet away, propped against the fence, the shotgun not the rifle. The breech had not been broken for Mr McCallum had been on his own with nobody in sight for miles and had thought it safe.

Gavin had waited, pressed against the ground, a strange exciting, uncomfortable feeling in his stomach, as if he needed to pee. But he had not needed to pee and the feeling had got stronger when he thought what he would do to Donnie and how without Donnie he would become his Aunt Baverstock's darling and would go to stay with her in the big house, away from his mother and sisters. He would not go off to the city, though. He would stay with Aunt Baverstock and help his father look after her sheep. She would give him a gun of his own, a rifle to shoot rabbits with and, when he was big enough, deer.

He had lain in the ditch for ten minutes, listening to Mr McCallum move away, then he had looked up again. His big bottom stuck up in the air, Mr McCallum was crouched on all fours laying one of the weasel traps.

Gavin had lifted the shotgun from its position against the fence as carefully as he might have lifted a baby. He had whisked it down into the grass in two shakes of a lamb's tail. He had tucked the gun under his right arm and cradled the barrels with his left hand. Then he had risen just enough to make his legs work and had gone off down the ditch as fast he could. He had been half-way up the crumbling slope of the ridge before he had heard the gamekeeper's shout.

He had thrown himself down full length, the shotgun between his thighs, and had lain motionless until the gamekeeper had stopped shouting.

He had been sure that he had not been seen. Not being seen was a vital part of his plan. If he was seen then he would not be able to tell them that he had never touched Mr McCallum's gun but that he had noticed a man, a stranger, a tinker with rings in his ears, a packman with a black beard – someone – on the track north-west of the Crove road, that it must be the stranger who had done whatever had been done to Donnie.

On reaching the crest of the ridge he had got to his feet and, carrying the weapon in both hands, had skiddled down the diagonal path towards An Fhearann Cáirdeil across the wildest part of the moor. Finally he had found a good quiet spot among a tumble of boulders and seated himself there.

He sat for a little while with the shotgun across his knees, tracing its beautiful combs and curves with his small, brown hand.

Overhead two buzzards circled in the dusty blue April sky. He could hear their high *kee-keeing* as if it was inside his head.

He was damp with perspiration and his hands trembled slightly as he clicked off the safety and pushed over the top lever.

Butt against his chest, he let the barrels drop away from the face of the body. He stared at the round brass eyes of the cartridges. Until that moment he had not even been sure that the shotgun was loaded.

Mr McCallum had told him that a 12-bore all-round game gun was built to shoot a 2½-inch cartridge with 1¼ ounces of shot. The cases looked larger, though, huge in fact. He slid the gun upward until he could touch his tongue to the brass, taste the clean, new, acrid powder and pressed card.

He closed the breech with a little snap, snapped on the safety, and got to his feet. He held the gun above his head, pumped it towards the sky and let out a little cry, a little *kee-keeing* sound of his own.

Then, with cold joy, he set off to hunt down his cousin.

They had drunk tea and devoured the bread-and-butter that Janetta had made for them, then Evie, Bobby and frisky young Pepper had gone out to play, and Donnie, mindful of his duty to his aunt, had said that he must be getting back to the big house as he had chores to do before dinner.

Tricia had made a sad face. 'May I walk a wee bit of the way with Donnie, Dad?'

Gillies glanced up from his newspaper, caught Netta's eye for just a moment and then, absolutely straight-faced, said, 'Of course. We wouldn't want him to get lost, now would we?'

Donnie knew that the schoolmaster trusted him to behave like a gentleman but that the rest of it, particularly the hand-holding, was a source of amusement to the Brown family. He was mystified by their gentle mockery and could only assume that none of them knew what it was like to be in love the way he was in love. Mr Brown and Janetta were teasing rather than scornful but Bobby was openly scathing. He would pop out of the bushes, whooping, or, if he happened to catch them embracing, would utter a great gargling shriek, clutch his throat and fall backwards upon the grass as if struck down by plague.

That afternoon, however, Bobby and his young sister had gone scampering off in the other direction, chasing after Pepper who, in turn, was chasing the lukewarm scent of a roe-deer. Janetta accompanied Tricia and Donnie to the door and, rather wistfully, watched them start along the track towards Fetternish. 'Be home before dark, mind,' she called then, with a wave, went back indoors.

Reaching down Donnie found Tricia's hand and laced his fingers with hers. She sighed and laid her head against his shoulder. Saying not a word, the couple ambled on in the dusty blue evening light towards the line of birch and alder that screened the headland from the house. They had gone no more than a hundred yards when Gavin stepped out of the bracken.

He still wore the knitted vest that he had worn to school that day, and black breeches tucked into long stockings. He had removed his jacket, though, and had wrapped a red hand-kerchief about his brow and knotted it with a big soft knot at the side of his head. He looked smaller and more inconsequential than ever, dwarfed by the shotgun in his hands.

'What are you doing here?' Tricia said. 'Are you spyin' on us again, Gavin?' She shook her head. 'You really shouldn't go spyin' on folk, you know. If you don't stop it I'll have to tell your Mam.'

'Wait, Tricia.' With a motion so slight as to be almost indetectable, Donnie edged her behind him. 'What is that you have there, Gavin? Is that Mr McCallum's gun?'

'My gun.'

'Oh, did Mr McCallum give it to you?'

'Aye.'

He came out of the dead bracken on to the path. His limbs seemed stiff, his movements jerky. His eyes too looked odd, rolling a little in his head, the way his – Donnie's – mother's did from time to time. At the corners of Gavin's lips were two little hinges of sticky white foam.

Donnie took in a deep breath.

He flattened his hand and touched Tricia's skirt, eased her further behind him. He could sense her annoyance. She was too sensible to understand what was going on. He tried to make himself bigger, to cover her.

'Have you come to show us your new gun then, Gavin?'

'Not spying.'

'No, of course you are not,' Donnie said.

'Not spying. Not spying.'

Cautiously Donnie extended his right hand.

'Here then, let me have a look at it,' he said. 'By gum, but it is a fine gun right enough. I wish I had a gun like that.'

'Mine,' Gavin snapped. 'Mine, mine.'

In some cloudy corner of his mind Donnie held a memory of his mother uttering those very words in that same shrill, possessive tone. He tried not to think what the memory might signify.

He took in another breath and eased his weight on to his toes, staggering a little as Tricia leaned into him and shouted, 'Don't you lie to us, Gavin Tarrant. Nobody would give a gun like that to a wee boy like you. You stole it. Admit it, you stole it.'

'Mine,' Gavin said again. 'Mine.'

He was twenty yards away at most. A grown man would have fired immediately. Even if the aim had been poor the spread of shot would have brought both Donnie and Tricia down. But Gavin was not a grown man. The shotgun was heavy. He started to hoist it into a firing position, not at the hip but at the shoulder, thumb fumbling with the safety. For a split second he glanced down, glanced away.

Donnie seized his chance. He thrust his shoulder against

her, swept both arms out as if he was throwing a rugby ball, and flung Tricia bodily into the bracken as if she had been made of straw. He pounced after her, caught her by waist and shoulder and flung her from him again.

And the gun went off.

He heard the roar, as deafening as if the muzzle had been placed against his ear. His head rang and his nostrils were filled with the reek of powder. He felt the sting of stray pellets against his left cheek and heard another sound, a strange sound, like a sob of breath, as the shot dispersed.

And another sound still, a shout this time, perfectly audible even through the singing in his ears: '*Gavin, no, Gavin.*'

Donnie dropped to his knees in the bracken. He could see Tricia sprawling ahead of him, her long legs kicking. 'Down,' he shouted. 'Keep down.' Then he turned towards Gavin so swiftly that the little trickle of blood that one of the pellets had coaxed from his cheek ran into his mouth, hot and salt-tasting.

The recoil had thrown Gavin backward on to the path. He still clung on to the shotgun, though, hugging it to his chest. He scrambled to his feet. He too was charged with abnormal strength, it seemed, for he raised the gun without effort. He had fired only one shot. Another remained. He ran, spread-legged, down the path towards Donnie, the gun butt rammed into his belly, his little brown fist closed over the trigger guard, finger on the trigger.

Everything seemed to be happening at double speed now. At first Donnie thought that the man must be Mr Brown. But he was coming from the wrong direction and shouting at the pitch of his voice, '*No, Gavin, for God's sake, no.*'

Donnie realised that it was Quig and, standing upright, he called out, 'Here, Gavin, here I am,' to divert his cousin's attention.

Confused, Gavin stopped in his tracks. The shotgun sagged. His eyes rolled in his head, skimming with a kind of despera-tion, a kind of despair. He pivoted this way then that as Quig, running at full tilt, bore down on him. Crashing through the undergrowth behind Quig came Aunt Biddy Baverstock, her red hair flying.

Donnie felt Tricia tug at him, dragging at his arm to pull him down. He shook her off. He saw his cousin turn and turn, turn again, and the gun jerk up.

Donnie shouted, 'Me, Gavin. Here I am.'

He saw Quig lunge, heard the gun go off.

The echoes pealed away over the wilderness and a flock of little birds fled, chittering, from the alder brake. And Quig lay face down upon the track, his legs flung out behind him as if he were running still.

THIRTEEN

The Wind from the Hills

The day was winding down for the Fetternish shepherds. They met as usual by the fank at the road end within sight of Pennymain to exchange odd bits of news and opinion concerning the health of the flock and there was nothing in the air to indicate that they would never meet in this manner again.

Michael was cocky, though, just as he had been that morning and the morning before. He had lost much of his sourness now that the lambing season was over and he had nursed through another good crop for his mistress. That, at least, was how Barrett chose to interpret the change in his boss, for he was too innocent – or too cautious, perhaps – to ascribe the arrogance to anything else and ignored the broad hints that Michael dropped that he, Tarrant, had won Mrs Baverstock over and might soon have a piece of land to call his own.

They were leaning on the wooden gate at the mouth of the pen, elbow to elbow. Barrett had a tobacco pipe in his mouth, a recently acquired habit and one that he had not quite mastered. The pipe, a clay, was not yet fired, not even lit, and he rolled it cautiously between his molars in case he broke the fragile stem. He had become good at spitting, though, and would punctuate his remarks now and then with a little flick of the head and a dab of the tongue.

They had been there for ten or fifteen minutes and the conversation had taken a turn that Barrett found uncomfortable. Michael Tarrant was bragging, though just what he was bragging about was something that the younger man could not quite fathom. He might have asked outright, might have wrung the information from Michael without much effort for it seemed to him that his boss was full of himself and was just dying to confide in someone.

'No, she'll not be able to refuse me now, not after what I've done for her,' Michael was saying. 'Aye, she's not such a fine lady as she pretends to be, I can tell you. She'll be back for more.'

He glanced out of the side of his eye at Barrett who only had to say, 'More of what?' to have the whole wicked story poured into his ears.

Barrett took the pipe from his mouth and spat.

He settled his elbows on the spar again and pretended that he was staring into space. He was, in fact, thinking of Muriel and his children and wondering, in a vague sort of way, why Gavin had not turned up yet since the girls, Rachel and Becky, were visible in the garden of the cottage by the glen and it was well past the hour of six o'clock. He did not miss Gavin Tarrant's company, though. Gavin was too sullen and silent a lad by half and had none of the fun in him that a boy of that age should have. Barrett would have left, would have gone home for his supper but he was still under Michael Tarrant's thumb in that respect and would have to wait until his boss had had enough of him.

Michael said, 'It'll not be her ladyship's lambs I'll be feeding next winter. I'll be having lambs of my own to look after and the profit from my hard work will come to me, not to her. It'll be a fair exchange, though. Aye, she'll have what she wants out of it, and not be disappointed.'

'Is this,' Barrett hesitated, 'is this what Innis will be doing with her windfall then, buying you a croft somewhere?'

'Not somewhere,' Michael said. 'Here on Fetternish. She'll not want me to be too far away.'

'Innis, do you mean?'

'Nah, I mean Biddy.'

Barrett took the clay from his mouth, cleared his throat and peered into the unfired bowl. He did not know what to say next. He was too open a man to have learned the art of evasion.

He said, 'I think I should be going home soon.'

'Are you not going to ask me the reason for it?'

'Well, I am thinking it might be none of my business.'

'You'll have charge of the flock then, Barrett, have you thought of that?'

'Aye, I suppose I will.'

'You don't believe me, do you?' Michael said. 'You don't believe I'll have a piece of ground off Biddy Baverstock and a flock of my own. I will, Barrett. I tell you I will. She'll not be able to refuse me that, not after what I've done for her.' He nodded, slid his eyes towards the younger man, waiting. 'I'll do it again too, if I feel like it.' He raised his arm, stiffening it, and closed his fist. 'I have her like that now, just like that, and it's only a matter of time until . . .'

Barrett turned from the gate.

'Now who is that with your Gavin, I wonder?' he said, pointing across the fields. 'Over there, just going into your house?'

Michael frowned, then scowled.

'Christ!' he said. 'It's bloody Gillies Brown.'

'I wonder what he is after?' Barrett said.

'He's after my wife for one thing,' Michael said, without thinking.

'Had you not better see what he wants?'

'Aye.' Michael heaved himself away from the gate. 'I'd better.'

When she tried to draw him to her to comfort him he jerked away. He was ashen under his tan and did not blink. He wore an expression of stubborn hostility. She had seen that look on her father and on her husband too from time to time but written on her son's unformed features it seemed somehow more sinister. She did not know what to do with him. When it seemed as if he might try to dart through the open door it was Gillies who caught him by the arm and told him not to move, not to dare move until it was decided what must be done with him.

Innis seated herself on a kitchen chair. Through the door she could see the girls and Fruarch on the drying-green. They

429

were grown-up enough to sense that something was seriously wrong and that they were better off where they were. They stood by the line of washing, heads together, whispering as if they were part of a separate, female conspiracy.

'Is he dead?' Innis crossed herself. 'Is Quig dead?'

Trying to keep her voice even and the tears from flooding her eyes, she glanced at Gavin again. He glowered at her without guilt or contrition.

'No.' Gillies shook his head. 'He was very lucky. He caught the shot across his left shoulder. He's in a fair mess, though. It'll take all of Kirkhope's skill to get the pellets out. He's lost quite a bit of blood too.'

'Where is Quig now?'

'At the house with your sister,' Gillies answered. 'He insisted on getting up and walking there himself, with some help from Donnie and Tricia. Quite a lot of help, to be honest. He's a hardy soul, your cousin, but he'll be a long time mending, I think, particularly if there's been damage to the bones.'

'Gavin, Gavin,' Innis said. 'Why did you do it?'

'It was an accident,' Gillies Brown said.

'What? I thought you said . . .'

He looked grimmer than she had ever seen him before. His spectacles shone in the reflected light from the door and the planes of his face were hard as shell. He tightened his grip on Gavin's arm. He did not glance at him, though, did not, Innis thought, dare look her son in the face.

'Quig's orders,' Gillies said. 'Are you listening to me, Gavin? By God, son, you had better listen to me if you know what's good for you. It was an accident, pure and simple. Gavin found McCallum's gun up on the moor and decided to take it to his aunt's house. On the way he met Donnie and my daughter, Tricia. None of them realised that the shotgun was loaded. He was showing them the gun when Quig arrived and took the gun from them. The safety catch was off and the gun went off; one barrel only.'

'Is that the truth?'

'It's what Kirkhope will be told. It's what everyone will be told. If there's no complaint from Quig then there will be no

430

police enquiry, though in my opinion, there should be.'

'Where is the gun now?'

'On your sister's orders McCallum's taken it away.'

'To clean it?'

'Yes.'

'How many shots *were* fired?' Innis asked.

'Two,' Gillies answered. 'One at Donnie and my daughter, the other at Quig.' He felt the boy wriggle and, without compunction, clasped his arm even more tightly. 'My daughter could have been killed,' he went on in a harsh whisper. 'If it was up to me . . .' He paused and closed his eyes. 'No, I can't say that. I can't say what I would do. The decision has already been made.'

'By Quig?'

'By Quig and by Biddy,' the schoolmaster said. 'I hope you are taking all this in, Gavin, because it is what you will have to tell Dr Kirkhope or anyone else who asks. You *found* the gun, remember, and . . .'

Michael stepped into the kitchen. 'What gun? And what the hell are you doing in my kitchen?'

Innis and Gillies rose at once. Gavin sidled towards his father. Michael placed a hand on his son's shoulder. 'Well?'

'Quig's been shot,' Innis said.

A faint flicker of pleasure, almost a smile, passed over Michael's face.

'It was your son who pulled the trigger,' Gillies said.

'Did he?' Michael said. 'Is Quigley dead?'

'Fortunately he's only wounded,' Gillies said.

'Well, that's – that's not so bad then.'

'Not so bad?' Gillies said. 'Your son steals a loaded shotgun, deliberately discharges it at my daughter and your nephew, then wounds Robert Quigley and all you can say is "Not so bad".'

'Quigley won't press charges,' Michael said.

'No, but I might.'

'No, Brown, no you won't.' Michael smiled again. He placed both hands on his son's shoulders. 'For the boy's sake, you will support whatever story you were busy devising when I came in. What? An accident?'

Innis had never seen Gillies lose his temper before but she could sense the anger bubbling in him now, not far beneath the surface. He uttered a little growling. 'Not for the boy's sake,' he said. 'For your wife's sake. I've no wish to bring more grief to your wife than she already has to bear.'

Michael moved suddenly, fist raised. Gillies was ready for him. He raised not his fist but his forefinger, pointing it straight into Michael's face.

'Would you strike me? Would you, Tarrant? Would you attack me just the way your son attacked Donnie? For what reason? To protect your wife's honour? Then you're more of a fool than this boy here. You know that Innis would never betray you, with me or with anyone.'

'She has already admitted that she loves you,' Michael said.

'Be that as it may,' Gillies Brown said, 'it's not honour that moves you any more than it was mischief moved your boy to do what he did. It's envy, I think, envy pure and simple.'

'Why should I be envious of you?'

'You are envious of everyone,' Gillies said. 'You thought yourself superior to these humble islanders and when they refused to recognise just how marvellous you were and how favoured they were to have you among them then you resented them for it and became covetous.'

'At least I do not covet another man's wife.'

'Or another man's widow?' Gillies asked. 'Or the land the widow owns and that you might have owned too – if only, if only, if only . . .'

The clarity with which the schoolmaster had defined her husband's motives astonished Innis. Everything that Gillies had said was true. She had blinded herself to it to protect her children and in doing so, it seemed, had failed them. But it was not falling in love with the new schoolmaster that had carried a canker into her household, that had eroded her marriage. It was Michael himself, his cold, suppurating selfishness, the fallacy that he was owed more than he deserved, that what he had was not enough. She had no value in his eyes. His home, his children, his work, none of the things had value because he had pursued the chimera of independence without ever understanding what it meant.

Now her son, her odd, unbalanced son, would pay the price.

'This is not about you, Michael, or about me,' she said. 'It is about Gavin and what Gavin has done.'

'Gavin shouldn't have been allowed to handle a loaded gun,' Michael said. 'It's all McCallum's fault for leaving the weapon untended.'

'Good God!' Gillies exclaimed. 'Now it's McCallum's fault. Not *your* fault, Tarrant, not even *my* fault for not looking after Gavin properly, for being unwilling to admit that there's something seriously wrong with him.'

'Wrong with him? There's nothing wrong with my . . .'

'No? Oh no, how could there be?' Gillies said, sarcastically. 'Better to accuse McCallum, to declare that it's all McCallum's fault, or Biddy's fault, or Donnie's fault for being so bright. Next it'll be the fault of the man who filled the cartridge or the craftsman who fashioned the gun. Anyone's fault but your own.'

'If you're saying I'm responsible for what Gavin did . . .'

'I am. Yes, damn it, man, I am.'

Perhaps, Innis thought with a jolt, it is no one's fault but mine. She was Gavin's mother. She had carried him in her womb, had given him birth, had suckled him. She had taught him what the world was about up to that time when he was old enough to choose; that tender age of choosing when he, a little male, had selected his own pattern according to whatever Nature had planted in him. The unfathomable legacy of Campbells and McIvers that lay behind him, divided and split and divided against like some vast tract of land, some wilderness estate that no individual could ever hope to tame and cultivate.

Michael released a hand from his son's shoulders. He swung the boy violently around. He, Gavin, had been utterly still and quiet up to that point as if his father's hands had gentled the animal instinct that ran within him, had calmed and soothed and brought him into harmony with himself. He looked dull, as shuttered and enclosed, as harmless as any small boy.

Michael struck him a sudden back-handed blow that shook the dullness out of him, made his blue eyes roll in his head and drew a thin, defiant cry from his throat, a cry that did not

433

indicate shock, disappointment or even pain but mimicked the dry unruffled savagery of a hawk or buzzard, and that in that moment gave him away.

'Why?' Michael shouted. 'Why did you do it?'

As the big flat fist slapped hard against the side of his head once more Gavin put his hands on his hips and yapped an answer that was no answer at all.

'Tell me, you little beggar or I'll beat it out of you?' Michael sank to his knees on the stone floor. 'Why, Gavin, why?'

Gillies touched him sympathetically on the shoulder. 'It's no use, Tarrant. He can't tell you why. He doesn't know himself.'

Brow resting on his son's narrow chest, Michael did that thing that he had never done before – he wept.

It was early, very early, when he wakened her. She had been asleep for no more than a couple of hours. Sleep had been hard to come by and he, Michael, had not come to bed at all. She would have welcomed him beside her that night, for she could not stop crying. She was filled with so much remorse that even her prayers to Our Lady seemed like broken promises. She was convinced that she had let her son down, that what he had done that day had been more her fault than his.

She had lived in the shadow of selfish men all her life, men whose strength was based on false principles, on greed that had no focus. Even her grandfather had been tarred with that brush, for he had created a kingdom over which only he had had dominion. Gavin, though, was different. Unprotected by adult guile, he had acted out of motives too raw to be fathomable. Envy was there, yes; rage, yes; a grudge against everyone and everything, a pettiness that Gillies defined as 'covetousness'. She knew exactly what Gillies meant, and as she lay in bed that night, tearful and sleepless, she searched her soul for signs of it within herself.

'Innis.' He shook her gently. 'Innis, waken up.'

It was still dark. She could hear the clock ticking and the silence of the house and sensed the misty stillness of the April morning.

She opened her eyes and sat up and saw the glimmer of a candle in the kitchen, the flicker of firelight and glimpsed her son at the table, eating bacon with his fingers, all neat in his outfit of black serge, collar clean, hair combed.

'What time is it?' she asked.

'Early,' Michael whispered.

'The girls . . .'

'Still asleep. Be quiet and don't waken them.'

She slid out of bed, groped for her shawl and wrapped it around her shoulders. Puzzled and apprehensive, she followed Michael into the kitchen.

Gavin did not look at her. He continued to nibble at the bacon strip until it was gone then he picked another from the plate. He had bread on the plate too, milky tea in a tall mug. Shod in his Sunday boots, his feet were tucked under the spar beneath the chair and he hung forward, poised, intent upon his breakfast.

'We're leaving,' Michael said.

'Leaving?'

'Gavin can't stay here after what's happened. We daren't send him back to school, even if Brown would have him.'

Michael too was dressed in his best suit and black boots, his heavy working overcoat draped over a chair-back. Two worn old packs that had gathered dust in a cupboard for years had been set beside the door.

Innis put her hands to her breast and pressed against the bone.

'Where will you take him?'

'To Ettrick,' Michael said. 'My mother will look after him. If she won't take him in then I'll find a good lodging. He can go to school there until he's old enough to work.'

'What sort of work?'

'There's never any scarcity of work for herders in my part of the world.'

'I thought this was your part of the world, Michael?'

'It is, aye, of course it is.'

'Will you be wanting us to follow you?' Innis said. 'The girls and me?'

His warmth had a false quality, just too solicitous, too affable. 'Oh, no, no. Don't you worry. I'll be back as soon as I've seen Gavin settled.'

'Will you?'

'Do you doubt me, Innis?'

She stared him for a moment and then, shaking her head, she lied.

'No.'

'Don't you understand that I have to get him out of Crove, Innis, just in case Quig changes his mind. Gavin's not too young to be put into an institution, you know. He'll be safer in Ettrick with me, at least until the fuss dies down.' He brushed Gavin's hair with his palm. The boy looked up. 'He's looking forward to making a trip with his Dad, aren't you, son?'

'Yes,' Gavin said, flatly.

'Barrett can take care of the flock,' Michael said. 'You'll be safe enough here. Biddy won't throw you out. You've more than enough in the bank to pay for what you need until . . .' He applied a frown. 'Oh, that reminds me – I could do with some money. If you give me a banking cheque made out to "Cash" then I can exchange it when we reach Oban.'

She went back into the bedroom. She opened a little drawer in the chest-of-drawers, took out the cheque-book that the bank had supplied, an ink bottle and pen and brought the materials to the kitchen table. While Gavin and Michael watched, she wrote out the cheque as he had requested. She extracted it carefully from the pad and handed it to him.

He held it up, and whistled.

'Four hundred pounds?' he said.

'That will be all there is, Michael.'

'Oh, that's more than enough to see us – to see Gavin settled. Well, we had better be on our way.' He tucked the cheque safely into his vest pocket. 'I'd like to have us on board the boat before anyone sees us.'

'How will you get to Tobermory?'

'Walk,' Michael said. 'We're good at walking, aren't we, son?'

'Yes,' Gavin said, and hopped down from the chair.

He put on his cap, picked up the smaller of the packs, slung it across his shoulder, went to the door and opened it.

And then, just then, Innis felt her heart break.

He looked so small, so defenceless – yet there was nothing in him that he was willing to yield to her, nothing that he would surrender at the last. She had raised him, she had given her love but she had remained a stranger to him. He dwelled with his own thoughts, his own perilous and violent desires.

She knelt and hugged him.

Standing stiff and obedient he allowed her to kiss him without pulling away, made that one small concession before the link between them was broken.

She got up, lips pursed and quivering.

'I'll look after him, never fear,' Michael said.

He kissed her, his arm about her waist. She knew that he would not come back to Mull and that she might never see him again.

'Goodbye, dear.' He hefted the pack and picked up his crook, the same crook that he had brought to Mull over a dozen years ago. 'Listen, tell Biddy, that if she . . .'

'What have I to tell Biddy?' said Innis.

'Nothing.' Michael grinned wistfully. 'Nothing important.'

And then, steering his son before him, he was gone.

Somehow Innis struggled through the spring. She felt that she had to put a brave face on things for the sake of the girls. Rachel and Rebecca were more resilient than she gave them credit for, however. They had so much pleasant company about them and so many diversions, in and out of school, that they missed their father only occasionally and their brother not at all.

Throughout May Innis continued to pretend that Michael's absence was temporary. But gradually Rachel's questions dwindled and Becky's little bouts of sulking ceased and other men – Quig and Mr Brown in particular – assumed a paternal role in the lives of Innis's daughters.

Only three letters arrived from Ettrick, each more stilted than the last. Gavin, it seemed, was happy in his new school, was growing rapidly and would soon be 'quite the little man'. They were lodged with a widow on a farm not far from his mother's cottage. Both he and the boy were well. He had accepted a temporary post as shepherd with the Roxburgh flock. He had hopes that he would soon be in a position to buy sheep of his own and a rent piece of ground to graze them on. When that came to pass of course he would expect Innis to join him. In none of the letters did he mention the shooting.

Biddy also received letters from Michael; mad letters, full of bragging, false passions, promises and threats. She replied only to the first of them. In it she informed him that she had promoted Barrett to flockmaster and that if he, Michael, did not return to Fetternish soon she would be obliged to employ another shepherd to replace him.

Late in May, however, she wrote to Michael again; a crisp, gay little note to tell him that she had married Robert Quigley.

It was a quiet wedding in Crove parish church with no great celebrations afterwards. Besides, there too much to do on Fetternish. Even with Donnie gone to Edinburgh there were plenty of guests, temporary and permanent, to keep the place humming and, at Willy's suggestion, two day-maids – nieces of his wife – were employed to assist in the running of the household.

By now Vassie was permanently installed in Fetternish house and there was no more talk of her returning to Pennypol.

Aileen and Mairi Quigley had moved out of the turf-roofed cottage to stay in the big house for a while. Quig was more than capable of dealing with Aileen's wayward moods and, for the most part, kept her out of mischief. And the Browns were always willing to take her off on 'expeditions' or accompany her back to the haunts she had known as a girl. Aided by Barrett's brother, Innis assumed temporary responsibility for the cattle herd and continued to live at Pennymain. In the course of that long summer there was simply too much going on for long-term plans to be laid or the future settled.

If Biddy's marriage to Robert Quigley was a surprise to the folk of Crove, the minister's marriage to Quigley's mother a month later came as a shock.

Tom Ewing chose to be wed in Dundee. Mairi had no objection. Indeed, she would have married him on a coconut island if that had been his wish.

The banns were announced from the pulpit in Crove. Reverend Ewing read them out in a bold, droll voice, and if he derived any satisfaction from the reaction of his little flock he gave no sign of it. Spurred by Hector Thrale, some of the elders endeavoured to put a stop to the nuptials by complaining to the Presbytery. Tom simply stood back and waited. He knew that the Presbytery would find no impediment to the marriage of a bachelor and a widow lady to whom no scandal had ever attached itself, if, that is, you disregarded her fondness for fancy ear-rings.

Biddy and Quig travelled to Dundee for the wedding. Gillies Brown stood as best man to the groom and his daughter, Janetta, as maid to the bride. Vassie and Willy Naismith went too but Innis, a Catholic, remained on Fetternish to look after the children.

Father Gunnion died in July. Innis missed the old priest. Young Father O'Donnell was energetic and enthusiastic but Innis was no longer inclined to make the long journey to Glenarray and attended mass in Tobermory instead. She did not regret her conversion to Catholicism. Sometimes she thought that it was the one good and lasting thing to have come out of her marriage.

Gillies Brown was too decent a man to challenge Innis's beliefs. If he desired her – which he did – he was willing to settle for the cinder path of chastity. He wanted no other woman but Innis Tarrant and if he could not have her as his wife then he would have her as his friend.

The weather that August afternoon was not oppressive but all the sounds of land and sea seemed lazy and languorous in the late summer heat. The lawns in front of the house had recently been mown, the odour of freshly-cut grass lingered in the air and the big brown bumble-bees from the hives in the walled garden droned over the last of the clover.

They were all there at the picnic, all the folk that mattered to Vassie Campbell's daughters.

Vassie was throned over them, seated on an upright chair that Donnie, home for the long weekend, had carried down from the house. The others sprawled on rugs and blankets spread upon the lawn, the ladies' less-than-delicate complexions properly protected by wide-brimmed hats and parasols while the men, less bound by convention, had shed their jackets and stiff collars and basked, all loose and idle, in the rays of the westering sun.

Even the children, stuffed with boiled egg and chicken breast, sticky with sugar cakes and raspberry cream, had almost expended the last of their energies. They lay in the shade of the parapet, weaving daisy-chains, debating the properties of buttercups and, now and then, tickling Aunt Aileen's nose with a leaf of cut grass and giggling when she pretended to snore.

Safe from his elders' disapproval, the Reverend Thomas Ewing was stretched out upon a tartan rug, his head cushioned in his wife's lap while she fanned him with a docken leaf and shaded his face with her forearm. Donnie and Tricia Brown had wandered off a little way. They were seated, tête-à-tête, on the slope of the lawn, kissing – unnoticed, so they thought – beneath the brim of Tricia's hat and murmuring endearments so softly that only the bees could hear.

For Innis and the schoolmaster there could be no such obvious intimacy. She sat close to him, though, shoulder resting against his arm. She watched him sip from a glass of beer, saw the wetness on his lips and the bob of his throat when he swallowed and thought how dear he had become to her and how well she might love him now that her longing had been satisfied. He was all that she had longed for, all that she had desired, and if some folk thought that he had come too late to bring her fulfilment then she would live to prove them wrong.

Biddy stirred. She had been resting too, leaning against her husband.

He had braced himself, arms out, shirt unbuttoned to let the sun get at the ugly blue-brown rash that still pocked his chest and shoulder. The ache had gone but the stiffness and scars would remain, a reminder of all the trouble that he and Biddy had endured before they had been brought together at last.

'Do you not think you should tell them, dear?' Quig said.

Vassie leaned sharply forward. 'Tell us what?'

'I – I want to be sure.'

'Come now,' Quig said, 'you are as sure as you will ever be. Tell them, Biddy, since we are all friends here.'

'I am expecting a baby,' Biddy said.

'Hmmm,' Quig said, nodding. 'Dr Kirkhope has confirmed it.'

Tom Ewing sat up. 'Well, well, well.'

'At last,' said Vassie, sitting back. 'It is not before time.'

'Congratulations,' Gillies said. Rising, he shook Quig by the hand and kissed Biddy's brow. 'Many, many congratulations.'

Innis got to her feet.

She did not go at once to her sister. She looked up at the house, at the lowering facade of Fetternish planed out against the soft blue sky.

She felt within her a little jolt of displeasure, almost of envy, an eddy of the rivalries that had existed between them since they were girls. Once she had had a husband and children and Biddy had had everything else. How fair that had seemed, how fitting; a sort of justice. Now that advantage had been taken from her and she was not woman enough, not Christian enough to share her sister's joy without bitterness, without compromise.

She knew that they were waiting, watching her: Quig and Tom Ewing who, once upon a time, had been brave enough to defy convention and attend her Catholic wedding in the chapel at Glenarray: her mother, Vassie McIver Campbell, who had exchanged love for duty and duty for revenge, who had endured long enough to make her husband pay, not for just his wickedness but also for her folly. She glanced up at her daughters, Becky and Rachel, who seemed to be watching her too. And then she realised that she was wrong, quite wrong, that it was not up to her to judge what was fair and what was not and that in the final accounting Biddy was no less entitled to happiness than she was.

She looked first towards the mountains, then towards the sea. She felt the evening breeze cool against her cheek, the clean little wind drifting in from Foss, from Pennypol and the hills beyond.

She must put bitterness aside. She could not, would not let it spoil her life and blight the love that lay around her.

'What do you say, Innis?' Quig said. 'Are you not pleased for us?'

'Of course I am,' she said, smiling. She stooped to kiss her sister's cheek. 'I am delighted for both of you. But tell me, dearest, when is the baby due?'

'In February,' Quig answered.

'Or thereabouts,' said Biddy.